ONTRETO

OTHELLO

PETER CRAWLEY

ONTRETO

A NOVEL OF LIPARI

Matador
9 Priory Business Park,
Wistow Road, Kibworth Beauchamp,
Leicestershire. LE8 0RX
Tel: (+44) 116 279 2299
Fax: (+44) 116 279 2277
Email: books@troubador.co.uk
Web: www.troubador.co.uk/matador

ISBN 978 1784622 213

British Library Cataloguing in Publication Data.
A catalogue record for this book is available from the British Library.

Printed and bound in the UK by TJ International, Padstow, Cornwall
Typeset in 12pt CentaurMT by Troubador Publishing Ltd, Leicester, UK

Matador is an imprint of Troubador Publishing Ltd

For Daisy

Antoine de Saint-Exupery,
the aviator poet,
proclaimed there is but one freedom
and that is the freedom of the mind.
Yet there are many who enjoy no such freedom.
To set them free requires not only great understanding,
but also courage, patience and compassion.
Of these, the most elemental is compassion.

Also by the author

Mazzeri
Boarding House Reach

Foreword
&
Acknowledgements

It doesn't matter which Aeolus one believes in, that he was the father of the Aeolian Islands is not in doubt. Was he, though, the son of Poseidon, the God of the Sea, or was he the son of Hippotes, a mere mortal but a king nevertheless? What we believe from the writings of Homer in his epic *The Odyssey*, is that Aeolus presented Odysseus with a bag of winds to speed him on his journey back to Ithaca. Unfortunately, mistaking the bag to contain gold and silver, Odysseus' crew opened it and in so doing released the winds. Because of their greed, Odysseus' ship was blown further from its destination.

However, all I am certain of is that one doesn't find the Aeolian Islands; one is drawn to them.

Some years ago my friend Jo Salamone, who hails from the pretty village of Suteria in the province of Caltanissetta, Sicily, suggested I visit Lipari in the Aeolian Islands. Jo proposed I stay in the hotel of a friend of his. His friend would arrange the taxi from Catania to Milazzo; he would arrange the connection to the islands on the hydrofoil; he would meet us at the harbour. In short, Jo's friend would arrange everything. He did. Adriano was true to his word.

This small, volcanic archipelago of seven main islands lies just to the north of the Sicilian coast near the Straits of Messina. They are known to some as the Seven Sisters and together they comprise one of the best kept secrets of the Mediterranean. The islands are a string of radiant pearls, a necklace of iridescent gems, a handful of jewels so elegant and beguiling that one is inclined, on hearing of their beauty, to disbelieve they exist.

Adriano Longo is the proprietor of the very beautiful Hotel Rocce Azzurre, which overlooks the bay at Portinente. Adriano and his daughter, Ariana, introduced me to the many delights of the islands: the white pumice beaches of the Spiaggia della Papesca, the clear waters of the Mare Siculum, the wine of Salina, the imposing citadel of Lipari and, perhaps best of all, the people. It was only later and by chance that I found out the island possesses a darker history.

Wandering through the *città bassa*, the low city which is comprised of a warren of narrow *vicolos* running below the citadel, I heard someone whisper that the island had, during the Second World War, been home to a number of political deportees, most of them men of conscience and principle who spoke out against the tyrant Benito Mussolini. Further to this rumour, I heard that three of these political deportees had, with the help of certain islanders, planned and executed a daring escape.

Late one night, as I sat with Adriano fishing for *totani* in his little *barca*, I began to learn more about the island and its remarkable people, and charged myself with the task of researching the island in greater depth.

A few months later, sitting at my desk, I stumbled across a newspaper article from 1929, which reported George Palmer Putnam, the titular head of the New York and London publishing house, as receiving a number of death threats if he published Francesco Fausto Nitti's *Escape*. The forthcoming publication of such a personal narrative by a political prisoner who had escaped from Lipari, the Fascist's Devil's Island, so angered Il Duce that he set his spies and secret agents, The Black Hand, to see that *Escape* never made it to the shelves. Fortunately for us, Putnam was no shrinking violet. He ignored the danger, was damned by Mussolini and went ahead and published.

Some weeks later I procured a fourth impression copy of Nitti's book from South Africa; there are few left in existence. It is, by any stretch of the imagination, a crucial and fundamental work exposing the brutality and ugliness which lies at the heart of Fascism. But further than this, Nitti's book is also proof that truth is often stranger than fiction.

There are, though, more than a few works I have drawn inspiration from. The Archduke Ludwig Salvator's volumes on *Die Liparischen Inseln*, provided by the Bavarian State Library, contain much useful information, though I am not aware of any translations from the original German language version. Philip Ward's *The Aeolian Islands*, Oleander Press, has proved invaluable and I would not advise the traveller to visit the islands without first having read this beautifully written and very informative book. Alberto Denti di Pirajno's *A Cure for Serpents*, Eland, sheds much light on the attitudes of Italians working in the North African colonies of Balbo's Grande Italia. John Julius Norwich's illuminating tome *The Middle Sea*, Vintage, explains the history and politics of the region from the Roman Empire right up to the Risorgimento. M. Emma Alaimo's *Proverbi Siciliani*, Giunti, and Mariolina Venezia's novel *Been Here a Thousand Years*, Picador, have been most useful companions when attempting to understand how first Sicilians and second Italians view their part in the great scheme of things. Finally, if you think fairy tales began with the Brothers Grimm, read Giambattista Basile's *Lo Cunto de li Cunti — The Tale of Tales* — first published in the seventeenth century, and think again.

As always, the most fruitful research is conducted out engaging with local people. Many have given freely of their time in this respect, none more so than Ariana Longo and her father Adriano. Without their time and enthusiasm, *Ontreto* would never have made it past the first few pages. As a caveat, though, I must add that I have played fast and loose with a couple of details, if only to complement the narrative. Homer's coffin, for instance, sits just below the surface a few metres off the pontoon of the Hotel Rocce Azzurre and not near the Punta San Giuseppe, and La Casa dei Sconosciuti is a work of my own imagination, as is the character Massimo Farinelli.

There are, of course, other fictionalised happenings and characters. Yet, Francesco Nitti, Edda Ciano, Leonardo Bongiorno and Benito Mussolini all take their seat in our history class; they have left their mark upon our world. However, apart from historical reference, none of the characters who take an active part in this book bear any relation to any persons either living or gone before.

I sent a final draft manuscript of *Ontreto* to Ariana Longo in Lipari, asking if she would mind checking my use of local dialect. She responded immediately and very enthusiastically, and within a couple of days I was returned the manuscript with her suggested alterations for which, naturally, I am very grateful. What I had not expected, though, was her mention of a character from my novel who, it turns out, actually exists. This character, a man for whom I had created a profession, a nickname and a home village, is not only flesh and blood, but also flesh and blood in exactly the manner in which I had conjured him. I was, to say the least, surprised. After much thought and taking into account the risks of litigation, I decided it would be better to rewrite the character. Yet, having grown rather attached to him, I was sorry to let him go. Spooky, uncanny, weird, creepy, chilling, or perhaps even auspicious: call it what you will, but it proves yet again that truth is stranger than fiction.

To Ariana, I say a considerable "thank you". If I have made mistakes, they are mine and not hers.

As ever, I am also indebted to Sally Duhig, Ba Collinson, Peter Matthews and Christine Ellerbeck for their time, their assistance and insightful critique. Anlouise Snedden introduced me to Opera and in doing so she has brought light to my previously blinkered view of this wonderful art form. For her generosity and enthusiasm, I am grateful. My thanks go, of course, to all the team at Troubador Publishing.

As with the launch of *Mazzeri*, I handed over the organisation and presentation of the launch of *Boarding House Reach*, my second novel, to Peter Matthews. And Sue Woods of Mintsource-uk.com and Jack Newman at boodesign.co.uk produced the artwork and banners. I will be more than happy to hand Peter the responsibility of organising and presenting the launch of *Ontreto*.

Finally, and as always, I have to thank Carol, my wife, who pores over every draft, provides copious quantities of tea with dashes of sympathy, and who puts up with the author's occasionally capricious vein.

Be drawn to the Aeolian Islands, I urge you. Though their past may have been dark, their future is so very bright. Or, as Giambattista Basile might have written it: each dawn the shepherd of the moon calls the stars to pastures new, so that we, the windblown seeds of the islands, may wake to flourish in the warmth of the sun's smile.

The Aeolian Islands in the Mediterranean

The Seven Sisters of the Aeolian Islands

The Island of Lipari

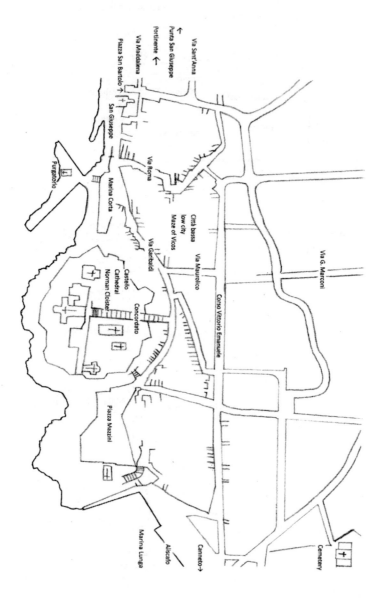

The town of Lipari showing the Castello and the Città bassa

I

Midsummer 1930

Tonio scrambles up the path, reaching out to grab hold of anything that will stop him from slipping back down. As far as Tonio is concerned, he is going nowhere fast.

He mutters constantly, urging himself to greater effort and at the same time scolding himself for making so much noise. There is a checkpoint manned by the Carabinieri on the road not a stone's throw below him and the last thing he needs is to stumble across some dark-skinned oaf from Perugia relieving himself in the scrub.

They are lazy good-for-nothings, the Carabinieri; thugs and bullies, men who would sell their own mother for a weekend with a whore in Naples. "I bet your sons wear *Balillas* and sing the *Giovinezza,*" he whispers, of the black shirts the school children wear and the Fascist hymn they are forced to sing. But, at least their low scruples mean they can be bribed; that is perhaps the only good thing about the filthy bastards. A couple of *salpe* or a handful of *seppie* can buy one much valuable information.

Although it is nearly midnight, the moon and the stars reveal the winding path up over the saddle which connects the twin peaks of Monte Rosa to the island.

"One day," he mutters, "they will dig a tunnel to connect the two bays and when they do, I will not have to make this climb every time

I need to get into town." But then it dawns on him that even if there was a tunnel, the Carabinieri would be guarding that too.

The conversation he has overheard in the café in Canneto has chilled him to the bone, and if he does not make it over to San Giuseppe in time, there will be three less *deportati* for the islanders to feed.

There is no breeze and Tonio pauses to breathe in the sweet fragrance of honeysuckle and rock carnation. He knows he shouldn't talk to himself so much, but the sound of his own voice heartens him. And creeping about in the scrub at night is strictly for fools; he knows that too. He is as likely to be shot out of boredom as he is for breaching the curfew.

He slips and reaches out to the branch of a carrub tree, but by mistake grasps the thick fleshy leaf of an agave and as his hand slips down the spiny edge, he cuts his palm.

If the long, hot day grading pumice in the warehouse up at Porticello hasn't tired him enough, hurrying to find Vincenzo has. And then, when he found him and related the conversation, Vincenzo told him he would have to go at once to the house at the Punta San Giuseppe to warn the others. And San Giuseppe is beyond the *città bassa* of Lipari. Even if it was daylight and he could run by the most direct route, it would still take him an hour. In the dark, and trying to avoid the patrols, he knows it will take him twice that long. He can't risk going by the road. He will have to scuttle round the back of the Timpone Croci, steal through the lanes at Diana and pick his way through the narrow alleys that lead round the back of the town through to San Nicola. He shakes his head, knowing it is asking too much not to get stopped at least once.

Again, Tonio scolds himself for his grumbling. The luminosity of the moon makes him easier to spot, but the pitch black shadows created by it make it easier for him to hide. That is how it is; some bad, some not so bad.

He picks his way between the headstones and mausolea in the cemetery, pausing occasionally to apologise for his haste: his sister-in-law, Grazia, a victim of starvation, or so Innocenzio the *comunista* maintained; Gaetano, his cousin, drowned by the police spies; and Peppino, who Tonio was never certain was a relation, poisoned by the authorities for taking part in the riot. But, Tonio knows full well that Grazia was consumed by her tumour and that Gaetano fell overboard in a storm. And Peppino? Well, he'd mistakenly drunk from a bottle of detergent thinking it was Malvasia; there was nothing sinister about that. But then, Innocenzio likes to blame everything on the Duce, including his facial warts and his terrible breath. After all, he is a disciple of Bongiorno.

"Oh, why did I not go with my brother to that place he called Argentina? I bet the people there don't have bad breath."

As he leaves the back of the cemetery he glances over at the forbidding mass of the Castello. The fortified gate beneath the Greek Tower is well-lit and he can see the Carabinieri loitering beneath it. And he knows the other entrance, at the bottom of the broad steps of the Via del Concordato down on the Garibaldi, will be watched too.

Until a few years before, the Carabinieri guarded common criminals, the curse of the island. But the people, Tonio amongst them, stormed their own citadel in protest and as a result the authorities replaced the thieves and murderers with political deportees, with gentlemen. So, while Tonio labours in the pumice quarries, the people of the island do their level best to relieve the former members of the Italian Parliament — men like Volpi from Rome, Beltrimini of Como and Rabezzana of Turin — of as much of their living allowance as they can. With over five hundred of them billeted in basements and hovels in and around the *città bassa*, they are the reason Tonio cannot take the quickest route to his destination; the *deportati* are watched day and night.

3

Something over half an hour later the moon sees Tonio slip past San Nicola. He is surprised by a patrol near the church of Santa Anna and has to hide for a few minutes in the doorway of Bartolo the cobbler.

"I must be making too much noise," Tonio whispers as the old man unlatches the door and ushers him inside.

"If you are going to play spies, Tonio, you really should wash first. They won't need to see you coming; they'll smell you."

They stand and whisper for a minute or so, but old Bartolo knows better than to ask Tonio what he is doing out at this late hour. Questions only demand answers, and some answers are best not heard.

"And please, stop scratching; they'll hear you before they smell you. Next time you come to visit, stop by San Calogero and take a bath; your lice are a greater threat to your wellbeing than the Carabinieri. Go on, get out, they have gone now."

Tonio takes the lane out to Capparo, the southern tip of the island, and scurries off towards the sea just before the land rises up to the small settlement of Capistello.

The house at Punta San Giuseppe is difficult to approach; there is only one narrow lane in and it twists and turns down the steep hillside, running out at the small house which sits up on the blunt promontory, a tall man's height above the sea.

Vincenzo has told him that a motor launch will come in to the *punta* at midnight and that the three *deportati* will be waiting in the water, perching on Homer's coffin; a rock which rises up from the seabed and crowns just below the surface, not fifty metres from shore. It is a similar escape route to the one taken by Nitti, Lussu and Roselli the year before; except that they met at a house on the Maddalena and were collected from the point near Portinente.

What Vincenzo has also told him is that these other, new men are clearly betrayed, that the Fascist authorities will now be lying in wait for them and that he, Tonio, must warn them. But what Vincenzo has singularly failed to tell Tonio is just how he is supposed to warn them. Is he supposed to swim out to the coffin and casually tap one of them on the shoulder and say, "*If you please, gentlemen, we are very sorry to have to tell you that we have a traitor amongst us. Perhaps it would be better for you to postpone your departure?*"

He knows only one of the three men trying to escape: Farinelli.

He admires Farinelli. It is known that he is brave, an *Ardito* from the Great War, and that he started out as a supporter of Annunzio. But, like so many others, when he learned how the poet's words were nothing but empty promises, he followed Matteotti into the opposition Reformist Party. Then, when the *Fascisti* assassinated Matteotti, Farinelli was deported, first to Lampedusa and then to Lipari.

"That is how it is if you are political; that is why I have no time for such matters," Tonio mutters. But, he also knows that Farinelli and Vincenzo's daughter, Katarina, are close. He has seen them out together at *passeggio*. And that is why it is only natural that Vincenzo should take such an interest in the man's welfare. *That is not political, is it, eh?*

The sea is but a short walk away now and the moon shines so bright, it might as well be the sun. Tonio shudders to think how anyone is supposed to hide themselves in such light. And, as he shudders, he makes out the heads of the three men bobbing just above the water out about where Homer's coffin would be. They are waiting patiently like buoys waiting for a boat, which, he supposes, is exactly what they are doing.

Tonio creeps down between the small holly oaks and cistus. He is afraid. He hates the silence; it has never been a friend to him. Even at this late hour he would expect to hear a fishing boat setting out for the night or a herring gull shrieking from the cliffs beyond the point. But there is nothing, only silence; not even the glow of a lamp from within the little house.

He works his way as quickly and quietly as he can down to the water's edge. It is not easy; in places the scrub gives way to bare rock and the slope drops away sheer into the water.

Tonio loses his footing and slips, stumbles and falls down the last of the slope, pitching headlong into the black water. He lands with a thunderous splash.

But the water is, if nothing else, cool and refreshing on his skin. *Bah, Vincenzo,* he thinks, *at least there is some pleasure.*

There is little point in his trying to keep his presence quiet any longer. "*Signori?*" he calls, cupping his hand to his mouth and not really understanding why; in all probability they will have heard his grand entrance over in the Marina Corta. "*Signori,* you must come back."

But as he calls, Tonio becomes aware of the noise of a boat engine some way off shore. It is a growling noise, like the noise of the generator at the quarry, only more urgent.

Tonio begins to swim in the direction of the men; his stroke is raw and uncultured. "*Signori, gentili,* you are betrayed!" he calls again.

The sound of the motor grows and echoes around the gullies of the hill behind him. He is worried that the boat will run him down if it doesn't slow up soon. It is somewhere close; he is sure of it. Still, though, he cannot see it. He stops and treads water for a moment, hoping to catch a glimpse of the boat as it approaches. He can see the heads of the men not far away. "*Signori,*" he calls once more.

Now, he can just make out the white shimmering bow-wave of the boat, carving through the night towards him. It is a beautiful sight, bright and shiny like the silver paint on the statue of San Bartolo up in the cathedral. The boat is low and long. It slows and halts. The motor dies and a torch is played over the heads of the men. There is much excited talking.

Then, all that is dark is light and all that is silence is noise. And where there were three men waiting for a single boat, there is now a great commotion and more boats than Tonio has ever seen, even at the festival of San Bartolo.

The long motor launch lies not thirty metres before him. Hunched figures lean over the rail, reaching down to haul the men from their precarious perch in the sea, and Tonio can see this quite clearly because all are now bathed in the white light of a thousand candles.

A rifle is fired, then a machine gun and then more guns.

The water around the launch boils and jumps, like when fishermen herd tuna towards a net. The figures fall back, some into the boat, others into the water.

A man screams and waves his hands in the manner of a Sicilian puppet.

Another man stands still and raises his arms in surrender, pleading. But, the water continues to boil and the bullets continue to strike. And the man lurches and crumples and falls headfirst into the sea.

One of those in the water attempts to climb into the boat, exposing his broad back to the searchlight. It spots black in several places and the man slumps back down, one of his arms slipping so slowly, ever so slowly, from the rail, as if in one final, desperate plea for help.

And the side of the motor launch is exploding into tiny fragments and splinters, and someone is shouting. And suddenly there is no more shooting because there is no longer anyone left alive to shoot at. The gunfire echoes around the shore and gradually fades away. The silence is interrupted only by a weak, pleading moaning, like that of a man who knows he is about to close his eyes for the last time.

Tonio has heard this moan before. It is the same moan his father gave out when he fell through the floor of the drying house at Porticello and broke his back across the wheel of the cart below. Even Innocenzio had not been able to blame that terrible misfortune on the authorities.

7

There is little else to be done. The carnage Tonio has witnessed will live in his memory; that is, if he is to live long enough to possess a memory. He is too late; all his efforts have been in vain. He slips slowly beneath the water, turns himself round and strikes out for the shore, careful not to break the surface with his strokes.

Oh Vincenzo, he thinks as he clambers ashore, *if you have killed me, there will be trouble.*

2

Early summer 2013

During the night Ric slips into the fitful doze of the lone yachtsmen. He doesn't allow himself to fall fast and deeply asleep which, given half the chance, is exactly what he would like to do. All it takes is the briefest trembling of a sheet or the thinnest slap of a wave to jerk him rudely awake.

And yet, during the moments in between, he dreams.

And he dreams light, frivolous fantasies of Manou and the boy he came to know in Corsica. And he dreams of Camille, the white-haired old fox whose boat he now sails, and the kindness and generosity of the people he has met in the small harbours of the east coast of Sardinia: Fabrizio the mechanic in Santa Maria Navarese, Giuseppe the carpenter in Arbatax, and Carmelo the harbour master of Cagliari, where he has passed most of the winter.

Camille, in signing the small yacht over to Ric, has sent him on his way with various letters of introduction, which is fortunate, because in just about every harbour along the way, some old salt pitches up to press him: Where is Camille? Why is it that this stranger is on board the Mara without him? And, perhaps more to Ric's liking, will the new owner come ashore and take a little wine, as Camille surely would have?

The Mara is old, like her previous keeper, and many of her small things — her padeyes, bails and the snap shackles of her rigging — are brittle and occasionally break beneath his clumsy fingers. She is old, but she is not ancient. Rather she is old in the way that one instantly recognises a great aunt who is old and therefore very naturally deserving of respect; as though the moment you recognise the light of wisdom in her eyes, you understand that she has seen much and knows more.

The Mara is an elegant and distinctive sloop; ten or so metres of hand-planed Cedar of Lebanon, slim at the hips and lithe through the water. But, what she wants more than anything from Ric is his time; time for him to understand that she is happier just off the wind as opposed to running fast before it; time for him to attend to the helm, which jams occasionally; and time to sort the rigging, which snags whenever he reefs the main. And that is not to mention the bilge pump, which runs only when it sees fit.

But it is Manou he misses most. Eight months have passed since he left the tiny bay at La Tozza on the south-eastern coast of Corsica and every time he closes his eyes she appears before him. It is as if she commands the approaches to his sleep in the same way Cerberus commands the gates to the underworld.

But, though Manou monopolises his sleep, there is good news. For Ric knows that if it is Manou's face he sees whenever he closes his eyes, it means the dream hunter has at last departed and with him he has taken the faces of the dead.

Tonight is Ric's fourth night out of Cagliari. A strong and steady Libecciu has been blowing out of the south-east and he hopes it will take him only another day or so to reach his destination.

But Aeolus has other designs for him. The devious son of Poseidon prefers to toy with Ric, just as he has toyed with so many other seafarers who pass too close to the islands of his birth. The God of Winds is bored and, by way of distraction, turns his eye to simple amusements. He stills the Libecciu and replaces it with a thick, clinging sea mist.

The choice, for Ric, is simple: either wallow at the mercy of the current or run up the motor so the Mara can make some way. He furls the jib, hauls down the mainsail and returns to the cockpit to start up. After a few juddering objections, the engine coughs, clears its throat and settles to a purr.

Ric maintains his westerly heading; gliding like a lean ghost through the white mist, which opens and then closes swiftly behind him.

If the Mara possessed even the most basic radar, he might sleep more restfully. But, she doesn't have radar in the same way that she doesn't have any other more conventional navigational aids and conveniences; the mast head and crossbar lights being the only concession the Mara makes to modernity. The old boy, Camille, hadn't needed them. He'd merely gone wherever the wind had taken him, just as Ric is now going wherever Aeolus drives him.

He wakes, startled. The deck beneath him stirs and he grows aware of small waves lapping at the side of the hull.

But the night mist still blinds him and he wonders how it is that without the wind, the sea is disturbed. He hears a muted thump, like a bass drum beaten once, and becomes aware of a dull crimson glow high up ahead.

From disturbed, the sea is very soon distressed and the Mara begins to pitch and yaw. The waves increase in height and weight and he has to hold the wheel firmly to maintain his heading. Ric glances at the compass and notices the needle is uncertain about its bearing.

The crimson glow, an explosive incandescence he recalls from a far-away-field, burns bright and intense; an eerie fire on a hillside high up beyond the prow of the little boat. And the odours of the very same far-away-field now lay siege to his senses: sulphur, mustard and bad eggs, and the bitter, stinging, acrid edge of cordite, of urgent exercise in oppressive heat and, inevitably, of decomposition.

Ric is unnerved by nature's sudden display of energy. He is

11

humbled and apprehensive. He cannot think what this lurid apparition means.

A second thump from the same drum results in a thick spray of garish liquid; a vivid spout of fresh blood, like that from a bullet wound. It shoots high up from the summit and falls back to earth, radiant and piercing to his eyes: the dazzling reds of the cherry orchard at dawn, the blazing yellow of the desert sun at midday and the deep purple of last light in the mountains. And the nearer he comes to the volcano, the greater grows his fear.

The sea is bewildered; the waves wash this way and that, not knowing which way to run. The compass still swings wildly and Ric, now standing at the helm, his blood thundering through his veins, realises that immediately in front of him must lie some significant land mass and that he must turn away to avoid it.

He feeds the helm to starboard and steers the Mara away so that the volcano comes to rest over his left shoulder.

The drum is, for the moment, silenced and the fire, though casting its strange glow about the boat, grows dim. The sea settles, the waves drop in strength and frequency, and the compass is once more steadied.

Ric stays standing, alert, at the helm. Whoever was beating the drum has decided to leave him to wander through the mist.

Thinking to give the island a wide berth, he steers south-south-west. There is a small group of islands lying to the south of his projected route and, because he can't recall their names or their disposition, he makes a mental note to check their lie at first light.

He looks at his watch: there are still a couple of hours before dawn. Now wide awake, his senses heightened by the sudden emergence and slow disappearance of the strange light, he figures he'd be better to stay on watch. If he has drifted south, he might be somewhere in the shallow channels between the islands. In the fog, where he has no hope of making out any of the harbour lights, and without radar, he will have to stay awake until the morning sun burns away the mist.

The Libecciu has given up on him and Ric is now beholden to the Mara's screw and the rhythmic swell beneath his feet.

Aeolus, like the gamekeeper and his dogs, is stalking his prey.

3

Dawn is too long in coming and the mist persists, coating every surface in a cool, sticky film of moisture. Ric is still awake and alert, listening for the slightest sound that might warn him of another vessel or his imminent landfall.

Every now and then the wake from a much larger boat some way off in the gloom unsteadies the Mara and she lurches, like a drunkard.

The assembly of ropes which, when tied to the helm, go to make up a rudimentary autopilot, allow him time to go below to fetch his chart. When he studies it, he realises the swell has pushed him south and that the source of the curious, crimson eruptions during the night must be the volcano on the island of Stromboli. If that is the case and he has been motoring slowly south-south-west for a few hours, he reckons he is somewhere near Lipari, the largest of the Aeolian Islands.

Ric sits down and rests his hand against the helm. He munches his way through a few of the cigar shaped *aranzada*. The orange peel, honey and almond biscuits rouse his taste buds and replenish his energy reserves; the marmalade flavours suggest his day is only just beginning.

The chart, he notices as he folds, is getting damp; the heavy condensation is soaking into the paper and softening the pages, which are splitting along the creases.

Ric stares into the opaque wall of vapour that surrounds him. He stands up and stoops, climbing down into the cabin to lay the chart back on the small folding table.

As he pulls himself back up the steps to the cockpit he looks aft. The sea is now so calm and flat that, bar the small swirls and eddies caused by the slowly turning screw, the Mara leaves little evidence of her progress. He wonders what Manou is doing? Probably, he decides, she is preparing the campsite at Renabianca for the first of her early season sun-worshippers. He pictures her strolling through the pines to the white sandy beach, stopping here and there to collect debris blown by the winter winds or sheaves of sea-grass washed ashore by the spring squalls.

Ric turns round to face forward and is astonished to see a tangle of iron girders stretching up out of the sea like the petrified limbs of a partially submerged forest.

He pulls back the throttle, jams the motor into reverse and throws the helm to port to avoid ramming the pilings head on.

At first he doesn't know what to make of the assembly of iron props. He stands in the cockpit, the Mara idling, drifting, and studies them, mystified as to what the bent and twisted construction might be.

Slowly, he realises they are more substantial than merely a disordered collection of broken metal beams and angled stanchions. They are, or rather were, the makings of a pier; the framework of a dock or wharf, which has at one time been filled out and clothed in concrete and wood, but which is now decayed and decrepit, rusted and gnawed back to its bare chassis by the chemical corrosion of the salt water and the relentless onslaught of the waves. In places the girders have buckled and warped as though the frame has been stamped on by a giant.

Ric edges the Mara up close to the nearest of the vertical iron posts. He pulls hard against it; it remains unmoving. And as he looks down, he sees that not only does the ocean floor reflect the white of the mist, but, somehow, it also holds a richer, deeper, more textured alabaster tone to it, as though the seabed is overlaid with crêpe batter.

The rectangular structure is solid; it rises up to just higher than the Mara's mast and the stanchions are spaced a good twenty metres apart. They stretch away into the mist, promising no end.

Clearly, it is a mole or jetty or landing stage of some kind, and just as clearly, if it is such, then it is attached to the land and it has prevented him from running aground. But, and perhaps more importantly, he can tie up to it and get his head down for a few hours, secure in the knowledge that the Mara won't go anywhere.

Sleep, Ric decides, is higher up his menu of needs than the square meal his stomach so noisily demands.

He ties up fore and aft to the iron skeleton, paying out just enough line so that, if the wind does get up, the Mara will simply swing between the stanchions. Ric turns off the motor and sits down. He listens for the gentle swell lapping at the shore and guesses that the beach or cliff, or whatever shape the land takes, is not much more than a few yards out of sight behind the white curtain. He lies back and stretches out his weary limbs, savouring the moment before he goes below to lie in the arms of Hypnos and surrender to Manou's sky-blue eyes. Wherever he is, and he supposes it must be the island of Lipari as his chart suggests, he is glad he and the Mara have arrived in one piece.

He stands up very slowly and rubs his fingers through his hair. His eyes are tired; they sting from the salt and the hours of concentration. His ears buzz with the silence, and his arms ache and his back is sore from standing too long at the helm.

Ric decides to lie down and sleep for a few hours, hoping that when he wakes, the fog will be gone and he will find out exactly where he is.

He shakes his head. He can hear someone shouting.

4

At first he wonders if, after his recently extended solitude, his mind is beginning to play tricks on him. He shakes his head again and rubs his eyes, and when the pounding of blood through his brain has reduced, he looks up and listens.

The voices are indistinct and muffled by the heavy blanket of fog. One moment he can hear people talking and the next, their conversation is swallowed up.

Ric strains to listen harder. There are two men, both Italian. One voice is low and guttural, harsh and unforgiving, like that of an officer chewing out a junior rank; the other distinctive, higher pitched, not that of a young man or boy necessarily, more that of a man pleading or apologising.

Their conversation grows ever more heated, the volume increases and some of the individual words become clearer. The pauses, too, grow longer and carry more weight, as though each argument is carefully considered before being contradicted. And every now and then, one softens and addresses the other in sentimental tones, as if they are friends or, perhaps, relations.

After a prolonged pause, the conversation develops an angry, threatening edge; the higher-pitched of the two voices pleads more desperately, whilst the other continues to accuse with greater authority.

Ric hears the words *"bastardo"* and *"cagna"*.

The two men are at loggerheads and their rhetoric is being ratcheted the way a wind-filled sail is tightened. The pleading grows more hysterical as the rebukes increase in certainty. Whatever wrong the one man has done, it becomes apparent the other is not inclined to forgive him.

The mist closes in and muffles the voices.

Ric walks up to the prow and stands, holding on to the forestay, waiting and listening.

The mist thins momentarily and he hears the words *"traditore"* and *"vergogna"* and the phrase, *"Tesoro mio, sei una cagna. Vai con Dio,"* and finally, silence.

One of the men begins to scream and plead, *"No, per favore, no, Ci–"* followed by a second muffled, choking sound and the scuffling of feet.

And silence. A silence both profound and chilling, and pressed beneath the enormous weight of the fog.

Ric listens hard, but… nothing. The seconds slow as somewhere out in the mist a life slips its mooring and fades away.

The deep, lasting quiet is suddenly punctured by the word *"Puddaciaru!"* not so much spoken as snarled by the man who has just murdered another.

5

That he cannot tell how far off in the mist the action is happening, concerns him. The blanket of fog shows no sign of lifting and Ric knows that if it does, he will be alarmingly exposed, moored as he is to the rusty old dock. For the moment, there is not much he can do. The wind, or rather the lack of it, lends him no means of escape. And though he can start up the Mara's motor and disappear swiftly into the clinging white vapour, the noise of the motor will no doubt give his presence away. The Mara is genteel; she does not take kindly to being hurried to the door.

He creeps aft and slips down into the main cabin; the sleep he craves now forgotten. The hairs on the back of his neck are standing at attention and his previously aching limbs are feathered by cool tendrils of adrenalin.

A square of the planked floor beneath his bed lifts by means of a small finger-hole and beneath it lie two plastic bags: one contains two passports and money; the other, a semi-automatic pistol.

Ric removes the pistol, tucks it in his belt and stands up to examine his chart. Sicily is thirty or so miles due south, but there is another island, Vulcano, he would have to sail round before he could get into open water. His best bet is to sit tight and hope the fog conceals him until he can gain a better look at the terrain.

He slips back up into the cockpit of the Mara and wonders what kind of dock he is tied up to. Clearly it is no longer in use, but he wonders for what purpose it was built. In the course of his journey, he's seen no oil derricks and there are none marked on his chart; neither is there an Italian naval station in the area. And he can't imagine what industry would exist on such a small island that it requires such an imposing structure.

He thinks about the word *puddaciaru*. It is not an Italian word he recognises. But it was spoken with such venom that, even though he hasn't the first clue what it means, Ric is in no doubt it must be some kind of insult. Some of the conversation he understood: *bastardo, figlio di una cagna*, meaning bastard and son-of-a-bitch; *traditore*, he thinks, suggests one man thought of the other as a traitor, and *vergogna* he recognises from the Corsu for shame. So the killer called his victim names that suggest the poor unfortunate did something to bring shame on the man who murdered him.

For a moment, Ric wonders whether he has stumbled into some ghastly Sicilian opera, but knows however much he would prefer to believe it, it is unlikely. All winter he has cruised down the eastern coast of Sardinia without so much as a crossed word. Now, wherever it is he finds himself, he has drifted into someone else's domestic disagreement.

Eventually, the adrenalin marching through his limbs disperses and tiredness overcomes him. Ric realises his head has dipped onto his chest and his eyes are no longer open. He knows that if he doesn't get below soon, he'll fall asleep sitting awkwardly in the cockpit of the Mara and, later, when his neck and muscles object, he will hate himself for not going below.

Ric folds his weary frame through the narrow hatch, puts the Beretta down on the small chart table and collapses on his bed.

6

When he wakes, the air is clean and cool to taste, and the Mara is rising and falling rhythmically on the wash from another vessel. Ric is aware of a dull, drumming, droning noise fading into the distance.

Up on deck, he is met with a bright, new world. The heavy, filmic moisture and the cloaking pale of the night fog have been replaced by a shimmering, sparkling spectacle of blue and white. A dazzling path of reflections stretches out across the Mare Siculum towards a burnished sun; Poseidon's temple handmaidens have gilded the sea with a thousand leaves of silver.

However, when Ric turns round he is confronted by a surreal landscape. The Mara is moored to the bare frame of a pier, only the delicate metal spines of which remain sticking up above the water. The cladding of the pier, which was once supported by the now rusting girders and pillars, has long since fallen away. The structure runs a hundred metres or so to a broad dock; it is bent and warped in places as though it has been deformed by the weight of many cumbersome ships. A concrete apron fronts a handful of grey stone, derelict warehouses standing four stories tall. Ric assumes they are derelict, because none of the rows of apertures possess glassed windows and most of the wooden doors hang haphazardly on their hinges. They aren't completely rundown and overgrown, and yet they are devoid of both human presence and industrial purpose. The vacant enclave reminds Ric of a city deserted and swept clean by a fire storm; a fire which penetrates and kills, rather than an explosion from a shell which detonates and destroys.

The buildings, once the domain of the LA CAVA family, according to the name painted in faded letters across the façade, crowd round a small track that winds its way up a hundred and fifty metres or so to the crown of the slope at the back. And away behind the sombre ghost town stands a huge grey mountain of screed, evidently the source of whatever stone it is that the labourers once mined and shipped from the jetty. Ric assumes the aggregate is also responsible for the curious chalky-whiteness to the sea floor. At odd intervals and varying depths, strange white sponges, like bowls of mistletoe, cling to the stanchions and wallow and sway with the swell.

Ric recalls the shouting and the hopeless pleading and decides that rather than sit and brew a cup of tea, it is probably best if he moves on. He glances through the hatchway and is relieved to see the gun right where he left it.

He makes a mental note to put it away, fires the Mara's motor, slips the fore and aft lines and backs her out from beneath and between the mooring. Ric shivers in the breeze; a reaction caused as much by the haunting of the previous night as by the cool zephyrs gliding in off the sea.

A minute or two out, Ric spins the Mara round and is treated to a view of a coastline which runs pretty much north to south, and he understands he has landed at a substantial island. The large slope of grey screed behind the rise of the seashore turns out to belong to a considerable hill of similar coloured rock; a volcanic grey of some form, lacerated here and there by huge striations as straight as roads. Mines and quarries have been cut and carved in the face of the hill which rises up five hundred metres. But the slope lies quiet and lacks even the smallest suggestion of any current or, for that matter, recent activity.

A few miles to the south and beyond a village clustered at the water's edge, the shoreline curves round towards the east, where a point is backed by a pair of small hills. At the back of the village the ground rises steeply to yet more rich-green hills, the highest of them standing about as high as the grey peak away to the north. To the north-east, over his left shoulder, Ric can see a small island, some fifteen or so miles distant, and further behind it, perhaps the same distance again, a larger, taller, cone shaped island which is topped by a singular, cotton-wool puff of cloud. He supposes it is this island that was responsible for the peculiar, unnerving, fiery images he came upon late the night before.

He goes below and retrieves a letter Camille has left for him. The penmanship is remarkably precise for one who he remembers as having stubby fingers and poor eyesight. Ric rests his leg against the helm and leans back to read the letter once more:

Ric,

When you have been recovering, I have been to the old Legion garrison at Bunifaziu; the same place in the photograph of your great-grandfather you have shown me. It is as you found out, the garrison is no longer in use, but I was able to meet with an old friend who remembered a rumour he had heard about your great-grandfather, the Legionnaire known by the surname of Rossi.

Yes, you are correct in thinking he served at Gallipoli with Amade's regulars, but you are incorrect in thinking he returned from Gallipoli to Britain. After Gallipoli, he returned to Bunifaziu with the Legion. He served for many years, but after a dispute with his superiors he deserted. I am told the story was that in order to make his escape, he swam across the Bucchi di Bunifaziu to Sardegna. As you will by now know, the Bucchi is 11 kilometres wide and it is thought he must have drowned, so the Legion did not bother to search for him. He was not seen again in Corsica. This old friend of mine remembers your great-grandfather as an exceptional swimmer and he is convinced he would have made the journey to Sardegna. Perhaps it is he who has given you your love of the sea. My friend also remembers that his real name was Antonio Sciacchitano and that he came from the island of Lipari, near Sicily.

23

Lipari is a place I know well: I have visited it often in winter. If you have the opportunity to do the same, perhaps you should call on a woman I have stayed with there. Her name is Valeria Vaccariello and she lives in La Casa dei Sconosciuti on the Punta San Giuseppe. She is, as you will no doubt find out, very beautiful; though I am not sure anyone knows exactly how old she is — such a question I have always been too polite to ask. And Vaccariello was perhaps the name she used for her acting; although this I do not know for certain either. But, she has lived on the island of Lipari for many years and so knows many people; she may be able to help you find out more about your ancestor.

For your travels, I have given you many 'lettres de recommandation'; they will help with your passage through Sardegna and on to Lipari. One of these letters is for Valeria. Please pass to her my letter with affection.

As you are now the master of the Mara, I doubt that I will see Valeria again, but as she will tell you, we have enjoyed many good times together. I hope, when history has been provided with sufficient time to forget what has passed this last autumn, I will see you return to your friends here in Corsica.

Votre ami dévoué,

Camille

Ric puts down the letter and picks up a chart. Before him lies Lipari, the largest of the Aeolian Islands; behind him, Panarea and the island volcano of Stromboli. The village before the southern point is Canneto and beyond the point he should find the main town of Lipari.

Ric unfurls the Genoa and hauls up the mainsail. The breeze through the islands is even and holds enough weight for three or perhaps four knots. He grabs a bottle of water from the cabin and swings the helm over to port: the promise of a square meal in Lipari appeals.

7

The Mara makes good time across the bay at Canneto, a village squeezed between a slender white strip of volcanic sand and the steep slopes of Monte Sant'Angelo towering behind it.

Ric has no detailed local charts and so gives the point below the barren and breast-shaped hummocks of Monte Rosa a wide berth. The sea around the point cuts up a little and he bounces and lurches in the wake from a hydrofoil scurrying northward.

As he rounds the point the town of Lipari comes into view. To starboard, a cluster of masts emerge from the low seawall of a modest and modern marina, and directly before him, spread either side of its citadel, sits the town. To the right lies the municipal port: a sizeable fuel dock beside a ferry terminal, a cemetery arrayed up the slope behind it. To the left lies the old town: a press of whitewashed, sun-bleached houses, most of them two storey dwellings watched over by a cathedral and a monastery, which grace the citadel like ageing chaperones.

In the cradle below the citadel, lies a small harbour from which small boats come and go, and beyond the town the coast runs down in a succession of shallow bays and rocky points towards another island, Vulcano, a mile or so further south.

Ric isn't minded to tie up in the marina away to starboard and, though the wind has tailed away in the lea of Monte Rosa, he is making easy passage. As he gets closer to the town, he sees small water taxis plodding this way and that, and notices a few, broader-beamed, day-trip launches lined up along the seawall.

As the Mara slips quietly beneath the hotels perched on the cliffs to the south of the town, he observes a small *barca* cruising twenty or so metres off and slightly behind his starboard quarter. A man sits in the back while the helmsman stands in the wheelhouse. Their course is taking them too close to the Mara, but thinking that the motor boat will, according to the laws of sail over motor, give way to him, Ric ignores them.

The *barca* does not though: the helmsman is for some reason ignorant of the Mara's presence.

The passenger calls to the helmsman to make him aware of their proximity to the sailboat.

The helmsman nods in reply, slows his motor and bears away, making to pass behind the Mara.

Ric acknowledges the helmsman's reaction with a brief wave, but the helmsman, a short, stubby man with grey curly hair, simply scratches his cheek and ignores him.

But for the stubby helmsman, the scene reminds Ric of an aftershave advertisement: a gentleman of Latin descent sits upright on the aft deck of a motor cruiser as it sweeps swiftly across a bay in the evening sun. He sports wrap-around sunglasses, is suntanned, chisel-chinned and is blessed with a full head of wavy black hair. His open-neck, white cotton shirt flutters over a frame that is the answer to a woman's dream, which is both appropriate and fortunate because just such a woman waits expectantly on the far shore.

The passenger in the *barca* is watching Ric as though reading his thoughts. He bows his head, politely.

Ric drags himself out of his reverie, smiles and raises his hand in both apology and appreciation.

The man waves back and grins. He knows how good he looks; his teeth dazzle white against his tan.

A way further on Ric comes upon a secluded, half-crescent bay, the waters of which play host to a handful of sloops and ketches similar in size to the Mara.

A slim, shingle beach accommodates a slipway, just large enough to provide for the launching of a dinghy, and a narrow track from the slipway curls and twists up at a steep angle out of the bay. Overlooking the bay, and set back up on a protective wall, stands a stone cottage so small it could easily be mistaken for a garden shed were it not for the satellite dish on its roof. A green hatchback is parked outside and a table and chairs are arranged out front on a patio.

Ric drops sail, starts the motor and potters into the small bay. With the sea out of the north-east behind him, the sailing boats lie bow onto him; a squadron of naval corvettes zealously guarding their station.

As he motors to the right of them, he notices a change in the colour of the water ten metres or so on the nose. He spins the helm over to port. The Mara swerves and yaws, and Ric watches as a bright turquoise rock threatens the surface a couple of yards off his starboard quarter.

There are enough spare buoys to go round, so he heads up to the furthest on the line, hoping he isn't about to take someone else's favoured mooring. His body protests a little as he lies over the bow and ties up, but that done, he squares away the sheets, checks the bilge and, noticing it is a little full, runs the pump for a few minutes. He goes below to set the main cabin straight and replace the Beretta in the locker beneath his bed. If there is a drawback to the Mara, it is that she lacks a dinghy with which to get ashore.

The breeze, which has helped him make such good time down from his overnight stay, has settled in the midday heat and there is little in the way of swell that will hinder his swim to the beach. He locks the main cabin hatch, hides the key in the recess beneath the cockpit seat and stows his shoes and clothes in a plastic bag, which he makes watertight with a length of line.

Ric pitches the bag over the stern, climbs over the rail and dives into the sea. The sea is colder than he thinks, but, he is glad to notice, not so cold that it takes his breath away. He swims ashore towing the bag behind him.

The small beach is deserted and no one comes from the cottage to tell him he is not allowed to moor in the bay without paying a surcharge. He towels himself down and changes into his shorts, shirt and shoes, tucking his trunks and towel back in the plastic bag and hiding it behind a thriving oleander at the back of the beach.

The track up out of the bay is steep and he is forced to take a breather halfway up. Though he has stretched and run through a limited routine of callisthenic exercises most mornings of late, his muscles feel tight and take too easily to filling with lactic acid whenever he slows.

The walk along the narrow road, which undulates and curls as it follows the contours of the slope up from the sea, takes him a good half hour. He keeps to the water's edge whenever possible and arrives at a bay a little broader than the one in which he has just left the Mara. A whitewashed hotel looms tall above an alley that rises steeply up, over and into the town. At the top, he has to stand back in a doorway as a three-wheeled *Ape* van approaches.

The battered *Ape* is a cross between a moped and a flatbed van; it has no doors and only a bench seat. The driver, a stringy individual with short, light-brown hair, thick glasses and a wide toothy grin, leans out of the cab and salutes his thanks.

The alley is shaded and cool, and the humble terraced dwellings lean in, squeezing the heavens into a thin strip of blue. Washing hangs down from the balustrades and if it was not for the white plaster façades reflecting the sunlight down into the cobbled passage, the alley would lie in darkness. Old ladies swathed in black, chew their gums and watch.

A small maritime chapel on the corner, its doors swung open, is vacant but for the Virgin Mary waiting patiently for her congregation. Hollow debate echoes from a wireless behind the shuttered windows of a single room dwelling. Dishes clatter, children cry, mothers comfort and husbands doze; the atmosphere is calm. And, as he strolls through the Via Maddalena, Ric can feel the tensions of his journey fall away and his heart settle to beat a little slower.

He trips down a flight of stone steps winding round a corner and is confronted by the portal of a church, which faces the old harbour. The murmur of those at prayer swells and shrinks, and church bells chime the hour. Ric realises by the strangely thin metallic peal of the bells that the sound emanates from a loudspeaker in the belfry of the campanile adjacent to the portal.

Walking down past the scuba-diving school and the clothes shops, he is accosted by a young, curly-haired individual; young in as much as he is probably as close to twenty as Ric is the other side of thirty.

"Panarea, Salina, Stromboli?" offers the young man. He brandishes a selection of brightly coloured flyers in Ric's face, as though if he doesn't hurry up and choose one right here and now, they will disappear in an instant.

Ric recognises the *escurzionista* for what he is, neither threatening nor an inconvenience, and certainly not a magician. He met a few of them in Cagliari; they are not a bother, leastways not to him. All they are set upon is earning their crust by selling boat trips out to yet another blue grotto or secluded beach or, in this fellow's case, the adjacent islands.

"No thanks," Ric replies, smiling.

"You are English?" replies the *escurzionista*, his eyes lighting up.

"Sort of," Ric states. He makes to move around the man, but the fellow steps into his path.

A cloud passes over the young man's face. "You have been to Salina? You have had lunch at Da Alfredo? It is what one must do before one..." he lets his voice tail away, implying the restaurant holds some extraordinary mystery.

"Dies?" Ric finishes the sentence for him. "Death and food! Nice angle!"

The *escurzionista* is wearing a two-day stubble, which enhances his poor-man-of-the-town look. His olive skin is heavily tanned for so early in the year and he stands a shade shorter than Ric. His shoulders slope down from his neck, giving him the aspect of a slim pyramid.

"You think it is funny?" he asks.

"No," Ric replies, studying the curly black hair which falls either side of the man's face. "Keep your wig on. I've just come past Panarea and Stromboli, and I'm sure I'll get around to Salina in good time. But, right now, I need food sooner than I can get by taking a trip out to Salina."

The *escurzionista* allows his frown to linger for a couple of seconds before his face breaks into a wide beaming smile. He steps back out of the way and at the same time gives Ric the once over. "Okay, English, maybe some other time." His smile is practiced; it is both easy and endearing.

"Not that it matters, but I'm not English," Ric replies, turning to walk away, "I'm Welsh. *Ciao.*"

Ric walks down into the square and realises the *escurzionista* is keeping step with him.

"So, you are *Gallese*. If you do not want me to know your name, this is how I will address you. I am Alessandro; everyone call me Sandro," he pauses waiting to see if his information has been absorbed. When he is confident it has and they have reached the bottom of the steps down into the square, he wipes his right hand on his shirt and holds it out. He wears an off-white cotton shirt, shorts and flip-flops. A small gold medallion swings from a chain

30

around his neck as he leans towards Ric. "Sandro," he says and makes to bow.

Ric shakes his hand, "Pleased to meet you, Sandro."

"Yes, *Gallese*, it is good to meet you, also. This café, over there," he points. "Tell them Sandro sent you." Then the young man is gone, off after virgin prey: a greying couple, sandals, socks and shorts, stealing nervously into the piazza. There are others of Sandro's type mooching about the place, but lunchtime is not a favoured period in which to flog boat trips out to the other islands; most of the tourists, like Ric, are more interested in food and shade.

He takes a seat at a café and orders a beer and a plate of salami, tomatoes and lastly mozzarella which, the pretty waitress informs him, is sent over from Naples.

Ric has only been sitting for a couple of minutes, watching the small boats come and go from the harbour, when the *escurzionista*, Sandro, reappears at his table.

Without asking, he sits down opposite Ric and lights up a cigarette. His dark eyes gleam and a mischievous smile plays across his lips, "You sail here?"

"Uh-huh," Ric replies, chewing.

"How many days?"

Ric hesitates and then holds up three fingers.

"Where from? Napoli, Capri?"

Again Ric makes him wait.

Sandro studies him, calculating and for some reason squinting briefly up at the sky. He drags heavily on his cigarette and speaks as he exhales the smoke, "Libecciu has been for the last week blowing." He grins cheekily. "I think perhaps Cagliari. Yes, I believe you have come from Sardegna."

"Give the man a cigar," Ric mutters.

But Sandro, his confidence high now that he has placed his quarry and, even more importantly, not yet been dismissed, carries on, "But

31

where is your boat? One man in a boat; it cannot be very big. You are in Porto Turistico?" He appraises Ric, lingering to look at the small strawberry birthmark above his right eye, and then corrects himself, "No, I do not think you are a man for the tourist marina, you have your boat somewheres else."

"You like to ask questions, Sandro," Ric observes dryly.

Sandro frowns as though his new friend has insulted him, although not insulted him so much that he feels the need to dispute the veracity of the insult. He grins again. "There is not much to do here when business is quiet. It is a little game I like to play; to guess where all the peoples are coming from." He pauses. "So, where do you stay? You want a hotel for a few nights?"

Ric chuckles. He has to admire Sandro; he has nerve and no little charm. "No, I don't need a hotel. I'm moored in a bay just up from Portinente, if I've pronounced that right. But thanks for the thought, anyway. Rest assured, Sandro, if I need a place to stay, you'll be the first person I ask to recommend it."

"Okay," he hesitates, "*Gallese*. When you want something, you come see me, Sandro, okay?"

"Be happy to Sandro," he replies and returns his attention to his plate.

Fortunately, Sandro understands he's exhausted his share of his new friend's patience, so he gets up and wanders off.

Ric watches him lope across the square; his gait is relaxed and rolling, a slight swagger to it, but the kind of swagger that comes from enthusiasm or perhaps bravura, not from any kind of physical intimidation. Sandro strikes up a conversation with an old man sitting in the shade of a statue.

As Ric's taste buds grow more accustomed to the lively profusion of flavours, the comforting sustenance and the unmoving ground combine to accelerate the lethargy seeping through his system. Soon he drops off to sleep.

Ric is not aware of how long he has been out for, but he is woken by a gentle hand on his shoulder.

It is Sandro, again.

"No good to sleep in the sun, my friend." Sandro changes the angle of the umbrella, returning the table to shade.

Ric sits up and rubs his eyes: "Sure, you're absolutely right, Sandro. Thank you for thinking of it. I must have been out for the count."

"Out for the count?" Sandro sits down, again without asking permission.

Ric feels his own face and wishes he'd remembered to wear his cap. "Yes," he replies, "out for the count." But when Sandro is clearly none the wiser, he continues, "Out for the count. You know, when a boxer gets knocked down. The referee counts to ten, if the man doesn't get back up, the fight's over."

"*Ah! Si!* Boxing! I have seen this. It is a saying, yes, out for the count?"

"You want a beer, Sandro?"

Whether it is the beer he wants or the acceptance lent him by the offer, Ric doesn't know and doesn't really care. Sandro has saved him from waking up burnt to a crisp, so he reckons the young man deserves a reward. Ric hopes too that the bilge pump of the Mara has kicked in. He turns to look for the pretty waitress, but as he does so, she appears as if by magic and sets a Birra Messina in front of Sandro.

"*Grazie, Giuliana,*" Sandro says. But the girl is making eyes at Ric.

"*Ciao, Giuliana,*" Sandro encourages, more than a little irked.

She walks away, swaying her hips.

"I have this for you," Sandro leans over and drops a map of the island on the table. "It has streets for the town, and roads and information. It is useful, eh?"

Ric sits up and reaches into his pocket for some coins.

"No," says Sandro firmly, "you buy me beer, I give you map. It is fair, no?"

Ric lowers his head and frowns theatrically.

Sandro winks, a curiously lop-sided, grimacing movement which requires him to tilt his head. Again his eyes linger on the red mark above Ric's eye.

They talk a while and Ric asks Sandro about the monastery looking down over the square, the boats in the harbour and the hydrofoil which drones in and out of the municipal port on the far side of the citadel.

"*Aliscafo*," corrects Sandro, "The hydrofoil; we call it *Aliscafo*."

An enormous metal ship resembling a car ferry lumbers out of the port beyond the citadel. It appears to be full of rubbish trucks.

"Yes," Sandro sighs when he sees Ric watching it, "it is a garbage ship that comes from Milazzo. We are UNESCO World Heritage Site, so there is no place for rubbish here. The ship comes here empty and leaves with all our garbage. The water ship comes here full of water and leaves empty. Everything that comes here brings something we need or takes away something we don't need; just like the tourist boats. They bring the *Romanacci*, the *Catanesi* and the *Calabresi*. We need them; they are a source of income. But we need them to go home too." He raises his right hand and touches his thumb with his forefinger. "It is a delicate balance," he states in crisp, educated English, as though repeating a phrase he once heard spoken by a visiting university professor.

Ric finds Sandro's caricatures amusing and they help pass the time until the sun drops behind the church without bells.

"You want I give you lift back to your boat?" Sandro asks, anticipating Ric's mood. "I have Vesper—scooter?"

Ric thinks about the offer for a while; he finds the fellow likeable in a fresh sort of way. "No thanks, Sandro. The walk will do me good. But I appreciate your company. Perhaps we'll have another beer some other time."

Sandro moves to object to Ric's refusal to his offer, but then suddenly thinks better of it. "Okay, *Gallese*, perhaps another time. You are staying long?"

"A while," he replies, "not sure how long. I guess that depends on the breeze."

"Okay, Ric. We will wait for the breeze."

Ric settles the bill and is unsurprised that no offer of contribution comes from the *escurzionista*. The waitress lingers a minute by the table, watching and waiting.

"Okay, okay," Sandro sighs. "Giuliana, this is my friend the *Gallese*. *Gallese*, this is Giuliana."

"Hi!" She raises her hand in recognition.

"Pleased to meet you, Giuliana."

She nods and supplies him with her widest smile.

Sandro, very obviously needled that Ric has leapfrogged him up the ladder of her affection, waves her away: "Okay, *adesso basta! Ciao, Giuliana. Grazie.*"

"Eh, *Gallese*?" He nods towards Giuliana who, though she has retreated to the back of the café, is still watching them, smiling. "This one; she is from Rome; a cousin or something of the owner. She looks at men the way city girls do, eh! It is like she knows what we are thinking and she doesn't care. The other girls here are not like this." He hesitates. "Or maybe they are; I don't know. Maybe it is the fathers who care more than the girls."

Ric shakes Sandro's limp hand, gets up from the table and strolls across the piazza beneath the citadel.

A cobbled street, wide enough for one car but not two, curves up a shallow incline out of the harbour. World-weary women adjust the displays outside their shops and make gossip with their competitors. Pensioners take time out of the late afternoon sun to stare at passers-by.

Rather than follow the rise of the street, Ric consults the map Sandro has given him and takes a left turn. The Via Maurolico leads him down to the Corso Vittorio Emanuele, the town's high street. The Corso is wider, and the tables and chairs of the cafés spill off the pavements onto the road.

He stops at the café La Precchia, takes a chair by the entrance and orders a coffee.

A mix of townsfolk and tourists stroll up and down the Corso, and Ric is content simply to sit and watch, comfortable in the company of strangers.

After a few minutes, the waiters begin to usher away those seated at the tables in the street and, once the customers have left, they drag the tables and chairs back, and stack them away.

Ric starts to rise, but a waiter motions to him to stay seated; it is only those in the street who need to be disturbed.

Shops up and down the Corso draw their shutters and close up. Owners and staff alike emerge from inside and loiter, evidently waiting. They chat amongst themselves, though they resist the chance to wave when they see a friend or the shopkeeper opposite; the mood is sombre, respectful.

Softly and very gradually music drifts from the top of the Corso: a trumpet, trombone and tuba, flutes and a drum herald the approach of a funeral procession. The dozen musicians in the vanguard are, with a few exceptions, young. They wear gold-buttoned light-blue uniforms, epaulets and plumed caps, and file slowly, but not to any step or keeping time, down the street.

The pavements are now crowded and though the band continues to play as it marches past, the air is strangely stilled. Those in the cafés quiet. They stand and join the assembled gathering in bowing their heads.

Behind the band trails an old, green three-wheeled *Ape* with a flat bed on which are arranged bouquets of brightly coloured flowers. Close on the heels of the *Ape*, file the clergy: altar boys dressed in white surplices over blue robes, priests in similar vestments bearing the cross, and a senior cleric wearing his mitre, pallium and pectoral cross, and thrusting his crosier before him, as though without it he would collapse onto the cobbles.

Next, a modern, shiny black hearse bears a coffin draped in more bright colours. The family and friends of the deceased follow close behind; the men, clean shaven and black-suited; the women gazing down at their feet, their heads veiled in black lace, their hands gloved. As the hearse inches down the Corso, it is pursued by an eddy of whispers. Like a slow-moving boat rippling the water of a still pond, so a ripple of conversation spreads in the wake of the hearse. Bystanders mutter and mumble aside and point furtively, sharing knowing looks.

The man at the head of the cortège walks with his head held high. He is barrel-chested and broad-shouldered, and pain and sorrow are etched deep in the lines of his face. He ignores the discourteous babble from the onlookers, but when he recognises a face amongst the crowd, he sets aside his sorrow to offer a weak smile of appreciation.

He glances at Ric by accident. The man's eyes are as dark as coal and glow with the embers of emotion.

Ric is startled by the intensity of the man's gaze, but he returns the look with an appropriately respectful nod.

In turn, the man acknowledges Ric's response with a slight bow. His glare yields for a moment and he walks on.

As soon as the last of the mourners have passed by, the low murmur of conversation returns to busy chatter. The young amongst the crowd offer the elders their sympathy; the elders eventually falling silent and wandering away.

The shopkeepers unlock their premises and stand back to allow their staff inside. The café waiters bring out the tables, chairs and parasols, and restore the street to its former symmetry. The melancholic atmosphere quickly evaporates and the movement of life returns to the Corso.

Ric sits back down, finishes his coffee and wonders what it was about the man that made those looking on so unsettled.

He pays his bill and sets off back up the Corso, reading the map as he walks. He's enjoyed his meal and, curiously, the company of the *escurzionista*, Sandro, and as the coffee works its magic with his weary limbs, he is taken with the feeling that he will enjoy his time in Lipari.

But when he gets back to the top of the road down to the small bay in which he's moored the Mara, he notices she is sitting low in the water. And by the time he gets down to the beach, he is alarmed at just how low.

A tall, elderly woman stands on the retaining wall, gazing, with her right hand shading her eyes, towards the Mara. She wears a floral blouse and long skirt, and–

"Your boat," she says as he reaches her side, "is sinking."

8

Unfortunately, the woman is right; the Mara is sinking. That she is down by a foot and some is obvious, but, thankfully, the water isn't yet up to her gunwales.

"Damn!" Ric swears, looking round, hoping to see a solution materialise out of the rocks around him. But, when he looks back at the woman beside him, he realises she has retrieved the plastic bag containing his towel and trunks from behind the oleander and it now sits at her feet.

"Yes," says the woman, in answer to his questioning look, "I thought you might need them quickly when you returned, so I took them from the bush. I thought it was a good idea."

"It was. Thank you," he replies, glancing at the woman. Ric kneels to open the bag, changes quickly and immodestly into his trunks. "Excuse me," he says, "if I..."

"Yes, of course," she says, as though she hadn't been expecting him to hang around to make polite conversation, "but I have a—"

He runs down to the beach, charges into the sea and swims the twenty metres out to the Mara as quickly as he can.

Ric scrambles on board, grabs the key from beneath the seat and unlocks the main hatch. He slips down inside. The cabin floor is already flooded, the water washing around his ankles.

Ric turns on the bilge pump. By rights, it should have kicked in automatically, but it hasn't and when he flicks the switch, he is rewarded by an irritating silence.

"Damn," he swears again. Water has been seeping in through the packing gland on the propeller shaft; not much, but enough for the bilge pump to have to put in some overtime and blow its fuse in dissent.

Fortunately, Camille has had the foresight to fit a manual pump as well as an electric one. So, the only avenue left open to Ric is to get on and pump the water out by hand. There is a lot; he will be a long time pumping.

Ric sits down in the cockpit and begins to work the pump handle back and forth in slow rhythm. There are only a couple of hour's daylight left; obviously not enough time to pump the bilge and prepare and pack some more homemade sealant around the shaft, so all he can do is to carry on pumping until the seawater in the bilge has sunk to an acceptable level. Then, maybe he'll be able to fix the pump.

In all the brief excitement he realises he's left his clothes with the tall woman. He twists in his seat and looks over at the beach.

She is still standing on the retaining wall, watching him. He can see she has long, wavy hair, but remembers that when he turned to thank her for retrieving his kit, he noticed that her hair was greyed at the crown and fine and blonde down the side. She is heavily tanned, as though she is used to the sun year round; as though, in spite of her good English, she is a native of the island.

Strange, he thinks, he didn't really look at her at the time, being as he was more concerned about the state of the Mara. And yet, from the brief glance he afforded her, he now recalls what she looked like in considerable detail: her frame slender and willowy, her shoulders broad and her collarbone well-defined. Her eyes, he remembers noticing, were grey; grey and possibly a touch cold.

Ric waves a brief acknowledgement of her. There is not much

more that he can do; he can't stop pumping for the moment, so he will have to sort out what he is going to do about his clothes later.

Then, as if she is reading his mind, the woman bends and collects his shorts, shirt and shoes and folds them neatly, before putting them in the bag. Expecting her to replace the bag where he has left it, Ric is surprised when the woman simply tucks the bag under her arm and walks back to the house set up above the shingle beach. She walks smoothly. Her poise, her deportment, is elegant and graceful, and he wonders if perhaps she was at one time a ballet dancer.

When she gets to the front door of the dwelling, she turns to gaze rather dreamily at Ric and, as she gazes, she raises her hand and waves at him.

Ric acknowledges her and watches her go inside.

The grey stone cottage is small, more garden shed than holiday retreat, and the roof, like those he's already seen, is pitched low and tiled in terracotta. But, at most, the place cannot accommodate more than a couple of rooms.

He glances out towards the eastern horizon. He knows from his winter in Sardinia that when the Levanter blows, as it does out of the east, the waves which beat the windward side of the island can swell to fifty feet or more, and he wonders if the cottage is set sufficiently far back from the retaining wall to be protected from them. The wall is, he judges, twice his height, maybe a bit more, and the garden between the house and the walls no more than ten or so strides back.

Ric pumps. His arm grows sore, so he switches hands and stands for a while, preventing himself from looking down into the cabin in case his efforts have not yet produced a noticeable reduction in the water level.

How many minutes have passed he isn't sure, when a small white skiff appears round the northern corner of the shallow bay. The outboard whines excitedly and the prow stands proud, obscuring his view of the occupants.

There is little wind to speak of and the sea is calm but for a broad, docile undulation. The sky is a silken light blue and cloudless, and the temperature languishes in the early twenties; it will cool, later, without any cloud cover.

The little skiff ploughs steadily towards him.

Ric works the pump to and fro, and watches the boat. A movement out of the corner of his eye makes him glance shoreward. The woman is once again standing on the retaining wall, but now she is between the Mara and the cottage. She is gazing in his direction and when she sees she has his attention, she points in the direction of the small skiff. The woman seems to be signalling that there is something, or someone, in the boat he should take note of.

When the skiff draws close to the Mara, the driver slews it round broadside so that with the wash from the turn the skiff drifts very smartly alongside. The act is precise, practised. The man at the tiller is short and wiry of build; his hair brown and shorn in a rather amateur fashion. Thick glasses perch on his wide nose and he wears a pair of faded blue shorts and a short-sleeved shirt, which probably started out white, but is now a tired shade of grey daubed with oily, smudged finger marks.

He grabs hold of the guardrail and stares at Ric through the thick lenses of his glasses: it is the man who was driving the *Ape* down the narrow Maddalena; the man who saluted Ric as he stood aside to let him pass.

"*Salve,*" Ric greets.

The man nods and grins in reply; his teeth are extremely white and even for a man who doesn't look as though he possesses the funds necessary to procure the services of a dentist.

Ric continues to work the pump.

The man just stands, holding the guardrail, watching.

"Well, I guess you've come to help?" Ric says, "Better come aboard then. *Vieni... a bordo,*" he adds.

And that is all that the man is waiting for. He ties the skiff off to a cleat by the pushpit and climbs over the rail.

"*Si è rotta la pompa di sentina elettrica?*" he offers, looking puzzled.

Ric shakes his head, "*Si*, dead right, my friend: the electrical bilge pump is on the blink."

He steps towards Ric and motions to relieve him of his onerous task.

"*Grazie*," Ric replies with considerable feeling, "*mi chiamo Ric.*"

"*Salvo*," says the man. He grins again and adds for good measure, "*Salvatore.*" He works the handle more smoothly and seemingly more easily than Ric, as though he and the pump are old friends and now that they are reacquainted with each other, the pump will transfer the water out of the Mara quicker for him than it will for Ric.

"*Grazie, Salvo, mille grazie*," Ric offers by way of encouragement.

"*Prego*," he replies and proceeds to work the pump. Great jets of water spurt from the outlet just below the gunwale, punctuating his effort. And although Salvo pumps assiduously, his expression betrays a casual indifference to his exertions, as if it would not bother him to have to pump all night.

He grins, a wide toothy grin. "*Albero motore, trasmissione? Elica? Stagno?*" he asks, letting go of the pump handle briefly. He sticks the index finger of his left hand out straight and makes a winding motion around it with the same finger on his right hand.

"*Possibile*," Ric replies, and then says more positively, "*probabilmente.*"

"*Okay*," Salvo decides, "*nessun problema*," and he continues to grin as though the leak is nothing more than a manifestation of the Mara's age and therefore nothing that one should be ashamed of.

They take turns at the pump for the better part of an hour and when the water level has receded sufficiently, Ric replaces the fuse in the electric bilge pump. It whirrs, cuts out, and then whirrs away continuously, allowing them time to take a breather.

"*Scusa, Salvo*," Ric apologises, "*non ho birra, posso offrirti un bicchiere d'acqua?*"

He shakes his head, *"No grazie. Nessun problema. Grazie."*

Salvo has brought tools with him. Strewn about the bottom of the little white boat lies a collection of wrenches, screwdrivers and spanners, and a box of assorted lines, weights, tins of grease and various off-cuts of material.

He climbs down into the skiff and returns with a lump of dull, cream-coloured waxen substance, which he begins to work between his large hands the way a cigar wrapper rolls tobacco leaves. *"Stucco,"* he says allowing Ric to sniff it.

"Sure! Okay, putty?"

Salvo nods enthusiastically. *"Si,"* he says and then tugs at his eyelid to suggest Ric pays attention. He lays the little pipe of putty carefully on the deck, strips off his shirt and shorts, and climbs down into the skiff. From it, he grabs a diving mask, which he puts on, and then he slips, carefully, into the sea.

"Ric, lo stucco, per favore?" he asks, sounding as though his head is thick with cold.

Ric leans over the rail, passes him down the putty and Salvatore disappears beneath the boat. From where Ric is standing in the cockpit, he can feel the little Italian fumbling about somewhere around the prop.

While he is left alone, Ric tries to understand why Salvatore has materialised out of the blue and, perhaps more importantly, where his saviour has come from. Apart from passing him in the narrow passage on his way into town, he doesn't know the man from Adam. And apart from Sandro who, like an unwanted pet, seems to have attached himself to Ric and the tall lady with the cottage across the way, he has so far spoken to no one else.

Salvo reappears, gasping for air. He pushes back his mask and treads water. *"Aspetti,"* he says, half-climbing into the skiff and grabs what looks to Ric to be a reel of clingfilm. Tearing off several strips, he winds them around his forearm, repositions the mask on his face and disappears down beneath the Mara's hull once more.

Again, Ric can feel Salvo tugging at the propeller shaft. And again, just when Ric reckons he must be out of air, Salvo reappears, panting and puffing.

He slips off his mask, tosses it over into the skiff and clambers up on board the Mara. "*Okay! Finito!*" he says, pointing at the deck.

"Sure," Ric replies and guesses at what it is that Salvo wants him to check. The bilge is, by now, pretty much dry and he can see that whereas before, where there had been a steady succession of drips from the stuffing box around the prop shaft, now there is only the very slightest and very occasional drip of water coming through the seal.

"*Fantastico, Salvo!*" Ric exclaims, hoping his pronunciation doesn't make him sound too British.

"*Prego,*" replies Salvo, with a nod of his head that almost qualifies as a bow. He is evidently a little embarrassed at the reaction his efforts have drawn. Then he seems to want to say something to Ric, but clearly doesn't want to put his point across in words of more than one syllable, so he just points to the deck again and says, "*Presto, eh?*"

Ric smiles. For sure, he knows the packing needs replacing soon; to ship water in a heavy sea would be disastrous. He looks at his new-found deliverer and notices the deep squint lines at the corners of his eyes and the long-cured scars on his knuckles and forearms. Whoever he is, Salvo is no stranger to work.

"*Si,*" replies Ric, "*Presto. E mille grazie. Mille grazie.*"

"*Prego,*" says Salvo, with another vague nod. Then he looks around the Mara as though seeing her for the first time. "*Mara! Una bella barca, eh?*" And with that he slips over the rail down into the skiff, unties his line, yanks the starter cord on the outboard, waves at Ric with his free hand and beetles off towards the town.

Ric stands and scratches his head. What he's done to deserve such kindness, he can't think.

The sun is sinking with what is left of the breeze, but now, thanks to Salvatore and his tuck box of homemade remedies, the Mara will not go the same way. He thinks briefly of his shirt, shoes and shorts the lady in the cottage has picked up off the beach. He supposes they'll be just as well in her care as they would have been in his. And he realises he's forgotten to ask Salvo if he has moored the Mara to a free buoy and decides it doesn't matter either way. He'll run the risk of being harangued by some late-returning sailboat; he's run greater risks in his time.

9

For the second time in two days, Ric is aware of a distant, mechanical droning; only this time it is much louder and much closer than before. He rolls off his bunk and stands, head up through the main cabin hatch.

A mile or so out, an Aliscafo, which ties the islands and acts as their umbilical to Milazzo on the Sicilian coast, thunders northward towards the town. It is a mean, wailing banshee hastening across a mirror-like veneer; a mad mullah, robes raised, charging along the Mare Siculum in search of the infidel.

There is not a cloud to poison the sky and only the faintest hint of a breeze out of the east. The first aid the little Salvo has applied to the propeller shaft seal has slowed the ingress of water to an acceptable level. But Ric knows he will not be able to leave the island until he has attended to the greater problem and hopes there is a dry dock over in the bay beyond the citadel. In the meantime he makes a note to keep an eye on the water level in the bilge.

He heats up a pan of water with which to make a cup of tea and shaves in what is left. As is the way of things, just as he's lathered his cheeks a small Rib comes alongside and two youths, wearing T-shirts and shorts and looking more like beach loafers than port officials, greet him casually.

"*Salve,*" says the leaner of the two sitting in the bow. But Ric loses the gist of what the lad tries to tell him next.

"*Scusa*," Ric interrupts, "*Non parlo l'Italiano. Parla Inglese?*"

"*Ah, Si*," he replies, grinning and pointing at the Tricolour of France hanging at the stern. "*Inglese!*" he adds as though everything is now clear to him. "*Inglese*," he repeats and turns to his associate standing at the helm. They bat whatever issue it is they have with Ric back and forth between them in a staccato of conversation, weighing their alternatives.

"Moment, I come," the spokesman says in stilted English and they motor away towards the beach.

As they near it, Ric sees the woman from the cottage watching them from her customary position on top of the retaining wall.

They greet each other with much smiling and polite recognition. A familiar, but respectful banter passes between the boys and the woman. The exchange lasts but a few minutes and ends with a happy salutation from both sides.

As the Rib passes by the Mara, the spokesman calls, "Is okay. *Grazie*. Thank you." And they are gone, speeding off towards the old port.

The woman waves at Ric, then walks back to the cottage and reappears a moment later with a pair of oars. She walks down to the slipway and turns along the gravel beach to where a small inflatable dinghy is lying tied up to the retaining wall. She unhitches the dinghy, drags it into the sea and sets the oars in their locks. Then she slips elegantly on board and rows in the direction of the Mara.

Ric hurries to finish shaving, looking round every so often to gauge her progress. He cleans up as she pulls alongside.

"Good morning to you in the Mara," she hails, shipping her oars.

Ric bends down through the rail to grab hold of the dinghy. "Good morning to you," he replies, straining a little. "Please, come aboard." He steadies the boat while the woman reaches up and places the plastic bag containing his clothes and shoes on the deck.

She is as tall and willowy, as he had at first thought; not as tall as

48

him, but tall for a woman nonetheless. Her hair is long and wavy, like the ripples created when a stone is dropped into a pond from a bridge, and she wears a white linen chemise with the sleeves rolled back and similarly coloured shorts which extend over her knees.

"I am Valeria," she says, holding out her slender hand for him to shake.

"Ric," he replies. Her hand is warm, sinewy and slightly calloused, as though she rows often. And he notices the grey of her eyes once more; that grey he has seen so many times, the cold grey of first light. He tries to guess her age, but cannot arrive at a conclusion; she may be in her seventies or even her eighties, but, then again he thinks, she may be younger if life has been unkind to her. "Thank you for looking after my kit."

"It was my pleasure," she says, smiling easily.

"Welcome aboard. I don't have much except for coffee and tea. Which would you prefer?" He stands back to allow the woman to step down into the cockpit.

"Coffee," she decides, "will be very acceptable, thank you; black, without sugar, as you will make it. I believe there are two kinds in this world: the coffee that the Italian cafés make and the coffee that we make ourselves, but I am not fussy."

Even though her English is good, Ric notices a slight Italian cadence in her pronunciation. "Well," he replies, "I can't compete with the average Italian café, so I am grateful." He inches past her and climbs down into the cabin to fill the kettle from a large plastic water bottle and, having done so, sets it on the small gas stove.

"You are grateful?" she asks.

"Yes," he calls up, "for your not being fussy. The Mara doesn't extend to anything as grand as a coffee-maker, but I do have a cafetiere and some freshly ground coffee. Well, ground anyway. I'm not so sure how fresh it is; I don't enjoy the luxury of a fridge."

"Oh, yes, of course, I know."

What she has said doesn't strike him as odd to begin with. His initial reaction is to think it is merely her use of English which has confused him and that she has probably meant him to know she would take it for granted his amenities are limited. But then he realises she must be Valeria Vaccariello, the woman Camille has mentioned in his letter.

Once the kettle has boiled and he's filled the cafetiere, he picks out a mug. "You know the Mara," he says.

Valeria smiles again, a warm reassuring smile which suggests she is pleased with him: "Yes, I know Mara. And because I know Mara, so I must know her owner, Camille. Last autumn was the first for many years he has not visited. I hope he is well."

"He is," Ric replies, "or rather he was when I last saw him in the back end of last summer." And, though he is reluctant to tell her what happened in Corsica and, particularly the sequence of events that led up to his leaving, he understands he must explain how he has come by the Mara, otherwise she will be suspicious of him.

"Camille has," he begins slowly, "decided to call time on the Mara. His years have finally caught up with him and he told me he no longer has the energy to look after her. He thought the Mara would be better off in younger hands. He asked me to give you a letter."

Ric retrieves the letter from the drawer of the chart table and passes it to Valeria. He expects her to open it, but instead, she hesitates and examines it briefly, her brow furrowing in concern as though the letter might contain bad news.

She realises Ric is watching her closely: "And not a day too soon. I was always pleased to see him. Two winters before, when he was last here, I was taken with the feeling that I would not see him again. I did not know it for sure; I just felt it in my heart." She pauses and smiles a little wistfully, before putting the letter in the pocket of her shorts. "Age is a blessing granted only to the fortunate few. But, like all blessings, it comes with conditions." She falls silent for a moment.

"You've seen Camille often... over the years, I mean?"

Valeria hesitates and studies her long, elegant feet, the toenails of which are painted a bright red. "Usually in late autumn he would come. And if he did not come in the autumn, he would come in the spring on his way home."

"So the Mara is known here?"

"Naturally, the Mara is well known throughout the Mare Siculum; from here to the Calabrian coast, down to Messina and along to Palermo. Mara and Camille; they are one and the same." She raises her head and studies him for a few seconds, as though she is placing him beside Camille.

Ric wonders whether the woman has enjoyed a casual liaison with the old boy. "The two young lads in the Rib, what were they after?"

"Oh," she wakes from her imaginings, "they wanted to know if you had reserved the mooring."

"And?"

"I told them you had only arrived last night and that it would be sorted out later."

"So, where do I go to do that: to sort it out, I mean?"

"Oh, I wouldn't worry," she dismisses, and adds with a confident dose of certainty, "they will not ask again."

Ric pours her coffee, passes her the mug and wonders what she said to the boys that it might incline them not to bother him again.

She examines the mug, giggles and sips; clearly she has drunk from it before. "Your coffee is good," she proclaims, "much better than Mosca's."

Now that she has referred to the old fox by his nickname, Ric is more certain that he is in the company of a friend.

Valeria is watching him again, watching and reading his thoughts, and studying the small, red birthmark above his right eye. "Mara is sick?" she asks.

He likes the way she refers to the old sloop as though she were

51

an acquaintance rather than a rudimentary construction of wood, metal and sheet. "Yes," he replies, nodding. "It is as you said: the blessing of age, but with conditions. I'll need to get her out of the water. Is there some place I can do that?"

"Of course," she replies, but she doesn't go so far as to tell him where or how he is supposed to go about finding out where.

"Thank you, that is good coffee," she repeats as she hands him back the mug. "And now I must be going. Perhaps if you would like to take me to the beach, you can return using my small boat. You are welcome to use it while you are here."

Ric raises his eyebrows in pleasant surprise, "Thank you. That will make life a lot easier. You must have got to know Mosca pretty well if he stopped off here so many times, though I'm not sure what I've done to deserve such kindness."

She stands up and looks down at him: "Oh yes. I know Mosca well enough." Her smile glows warm: "And, as to deserving kindness? Don't worry, Ric. This is Lipari. This is how it is here."

10

Early evening, once the sun has lowered and the heat has drained from the air, Ric checks the stern tube; it is no longer leaking. He takes the dinghy ashore and tethers it to the retaining wall. The tall Valeria is not at the cottage, so he strolls into town through the narrow Maddalena.

Sandro, the *escurzionista*, is absent from the Marina Corta and that makes way for others similarly keen to promote their cause. Doe-eyed daughters and sharp-eyed sons of café owners are dusting down, adjusting parasols and laying up tables. Old men congregate beneath the statue of San Bartolo; they lean on their walking sticks, gesticulate and chatter in urgent and sincere tones. Rock music filters from cafés and the waitress who had taken a shine to him the day before, smiles and waves.

The town rises back a hundred feet or so from the old harbour and the Via Garibaldi winds up out of the Marina Corta between restaurants and pavement cafés, rising over a shallow saddle which separates the main part of the town from the walled citadel above. The narrow streets are cobbled and crowned, with high pavements and grated drains.

Ric turns into the Via Maurolico in search of the supermarket, which he has learned is to be found some way towards the bottom of the Corso Vittorio Emanuele.

Caught up in the sights and sounds of the busy street, Ric strolls past the supermarket and lingers at a stall to admire the colourful array of fruit. A short, round-faced, gravel-voiced old woman calls her boy to the front. She weighs Ric up, wondering whether he is nothing more than just another tourist out to waste her time with banal queries concerning the pale complexion of her apricots or the extraordinary lustre of her tomatoes.

He picks up a lemon the size and shape of a hand grenade, and examines it. The skin is lumpy, rumpled and pockmarked like the face of an old soak. Ric has not seen its like before.

"*Cedro*," says a woman behind him.

He turns: it is Valeria.

"*Cedro*?" Ric repeats, trying his best to mimic her pronunciation.

"No, *Cedro*," she repeats, "with a *C* like cheese, a *D* like dame and an *R* that rolls. *Cedro*," she says again slowly. "It is like a lemon and a little like a grapefruit, but not so tart, you would say. The pith is very thick. Some people make a conserve with them, some candy the peel and others flavour drinks and make a salad with them. But most simply slice them very thin and eat the fruit of the centre."

"I've not seen one before," Ric says and asks the old lady, "*Quanto costa?*"

The old woman nods in Ric's direction, scoffs and barks a scathing remark at her boy.

He ambles over and says, "One," and then, "Euro."

"They are from the island," Valeria says.

Ric's attention is drawn by a young woman wearing a broad straw hat and oversize sunglasses walking by. She smiles back at him; a slightly deprecating smile, but not so deprecating that it suggests she disapproves of his attention.

"You've been in your own company too long," Valeria observes. "And you look like you could do with a decent meal."

But before Ric can reply to her vague offer, she adds, "And, I think, perhaps a shower?"

Ric steps back.

She recognises the distress in his reaction, "No," she says, shaking her head, "that wasn't what I meant." She tut-tuts mischievously. "It is what Camille always wanted when he arrived: a cold beer and a shower, amongst other things, but always those two before he turned his mind to food. Come, this evening. You are not allergic to fish?"

"No," he replies, "thank you, a shower and a meal would be very welcome."

"Some time around eight-thirty then," Valeria says, glancing at his wrist, and adds, "around sundown," in case the clock on the Mara is not working.

"Thank you, Valeria. I look forward to it," he replies, and then realises the right course would be for him to contribute towards the meal. "Would you like me to bring wine?"

She smiles and says, "Yes, that would be good of you."

Ric raises an eyebrow in question.

"The Caravaglio, a white wine, is good," Valeria replies, "it is from Salina. You will find Caravaglio in the supermarket."

She turns and strolls gracefully up the Corso Vittorio. Valeria walks slightly head down, as though carefully studying the cobbles before her, but now and again she acknowledges the greetings of the café owners with a smile and a slight inclination of her head.

Ric watches until she disappears round the corner into the Maurolico, then turns and continues his stroll down to the municipal port.

The Corso empties its gaggle of lazy strollers into the Marina Lunga; a colourful crowd amidst a warmth of gentle chaos. Eager *escurzionisti* petition tourists freshly arrived off the Aliscafo. Enormous, pin-clean coaches, seemingly too sophisticated for such a plain island with so many narrow roads, lurk menacingly on the corner. And older, smaller minibuses stand idle as stooped pensioners file out for their day's shopping. Antique Fiats and Lancias appear from the colosseum of winding lanes, bearing all the hallmarks of combat. A tinker, hunched over the back of his three-wheeled *Ape*, sharpens knives and works metal on request. The garbage ship is leaving and the loud speakers atop the small ticket gazebo proclaim the onward destinations of the Aliscafo: "*Salina, Panarea, e Stromboli.*" In the middle of all the organised confusion, a policeman stands chatting to a pretty girl.

But it is the walled cemetery, stretching up the hill behind the Marina Lunga, which catches Ric's eye. It reminds him of his first time in the citadel of Bonifacio on the southern tip of Corsica.

Even though he'd located the arched entrance into the long-deserted Foreign Legion garrison – the location of the black and white photograph of his great-grandfather – it was the *Cimetière Marins* in the Bosco that drew him. It was as though the rows of mausolea exerted some gravitational influence over him, beckoning him to the narrow walkways between the whitewashed tombs as though the dead knew he would be fascinated to hear their histories. Curiously, although he doesn't understand why, it is the same now.

Tall, grey iron gates are flanked by four even taller columns, the outer two topped by white pillars supporting stone urns which throw out petrified eternal flames; the inner, shorter pair support two conical vessels draped with sculpted cloaks. And in between the columns stand ornate gates crowned by a delicate iron cross, the centre of which is ringed with a crown of thorns, the words *Omnia Traham* inscribed beneath.

Ric strolls up the long avenue of cypress trees between the modest headstones and the simple graves. In crowded beds the young sleep beside the old. A marble headstone adorned with an anchor notes the year of passing, but there is often no note of the year of birth.

Geckos skitter in and out of the shade, and ants trail to and fro like supply vehicles on a busy mountain road.

The further he strolls, so the modest headstones are replaced by elaborate, raised sarcophagi, presided over by Jesus on his cross, miniature angels with mournful faces and the bust of a noble patriarch. And, nearer the back where the hill rises more steeply, substantial neoclassical mausolea, some art deco, others plain, some black granite, others white, grace the terrace and bear witness to the comings and goings in the port below. The deceased wait patiently for the return of their children, children who long ago left in search of greater opportunity.

One of the grander mausolea belongs to the La Cava family and Ric recalls the name written in large-but-faded letters on the façade of the run-down warehouse by the tangled steel pontoon to which he'd moored. That, in turn, reminds him of the argument he heard through the fog and he wonders whether he managed to get away from the place without being seen.

As Ric walks out of the cemetery, he hesitates. Though it is still warm and sultry, he shivers and turns, for some reason expecting to see the ghosts of the departed following him. But there is no one behind him except for an old man, who leans against his witches broom and watches him, waiting to see which way he will turn out of the gate.

He wanders through the milling crowd to the Corso Vittorio, stops off at the supermarket to pick up a couple of bottles of wine and climbs the narrow, winding steps between the houses of the Salina Meligunis up to the cool of the Piazza Mazzini in the citadel. Ric pauses to read the commemorative plaques on the walls of the municipal offices.

He checks his stride as he walks down out of the cool piazza, turning, expecting to see a line of *Soldati* and *Militari* stalking him. But again, there is no one.

II

After his shower, they sit out on the patio and watch the shadows lengthen over the water. Valeria serves him a plate of *fettuccine* garnished with small, sweet tomatoes, feta and basil, and follows it up with thin slivers of rapier fish, minced herring and capers.

Ric has neither showered nor eaten so well since leaving Sardinia and now he's scrubbed off the layers of sea salt, he feels clean and full, and pleasantly rested. The wine dances through him with light feet: peach, lemon, delicate minerals.

Valeria sits and smokes long, thin white cigarettes. She seems comfortable in his company in just the same way Camille had been easy with him; neither of them driven to unnecessary conversation and neither of them offended by silence.

Later, she serves him a small glass of limoncello. "You had trouble in Corsica? Camille writes this in his letter. He says it is better for you to keep away from the police." She frowns, as if he is her pupil just returned from an hour on the naughty chair. But her frown soon melts into a reassuring yet vaguely amused smile. "You can relax here; they will not bother you. My god, it is not as though we don't have enough police: Port Police, Carabinieri, Finanza, Urbani and Forestale. Most of them I know, including the chief of the Carabinieri. It is La Polizia from Milazzo you will have to be careful of; they play by different rules. And remember, if Camille says you are a friend then what trouble you have had is not important."

She pauses and glances at the signet ring Ric wears on the slender chain around his neck. "The ring?" she asks, "It is Camille's?"

"No. It is a similar ring. It belonged to his friend, Gianfranco Pietri."

She nods: "Manou's father."

"Yes. He's told you about her?"

"Oh, yes," Valeria replies, smiling again. "To give such a ring to a man implies great affection."

Ric's face colours: "I'll take on board what you say about the police. Thank you."

"Oh, don't thank me; the chief of the Carabinieri doesn't like waves any more than the fishermen. Storms we have in good supply and wind too? Well, this is the Isle of Winds, the home of Aeolus the King of Winds, so we are used to living with his capricious temperament. But, I have also learned waves make it difficult for us to navigate through life; we can do without them."

"The Isle of Winds?"

"Yes," Valeria replies, gazing out at the flat, oily sea: "Also the Island of Grief, of Drama, of the Damned, and, for many years, an island that belonged to the Devil."

Ric studies her face. Her nose is slender and straight, not acquiline, like so many, and her cheekbones are high and proud.

"Why Grief and Drama?" he asks, "Why the Devil's Island? To the naked eye, it looks like a small slice of paradise." But, as soon as he has said it, Ric realises he had thought the same about the south-eastern corner of Corsica until he was dragged, kicking and screaming, beneath the surface.

She smiles a resigned, slightly amused smile, "Because history has a habit of cursing small islands like ours. Lipari is out of the way and there are always people who are in the way. Caracalla, the Roman

59

Emperor, sent his wife, child and brother-in-law to Lipari in the third century; he had them murdered here. Later, when the Bourbons ruled the Kingdom of the Two Sicilies, they expelled their political opponents and many criminals to Lipari. And yet the Bourbon Queen Maria Carolina, Marie Antoinette's sister, built a refuge here; although we think this was because she wanted to get away from her filthy commoners, not because the British Governor of Sicily exiled her to the island.

"But the blame for why Lipari became known as the Devil's Island lies with Mussolini. Il Duce deported many of his political adversaries here. In fact," she mocks gently, "you had only to sneeze in public to be deported here in the 1930s; you didn't have to be openly disrespectful of the Fascist ideal. During the years of crystallised disorder, you could be expelled here for saluting the Militia in the wrong fashion or simply by knowing someone who was on their black list. That was enough to get you locked up in the Regina Coeli in Rome before being transported like cattle to Lampedusa or Ustica or Favignana."

"I can think of worse places to be banished to," Ric replies.

Valeria shakes her head. "No, it was not so nice in those days. Before the political deportees came, the citadel was a prison for murderers and bandits, sometimes even Mafia. The citizens protested to the authorities, but all they did was to replace the criminals with politicians; at least *they* didn't rape and beat the people of the island. But the deportees had to live in hovels and basements, and pay much in rent. On ten liras a day, if you did not get money from your family, where else were you supposed to live? The conditions were terrible. As we say, poverty is one thing, squalor is another."

She sighs as if the island is still unclean. "One man," she pauses, remembering, "Leonida Bongiorno, a teacher of English. He helped some of the deportees escape from Lipari. He was a man of conviction; not like so many others who wanted only to make money from the misfortune of others."

The sun has now set away behind the island and the patio is lit by a bright full moon, suspending like a lantern low in the eastern sky.

"It's not exactly Siberia though, is it?" Ric says, trying to lift the conversation from the doldrums of Valeria's recollection.

"No, Ric, you are right. It is a small slice of heaven." She lights another cigarette and exhales heavily. "We are famous for our volcano, Stromboli, and our pumice and our obsidian. But, for how much longer, who knows? There are people who want to build hotels here; to bring prosperity to our little island. If they do, we will lose our status as a World Heritage Site. As for the politicians, they continue to promise us prosperity like it is a light at the end of a tunnel. But this is a dream which should not be realised by us, the *Terroni*." She glances at him. "The promise of prosperity is nothing more than an illusion: it is a false horizon which delivers only a poverty of spirit."

Her pronouncement hangs in the air like a pregnant moth.

If Ric didn't already know from Camille's letter that she had been a film actress, he is sure he would have guessed so. In spite of her years, she is strikingly beautiful and even more so when stirred. She reminds him of Manou.

Valeria turns to look at him very directly, "I apologise for my rather monochromatic view of the world. It is state of mind that comes with age."

"You've no need to apologise, Valeria. It's perfectly natural to want to protect something you love. How long have you lived here?"

She gazes at him; her expression balanced between bitterness and regret: "Since the seventies. Since I realised the world is full of ugly, unforgiving and dishonest creatures."

Valeria sighs once more. "Luchino," she glances again very briefly at Ric, "Luchino Visconti, he promised me the part of Angelica in *Il Gattopardo* – The Leopard. It was good casting; it made much sense. I come from near Palermo, not far from where the Salina estate of Lampedusa's book lies." Valeria stands, as though it is the only way she can accommodate the pain of her memory, and Ric is reminded of how tall she is and how gracefully she moves.

"Then, out of the blue, he gives the part to that Tunisian slut and the film wins the *Palme D'Or* at Cannes. The rest, as one might say, is history." She floats back down; a gossamer throw settling over a chaise longue. She sips her wine.

Ric searches for some words with which to apologise for the many great injustices of the world, but nothing that comes to mind seems either adequate or appropriate.

"*Non è giusto*, Valeria," she mutters and immediately giggles. "That is not fair of me; La Cardinale was the better age for the Sedara virgin and she had worked with Luchino before. No, I should not speak ill of her, or him. He was a good communist and it's not as though she was his paramour. Luchino was not one for the girls, if you understand what I mean by this."

Ric feels his head weigh under the fierce glare of her emotion, and the wine and the lack of true sleep during his journey begin to tell on him.

"Please don't think me rude, Valeria: dinner was wonderful and light years ahead of my diet of the last few days. I'm grateful to you, but I think I'd better hit the road or the water, or whatever the correct expression is."

Valeria smiles warmly, her moment of irritation passed. "Of course, Ric; I understand perfectly. A good night's sleep is of greater benefit to youth. When one is older, sleep, like lovers, can be elusive. And the only lover available to a woman of my years is Morpheus; to find him, I take a sleeping draught. Even our lighthouse, Faro del Mediterraneo will not wake me."

They clear the table and take the dishes and glasses into her modest kitchen.

As he turns for the door, she says, "In the morning we will talk of this ancestor you come to look for. And we will talk about how to improve Mara's health." She hesitates, "If you would like, Ric, you are welcome to sleep on the sofa. I have spare blankets and I am certain you will find my sofa more comfortable. Mara will be quite safe without you; there are no storms forecast this night."

Ric smiles in appreciation.

"I would offer you my bed," Valeria grins, playfully, "but you are not Camille and I am not young. In the morning, bring me your washing and I will see to it; this is one luxury you can share with Camille."

12

Her sofa provides a better night's sleep than his bed on board the Mara. But it is narrower than he might have hoped and several times in the night he dreams he is balanced on the edge of a cliff, staring at rocks and shallow water.

Over a breakfast of fresh apricots, sweet cake and coffee strong enough to tar a road, Ric again asks Valeria if there is a boatyard where he can get the Mara fixed.

"Il Velaccino, Marcello," she replies. "He will take Mara out of the water at Canneto. He knows all there is to know about making her better. He lives at Capistello, the village up there." She points over her shoulder at a hamlet on the hillside. "I will give you directions. You must tell him you are a friend of mine, that way he will be fair with you."

The air is cool and clear, and, as they sit out on the patio, Ric watches the Aliscafo charge towards the Marina Lunga.

"Camille says in his letter that your family name was Sciacchitano."

"Or so he thinks," Ric replies.

"It is more than possible," she says, considering. "It is a Sicilian name and there are families with this name in Lipari. That will both help and make it difficult for you to find out anything. Sadly, many people of the islands emigrated in the last century." Valeria looks for all the world as though she's just come out of make-up and her carefully constructed repose suggests she is expecting a photographer.

"Even now, after *scuola media* most of the children go to Milazzo or Messina for further schooling. They don't always return. Once they have seen what the world has to offer, it is hard for them to find enough reason to come home."

Valeria lights one of her thin, white cigarettes and ponders for a minute. "Your grandfather or great-grandfather, he left Lipari for Britain, when?"

"We think, in the thirties," Ric offers.

Valeria frowns, turning figures over in her mind. "In the last years of the nineteenth century, to emigrate made much sense. Of course, the island exported pumice for the building of skyscrapers in New York and many of the men went to help build them. But the only work for men was fishing or working the pumice quarry, so in the first ten years of the last century nearly 10,000 left for America, a quarter of that number for Argentina and many to Australia. Now we have only 10,000 people on this island, although in the summer the Aliscafo brings as many people again. But… but in the thirties, life was hard; the only way to get off the island was to volunteer to go to *Quarta Sponda*, to Libya or Tunisia."

Ric is listening. But it comes to him that if the population of Lipari is so small, then it is likely that most people know each other and, therefore, it is likely that any one of the people he has met since his arrival knows either the victim or the murderer from the charade he heard played out in the mist.

"As part of the forced colonisation, you mean?" he asks.

"Yes, as a part of Balbo's dream of Grande Italia. You could not leave the islands unless you had a permit. Many of those who could not get work sold their souls to the Fascist State. Before the war, the police force in Italy was greater than that of the police forces of France, Germany and Britain combined. It is unlikely that your ancestor would have emigrated from Lipari; it is more probable that he would have escaped."

Valeria chews her lip for a moment before adding, "I will commit some thought to this. A diversion would be most welcome. But first, you must see to the Mara. Here," she scribbles a map of directions, "this shows you where Marcello's house lies. He knows all there is to know about boats; even his name means he is of sea. Tell him I sent you."

13

"La Strega, you say, eh? At La Casa dei Sconosciuti?"

Ric assumes he's referring to Valeria and the cottage, and he expects the man to follow up his questions with some sharp remark about how Ric is living with a woman old enough to be his grandmother. But he doesn't. He busies himself poring over the tow-hitch of an archaic tractor, so Ric replies simply, "Yes."

Signor Maggiore is medium height and barrel-chested, and his jet-black hair frames a wide face dominated by a heavy brow, a brow which extends like a broad lintel over his arrow-straight nose. Ric recognises him as the figure who walked behind the hearse and who led the mourners of the funeral cortège two days before.

"You are English? We can speak English. It will be easier." He lights the stub of cigar wedged between his teeth.

"Well, I'm probably more Welsh than English, but that would be splitting hairs given the circumstances."

The man frowns, but Ric feels this more from the brief and intense flash of his eyes, rather than any obvious alteration in the contours of his forehead.

"No, I understand what you say, but it is important to split hairs. The people from Wales are not the same as the people from England. This will be like saying the *terroni* are the same as the *polentoni*, which is not true. The *polentoni* are from the north of Italy; they have money and die young from stress-related illness. We are the *terroni* of the south; we live long because we understand that life is simple." He clears his throat, spits aside and bends to the coupling of the trailer.

"You get many British tourists here?" Ric asks.

"A few, not many. We are not sophisticated enough for the British. Or, maybe it is that we are too sophisticated. Who knows?" He wipes his hands on an oily rag. "Why? You want to meet people from your own country? You have a boat, why would you want to meet people of your own kind? Usually people with boats don't want to meet people of their kind; that is why they travel by boat, alone, eh."

"No, it's not that. It's more that so many people here speak English, I hadn't expected it this far south."

Signor Maggiore leans back, hands on hips and stretches out his short back: "Many different reasons for this. La Strega speaks good English because she was a film actress. *Escurzionisti* speak good English because they must speak it to earn money. I speak good English because I had a good teacher."

"Bongiorno?"

The broad Liparotan eyes Ric a little suspiciously. "Si, Leonida Bongiorno, the *comunista*. I was not one for learning, but he was a good professor for me." He pauses for a moment and weighs Ric in his mind. Whatever conclusion he reaches, he dismisses it.

"But, I have to fix boats for every nationality, so it is a good ability for me. Not," he says, pointing out to sea, "boats like this, eh?"

Ric turns and shades his eyes to watch a gargantuan motor yacht open at the transom to disgorge a sizeable tender and several jet-skis. It is absurdly monolithic in proportion; at least twice the size of the Kohar, the Armenian's yacht in Corsica: "Not so much gin palace as champagne palace."

"*Si*, they get bigger and bigger, like big hotel, perhaps one day even bigger."

"You could hide a small army in one of those."

The man Valeria has referred to as Il Velaccino glances up at Ric. "*Si*, or many bad people, fugitives, illegal immigrants… last summer a little bird told La Polizia in Milazzo that one of these boats, a Russian boat, was taking a Serbian war criminal to Africa to escape the Court of Hague. They arrest the boat and bring it here, to Marina Lunga. Big important happening: much chest puffed out and growing taller for La Polizia. Then," he begins to chuckle, "then they find out it is not a Serbian war criminal, but it is a member of the Russian Parliament – the Dumas – on his way to a party with Il Cavaliere – Berlusconi – in Panarea." He laughs, bends, slaps his thigh, and wipes his eyes with the same oily rag with which he has just wiped his hands. "Ah, it was what you would call priceless. Many red faces; many cocks suddenly walking like hens. Much amusement for us, eh? La Polizia, they go back to Milazzo to argue with each other. Perhaps they don't come to feel the heat in our kitchen for a while, eh?

"Now, I have work and soon the sun will be high. What can I do for the Mara?"

Ric explains the problem with the packing around the stern tube seal and Marcello Maggiore says he can fix it, only the boat will have to be out of the water for a few days.

He plucks the cigar from between his teeth, examines it and then rubs his lower lip in thought: "You cannot stay on Mara while she is out of the water. This is not possible, I don't have the correct braces; only enough to keep her up while we work. You can stay at La Casa dei Sconosciuti, with La Strega?"

"How long's a few days?"

"Maybe five, maybe a week? I have others waiting and it will help me to have Mara at my yard if I need to order parts."

"Five nights might be too long on Valeria's sofa. For her, I mean. I'd be better off taking a room in town."

Signor Maggiore examines his cigar once more. "I have an idea. Your name is…?"

"Richard Ross, Ric will do."

Il Velaccino examines his own hand before offering it. "Marcello, pleased to meet you, Ric." His fingers are lean and strong. "You are a friend of La Strega?"

"Sure."

"Then, I have a *monolocale* in the town, in a vico near the Garibaldi. I rent it out in the summer. Now it is empty, so you can have this for as long as it takes me to make the repairs."

"Sounds good to me," Ric replies, surprised the man has not demanded a fee for the accommodation. "Thank you."

Marcello relights his stubby cigar, takes a couple of drags and walks away, checking the straps on his trailer as he goes. "Now I must work; we can talk later. You want me to come to Casa dei Sconosciuti or I see you in Marina Corta?"

"The Corta will do. I don't have that much kit. What time?"

"Oh, I see you at *passeggio*." He waves his cigar in salute.

14

Valeria is hanging his washing on a line behind the cottage when he returns.

"You should let me do that."

She sucks her teeth, "When I can no longer hang out the washing, then I will lie down for good. What did Il Velaccino say?"

Ric chuckles.

"Oh, of course, he told you I am La Strega. Well, you will find the Siciliani are not offended by their sobriquets. To most, I am known as La Strega, the witch, and Marcello is known as Il Velaccino, the sailmaker." She gathers her basket and he follows her inside.

"I'm afraid the Mara is going to be out of the water for a few days," he says, "and I won't be able to stay on board while he does the work."

"It is not a matter, you can stay here."

"Marcello, Il Velaccino, has offered me a place in town and I don't want to put you out: fish and house guests and all that."

Valeria turns to look at him, clearly none the wiser for his expression.

"Sorry, it's an old saying: the similarity, fish and house guests, they both start to go off, to smell, after three days."

But, Valeria is still studying him, dreaming or perhaps trying to find a deeper meaning in what he is saying.

"Something my mother used to say," Ric offers. He wonders for a moment whether he has offended her by rejecting her hospitality and appearing to throw his lot in with the man to whom she has just introduced him.

Then she comes out of her stupor: "As I said, it is not a matter. You can come and collect your washing tomorrow, but first a little coffee and biscuits."

They sit out on her patio and watch the sailing boats beat the breeze down towards Vulcano. The air is clear and from where they sit the coast of Sicily is a faint blur on the horizon. Yet another Aliscafo hastens noisily around the citadel.

The *nacatuli* biscuits are small and round and decorated with flowers and leaf shapes; they taste of almonds and cinnamon and rose water.

"*Cavazza*," Valeria says, pointing at a herring gull circling the cliffs away to their right. The gull's cry is jarring and scornful, as though it objects to carrying the ills of the world on its broad, black-tipped wings.

Beyond the cliffs, the tall, grey-white, bald cone of Vulcano dominates the horizon. "Is the volcano still active?" Ric asks.

"No, no longer. The white smoke comes from sulphur fumaroles at the rim of the crater. There are four volcanoes, all dormant now. A Scottish man, Stevenson, bought the island in the nineteenth century. He mined sulphur for making explosives, for treating skin conditions, making paper, that kind of thing. Stevenson also mined alum for purifying drinking water and for cosmetics, but he built houses, and planted vineyards and orchards. Then in 1888 the volcano erupted for two whole years; Stevenson left and nobody went back until after the Second War. Before Stevenson, the Bourbons sentenced their condemned to work in the mines. People say Vulcano is the closest place to hell on earth, which is probably why the Romans thought it was the entrance to the underworld."

"Seems a pretty uninviting spot," Ric says.

72

"Oh," Valeria drags on her cigarette and exhales a long stream of white smoke not unlike those issuing from the crater, "there are some hotels on the coast, just across the straight. And, sometimes I go to Acqua di Bagno for the hot mud. It is good for the skin. But you cannot get away from the smell of the sulphur; it can be overwhelming. Some days, when the Scirocco blows, you can smell it from here."

"I suppose one can get used to most things," Ric adds, "but living with the many volcanoes must be like living in the shadow of several time bombs."

"Yes, it is. The volcanoes can be destructive, and yet they can be benevolent too; over the years they have provided the islanders with the means to make a living. First they provided obsidian; the black glass which you find on the beaches. Pliny, the Roman naturalist, named it this way; it was first used as a cutting tool in the Stone Ages. It is said that Pliny died trying to rescue a friend from the eruption of Vesuvius: ironic, eh, don't you think?

"Many people died mining the sulphur and alum, and later they began to mine the pumice. As recently as the seventies Lipari exported 150 million lira of pumice. It was one of the few regions of Italy which were not in debt. However, that has stopped now; there are cheaper sources of pumice and the idea of child labour no longer sits so easily alongside the idyll that is Lipari. Stromboli is now the only time bomb, as you put it."

"I stumbled across Stromboli on my way here," Ric says, recalling the colourful aberrations which had interrupted his night, "didn't seem to be sleeping too soundly to me."

"If you were coming from Sardegna, what you saw was probably the Sciarra del Fuoco, the Path of Fire, on the north-western side. But you are correct, Faro del Mediterraneo never sleeps. For thousands of years the sailors of the Mare Siculum have relied on her light to guide them home."

"She?"

"Yes, *she*: Mount St Helens, the Three Virgins and the Saints Ana, Clara and Isabel. They are all women." Valeria turns to face Ric, smiling and yet calculating. "Is there a man who can match a woman for her emotion, her ferocity? And who can look at a volcano without seeing a woman's breast rising out of mother earth? Yet, I have heard it said that when a volcano is active, she is a woman and when the volcano sleeps, he is a man. Strange, no?"

Away to the north Stromboli sits quietly electing a new Pope. Ric smiles back. "But I thought Stromboli was a character from *Pinocchio*, the Disney film?"

Valeria nods, "Yes, you are correct. In Collodi's novel Mangiafuoco is the fire eater, but in the film he is a puppeteer. But," she adds, "as much as Faro del Mediterraneo can be a blessing, she can also be a curse."

"A curse? Why?"

Valeria frowns and pauses. "Yes, a curse. Her flames attract people in the same way a light attracts insects; people, like insects, become transfixed by her brilliance. But, when one gets too close to her flame…"

"Your house, La Casa dei Sconosciuti?" Ric asks "The House of Strangers?"

"Yes." She stubs out her cigarette and sips her coffee. "You remember I told you about the island being a prison during the time of Il Duce. Well this house was used as a meeting place for the political deportees. La Casa dei Sconosciuti brought many strangers together."

Valeria lights another cigarette and gazes out at the sea. "I was drawn to the house when I came here. It was appropriate. I needed to find peace – a certain anonymity – and it is often to be found in the company of strangers. They may be silent strangers, long dead, but their souls still walk the shoreline at night. I find their presence comforting."

Though the sun is by now close to its zenith and the heat haze has reduced the view of the mainland to a faint smear, Ric shivers. Valeria is the first person since Manou in Corsica who has referred to the dead as though they still walk in the land of the living.

15

Ric knows from his time in Sardinia that to meet at *passeggio* means meeting at some time between the end of the working day and dusk. He takes a seat at the back of a café and waits.

Couples walk to stimulate their appetite, while others walk to ease the course of their digestion. Old men sit beneath the statue and lean on their walking canes, ruminating about political stagnation. Boys play hide-and-seek and kick plastic bottles between them. And older boys, sporting pork-pie hats, lounge on the low harbour wall, laughing and applauding their friends as they show off their latest bicycling tricks. Young girls, dressed to the nines, push prams and cluck over imaginary infants, and new mothers parade their babies in multi-coloured underwear. Other girls, too old for pretend and too young to engage, stroll slowly, though not so slowly that their aged chaperones might think they risk indecency. The sun has dipped below San Bartolo al Monte, throwing the Marina Corta into shadow. The air is still and vaguely humid. But, to walk is to be sociable…

"*Salve*, Ric," the pretty waitress, Giuliana, greets him and with a sweep of her hand she suggests he take a table of his choosing.

Giuliana lingers when he has chosen. She is, he thinks, in her early twenties, not perhaps as young as some of the waitresses working tables in adjacent cafés and she dresses differently too; her straw-blonde hair is short-styled, her blue skirt not quite to her knees and though she is slender, her Dolce and Gabbana t-shirt is a size too small.

Marcello pitches up just as the lanterns around the piazza begin to shine. He acknowledges Ric with a wave of his cigar, but has business to discuss with others before he has time to share. Now and again Marcello's acquaintances glance over at Ric as though Il Velaccino is advising them of his status.

"Excuse me," he says, when eventually he pulls a chair up, "but this is the only time of day I can speak to others. How was your day with La Strega?"

"Interesting," Ric replies, "she would appear to be the font of all knowledge."

Marcello raises his eyebrows and says, "I think I know what you mean when you say this, but surely the font is what you have in the church for keeping holy water?"

"Font, fount, fountain of knowledge: same thing only different, I guess."

"You have been spending too much time with that old witch. She speaks in riddles too, eh?"

"Is that why you call her La Strega, because she speaks in foreign tongues?"

A thin individual of pensionable age with a pinched face, hard eyes and thin lips approaches the table. When he realises Marcello is in conversation, he nods politely, almost deferentially, and takes a chair far enough away that he cannot be accused of eavesdropping. Marcello nods at the man, who in turn speaks aside to the waitress. A bottle of Birra Messina and glass appear in an instant.

"No, we call her the witch because she believes she can communicate with the spirits who live out in the water near La Casa dei Sconosciuti. People have seen her walking out by the cliffs at Punta San Giuseppe at night, dancing and calling out. There are some old stories of this house." He scoffs gently, as though he is not inclined to condemn her for her beliefs. "Perhaps the house is haunted? Who knows?" He waves his hands in the air and laughs, "She is old. Old people are allowed to think what they like. And if talking to imaginary friends is what they are happy doing, then…"

A scrawny-looking youth with long, straggly hair and low-slung jeans sidles into the café and flops down at an adjacent table. He glances around nervously.

In an instant the patron of the café is standing beside him. He growls at the kid, who jumps up and leaves as though he has sat on a scorpion.

Marcello shakes his head in pity, but, as if to distract Ric, says, "You see this old man who sits beneath the statue of San Bartolo; the man who sits up straight; the man with the black glasses and the nose like a Roman?"

There is more than one old man sitting at the foot of the statue wearing dark glasses. Ric cranes his neck, "The one with the collarless shirt and braces?"

"*Si*, him. Old Nino. He is so old that no one knows how old he is. He is older than La Strega and has outlived his wife, two sons and six grandsons. If you talk to him, he will tell you how, as a boy, he used to slide down the Cave di Pomice, the hill of pumice at Porticello, all the way from the top right down into the sea. And, even though he is blind, he can describe this to you in such detail that you would believe he did this yesterday. I think he sees everything more clearly than we do. Every evening, one of his neighbours brings him to the Corta and takes him home after. The next day he can tell you exactly what was said the evening before. His memory is like a great computer. *Figlio di Troia!* And I can't remember what I said to my wife this morning!

"But, old Nino Cafarella believes that Il Cavaliere — Silvio Berlusconi — is Il Duce's illegitimate son and that the Fascists still govern through him. But, if that is so, it would mean that Il Cavaliere is Edda Ciano's half-brother, and that, my friend, is ridiculous." Marcello glances up at the heavens. "But, if Old Nino wants to believe this, what is the benefit to convince him it is not true, eh?"

"Ciano?" Ric asks, "Wasn't her husband fingered for Mussolini's shooting?"

Marcello scoffs, this time more dismissively, "Hey, everyone from Garibaldi's ghost to the Pope was in on that one. And if they weren't, they would all like you to believe they were." He drinks his beer and surveys the scene.

"I remember now," Ric says, "didn't Mussolini have his daughter's husband shot?"

"Yes," Marcello sighs, "but as we say, where there is smoke, there is fire. Nobody gets shot without a reason, eh? Maybe he was not complicit? Who would know this? The dead? And does it matter so much. He was Il Duce's son-in-law; perhaps that was enough reason."

"You know, Edda Ciano was a prisoner here, in a house in the little Piazza San Bartolo behind the Chiesa di San Giuseppe, over there." He points across the Corta to the church at the top of the steps by the entrance to the Maddalena. "She was sent here after she returned from Switzerland at the end of the war. It is said she had an affair with Leonida Bongiorno; I told you about him; my English teacher. They made a film about it. Just the other day they show it here."

"Can I get you another beer, Marcello?"

He thinks for a moment before replying, then turns and glances at the slender man sitting alone a few tables away. "No," he decides, "it is late and I must show you where you can stay; then I have more business."

"I'll settle my bill," Ric says and signals to Giuliana, who swans up to their table: "*Il conto, per favore?*"

She looks at Marcello, questioningly, and, when she receives no recognition, she turns to the man sitting across the way.

He smiles, but without any real warmth, and inclines his head: their drinks are his pleasure.

Ric nods his thanks, the man nods back and the waitress smiles.

"Come," Marcello says as though Ric is nothing more than one of his vassals, "I have been too long talking. It is a problem; too much talking."

16

The shops along the cobbled Garibaldi are closing. The women, bored, accepting, reluctant and relieved, are hooking down their carefully arranged displays of garments, packing away driftwood carvings, metal sculptures and fridge magnets, and exchanging weary moans with their neighbours.

Halfway up the rise dark-skinned, *hijab*-wearing women sit outside their shop. They bounce giggling children on their knees, cooing and poring over them as one might a favoured pet.

Marcello turns off the street and walks between the family, pausing and stooping to pinch a cheek. "*Buonasera,*" he says and the women smile and nod in appreciation.

Ric follows him into and down a narrow alley.

"*Melanzane!*" he mutters: "Arabs, Berbers, Tebos, even Jews," he says over his shoulder. "We inherit them all from Tripolitania: you would know it as Libya. Oh, and Somalis too. These days Africa begins at Rome, but then again," he chuckles, "ignorance begins at Perugia!"

The alley is narrow, only just wide enough to accommodate Marcello's broad shoulders, and bounded by a continuous terrace of houses whose iron balustrades protrude from low balconies. The passage is a meeting of shadows, and only the dim glow from corner lanterns and the occasional soft chevron of light projected through slatted shutters interrupts the dark. Murmurs and whispers, rhythmic and gentle on the ear, are broken only by a harsh exchange or the barking of a dog.

At the end of the alley, Marcello turns right into a second, slightly broader alley, but one that is little different from the first. Ric is trying to keep his bearings and searches for a sign on the walls to tell him the name of the alley.

"Not far," says Marcello, hesitating as though he has momentarily lost his way in the maze. He turns left, stops abruptly and fishes in his pocket for a set of keys.

The wooden door opens towards them. They enter and Marcello flicks a light switch.

Immediately in front of Ric is a staircase and to his left a modest room, which is both kitchen and living room. The tap at the basin, he notices, drips.

"There is a bedroom upstairs and a bathroom. There," he points to a door at the back of the room, "you will find a wash room with a toilet. It's not much, but it will be better than La Strega's sofa; a little more private too."

"What do I owe you?" Ric asks. The thought of sleeping in a real bed that is firmly tethered to the ground is all consuming.

"There are clean sheets in the bedroom and a towel in the bathroom. I have someone do this for you," Marcello replies, ignoring his question. "If there is something missing, you tell me, eh? I will ask her to get the right things? You didn't bring your clothes?"

"No, I'll get them in the morning. Valeria is washing them; I guess she'll tell me when they're ready."

Marcello stops and turns to look at Ric, studying him again as though he is trying to make up his mind about some doubt he harbours. "Yes, of course, I am sure La Strega will come here. È *una ficcanaso*: she is always curious, eh?" He touches the end of his nose briefly. "Now you must sleep and tomorrow morning we will take Mara out of the sea and try to find out her problem. You have all you need from the boat? Once it is out of the water it will not be good to climb up? You think it is the seal around the shaft for the *elica*, the propeller."

Ric is trying to remember if he's left anything on the Mara which he might need. "I reckon so. The morning I arrived at San Giuseppe, this guy turned up out of the blue, patched up the stern tube with something that looked remarkably like pasta; didn't charge me for the pleasure. Nobody seems to want to let me pay for anything, not even for the beers this evening. I hate to think what's going to happen if you all call your markers in on the same day."

Marcello is watching him as though reading his face: "Tell me: this man, what did he look like?"

"Wiry build, light-brown hair, thick glasses, constant smile."

"Oh," Marcello nods slowly, his expression strangely deadpan, "Salvo, yes, I know him. He works for me, sometimes. Curious, he did not tell me. *Ciao*, Ric. We will come to collect the Mara in the morning and together we will sail her to Canneto, eh?"

17

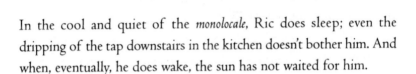

In the cool and quiet of the *monolocale*, Ric does sleep; even the dripping of the tap downstairs in the kitchen doesn't bother him. And when, eventually, he does wake, the sun has not waited for him.

He searches through the few of his belongings he has brought with him, but cannot find the keys to the Mara.

Ric swears in frustration and dashes out into the shaded maze of alleys. Once out in the stark light of the Via Garibaldi, he notices the neon sign above the doorway of the pharmacy flashing 12.00, and then 35 degrees. And, by the time he's taken the steps outside the Chiesa di San Giuseppe two at a time and hurried up the Maddalena, Ric can almost hear Marcello ribbing him for being late.

When he slows to negotiate the steep lane that runs down into the bay at Portinente, he glances seaward and is surprised to see the Mara several hundred metres out in open water, Salvo at the helm.

Marcello is walking up the Maddalena towards him, smoking a cigar. He looks serious. "Time is money," he says, but his expression cracks and he winks playfully.

"Sorry, Marcello," Ric replies, "no excuses; I overslept."

"Yes, tiredness will drive a man to sleep, but a woman... she will drive a man to drink." Marcello chuckles and raises an eyebrow. He puffs on his cigar, examines it, and adds, "Not my wife, eh, you understand. She drives me to work." He laughs out loud, a short staccato laugh, part *grappa*, part tobacco.

Not having met Marcello's wife, Ric doesn't laugh quite so readily. "How did you get her off the mooring? The keys, I mean?"

"It is not a problem, my friend. Your friend," Marcello nods out towards the Mara gliding serenely across the bay, "Salvo asks La Strega if she has the keys. She had them, so she gave them to him. She hopes you will not mind. The day is growing short, eh? I looked briefly at the stern tube; you were lucky she did not let the sea in on your way here. Do you know when she was last out of the water?"

"No, sorry. Camille didn't tell me and I didn't ask."

Marcello frowns, "You did not have a survey?"

Ric shakes his head and replies, "No. It wasn't that kind of transaction." But he's not inclined to let on what kind of a deal it was that he struck with the old man in Corsica, so he bridles his mouth and pulls a face that suggests he wishes he had.

"*Va bene*, it is not a problem." But Marcello is studying Ric again as if he is weighing whether his new client will be good for the money the repairs are going to cost. He decides. "It is okay, we can fix her. Come to my place tomorrow and we can discuss what there is to do. The *monolocale* is comfortable?"

"Sure, it'll do just fine. I'm obliged," Ric says, once more wondering exactly what his obligation might be.

"Okay," Marcello flicks the ash off his cigar and starts up the rise. "You will find my work place behind Canneto," he shouts over his shoulder, "on the road to the left after the tunnel. See you, but do not expect too much too quickly, we are very busy preparing many boats."

He hesitates and turns back, "Oh, hey, Ric! You like to fish? Perhaps we can go tomorrow evening. I will find you." Then he is off, marching up the Maddalena at a steady pace.

It is only when Ric has reached the bottom of the alley that he

85

remembers he has left the plastic bags with the passports and the gun in the stowage compartment on the Mara.

18

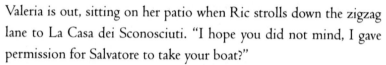

Valeria is out, sitting on her patio when Ric strolls down the zigzag lane to La Casa dei Sconosciuti. "I hope you did not mind, I gave permission for Salvatore to take your boat?"

"Not at all. Seeing as he stopped the Mara from sinking, I guess he's entitled. But where did he get the keys, I can't seem to find them."

"You left them here with your things. I gave them to him." She motions him to sit down. "I have your washing inside, not yet ironed of course." Valeria sips her coffee, slowly, and then says, "Now, there is a man you must talk with. His name is Nino."

"Old Nino? Tall, thin fellow, dark glasses?"

"Yes, you have seen him in Marina Corta? He is there most evenings."

Ric nods, "Marcello pointed him out to me; told me he knows as much about the island as there is to know."

Valeria smiles, "What Il Velaccino says is true. Nino knows much, but his memory is not constant. If you can talk to him on a good day, you might find out some information about your great-grandfather. And have you been to the cemetery above Marina Lunga? This would be another place to look; I am sure you will find more than one grave with the name Sciacchitano. Perhaps it would be worth your time to speak with Nino. We can go tomorrow. Nino speaks good English, but it will be better if I come with you. I can take you to Quattropani; it is where he lives, on the north-west of the island."

"I don't have a car," Ric says. "I could rent a scooter in town, but I'm not sure you..."

"No, we will go by bus. It will not take long; the island is only thirty-five kilometres around. I will meet you in the Corso Emmanuelle before the sun is too high."

"Thank you, Valeria; that is good of you."

"Oh, don't thank me, Ric. I have little to do here but see what Aeolus promises me in the way of weather. And besides, there is no guarantee that Nino will be enjoying one of his more lucid episodes."

19

The afternoon beckons and Ric wanders back into town. He isn't sure if he will offend the patron with the pinched face and hard eyes if he chooses an alternative café from the one in which he and Marcello sat the evening before, so, not risking it, he takes a chair and orders a beer. Giuliana is not on duty and Sandro is busy having his picture taken with a gaggle of tourists.

The Marina Corta is father to two humble harbours, divided by a short spit. A modest church with a pointed campanile graces the sea wall in the centre. In one half, fishing smacks, nets suspended from their frames, wait patiently for the sun to go down. In the other, a row of shiny, white rental dorys laze at their moorings. One boat, moored up by the fishing boats, stands out of place with the rest: it is a sizeable, blue police launch with a policeman standing guard.

When Sandro notices Ric staring at the police launch, he attracts Ric's attention with a sharp, flat wave of his hand as though the launch is to be ignored.

Ric looks about the square and notices sharply dressed policemen standing sentry at the three exits of the Corta. They are not the local police. They are not hanging about to make conversation with the shopkeepers and the passers-by, and though he is not inclined to think they may be looking for him, the possibility sits uneasily. The muscles in his legs tense and start to ache, and again he realises he has taken no exercise since leaving Sardinia.

But, as he wonders if there lies an exit through the back of the café, he hears a commotion from somewhere round the corner. Ric looks across the square at Sandro, who he sees watching him back, frowning with concern.

Sandro makes a second flat, fingers splayed signal as if telling Ric to stay put, and then touches the corner of his eye.

The disturbance, which grows in volume, is coming from the Via Roma, to his right.

Two policemen appear, hustling a kid towards the launch. Ric recognises the policeman's captive as the scrawny-looking youth who was thrown out of the café the evening before.

Clearly, the youth is trying his best to explain that he has been mistaken for some other felon and that he is not guilty of whatever it is he has been charged. But, the policemen are deaf to his appeals and haul him roughly across the Corta, down to the launch. No one intervenes on his behalf; the onlookers simply sit in mute observance, as though watching a scene from a movie.

The rest of the policeman, who have been guarding the entrances to the square, stride purposefully to the quay and clamber on board. The large blue and white launch coughs out a cloud of diesel fumes, rasps angrily and motors out of the harbour. The pilot feigns a casual indifference to the disruption his wake causes the dozen or so fishing boats bobbing up and down on their moorings.

"You don't like the police, eh, Ric?" Sandro murmurs.

Ric has not noticed him wander up. "No more than anybody. They put on a good show though."

"It is meant to be so; a jolly good show, as you would say. And that, my friend, is all it is: a show." Sandro sits down and sighs as though the police have just arrested his favourite nephew.

"What was that all about?" Ric asks.

"La Polizia. From Milazzo. This kid," Sandro nods in the direction of the departing launch, "drugs; small drugs. They never take the big dealers; they have too much protection. It is easier for them to arrest the small fishes. But we say, when the little fish is caught, the big fish is in trouble. So this show means that one of the dealers has upset another dealer who enjoys more influence. But, also, La Polizia likes to do this thing at the beginning of the summer; it makes the people think they are working. Also, they send a message to the dealers that they must show more respect and not be so public with their dealing."

Ric asks the waitress for a beer for Sandro. "You sure they're not pulling him in simply because he's committing an offence selling drugs."

"No, this is not how it works, my friend. This is Italy, not Europe: we are closer to Tunis than we are to Brussels and a very long way from London. If they wanted to remove this young kid from the street, they would have the local Carabinieri take care of him. This was for show."

"Some show," Ric offers.

Sandro ponders his own explanation for a moment, his mouth turned down as though he is considering whether the arrest was for something more than just show. "Perhaps they wanted to make an example of this boy, I don't know. We have a politician from Partito Politica Riconquista coming tomorrow evening to spread his poison. No doubt he will make a grand speech about how important we are, how our vote matters to his heart and soul, and how he is going to pay particular attention to our needs, because we are so unique." Sandro scoffs, theatrically, his voice rising as though he is delivering a monologue from a soapbox.

"I understand this politician will tell us we can create a geothermal power plant in the sea between here and Panarea; a power plant which will give us free electricity and enough electricity for us to sell what we don't need to the mainland. Maybe it will make us all rich? Maybe we will become part of a new age: the poor, rich relations of Aeolus?"

The gaggle of tourists to whom Sandro has been selling tickets for day trips, and for whom he has just posed for photographs, have gathered to listen to his sermon.

"This new benevolence may be good for Il Cavaliere and those footballers from Turin who own houses on Panarea, but for us? Pah! Perhaps the money will help Dolce and Gabbana pay the 500 million euros in tax the government say they should pay. But, I say again, for us? Do you seriously think they will give us this money from the electricity or do you think the money will go to those who have the power to decide where it will go?" He scoffs again, holding up his arms to appeal to the heavens. "I think I have more chance of winning the *Superenalotto.*"

The tourists laugh and egg Sandro on to further theatrics.

But Ric is not keen for the *escurzionista* to draw attention his way. So he says, hoping to calm Sandro's desire for oratorio: "A geothermal power plant seems a pretty logical idea, what with all these volcanoes on your doorstep."

"I tell you Ric, it may be logical and, yes, natural also, but this thing will cause much trouble. There are those who have much to gain, but many others who have more to lose. This is what money does; it divides and ultimately it conquers."

Ric is reminded of the Armenian he tangled with in Corsica. "I can think of a few that hasn't worked for."

"I will tell you a little story about Lipari," Sandro continues. "You see the citadel up here?" he points over his shoulder at the great lump of rock that is home to the cathedral and which overshadows the Corta.

"Hard to miss it," Ric replies.

"Maurolico tells us that before the Spanish came to make better the fortifications of the Castello, there came a devil, Khayr ad-Din; a corsair known by the name of Barbarossa. You have heard of him?"

92

"Sure," Ric replies. "Red Beard the Pirate, a sort of Muslim corporate raider, if you can call a Byzantine Pasha with 30,000 men under his command a pirate."

Sandro smiles, pleased he doesn't have to provide too much of a history lesson. "Good, okay. In 1544 he comes to Lipari; he lands at Portinente and tries to storm the Castello." He puffs out his chest. "But the cannons of the Castello are too strong for him and he has to camp out at Capistello. So he surrounds the Castello and makes a siege to starve the people inside out. When, eventually, they run out of food, twenty-six of the most powerful families – de Franco, Russo, Voi, Cremonese, and di Blasi – decide to send an emissary to Barbarossa to tell him that if he will leave them in peace, they will surrender the Castello and he can keep the weaker people as slaves. They ask to keep their freedom and their possessions and offer him twenty *scudi* for every one of them he does not kill.

"He agrees to their demands and they open the gates." Sandro smiles and makes flamboyant, sweeping, welcoming movements with his arms. Then he frowns: "But, Barbarossa is not a fool. Once the gates are open, he enters the Castello, burns the churches and steals whatever he wants, including the possessions of the twenty-six families. The families are upset. They say, "Hey, Barbarossa, you agree to let us go and keep our possessions." Barbarossa laughs and he says, "I am a pirate. Why do you think I will let you keep what is already mine?" Then he takes the whole population of Lipari – more than 8,000 people including the wealthy families – to be his slaves and to sell in the market place in Messina. As a result, in 1544 there is not one person left alive on the island; not one person, no one, *nessuno!*" Sandro hunches his shoulders, raises his arms and presents his palms to the sky. "An intelligent man, eh?" He slaps the table and sits back.

The crowd have been enjoying Sandro's performance and one or two clap and turn aside to nod in appreciation.

Ric ponders for a moment before saying, "Either that or the families were not very smart."

Sandro leans across the table, "And, my friend, this is where you are so correct. It was ridiculous of them to believe Barbarossa would let them go: their thinking was influenced by their greed. The wealthy families believed they would be allowed to keep their money at the expense of the liberty of the poor families. Nuts, eh? So, you see, this is an example of how money divides and conquers. And this is why, if the politicians sell us the idea of this free electricity, there will be trouble. Who will control it? The wealthy families? And who will make the most from it: those who already have more than enough money? It is possible that there will be free electricity and from it maybe comes a little money. But, I tell you, this money will divide the people."

20

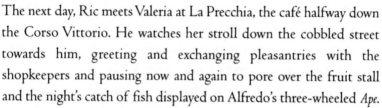

The next day, Ric meets Valeria at La Precchia, the café halfway down the Corso Vittorio. He watches her stroll down the cobbled street towards him, greeting and exchanging pleasantries with the shopkeepers and pausing now and again to pore over the fruit stall and the night's catch of fish displayed on Alfredo's three-wheeled *Ape*.

"*Salve*, Ric. You have not ordered?"

They dip slices of sweet, ring-shaped *Ciambella Della Nonna* breakfast cake in *cappuccino* and talk about the weather.

Valeria says, "*Cielo a pecorelle, acqua a catanelle*: when we have clouds that look like lambs, then we will have rain." She smokes her long, thin Vogue cigarettes and tells the waiter it is high time they visited the *Sorgente Termale* — the mud baths — in Vulcano. Though she must be three times his age, he responds to her enthusiasm as though they share many intimate delights.

Just before ten, they walk the last fifty metres down to the bus station at the Marina Lunga and wait for the small bus.

White-haired old ladies scowl, talk to themselves and examine their shopping as though they are certain they have forgotten some vital ingredient for *i Purpetta*. Short, dark, round-headed men of Sikelian extraction and taller, more slender, fair-haired and fair-skinned descendants of Normans, seek out the shade and roll their own cigarettes.

When, finally, the minibus has fought its way through the melee of vehicles filing up to the petrol station in the centre of the little roundabout, the old women grumble as a callow youth forces his way on board before them.

"It is the way of things," Valeria says in a voice just loud enough that the youth will hear her. "*Coatti* – the young ruffians – they no longer respect age. Even those as young as twenty-five now think the *Coatti* are too disrespectful."

The seats in the *Ursobus* are hard, the windows fixed and opaque with age, and it rattles and clonks over the many drain holes.

Valeria busies herself massaging cream into her hands. She chuckles when she notices him appraising the minibus: "We could have taken one of the more modern buses, but they travel too fast and a *pulmino* like this is slower and gives one time to admire the scenery."

The road winds up out of town and over the saddle between the hills to Quattrocchi on the western side of the island. Occasional white lambs of cloud graze in a cerulean pasture, casting dark shadows on a flat sea. They pause in the settlement of Pianoconte to exchange passengers, skirt the flanks of Monte Sant'Angelo through Castellaro, and then, twenty minutes later arrive above Quattropani. Valeria asks the driver to let them out at a bend just before the descent into the village.

"Four Eyes and Four Breads," Ric says as they alight, "all a little quaint."

Valeria chuckles, "Yes. They say Four Eyes because you need an extra pair of eyes to appreciate the view, and Four Breads because that is how much food you will need if you walk here over Monte Sant'Angelo. But I suspect nobody really knows." She shoulders her leather tote bag. "Come, we have to walk up; Nino lives in a small house near the Chiesa Vecchia."

The track is grassy, crowned and steep for the first fifty metres. Valeria strides up it as though the slope is merely an obstacle to overcome and therefore worth little in the way of consideration.

At the top, the track curves to the left and opens out to run north-east along a broad, bald ridge that ends in a high promontory. "Salina," she says, pausing and pointing away across the purple sea at a dark green cone resting in the shadow of one of her fluffy lambs, "it is where the Caravaglio comes from. Also they film some of *Il Postino* there. You have seen this movie?"

"Can't say I have."

"You must, Ric." Valeria stops and waits until he has noticed she is no longer beside him so that he, too, stops. "If you want to understand this place, the people, us; you must see this movie."

They stroll along the windswept ridge towards a low, square white church with a miniscule dome. Aside from the olive grove on the eastern flank of the church and a handful of small white houses dotted on either side of the track, the land around them is a mishmash of grey and green scrub broken by yellow Tyrrhenian broom, purple gillyflower, pink rock rose, and wild carrot and strawberry bushes.

Nino's house, like the Chiesa Vecchia just beyond it, is white-washed and square, but it is topped by a terracotta tile roof and graced by a pergola which overlooks the two mile stretch of sea separating Lipari from Salina. As they approach down the slope, Ric is minded to point out, "Hell of a view for a blind man!"

"Yes," Valeria replies, lifting her face towards the breeze, "it is strange how our perceptions are governed by physical limitations? I have always understood that Nino is able to sit in his *bagghiu* – his pergola – and feel the view: to feel the cool Tramontana from the north-east, to taste the moist seeds of cloud which rest over Salina, to hear the conversations of the people dining in *Da Alfredo's* in Santa Marina across the water, to smell the basil in the *Pane Cunzato* they are eating, and to feel the movement of the small boats that come and go between the islands. Just because one is blind, Ric, it does not mean one cannot see."

Nino is indeed sitting on a stone seat, staring out through his round, dark glasses across the strait as though timing the Aliscafo in its haste towards Salina.

"*Salve, Valeria,*" he says, clearly not startled by their arrival. "Come and join me on my *bisuolo*; there is room for both of us."

"*Vossia benedica, Nino,*" she replies.

The old man makes the sign of the cross and replies, "*Ortigia?*"

"Correct, Nino: *Ortigia Lime di Sicilia.*"

"It is unmistakeable," the old man says, "citrus and lime-wood and vanilla. Only you would grace the air so."

Ric had picked up on Valeria's scent whilst sitting next to her on the bus, but had not thought it so obvious.

Nino turns his head as if formally acknowledging their presence. His arms protrude like fragile sticks from his short-sleeved shirt and his black trousers are baggy and sack-like and tied at his waist with what looks like a scarf. The ridges of his veins stand proud on his hands and forearms as though it is they, rather than his cartilage and tendons, which are holding his emaciated limbs together.

"You have brought a friend, Valeria."

"Yes, Nino, I have brought a friend." She stoops and kisses his forehead.

Nino's smile reveals his teeth, which are small and carry the ochre'd tones of weathered ivory and which fix his high, round cheeks, long polished smooth by the wind. "So what is it that encourages you to provide this old man with such pleasure? Why should I be blessed with such good fortune?"

Valeria sits down beside him on the stonewall seat of his terrace. "My visit is long overdue, Nino; for that I have no excuse." She holds his hand and lifts it to her face. "And this man wanted to meet you: he is a friend of Camille Giovananngeli, from Corsica."

"A friend of Camille, you say. Well, how is the old fox? Is his humour still sharp like a blade?"

"He was well when I saw him last autumn," Ric replies. "I am sure he would want me to pass on his best to you."

"Any friend of the old fox is welcome in my house." His voice is cool like the breeze and clear like the view. "So how can an old man be of service? Come forward. Come, give me your hand."

Valeria offers Ric the old man's right hand; it is frail and brittle, like petrified root. He settles his left hand on Ric's wrist and holds it for a moment, as if searching for a pulse.

"Valeria, ask Ariana for a glass of *legbi*. It is early and she will resist, but she will get it for you."

Valeria stands and leaves them still holding hands.

"You are young and strong, that is good." Nino grins once more. "And you are too young to be Valeria's lover, which is good also; this way I have no cause to be jealous of you, even though I could do precious little about such a thing if it were so. We will be friends. But, you hesitate; there is much you are not sure of which, I suppose, is why you are here."

"Your English is good, Nino; much better than my Italian."

The old man takes a handkerchief from his pocket and wipes a thin trickle of saliva from the corner of his mouth. "I learn it from the men of Lyle Bernard in the second war. I was a guide for them at the landing of Sant'Agata di Militello. It was there that I lost my sight: a big explosion, a great light and then light no more." Nino shrugs and raises an eyebrow as though the event was of little consequence.

"Flash-blinded?" Ric asks. "Working for the Americans at the amphibious landing?"

"Yes, every man from the islands must know the coast of the mountains from Milazzo to Cefalù like he knows his own thoughts. When the Tramontana blows hard, Aeolus will take you there no matter where you want to go. It is important to know where to seek shelter. But you must be a military man, if you know about such things?"

99

Ric quiets for a moment as he tries to estimate how old the young Nino would have been in the summer of '43.

"I was a young man to lose my sight." Nino reaches out for Ric's hand and wrist a second time. After a few second's squeezing and manipulating, he declares, "Ah, yes, a military man. I thought so. One can tell these things: there is iron in the bone and courage in the muscle."

"A while ago," Ric replies.

Valeria reappears, followed by a short, gentle-faced young woman, bearing a tray with three glasses of cloudy palm wine and a plate of freshly-baked, small brown biscuits. She sets the tray down on a low wooden table fashioned out of driftwood, and she and Valeria lift it over in front of Nino.

He breathes in deeply, "*Ah, grazie, Ariana: Spicchitedda!* Cinnamon and almonds: music for the palate. Did she give you much trouble?"

The young woman smiles, blushes and scuttles back inside the house.

"None at all," Valeria says. "She simply shook her head and said if you wanted to be embalmed before you were dead, perhaps you could save her from having to pay the undertaker."

Nino chuckles, "But does she mean the wine in the biscuits or the wine in the glass? And tell me, why should the *giovintù* deny the *patri anticu* the few pleasures he has left?"

They sip the sweet wine in silence and watch the white caps skip across the sea away below them.

"So, what is your name?" Nino asks.

"Richard, Richard Ross. Most people call me Ric."

"Riccardo, mmm, you are given this name so that you will be powerful; a ruler of people. And it is so: you have been an officer in the army?"

"The Marines."

"You are not married?"

Ric is not prepared for Nino's interrogation. But, seeing as he has come to ask the old man a raft of questions, he does not think it fair to shy away from answering a few first: "No."

"Ah, you were. I am sorry; it leaves a mark when one loses the woman one loves."

Nino's response makes Valeria sit up and look questioningly at Ric, but as she does so, she asks, "How do you know this, Nino?"

"It is in this young man's voice. People can conceal many things when they talk. Some people speak in half truths and others can lie as if their life depends on what they say. But an immeasurable sadness such as this, one is powerless to conceal."

And, without thinking, Ric hears himself say, "My wife died the year before last, in a car accident. It was while I was away, serving in Afghanistan."

"So, forgive me for being... open, but you blame yourself for not being with her to stop this dreadful thing from happening, and now you are searching for somewhere to lay this guilt to rest. It is both understandable and forgivable. My wife," Nino pauses, "my wife was lost to me many years ago... The heavier the weight, the more difficult it can be to set down gently. You have my sympathy."

"And you mine, Nino," Ric replies, wondering if his sense of loss will ever leave him in the same way it has never left the old man.

Nino nods, slowly. "Now, enough talk of emotion. We know we have much in common: that is both good and bad. What is it you have come to ask of an old man?"

Ric takes a sip of his palm wine and says, "Camille told me he thinks one of my ancestors came from Lipari and Valeria suggested you might be able to shed some light on his family, my family."

"Oh," Nino sighs, "Valeria is always bringing people to my door to ask such questions; Australians, Americans and some from South America; not many British. But, I warn you: I am not an oracle, like Pythia, and I am not a recorder of history, like Tacitus. My memory often deceives me and sometimes I cannot remember what Ariana has given me for breakfast." Nino pauses and wipes his mouth again. He stares out at the far island as if he observes it in all the verdant splendour of its graded slopes and the starch-white cloud obscuring its summit.

"Although," he says, smiling once more, "of late I have found that my memories come back to me at the strangest moments. One minute I am back in the Marina Corta watching a film lit by magic lanterns; the next I am… What was your ancestor's name?"

"Sciacchitano or so Camille thinks."

"Sciacchitano," Nino says, pronouncing the name slowly. He scratches at a red mark on his face and Valeria reaches up to pull his hand away; she strokes the mark, softly.

"Sciacchitano," he repeats. "I remember this name, Sciacchitano. But what do I remember? What?" Nino drinks his palm wine, rests his elbow on the table and his chin on his fisted hand, his repose that of Rodin's Thinker.

Ric says, "Camille suggested he returned to the island after a spell in the Foreign Legion. It is thought he served with the Legion in Gallipoli, although we don't know when or why he would have joined."

Nino nods, slowly, "This is not so surprising. Even the Legion was to be preferred to fighting with the *Bersaglieri* in Gorizia. If you were not killed by the Austrians, you lived in fear of being hanged by your own officers. They practiced *decimazione* – decimation – a barbaric ritual from Roman times. The word means, literally, one in ten. They would select every tenth soldier and either shoot or hang him from a tree by the side of the road as an encouragement to the other soldiers not to retreat in battle. So, if you wanted to fight, to serve with another army was a far more attractive alternative. Perhaps that is why he left. But, do you know when he returned to Lipari?"

"'25, maybe '26, perhaps a little later."

Nino returns to his thoughts for a few minutes and then says, "I was only a small boy in these years. Perhaps you can give me time to remember. It is possible and if I can find the right lantern to help me see through the darkness of my memory, then perhaps I will remember some detail which will be of use to you. The late '20s, you say?"

His chin lifts and his lips purse in thought before he says, "I recall a family, not one of significance, but a family by this name; of this I am certain. And, there must be a reason why I would remember this name so quickly. Have you looked for the name Sciacchitano on a grave in the cemetery or perhaps on the memorials in the Mazzini?"

21

In the afternoon, after Ric and Valeria have parted, he walks up the steep cobbled road and through the Greek Tower to the citadel. On the memorial plaques either side of the entrance to the municipal building in the Piazza Mazzini, he reads through the names of the fallen; the *Gloriosi Caduti* of the island, not so much enlisted as conscripted and forced to fight in the great wars of the last century; wars of which the combatants understood little and cared for less.

The disparity between the numbers of officers' names and those of the local conscripts is marked. In the *Grande Guerra 1915-1918*, for every officer, ninety other ranks lost their lives. But what throws Ric is how many sons and fathers the local families lost: the Taranto family six, the Cincotta, the Rando and the Ricone families three each. And in the second *Guerra 1940-1945*, one *Ufficiale* was lost for over a hundred other *Militari*: the Biviano family five, the Rastuccia and Mandicio three, and the Saltalamacchia two. Recalling what Valeria has told him regarding the thousands who left for foreign shores at the beginning of the twentieth century, he is surprised there are any men left on the island.

The name Sciacchitano is not among them.

Ric turns at the sound of hammering and sawing. Behind him, in the gardens of the Piazza Mazzini, a wooden platform is being hastily constructed. The banners proclaim the name **Girolamo**

Candela and **Partito Politica Riconquista** and beneath that the words l'Energia Geotermico. The flags above the stage bear images of a fifty-something-year-old man; hair greying just enough to hint at wisdom, eyes sufficiently lively to imply youthful exuberance.

A heavy grey cloud passes before the sun, erasing the shadows, and as Ric walks down the broad steps of the Concordato it starts to drizzle. He takes a seat beneath an awning at a pavement café on the Garibaldi; the Birra Messina is cool and refreshing in spite of the rain.

The sailmaker, Marcello, emerges from the back of the café.

"Ah, Ric. Providence is kind to my legs. I was about to come and look for you at your, or rather my place." He sits down and a young waitress appears and sets an espresso and a glass of water beside him. "So how is the *monolocale*, comfortable?"

Ric thinks of the dripping tap at the kitchen basin: "It's perfect. Thank you."

"You have no need to thank me. For friends, this is a small service. You have had a good day? I see you in the Corso this morning; you were with La Strega. She makes herself *escurzionista* for you? Takes you on the bus around the island?" Marcello raises his eyebrows and yawns as though Valeria's personal tour of Lipari is famously boring.

"No, it wasn't dull at all," Ric replies. "She took me up to the north side of the island to see the old guy, Nino; the blind man you pointed out to me in the Corta. Valeria thought he might be able to shed some light on one of my ancestors who came from—"

"Lipari?"

"So I'm told."

Marcello stifles his surprise and chuckles, "Heh! Imagine this. A man comes to Lipari to search for the old life of a man who left Lipari in search of a new life. This is what we call irony, is it not? How many years ago, was this?"

"Some time around 1930," Ric replies.

The short, squat figure beside him sips his coffee, deep in thought for a moment. "And what was this man's name?"

"Sciacchitano, I believe. I don't have a first name.

If Marcello has heard the name, it does not register in his expression. "Many left the islands in these days," he scoffs slightly, as though only a weak man would do such a thing. "There is nothing unusual in this."

He finishes his coffee, washes it down with a mouthful of water and glances, first at the shiny cobbles and then at the heavens, "Ah, this rain will not last. This evening, we can go fishing. You would like to come, eh?"

"Sure. I have a rod, but it's on the Mara."

"No, for fishing *totani* – you would call them flying squid because they have bigger fins than *calamari* – we don't need this; only the boat, a little line and *ontreto*."

Ric repeats the word slowly.

"Yes, it sounds a little French, *ontre-to*, but it is our word. I don't know this in English. But this evening, I will show you. You know the Chiesa delle Anime del Purgatorio, on the harbour in the Marina Corta?"

Ric nods.

"*Bene!* This evening, when the cross is in shadow, come to Portinente."

22

The air is cool but not cold, as Ric slips his front door key beneath the flower pot beside the door mat. He winds his way through the narrow vicos which lead down to the Marina Corta.

Small clusters of the townsfolk are gathering; the men, smartly dressed in their newly-pressed best; the women, their hair coiffed and their make-up applied, as if ready for Mass. They greet each other and chatter earnestly, the tide of their conversation sweeping them up the short rise of the Garibaldi towards the Concordato, the broad steps of which lead up to the citadel and the Piazza Mazzini.

The evening sun still lights the campanile of the Purgatorio, so Ric takes a chair in the usual café.

Giuliana glides up beside him, beaming: "What would you like to drink, Ric?"

"You choose," he replies.

She grins as though he has just asked her out on a date. Moments later she returns with a tray bearing an Aperol Spritz and a plate of canapés.

"Dinner on the house?" he asks.

"*Stuzzicchini,*" Giuliana replies, "for your pleasure."

Sandro appears, scowls at Giuliana and pulls up a chair, "A good day, today, Ric?"

"I've had worse."

The *escurzionista* leans across and helps himself to a small pizza, a cherry tomato and a slice of egg wrapped in salami. As he fills his mouth, he remembers his manners and grins, "*Scusi!* It's okay?"

Ric nods, turns to Giuliana and asks her for a Birra Messina for Sandro.

"You see these people?" Sandro asks when he has finished chewing. "They go like sheep to a new field. They think the grass will be green for them because of this idiot, Candela."

Ric studies a short, round old lady, wearing a single-piece, Greek-style white *peplos* dress and a necklace of small *porcelluze* shells. She is shepherding her extended flock to brighter pastures.

"All going to hear about their brave new world?"

Sandro nods and grins in appreciation as Giuliana places the bottle of beer on the table. "Correct, my friend. As I told you before," he says, a touch of frustration creeping into his tone, "they think their faith will provide their salvation. Bah! I say, become a lamb and a wolf will eat you." He shakes his head in disgust. "I have no time for these empty promises; they are the cause of so many wars."

"Didn't make you out for a philosopher, Sandro."

"Oh, okay. But you don't need to be Machiavelli to know that it is only the fraudulent who escape poverty." He takes another couple of tiny pizzas and chews thoughtfully.

"So," Sandro carries on as he studies the herd shuffling through the Corta, "what would you like to do this evening, my friend? We can go to the Lunga? There is a very good restaurant. It is owned by a friend of mine. Very good fish! Fresh, eh?"

"Thanks, Sandro, I've already eaten and I'm about to go fishing."

His eyes light up, "Alone? I can show you the best places to fish for *occhiata*."

"No, but thank you, some other time. I'm going out with Marcello Maggiore; *totani*, as far as I know."

Sandro sits back and smiles, assuming a slightly patronising expression. "I get it. You want to be *Lampara*, to learn the ways of the lamp fishermen. Okay, this I understand. But, it's a little touristic for you, eh?"

Ric looks over at the Purgatorio; the sun lights only the very top of the cross on the campanile.

"Tourist or not, Sandro, I must be going." He stands and slips a note onto the table.

"Okay, Ric. *Ciao, buon divertimento*, my friend. Have fun."

"Don't you mean *buona pesca?*"

Sandro shakes his head: "No. If I say this it will bring you only bad luck and you will not catch any fish. *Ciao*, Ric."

Marcello is waiting in the small bay at Portinente; his *barca* is pulled up on the shingle beach. A rudimentary masthead and cross-spar bear crude navigation lights and a small outboard hangs over the stern. Lengths of line and a box of fishing tackle lie piled beside a small battery.

"*Va bene*, Ric," he greets, grinning. "This time you come at the right time; you are learning. Normally, Salvo comes with me, but tonight he has gone with the rest to listen to Candela." He chuckles, "Only Salvo and God know why he chooses to listen to a politician; Salvo cannot read and he does not vote."

They push the *barca* out into the water and Marcello rows out beyond the buoys before ripping the outboard to life.

"You sit in the front, Ric. Your weight will help keep it down." They whine their way out eastwards, towards the flat line of the horizon.

Ric watches the shadows chase them across the darkening water. The further out they motor, the more the island of Vulcano, to the south, comes into view. From the flattened summit of the grey cone, trails of yellowish smoke drift up into a cloudless sky, like the lazy tendrils of anemones waiting patiently for some nutrient to stray within their reach. A late Aliscafo drones out from behind the citadel and scurries angrily away towards Sicily. The two men hang on while they ride the roller coaster of its wake.

A mile out, Marcello cuts the motor and they wait for the *barca* to drift to a halt.

Last light cloaks the shoulders of the island in purple raiment and the harbour beneath the citadel glimmers, a string of pearls gracing the nape of a duchess. The echoes of a fanfare float down from the Piazza Mazzini.

"So," he says, "we connect the lights to the battery and we are set." Having done so, he stands up, the boat rocking a little.

"Here," he passes Ric a thick, elliptical pendant about the length of his palm. "*Fai Attenzione con l'ontreto!* It is sharp, eh." From one end of the pendant, an umbrella of vicious hooks curl out and up; the top half of the other end is made up of a domed light.

"A squid-jag," Ric mutters. "Evil looking things, aren't they?"

"*Si*," Marcello replies, "*ontreto*. The flashing light attracts the *totani* and they impale themselves on the hooks. It is not so much a sport as a harvest, eh? But first we have to find the *totani*. Tie this to the line and drop it into the water. Give out lengths of line and count them: twenty to start with." Marcello drops his *ontreto* over the side and measures off lengths of line between outstretched arms.

Having tied the squid-jag to the line coiled at his feet, Ric too drops his gently over the side. The light at the top flickers and then settles to a regular, pulsing flash. He watches, fascinated, as the blinking light fades into the inky black.

"Now," Marcello says, sitting back down, "we wait."

Sinister emerald and ruby eyes watch them from the dark as other small boats whine swiftly to and fro across the sea. Some of the *Lampari* have opaque lanterns, like upturned bee-keepers' hats, suspended over the stern and others have no lights at all.

"How long?" asks Ric.

Marcello's face glows like a lazy lighthouse each time he draws on his cigar. "Patience is the only friend of the fisherman," he mumbles. "If we have nothing in few minutes, then we let out more line. The *totani* will be here; what we have to find out is the depth where they are feeding. Ric, hold the line in one hand between your thumb and first finger. When you feel some playing on the line, then you pull it up."

The silence is punctured every now and then by the clamour from the citadel. There is no breeze and the sound carries so clearly they can make out the voices of the speech-makers.

Marcello instructs Ric to pay out another five stretches of line and says, "So, you are a friend of La Strega, eh. If you have not been to Lipari before, how do you know her?"

"I spent some time in Corsica last year, where I bought the Mara. The owner, Camille, said if I was down this way I should look in on Valeria."

Marcello's cigar glows briefly, "Ah, Camille. Yes, of course, the old fox with the white hair. I think maybe him and La Strega… eh? But perhaps it is not right to talk of such things with older people. What about this man, this relative of yours you come to search for. It was a very long time ago, the 1920s. What do you hope to find, if you can find out anything? Are not the dead best left to sleep? You might learn your ancestor was a bad person, what would you do then? You would not be as happy as when you were ignorant."

"I have thought of that," Ric replies. "Ignorance can be bliss, but…" And he is about to say, finding out about your forebears can only help you understand what makes you the person you are, when he remembers Corsica and Manou and Gianfranco and the men who died, and he wonders whether what he found there has made his life simpler, so he says, "I have time on my hands and—"

Marcello laughs loudly, "and the devil will find a use for them. Tell me, what do you know about this ghost you are searching for? You think he was from Lipari?"

"Camille looked into it for me. I had a photograph of my great-grandfather standing beneath the gate to the Foreign Legion garrison in Bonifacio. Camille found out he may have returned to Lipari after his service. The next we know is that he turned up in Britain, where he married my great-grandmother."

"And what was your great-grandfather's name again?"

"Far as I know, it was Sciacchitano."

"Mmm," Marcello murmured. "He was your great-grandfather on you father's side of the family or your mother's?"

"My father's."

"And what is your surname?"

"Ross."

"How is it so? Why is it not the same, Sciacchitano?"

Ric pauses, thinking he feels a tug on the end of his line. But when he draws the line up, it falls slack once more and he thinks his imagination is getting the better of him. "We think Rossi was his *nom de guerre*, his serving name in the legion. Camille thinks his real name was Sciacchitano."

"So why did he not keep this name after he left Lipari?"

"Beats me, Marcello, but that's one of the things I'd like to find out. Got any ideas?"

The wake from a boat unsettles them for a moment and they quiet as the waves slap.

Marcello takes the cigar from his mouth and blows on the end of it; it glows brighter and he puffs on it a couple of times. "At that time," he suggests, "many people wanted to escape from the Fascists. And, if you escape to another country, the Black Hand – the spies of the Fascists who work in other countries – they could find you and make you disappear. Maybe he changed his name because he lived in fear; to live in such fear was not unusual."

This time the tugging on Ric's line is not the product of his imagination and he can feel his companion tense as well.

"Pull it up, but be regular with the line, smooth and slow."

After ten lengths of line, whatever it is that is caught on the *ontreto* is beginning to object to being dragged upwards. The line feels heavy and aggravated.

Kneeling over the side, Ric sees the light blinking brighter with every metre of line he draws up, and eventually he pulls the *ontreto* out of the water and into the bottom of the boat. The moon now gifts enough light for him to make out, wrapped around and impaled on the hooks of the jag, a flying squid about the length of his forearm.

"*Bene*," says Marcello. He switches on his torch and shines it on the limp pink sleeve of sinewy muscle which lies staring up at them. In one movement, Marcello wrenches the *totani* off the ontreto and tosses it into one of the buckets by the mast. "Not so big, but now we know how deep they are. Put the line back in and give another metre."

For the next half an hour, the two fishermen are oblivious to all but dropping lines and hauling up *totani*. Some are as long as Ric's shin and others as thick as his arm, but they all stare helplessly back at him as he unhooks them. Soon enough, the buckets are full to overflowing and Marcello is muttering his approval.

"It is good, Ric. You bring me luck. And it is better to be a lucky fisherman than a good one. Here," he says, reaching forward from his seat in the stern, "I have a bottle of Fichera. We will drink for a minute and enjoy the peace. This mark you have on your forehead?" he asks.

Ric drinks from the bottle of brandy. He is not used to people questioning him so frankly about the coin-sized, strawberry birthmark above his right eye. "What about it?"

"Excuse me, Ric; I am too forward on occasion. But it is unusual, yes?"

"Guess so," he replies. "What's there to know?"

"I only ask, because we call this the *voglie*, which in English I think is translated as a yearning or a craving."

"Meaning what exactly?"

"No, please, Ric," Marcello clearly understands he is speaking out of turn. "I have heard people talk about this mark in the past. Doctors say this comes to a baby when still in the womb. They say it occurs because the mother is not eating enough food or vitamins to feed the baby; food like the wild strawberries which grow here. This need shows on the child when he or she is born in the way of the *voglie*."

"I wouldn't know if my mother went without strawberries during her pregnancy, Marcello. Guess you'd have to ask her."

The cigar glows for a few seconds. "Do you know if such a mark is passed from father to son, or mother to daughter?"

"Doubt it. Why do you ask?"

Marcello does not reply at first, he simply lounges in the back of the *barca* and puffs on his cigar. "No matter," he concludes. "It is just that I have seen such a mark before, on other people, and—"

A gunshot rings out from the shore: then a second and quickly a third.

Ric straightens up, immediately alert.

"It comes from the Maddalena," Marcello says.

They listen hard for a fourth, but... nothing.

Marcello turns and grabs the starter cord of the outboard. He pulls frantically on it, but the little engine refuses to fire. He pulls again and again, but the motor only threatens to start. It stutters and coughs, until eventually Marcello swears and hits it with his fist.

Other boats start up and move towards the shore.

Marcello is beside himself. He swears and punches and dares the motor to get going. And, like a child who knows he cannot put up with such a beating, eventually the outboard clears its throat and whines into life.

But as Marcello swings the little boat around towards the shore, another much larger boat appears from behind them.

Ric watches it come at them out of the darkness. It shows no navigation lights and its prow is at least two metres higher than the stern of their *barca*.

"Marcello, look out!" Ric shouts and points astern.

Marcello glances over his shoulder and pushes the handle hard over to steer away from the bow coming on behind him. But instead of steering away, Marcello turns directly into the path of the boat. In an attempt to avoid being broadsided, he turns again, this time towards it.

The *barca* pitches on the bow-wave of the bigger boat and slides down its hull. Ric hangs on to his seat and the mast, but the boat is in danger of being overturned. And, once it is thrown up almost beyond the vertical, the dark blue hull strikes Ric's head a glancing blow and he has no alternative but to half-dive, half jump into the water.

Below the surface, the engine of the larger boat shrieks in his ears. He dives straight down, as deep and as fast as his arms and legs will propel him; as far and as fast as he can to get away from the thrashing screws screaming their approach.

He doesn't stop until his ears begin to pain him and the noise of the boat fades. His lungs are ready to burst; he knows he cannot stay down any longer.

When he bursts back through the surface, he treads water, gasping and gulping in the cool night air. Ric is surrounded by the *totani* from the bucket in their boat; some floating dead, others waking up and thrashing about at his shoulders. He brushes them away and shakes the water out of his eyes.

Not unnaturally, he is expecting Marcello to be ready with a rope and some pithy comment about how other *Lampari* don't respect the laws of navigation.

But the little *barca* is nowhere in sight.

23

"Marcello?" Ric yells into the darkness. "Marcello? Where the hell are you?" The salt water stings in the wound to his temple and when he wipes the water from his face, his vision is obscured and the thin metallic taste of blood infects his mouth.

The last Aliscafo of the day drones out of the Lunga close to his right and other, smaller *barche* are crisscrossing the water between him and the shore; the whine of their engines drowns out his shouting.

Ric treads water and tries to pick out the shape of Marcello's boat against the shore lights, whilst wiping the blood away from his eyes.

"Marcello? Where the hell are you?" he shouts again, as loud as he can. But again, his words are absorbed by the noise of the other boats.

Slowly, it dawns on him that if he was thrown into the sea, then there's every chance the very same has happened to Marcello. The outboard had no dead-man's cord, so it's all too possible the boat has motored off, abandoning them both to the dark waters of the Mare Siculum.

Ric swims around, calling out, but receives no response. He realises that neither of them were wearing life vests, so either Marcello is lying unconscious, drowning slowly, somewhere nearby or the man is out in the darkness looking for him.

He continues to swim around in ever larger circles, hoping he might find him. But, after a good few minutes, Ric begins to tire and his head pains him.

Reason, eventually, gets the better of him and he decides it is time for him to start making for shore. He remembers they were the better part of a mile or more from the beach when Marcello turned off the motor and Ric knows he is a stranger to the current. If it should run north to south, he needs to start swimming hard to avoid being dragged out where the currents converge in the straights between the islands; there, he knows, the sea will not treat him kindly.

So Ric strikes out towards the lights of the harbour, figuring that if he heads that way and the current pushes him south, he should make it ashore somewhere near Valeria's house at Punta San Giuseppe. He tries the mental maths to work out how long he will be swimming: at a mile or more out and swimming at a speed easy enough to conserve some energy, he knows he's going to be in the water for at least half an hour and that's if the current isn't too strong and he can avoid being run down by a fishing boat.

That he has not found any sign of Marcello or his boat worries him, and whichever way he looks at it, whether Marcello has drowned or has left him out in the open sea, he knows there will be questions to answer when he gets ashore.

Fortunately, the current is not as strong as he fears and the water is neither too cold nor too warm to make life uncomfortable. The idea of drowning spurs him on, but if Ric needs any extra encouragement to reach the island in as short a time as possible, it is provided by the jellyfish. Their stings provoke a vicious and near paralysing tingling, like a second degree burn or the score from a sharp knife. And as he sweeps them out of the way with his breaststroke, he can feel the welts swelling on his fingers and forearms. The better part of an hour later, Ric drags himself up onto the beach at Punta San Giuseppe and lies, like a beached whale, gasping for air.

There are no lights on in La Casa dei Sconosciuti and Valeria does not answer the door when he raps loudly on it. So he sets off for the

Marina Corta, drying as he hurries. He has to alert someone to what has happened to Marcello, but hasn't the first idea who to report to.

In the Maddalena there are lights, and more. A police car, its blue light playing ghostly shadows against the flank of the Hotel Rocce Azzure, bars the way at the bottom of the rise and Ric remembers the sound of the gunshots as though they'd happened in another life.

When the two uniformed Carabinieri give him the once over, Ric hides his stinging hands behind his back and turns his head to one side to conceal the wound on his face. The policeman shrugs and waves him away towards the longer, steeper route into town.

"*Per favore…*" Ric begins.

"*No! Vada via,*" one of the policeman replies.

"*Commendatore, per favore,*" Ric tries again.

The Carabinieri shrug again and glare at him. "*No! Vada via,*" one orders, "*subito, immediamente. Non c'è nulla da vedere. Vada via!*" And they wave Ric away again. But, one of them catches sight of the blood on the side of Ric's face. He raises his head and frowns in question.

"*No, va bene, nessun problema,*" Ric explains, rubbing at his temple. He turns away to walk swiftly up the steep hill out of the bay.

Ric's legs cramp and his arms sting viciously. And through the chorus of discordant arias playing in his head, he wonders who he can talk to about Marcello and whether Sandro will still be hanging around down in the Corta sponging drinks off tourists.

He jogs up the steep road and has to pause at the turning into town to catch his breath. He realises he must look a sight, wet, bloodied about the face and tattooed with welts, but a vision of Marcello floating face-down out in the bay drives him forward.

The Via Sant Anna is strangely deserted. Although it is close to midnight, the houses are all shuttered and apart from the barking of a dog, the street is eerily silent.

Down in the Corta however, there is more than the usual collection of widowers lurking beneath the statue of San Bartolo.

They are talking earnestly and gesticulating at the police. A blue La Polizia launch, a few metres longer than the one Ric watched the policemen hustle the kid into, is berthed on the finger quay beside the Purgatorio and an ambulance sits waiting at the foot of the steps up to the Chiesa di San Giuseppe.

Ric is relieved to find Sandro sitting, drinking with Giuliana in the café at the foot of the Garibaldi.

Sandro notices him approach and hurries over to meet him.

"Oh, my friend," he says before Ric has a chance to speak, "what has happened to you? You are bleeding. Come, this way," he leads Ric by the arm, "I will ask Giuliana for the first aid."

"Hang on a minute, Sandro," Ric gasps. "We need to get a boat and go look for Marcello. We need to tell the harbour master, the coast guard, someone: Marcello's out in the bay beyond Portinente. His boat... we were run down... I think Marcello's still out there somewhere."

Sandro stares back at him, puzzled, "My friend, you have suffered a blow to your head. Are you alright? Are you confused? It is not a good sign to be so confused when you have such an injury. Come, sit down, I will get you a *grappa.*"

"No," Ric replies, tetchily, "I haven't got time for that. You're not listening to me, Sandro. Marcello's *barca* has sunk and I can't find any trace of him. I think he might have drowned."

"Il Velaccino? Drowned? Not possible, my friend." The *escurzionista* stands back and looks Ric up and down. "My friend, you are in a bad way; you are not thinking straight. Perhaps I should walk home with you and we will call for the doctor."

"Sandro, listen to me will you," Ric replies, now angry, "I tell you; we've got to get a move on; Marcello's boat has been run down. He's somewhere out there; for all I know, he may have drowned."

"No, Ric, this is not possible." Sandro frowns, his curly black hair framing his concern. "Il Velaccino was here in the Corta not five minutes ago."

24

Giuliana cleans Ric's face with a serviette. She is trying her best not to hurt him and she winces when she applies a steri-strip to his wound as though it is her injury she is dressing, not his. Sandro, too, winces as he dabs after-bite on the welts crisscrossing Ric's arms.

"But it can't have been Marcello. He wouldn't have left me out in the water like that."

"I assure you, Ric. As sure as you and I are sitting here and San Bartolo is standing there, Maggiore Marcello walked through the Corta half an hour ago. He wasn't injured like you. He even spoke with the owner of the café over there." He points to the café which is now closed up; it is the same café in which Ric had sat two evenings before with Marcello, the café owned by the man with the pinched face and hard eyes.

"But I don't understand, Sandro. If Marcello's back here, it means he left me out in the sea. Nobody abandons anyone that far out; it took me nearly an hour to swim ashore. God alone knows how I wasn't run down by any of the fishing boats. It doesn't make sense."

Sandro looks perplexed, but studies Ric, clearly thinking he must have suffered a concussion. "No, it does not make sense. To leave a man from your boat out in the water, in the dark, is not right. Come, perhaps I should take you home. You need to rest. In the morning you may remember something more."

Ric stares across the table at the shaggy *escurzionista* and wonders if he's playing some kind of game with him; wonders whether he is in league with Marcello Maggiore, and wonders whether they have set him up only to rob him.

And at that thought, Ric gets up and reaches into his pocket for a soggy note with which to pay for the drinks.

Sandro reaches out, "No, my friend, this time I pay: a man should not have to pay when he is... well, like you at this moment." He turns to Giuliana; her expression resembles that of a child whose favourite pet has just been run over.

"Come, I will walk home with you." Sandro takes Ric by the arm, forgetting the welts on it.

Ric pulls roughly away. "Thank you, but I can see myself home. Home?" he repeats loudly. Those remaining at the bar turn to watch him. "It's not even home; it's Marcello's place." He sighs and shakes his head, which thumps and is making him feel dizzy. Ric loses his balance and leans on the table for support.

Giuliana hurries to him, but Sandro takes him by his shoulder and leads him out of the café. "Come, you can walk with me. I would not want to find out in the morning that something even more unpleasant had happened to you. If a man cannot look after another who buys him a beer on a hot day, then what report will St Peter give me when the time comes, eh?"

However, Ric is still angry and shrugs away a second time. "Thank Giuliana for me," he growls as he turns to walk away up the Garibaldi. "By the way," he stops and turns back, "what was the ruckus in the Maddalena? Sounded like gunshots, or was it fireworks?"

Even with the hair hanging down around his face, Ric notices Sandro's eyebrows rise in disbelief, "*Fuochi?* No, this was not *fuochi*. Ah, of course, you could not know if you were out swimming." But Sandro is looking at Ric very sideways now; scrutinising him as though it is just possible he doesn't believe Ric has been where he says he has for the last hour.

Ric, though, is suddenly very tired and realises he hasn't had to swim that kind of distance since basic training. "Well, what? What was it all about?"

Sandro is no longer listening.

A gaggle of La Polizia and Carabinieri appear at the top of the steps up to the San Giuseppe. Close behind them follow four medics bearing a gurney. When they get to the bottom of the steps, they unfold the wheels of the gurney and start pushing it towards the ambulance. The retinue of La Polizia disengage themselves from the Carabinieri and stroll back over the humpback bridge towards the Purgatorio and their launch. Whoever it is they are pushing on the gurney is very obviously dead: the blanket is pulled up to cover the face.

Sandro looks around, leans towards Ric and whispers, "Girolamo Candela."

25

"Why don't we wait for a moment?" Sandro suggests. "We can watch them and later we will walk."

So they sit back down and order one last *grappa*.

"You know, Candela was to make a speech this evening in the Piazza Mazzini," Sandro tells him. "Well, everybody is there: the *magistrato* come with the Capitanerie di Porto and La Polizia from Milazzo, the power people from l'Energia Geotermico, the big families who own the desalination business, the electrical business and the hotel people, everyone. Even Old Nino comes to listen.

"So Candela... after much music and much standing like a cock in the *pollaio*, he says that if we vote for his party, Riconquista, we will receive all the benefits from this new source of power: scholarships for the schools in Messina, free health care, free travel," Sandro scoffs, "the children already have this, eh, and, of course, free electricity. It is as I have told you, yes?"

Ric nods, recalling the *escurzionista's* oratorio.

"At the end of the meeting there is much smiling and shaking of hands and everyone promises to vote for Candela. I tell you, Ric; it is as if San Bartolo has told the Liparoti his brother Jesus is coming to bless the islands. They went completely *pazzi*! After the meeting, Candela, or so I have heard, says to his bodyguards he has a rendezvous in the Piazza San Bartolo at the entrance to the

Maddalena. You know this is where Edda Ciano lived?" He pauses, waiting to see if Ric is keeping pace with him. "Candela, he does not want his men to go with him, so he goes alone.

"The bodyguards they stay here, at this café; they think he is going to meet with... you know, a woman friend." Sandro winks. "They are angry with Candela, because they are supposed to go everywhere with him, but..." Sandro pauses and nods towards the Chiesa di San Giuseppe, "the next moment there is shooting and suddenly the Corta is very quiet, like at a funeral," Sandro chuckles, "which is quite appropriate when you think about it. And then everyone is shaking fists and arguing and running round like women who have left their washing out in the Scirocco. Some people are arrested and then released and others are released before even being arrested. It is just like *opera buffa*. You know this type of opera?"

Ric shakes his head, but slowly.

"It is comedy without laughing; stupid, but not so funny when everyone is angry. Then one of La Polizia, a little man with a hat, one who must be very important because he is not wearing a uniform and all the police who are in uniform stop what they are doing and listen when he speaks... well, he tells everyone to calm down and that is the end of the fun."

Sandro feigns a curious sadness, as though he would've preferred the farce to continue. "Now they will take the body to Messina. They could have taken the body to the hospital here. But look! They bring it to the Corta to show all the people how terrible it is that a man should come to Lipari and be killed. It is like waving dirty underwear in your mother's face; they want us to feel guilty." Sandro sits back and clasps his hands over his stomach, "Now, you know all that I know. Come, it is late, we must go."

As they leave the table, Sandro looks to Ric to settle the account for the extra drink they have had.

Giuliana, though, refuses his offer of a soggy note.

Ric smiles and in doing so splits the cut at his temple. He feels around the steri-strips; they are damp.

As they walk up the rise of the Garibaldi, he asks, "So who would want Candela out of the way?"

Sandro scoffs again, hesitates and looks at his companion, "Are you sure you are alright, my friend? Your thoughts are a little muddled; perhaps you need a *medico* more than Candela. I don't think they will be much use to him now."

"Indulge me, Sandro."

They start walking again. "You English have a saying, how long is a piece of string?"

"Was he that unpopular?"

"You must look at the big picture, Ric. If you don't have an interest in politics, then whatever the politicians do does not affect your life; you can live happily and ignore them. But this is Italy, my friend, and everyone must have an opinion. The consequence of this is that whatever the politicians do, it affects our lives. If Il Cavaliere makes bunga bunga, then we lose faith in him. If we lose faith in him, we will have election. If we have election, we have new government. If the new government reduces our pension, we have to work for more years. If we have to work for more years, we die younger and we miss out on the pleasure of sitting under San Bartolo to discuss politics. So, because Il Cavaliere can't keep his *cazzone* in his *pantaloni*, I die before my time.

"Or, maybe one of the families from the islands does not want this brave new world Candela is promising. It upsets the balance of power; it changes things." He pauses and scratches his mop of curly hair. "Then, of course, it is much simpler to eliminate your political opponents before they become a threat to you, rather than when they have established themselves, eh?"

At the corner of the Garibaldi with the Maurolico, Ric turns to enter the narrow maze of *vicolos* that will take him to the *monolocale*. "You think it's that simple?"

Sandro wobbles his head from side to side. "Maybe; you can make it as simple or as complicated as you like. This is a different kind of politics; except, perhaps, in Italy, it is the same." He pauses and grins, "But then, it is possible he has been caught with his fingers in the wrong jar of cookies. Could be the money jar or maybe the honey jar? Or it could be one of those jars which is left in the *dispensa*, the place where you keep food and wine..."

"The pantry?"

"Yes, pantry; it is a nice word. But perhaps this particular jar was left for many years in the corner of the pantry because the contents were too bitter to taste. But the family, they did not want to throw the jar away because it is something they have inherited. And now, many years later, this family has opened it again and the smell is so bad they can no longer ignore it. These things, sometimes they happen."

"Why play that out here?" Ric asks. "Why out here on this island?"

Sandro chuckles again, "Why do it in your own back yard, in Palermo, when you can do this here? Many tongues in the mountains, eh?"

"You think Candela's family are caught up in some old blood feud?"

Sandro chuckles, "Possible, but I don't think so. *Ciao*, Ric. Sleep well. Perhaps in the morning you should go to see Il Velaccino and ask him why he left you to the fishes." He walks away down the Maurolico, a long, loping, confident gait which suggests that whatever tomorrow brings, Sandro will be ready for it.

Ric treads carefully through the alley. It is late, there are no lights on and only the slender reflections of the moon help him avoid the bins, bicycles and flowers left out for the night. He tries to remember the many twists and turns of the narrow *vicolos* which will lead him to the small rooms Marcello has let to him: Il Velaccino, the sailmaker, a man who shows him unnecessary kindness one minute and then abandons him out in the ocean the next.

Ric's head bangs and his muscles groan in disapproval of the demands made upon them; it is time to leave it all until the morning.

He locates the *monolocale* and bends down to fish the key out from under the flower pot by the door. The blood rushes to his head and when he straightens up, he is dizzy.

Ric reaches out to steady himself and is grateful to think there is no one about to mistake him for the drunkard he must resemble. But as the thought comes to him, he feels the hair on the back of his neck begin to prickle: someone is watching him from the shadows.

Glancing to his left, he notices a shadow shift at the corner of the alley.

Ric hesitates. "Who's there?" he asks, loud enough to wake up the neighbours.

The figure, if it is the profile of a man he can see and not simply a curious shape thrown by the moon, does not respond. The vico is cool, the night air trapped in the narrow confines of the alley; the silence absolute. The town, like Candela, is sleeping.

He waits a couple of seconds longer before turning the key in the lock. "Is anyone there? Sandro?" he calls more softly. Ric can think of no reason why anyone should be out at such a late hour and yet he has the strangest feeling that someone is watching him. But the shadow is frozen and Ric wonders again if his eyes are playing tricks on him. What little adrenalin the evening hasn't absorbed, seeps into his muscles; he can feel them begin to harden and bunch.

"Who's there?" he asks one last time. "Come out, I know you're there."

The figure steps forward, "*Sono io, Giuliana.*"

Ric sighs and then mutters, "Giuliana! You frightened the life out of me."

"Sorry, Ric." Her hair shines silver in the moonlight. She is wearing a quilted jacket which, he realises, is why he didn't recognise her shape.

"What the hell are you doing here?"

"I come to find out if you are okay. It's okay?"

He isn't quite sure if she's asking if he's okay, or if it's okay with him that she is asking. "I'm fine, thank you. You did a great job on my head." Ric doesn't want to open the door in case she takes it as an invitation. Giuliana may not be local, but he's not naïve enough to think that though old enough to know her own mind, her relatives might know it better. Yet, even in the pale moonlight Ric can see that her eyes are asking all the questions he'd usually be only too happy to answer.

Giuliana stands waiting, expecting.

He reaches out to her and rests his hand gently on her shoulder. "Go home, Giuliana. I'm fine, thank you. I'm grateful for your concern."

She pouts, childishly, "But Ric—"

"But Giuliana," he turns her round, "go home. I am very tired. Perhaps another time," he adds to help her save face.

She shrugs a little insolently, "Okay, Ric, perhaps some other time, yes?" And she steps back, pausing to throw him one last sulky look so that he should be in no doubt about exactly what it is that he is turning down.

"Sleep well, Giuliana," Ric says, with as much paternal sentiment as his weary mind can muster.

"*Ciao, Ric,*" she replies as she sways away down the alley.

But as Ric turns back to unlock his front door, he is sure he hears a scuffling sound from the other end of the alley. He sighs heavily and weighs up whether he should call out again. It has been a long day and, so far, too long a night.

He hesitates.

A cat rushes past his feet and is gone, swallowed up by the shadows.

26

Ric's head is dull and his mouth is dry. He wakes to find himself lying on his bed, but again has no idea of how long he has slept. Slivers of white light creep from between the margins of the shutters.

There is a noise from downstairs: someone is moving about.

He hauls himself upright and eases himself down the tight staircase, trying to remember if he locked the door after his unexpected rendezvous with Giuliana; perhaps, he thinks, she has returned to salvage her pride.

But it is Valeria. She has brought provisions and more of his clothes, which she has ironed.

"Ric, *Buongiorno*," she greets him, smiling. "Time to get up or the day will soon be as old as I am." She's left the front door open to allow a little light and fresh air into the room. The kettle is heating on the stove.

She glances up at him, but her expression changes quickly, "You look a little tired this morning – Ric, what has happened? You have had some trouble?"

He strokes the plaster above his right eye and frowns as he remembers the moonlit night and the hull of the fishing boat coming onto him, like a shark rising out of the depths. The crusted flesh splits and stings, but at least the chorus in his head has quieted.

"You want to tell me how you got this?" She inclines her head, frowning.

129

"Not really. It's a kind of unidentified squid-fishing injury; long story."

Valeria steps towards him and examines the plaster at the corner of his forehead and his temple. "Fishing?" she repeats with an air of scepticism. Satisfied that whatever the extent of his wound it has been adequately dressed, she stands back and says, "It must have been big, this *totani*."

"Actually it was a boat load of them."

"You went fishing alone or with someone?"

"With Il Velaccino, last night; didn't reckon on it being such a dangerous recreation."

"It isn't usually, but..." Valeria pauses.

"But what?" Ric asks.

"But..." she begins, and again she hesitates, "no matter." She shakes her head as if to banish some stupid idea and stands back to open the shutters.

Now that the little room is properly lit, she can get a better look at him. "Ric, you look terrible," she puts the shopping in his small fridge, "but from what people tell me, you were not the only person to have received an injury last night."

Ric sits down gently at the table. "I gather someone shot Candela."

"Yes, you are correct; it is a bad business." Valeria stares at the floor, her lips pursed in thought.

"Did you know him?" Ric asks to break the silence.

"Know him? Why would an old woman know a politician from the mountains, from Sicily," but then adds with a rancour Ric would not have thought she possessed, "they are all pigs. They are not to be trusted."

"Did you go to the meeting?" he asks, "I gather most of the town was there."

She hesitates before saying, "Such things, like looking into the future, do not interest me. When you have as many years as I have, the horizon appears nearer with each dawn."

Ric remembers hammering on her door after he'd swum into the point, but also remembers her telling him she takes a sleeping draught.

They are silent while she pours the boiling water into the cafetiere. The rich vapours of the coffee stir his senses.

"Interesting guy, Marcello," he says, as much to break the sombre mood as to keep her talking.

Valeria looks up sharply, "What makes you say this?"

"Only that he seems to know all there is to know about the island; seems to know everything and everyone, as though nothing happens here without his knowing about it."

"Yes, I suppose you could say that about him. But we are a small island; it is natural that people know each other."

But Ric wants to know more about the man who left him to drown out in the Sicilian Sea in the middle of the night. "His family must be one of the older families of the island."

"Yes," is all she replies.

"You mentioned a man to me the other day," Ric says: "Bongiorno, the communist who helped some of the deportees escape. Seems he taught Marcello English in school. Was Marcello's family part of the crew who helped deportees escape from Lipari?"

Valeria takes one of her long, thin white cigarettes from her bag and passes Ric her lighter. "I believe so," she says as he reaches over. "You know, only three of the deportees escaped."

"I didn't, no. Please, tell me."

"Francesco Fausto Nitti was a bank clerk, the nephew of a former Prime Minister, and Emilio Lussu was a lawyer. Lussu was one of the Aventine Secessionists who walked out of the Parliament after Mussolini's thugs murdered Matteotti. He was the founder of the *Sardo d'Azione*, the Sardinian Action party. The last of the three was Carlo Roselli. He, too, was a lawyer, but he came from a wealthy

Jewish family. Roselli founded the *Giustizia e Libertà*, the Justice and Freedom Party. All three were very different in character, but they were men of character and conviction, not like the politicians we have now."

Valeria stares into the distance and sighs as though the recounting of the tale is weighing heavily on her. "Because these men could not stomach Mussolini or his Fascism, they were sent here, to Lipari, to exile."

"How did they escape?"

Valeria stubs out her cigarette. "I believe it was a night in July 1929. They swam out to meet a *motoscafo* – a fast boat – which took them to Tunisia. Some people say they swam from a haunted house near the rocks below the citadel; others say it was from a house on the Maddalena, or perhaps the bay at Portinente. Nobody really knows. The smaller the number of people who knew; the smaller the chance of being betrayed."

"And after that?" Ric encourages.

"After that? All three of them went to fight for the Republicans against Franco. The French Fascists – the *cagoulards* – assassinated Roselli and his brother; Nitti fought with the resistance in France, was captured and escaped again; and Lussu helped the British defeat the Germans before returning to Rome, to the government."

"They sound like extraordinary characters," Ric says. He pours more coffee and studies her. From appearing so bright and full of life when he'd first come down the stairs, Valeria now seems weary; her eyes a little glassy with emotion.

"Did any others escape from the island?"

She wrests her gaze from the distance and focuses on him, "Many tried. Four escaped from the citadel using bedclothes tied together. Michelagnoli was one; he dressed as a woman and another man, Magri, as a priest. They hid in the hills, but they soon starved and begged a man for food. He gave them bread, but his wife told the

Carabinieri. The man was sent away to Ustica for five years." She chuckles in a sad, ineluctable way. "The irony is that without him, his wife probably starved to death. Perhaps it is true, eh? What goes around comes around."

Valeria sips her coffee, remembering. "A man named Spangero tried to escape on a ship, but the captain was German and returned him to the authorities."

"What about swimming to one of the other islands? Vulcano doesn't seem that far away."

Valeria shakes her head, "No, the currents in the Bocche di Vulcano are too dangerous. And in that time, Vulcano was a barren place; a few vines, nothing more."

"Seems crazy when you think you could keep anyone cooped up here when you can see the coast of Sicily in the distance. Only three ever got away?"

"Yes, only three." She hesitates, clearly wondering whether she should continue. But he can see that it is not that she is concerned she might be boring him; rather she is considering whether she should tell him something. Her eyes are unfocussed and for all his presence across the table, she appears momentarily detached.

"Go on, Valeria, please."

"There were three others who tried to escape in the same way as Nitti, Lussu and Roselli. Their names were Drago, Tamboia and Farinelli, but they were betrayed. The Carabinieri were waiting for them; they were all killed."

"You seem to know a good deal about these people, Valeria."

"I was told about them when I was young... and one reads," she says, dreamily. "The others, like Nitti and Lussu and Roselli are famous. They are in the history books. Drago, Tamboia and Farinelli are not so famous. After all, who remembers the names of the dead except their loved ones? For these three, there were no monuments."

"So, Marcello's family was a part of that underground network; the anti-fascists?"

Valeria nods, slowly, "So I have heard." She looks up from staring at the table and asks, "But why the interest in Marcello, Ric? It is unlikely that he would know much about your ancestor. Marcello's grandfather was one of the more... how would you say, more influential people in the island at that time, but he died many years ago. His father, Onofrio, passed away last week; the funeral took place the day you arrived. The Maggiore family are one of the oldest families in Lipari; they used to have the business for the transport between Milazzo, Palermo and the islands." She frowns at Ric, "So why so much interest in Il Velaccino?"

He shakes his head a shade dismissively, giving him time to conjure some answer other than wanting to know if there is any reason why the man should have deserted him out in the sea. "It's just that one of the *escurzionisti* told me Barbarossa wiped out all the old families in the sixteenth century. I was interested in just how old the old families are; that's all."

Valeria studies him for a moment, chewing the nail of her index finger. She takes a drag of her cigarette and points at him, "You know, Ric, if you ask too many questions, you may hear something you wish you had not. I told you: Lipari was once known as the Island of Grief and also the Island of the Damned. And, talking of the past, I must be going now. I have to visit my doctor to inquire after my health." Valeria stands up, very slowly, as though because she has sat for so long her bones have atrophied. "After all," she adds, as she stubs out her cigarette and gently loops her handbag over her shoulder, "these days, he knows my well-being better than I do."

"What do I owe you for the shopping?"

Valeria chuckles, "Nothing, Ric, you have already rewarded me enough with your company; that is as much compensation as an old woman can ask. *Ciao*, Ric, take better care of yourself. And stay away from such dangerous pursuits, eh?" She smiles warmly, turns and walks out into the vico.

The lemon and citrus of her perfume mingle with the odours of the coffee and cigarette smoke in the space she has vacated, and Ric is left wondering about her. Again, he tries to estimate her age and wonders if he was at fault in causing her to recall such unpleasant and perhaps even painful memories. She looks old enough to have lived through the second Great War, as the plaques in the Mazzini describe it, but he could not help but notice the consuming sadness in her eyes when she spoke of the deportees who had died long before it. He wonders if perhaps she shared some political affiliation with them. But he remembers, too, that she is originally from near Palermo, so there is no reason why she would be connected to a bunch of sorry politicos imprisoned on some island in the Sicilian Sea.

Ric shrugs and wonders: her age is of little consequence to him. Valeria has been kind to him since his arrival five days before, without her and her man Salvo, the Mara might be sitting at the bottom of the ocean.

And that reminds him; it is time to talk to Marcello.

27

The Corso Emmanuelle is a hive of activity, but all in typically slow motion. The *Apes*, loaded with vegetables, fruit and fish, are fringed by portly dowagers and skinny spinsters taking their time to make up their minds about what they are going to treat themselves to for lunch.

Sandro is chatting to a couple of middle-aged downbeats. He waves smartly, but he is commanding too big an audience to want to break off his spiel. And Giuliana appears from the door of the *panificio*, smiles and waves him towards a café, but he resists her offer.

Ric decides to walk up over the saddle to Canneto to Marcello's yard, rather than take the bus through the tunnel. The exercise, he decides, will drive the ache of the previous evening's swim from his limbs.

The Lunga is busy and the *escurzionisti* are, like a shoal of expectant piranhas, already limbering up for the arrival of the tourists off a colossal cruise liner wallowing in the bay.

An Aliscafo pulls in to the dock; a man announces its onward stops, the speakers atop the ticketing hut projecting his amplified voice in the tones of a tired bingo caller.

Stern-faced Carabinieri are checking the identity of all those waiting on the pier.

Before the road curves round to the Porto Pignataro and the tunnel through to Canneto, he cuts left up the hill and winds his way through a hamlet of low houses towards the saddle that connects Monte Rosa to the spine of the island. As he passes each gate, dogs rush at him, barking wildly, and in places he has to watch his step as the rough-and-ready road is potholed and uneven. The glare from the sun high over his right shoulder is relentless and the dust thrown up by his footfall hangs lazily in the air.

Ric follows the footpath at the end of the road and climbs up to the saddle. But, once there, the trail narrows and leads on up to the first of the twin peaks, Pietra Campana. He has to backtrack to locate the slender, overgrown trail which leads down to Canneto. The pathway is little more than a gulley-like run-off cut deep through the vegetation. He loses his footing and stumbles down, reaching out to hold onto anything that will slow his descent. In doing so, he grabs a handful of agave and cuts his palm on the serrated edge of the leaf.

He swears at no one in particular as he hops and jumps down between the steep banks of the path.

By the time he comes out by the entrance to the tunnel, he is sweating, one knee is grazed and his right palm is bleeding. "Next time, you idiot, take the tunnel like everyone else."

The yard, the Cantiere Nautico Maggiore, sits a hundred or so metres up a turning on the left. The road is deserted, dusty and crowned in the centre. A low white wall topped by a wire mesh fence runs along one side; old shacks with bleached-wood walls and doors held closed with heavy, rusting padlocks line the other. Marcello's yard is deserted.

Ric checks the sun and reckons it is a little early for lunch. He drags the heavy iron gate back and steps into the yard.

Scuffling and growling alerts him to the arrival of a hairy black mongrel. As he turns to face it, he realises it is too late for him to dash back out of the gate and so raises his arms to fend it off.

But as the dog leaps at him, the chain tethering it to the kennel extends fully and the dog halts in mid-flight, twists like a circus acrobat and lands on all fours in front of him.

The ferocious mongrel, eyes wild and frothing at the mouth, barks madly. It's frustration at not being able to reach him adds fuel to the fire of its fury.

They stare each other down until a mutual respect is established and the dog retires to the shade.

The Mara, supported by a crude assortment of jack stands and blocks, sits up in the middle of an uneven row of a half dozen more modern sailing boats. She looks uncomfortably out of place among the detritus of the yard and reminds Ric of a maiden aunt abandoned amidst a mob of drunken labourers. Hoists, chains, rusting engines, discarded outboards and broken spars litter the yard. And, at the back beneath a lean-to, a bench displays all the elaborate paraphernalia of the sailmaker. Coils of waxed cotton sailtwine, seaming and roping palms, sidehole cutters and hooks, spur grommets, turnbuttons, thimbles, jib hanks, slides, shackles and boxes of wooden and multi-coloured parrel beads are strewn about. And, under the bench lie rolls of sailcloth: yellowed flax, greying hemp and white cotton of varying weights, some crosscut and others radial, and all manner of more modern polyester and nylon, both laminate and woven.

Marcello is nowhere to be seen, so Ric walks over and around the back of the Mara. The propeller is missing, the stern tube has been disassembled and, in places, the hull is badly in need of anti-fouling; clearly, old Camille has not had the Mara out of the water for some time.

A wooden ladder stands up against the stern of the sloop. He checks it is secure and climbs up to the deck. The hatch cover is closed and, once he's pushed it back, he steps down.

Inside, the cabin is sweltering in the midday heat and the stale odours of drying cedar, engine grease and diesel foul the air.

Ric slides his mattress and a section of the bed aside, bends down and lifts the small cover off the hatch in the floor.

Where he expects to see the two small plastic bags, one containing the gun and the other the money and passports, there is only one bag. The gun is missing.

"Damn! What the hell do I do now?"

But before he can answer his own question, he hears the scrape of the gate outside and a car pulls into the yard.

Ric replaces the cover, slips the board and bed back into place, and steps up through the hatch to the deck.

Marcello is taken by surprise. "Hey, Ric," he calls up, taking the stub of his cigar from between his lips and shading his eyes from the sun, "you should have called. If I had known you were coming I would have brought cold drinks."

Ric slides the hatch cover in place and quickly, but not too obviously quickly, descends the ladder.

"No matter, Marcello, I thought I'd walk over to see how she was coming along."

But the short, curly headed Liparotan is, like his dog, suspicious of Ric.

"Hope you don't mind, my friend," Ric says, as innocently as his nervousness at being caught in the act will permit. "I thought I'd left something on the boat." Now it is his turn to watch the man back.

"Oh, yes? What thing is this that you have left on the Mara? We have been in the cabin, but I have not touched any of your things."

Ric waits, studying Marcello. If he is lying, he gives away no trademark tell.

"Sure. I mean I'm sure you wouldn't. I didn't think you would. It's just that I can't remember where I've left a couple of items of clothing. 'Suppose they must be at Valeria's. Maybe she's kept them back to iron them."

Marcello grins. "So, now La Strega is doing your laundry. Mm, well, be careful or she will have the shirt off your back, as you English say." He chews his cigar and raises his eyebrows. "A little old for you, don't you think?"

139

Then Ric remembers the other reason he has come to see Marcello and his expression darkens. "But, apart from the clothes I can't find, I wanted to see you. What the hell do you mean by leaving me out in the middle of the ocean last night?"

Marcello grimaces, examines his cigar, deems it not worth relighting and tosses it aside. The dog races over to consume it as though it is prime steak.

"Yes, of course. This was bad mannered of me. For this I must apologise."

But if Ric thinks he is worthy of any better treatment than the cigar, he is mistaken. "Just that?" he asks, incredulous. "I could have drowned out there. How did you know I wasn't knocked unconscious by the boat that ran us down?" He points at the wound above his eye, carful not to touch it.

The barrel-chested man scoffs dismissively, "How did you know it was not the same for me?" He takes a step back. "Come, let me show you something." He waves Ric over.

The dog makes to run at Ric, but Marcello snaps at it and it retreats, tail between its legs.

Over to the left of the yard lies the small skiff they had been fishing in the night before. But unlike the larger sail boats it is not up on blocks; rather it is lying on its side and halfway between the keel and the slender Plimsoll line the hull sports a gash large enough to put a boot through.

"You see this!" he says more than asks. "This is why I had to leave you." He waits for Ric to take in the extent of the damage. "How long do you think I would be floating with a hole like this? And what was the point of two of us swimming. The water was coming in faster than the motor can drive her through the water. I make it back just in time."

Ric remembers Sandro saying he had seen Marcello in the Corta some time before he arrived.

The breach in the hull of the little boat is overlaid with blue paint and Ric recalls the hull of the boat bearing down on him. He fingers the plaster above his right eye.

"Okay, Marcello, I'm sorry about your *barca*. I had no idea you'd been holed. I thought you'd run off and left me."

Marcello chuckles, "Oh, I did, my friend. I did. But I remember you telling me you were in the *Marina Militare* – the Marines – so naturally I think it will not be a problem for you to swim this little distance to the shore." He looks Ric up and down, lingering on the jellyfish welts on his forearms. "And I see, apart from caressing the *medusa*, you made it back in one piece. They hurt, eh?"

"They do."

"You must piss on the pain. I know it sounds unpleasant, but this is the best cure."

"Thanks, Marcello," Ric groans, "but I can do without the old wives' tales." He hesitates. "I guess I owe you an apology for thinking you'd run out on me."

The man bobs his head from side to side as he appreciates Ric's rather begrudging acknowledgement. "Okay, okay, now I have apologised and you have apologised, so let's go have a beer. It's too hot to stand out here playing *buone maniere*."

At a café down the front in Canneto, a waiter, wearing yesterday's clothes and a thousand-yard-stare, serves them a couple of beers and a bowl of green olives. Marcello pops an olive in his mouth, chews thoughtfully for a moment and then flicks the stone at a skinny dog which has sidled in to sit at his feet.

"How goes it with the Mara?" asks Ric.

Marcello shrugs, "Slowly. There is much that is a problem."

"Meaning?"

"Meaning, my friend, you will be here for a while unless you want to go somewhere else and return when I have finished." Marcello flicks another olive stone. The dog snaps and catches it in its mouth before dropping it at its feet.

141

"The seals are worn and as a result the propeller shaft is out of balance. This means that it is possible the main bearings in the engine are worn. If we put everything back together, there is no guarantee the engine will not have more problems." He holds up his stubby fingers in surrender. "I am at your command. You tell me what you want me to do."

Ric sighs, "Given the circumstances, what would you do?"

Marcello grins and looks up to the heavens and replies, "Oh, you have two choices: I take out the engine and replace the bearings or you pray that you do not meet a big storm and need to rely on the motor to get you out of trouble. It is simple."

"I'm not big on relying on the weather."

"It is wise not to be so," Marcello replies, nodding. "The weather can be a fine friend, but a cruel enemy."

Ric considers the shipwright's advice. "I noticed the hull could do with some attention."

Marcello nods again, "Yes, but it is not as bad as it looks. This you could do later."

"Talking of hulls," Ric says, sipping his beer, "the boat that ran us down last night?"

"Yes. What about this?"

"I noticed the paint on the hull of your skiff is dark blue. Any idea who has a boat that colour? You seem to know everyone hereabouts; I imagine you'd know who that boat belonged to."

Marcello glances at Ric; a brief, hard, penetrating glance. "Yes. I have given this much thought."

"And?"

But the Liparotan does not answer, he simply gazes out at the horizon; a flat line broken only by the low outline of Panarea and, behind it, the larger cone of Stromboli and the small cloud permanently suspended above it.

"No, this was not a boat from Lipari; it was both too big and not

142

big enough. It was not a *peschereccio*, a tourist *barca*, a *taxi mare* or a playboy's *motoscafo*. And it was not one of those boats like the floating hotel in Porto Salvo. This boat was both big and fast; it was from Milazzo."

Ric thinks for a moment and remembers the hull bearing down on him. "If I remember rightly it had a blue hull with numbers painted in white just below the rail."

Marcello is watching him, expectantly, "Go on, my friend."

"So it was an official launch of some kind?" And as he pictures the prow rearing up out of the night and the rail above him and the glancing blow, he realises, "It was the Carabinieri launch, wasn't it?"

Marcello is deep in thought, chewing an olive. When he has finished stripping the flesh off it, he picks it from between his lips and flicks it at the dog. "No it was not, my friend. It was La Polizia. It was they who caused you to swim back to the beach."

Ric frowns. "Can you make a claim against them?"

"Yes, I could if I thought it would be of benefit."

"So have you?"

"You see this dog, Ric," he nods at the scrawny hound sat at his feet. "You know why it sits so far from my feet and waits for me to throw it food it cannot eat?" He pauses, though not long enough to suggest he is expecting a reply. "It sits in the hope that one day I will throw it a piece of food it *can* eat. But, it will not sit so close to me that I find its smell unpleasant, because then it knows there is every chance I will kick it and no chance that I will give it anything to eat. It is the same with La Polizia and Lipari."

"But the boat wasn't showing any navigation lights."

"This is true and this is interesting."

"Because...?"

"Because it means they were expecting trouble at the opera and they did not want anyone to know they were waiting near the stage."

"Candela?"

"Yes, Ric: Candela." Marcello sips his beer and fidgets in his seat. "It means they knew something was going to happen. But if they knew something was going to happen; why did they not do something about it before it happened? This is also what is interesting."

His conclusion is punctuated by the nasal rasp from a scooter tearing past the café.

The beer suddenly seems flat and Ric feels curiously vulnerable; the matter of the missing Beretta is preying heavily on his mind.

"I was talking to one of the *escurzionisti* a couple of days ago," he says. "He told me word about town was that there was going to be trouble with Candela."

Marcello's ears prick up, "He did? Which one was this?"

"Don't know his name," Ric replies, hoping he has adequately sold his untruth.

"People here have nothing better to do than talk. It is the one commodity you do not have to buy, eh?"

Across the dusty road, the promenade is deserted. Like most sensible people, the beachcombers and strollers have settled for siesta. Even the dog resigns itself to finding a shady spot. It nurses its arthritic frame upright and turns a skinny tail.

"Talking of talking," Ric says, "Valeria and I went to see that old guy you pointed out to me the other night."

"Old Nino?"

Ric chuckles at the thought of the extraordinary, elderly blind man who could tell so much about him simply by shaking hands. "Yes. Valeria thought he might shed some light on my ancestor. Interesting guy! It's as you said the other evening; he has a remarkable memory."

Marcello scoffs; something Ric is beginning to understand he does whenever Ric brings other people into their conversation, "That old fool! You would hear more sense in the cemetery."

And, as Marcello mentions the cemetery, Ric remembers Old Nino suggesting he spend a bit of time there.

He stands and stretches. "I must be going, Marcello. Thank you for the beer."

"Don't worry, my friend," Marcello winks, "I will add it to your bill. What do you want me to do with the motor in your boat?"

"Damned if I know," Ric replies, wondering how he is going to be able to pay for the repairs with the small amount of cash he has left stowed in the Mara. "I'll see you later."

"Yes, Ric, later. Of course, we will see each other."

28

On his way back into town, Ric takes the easier option of the tunnel. The racket shouted by the cars, minibuses and scooters in the narrow passageway provides a deafening prelude to the activity beyond it. Whereas Canneto is an oasis of calm, the languorous atmosphere pierced only by a water taxi plodding offshore, the Lunga and Marina di Porto Salvo are all activity. A bright orange tanker lies up at the fuel pier, feeding the island like a gaudy wet nurse. The garbage boat is departing its berth below the citadel and even though it is siesta, the afternoon Aliscafo eases up, its hydrofoils sinking into the green waters of the port as it waits for its sister to vacate the dock.

The Carabinieri are still checking the papers of those leaving through the port, but outside of flagging down a helicopter or thumbing a lift on a yacht, the Lunga is the only gateway off the island.

At least the cemetery will be quiet, he thinks: even the dead must rest.

Ric pauses and looks up at the eternal stone flame, the cross of thorns perched on the high columns and the inscription *Omnia Traham* beneath. And from some dark corner of his school days he recalls the scripture: *Et ego, si exaltatus fuero a terra, omnia traham ad me ipsum.*

But, unlike the first day when his curiosity had gotten the better of him and he had walked straight in to wander amongst the mausolea, now he feels unable to enter until he has remembered the translation. He rubs his brow and searches his mind.

"And... and if I..."

A rumpled, wrinkled old man sits inside the gate, an expectant yet bemused expression on the stretched parchment of his face. He has long since lost his teeth and he is so thin, his flat cap and baggy trousers appear to be wearing him.

"Got it," he mumbles to himself, "And I, if I be lifted up from the earth, will draw all things unto me: Book of John."

The old man cackles at the sight of a much younger man bartering his way into the afterlife.

"Afternoon, Pop," Ric offers.

The man raises his hand in salute and rasps, "*Salve, mio amico.*"

The air beneath the cypress trees is cool, the mood of the cemetery appropriately calm. There are so many graves Ric is not sure where to begin.

Common sense tells him the cemetery would have begun its life either right by the entrance at the bottom or perhaps a little way up, a respectful distance from the harbour. The newer residents would have found themselves billeted further back up the slope as the cemetery expanded in the only direction available.

Ric imagines a grid and starts out inspecting the head stones and coffin-like mausolea. Some are ornate and intricate, some art deco in design and others plain and simple. But here and there a measure of wealth, standing or affection, or perhaps all three, is displayed in glossy black or shimmering white granite: the older the occupant, the more frugal and austere the style; the younger the occupant, the more polished and pretentious the aspect.

An old crone swathed in black, doubtless the better half of the fellow by the gate, is laying fresh flowers at the grave of the Conti sisters; twins born in 1890. She places a plastic bottle upside down in an earthenware vase and punctures the top so that the water will drip very slowly to feed her bouquet of clematis, cornflowers and blue violets.

More than a few of the headstones record the deaths of those interred as early as 1888; the year, as Valeria has told him, the island of Vulcano last erupted. And he comes upon the tomb of the Bongiorno family, a stone cross standing on top of a sarcophagus-shaped vault; stark and restrained and almost soviet in architecture, the word CREDO – Believe – is chased in the centre.

The terraces layer up into the hillside. Stone steps sweep around the Lombardo family: Luigi – dolphins, sails and tridents carved in the base and an anchor standing proudly on the plinth, Giovanna Arena – a simple eternal flame sculpted in stone, and Francesco – pictured in bas relief on an obelisk, a man of some standing at the turn of the century before.

An hour later, he finds a pedestal graced by a weather-worn angel of mercy standing alone in the lea of the chapel-house wall. The name of the family buried beneath the slab of stone is barely legible, but the Christian name seems to begin with the letter A and the surname S.

Ric bends to the gravestone and rubs the contours of the inscription. It is difficult to make out at first, but when he stands back the letters catch the sun and the name becomes clear.

It is ANTONIO SCIACCHITANO, the surname Camille has suggested his great-grandfather went by. There is no date of birth, but the details of his passing are inscribed simply as MORTO LUGLIO 1930. The headstone is heavily pitted and aside from the roughly hewn image of flowers and an incense bowl, he can make out only a couple of other words: INTEGERRIMO CITTADINO, which he roughly translates to a something citizen.

He kneels down on the corner of the gravestone and tries to read more of the inscription. But the words are illegible and after a few minutes he gives up. Ric can see no reference to a spouse and neither of the graves either side bear any relation.

Outsize black ants trail to and fro across the path and a gecko eyes him warily from the shadow of an adjacent pedestal. Down on the terrace below him, workmen toil, cleaning the stone edifices, restoring the mausolea which have succumbed to the ravages of the Aeolian winds and the Sicilian sun.

Ric recalls what Camille told him about the *guardiano* of the marine cemetery high up in the Bosco of Bonifacio; namely that if he wanted to find out any details of those buried in the cemetery, he should ask the men who attend the graves. But the labourers he is watching work diligently and silently, there is no radio to distract them and they do not whistle or sing. They seem, to him, to approach their tasks with all the appropriate reverence of men who know they are plugging away amongst the departed.

So the possibility is that this supposed relation of his passed away in 1930. Carmelo Corbino, across the way, made it to a hundred. How old, he wonders, was Antonio? But, if he is to take any comfort from his discovery it is that Antonio was thought of as an *integerrimo* citizen, which he believes must be positive. Surely, the loved ones of the departed were not in the habit of inscribing a headstone with anything other than terms of endearment. Right up at the back towards the final tier of the cemetery stand imposing and impressive mausolea; some twice a man's height and colonnetted and domed, like elegant pantheons.

As Ric turns, he notices a substantial, simple tomb set apart from the more recent, flashier copies.

The tomb is vaguely Roman in style, the roof squares to a pitch and the doorway is high and wide. The lintel is set in a recessed arch transcended by a semi-circular lunette, the columns in each corner carved from single pieces and their capitals convex and plain. The name inscribed on the lintel reads MAGGIORE.

Ric peers in through the wrought iron gate. A dozen or more plaques denote who is interred in the vault: the line of Maggiore runs far back into the nineteenth century. The women, Grazia, Isabella, Katarina and Maria are many; the men few. And Ric reasons this is because so many of the fathers, sons and brothers would have been buried where they fell in the mountains around Caporetto or the deserts of Abyssinia. He studies the names and dates for a while, looking to see if any of the plaques bear relation to his forebear's time.

There is one: a plaque bearing the name **Katarina,** her date of birth **25 Gennaio 1910** and her passing **18 Luglio 1930**. Katarina Maggiore died at the tender age of twenty. Clearly, Marcello would not have known her, but Ric wonders whether Antonio Sciacchitano might have?

Above Katarina's plaque is that of **Vincenzo**, who passed away on **13 Aprile 1951**. And alongside her, in his newly placed casket, lies **Onofrio**, born **1928** and died as recently as **10 Giugno 2013**, and Ric realises that this is the man whose funeral cortège he watched pass down the Corso a few days before. He also toys with the idea that Vincenzo may be Marcello's grandfather, and Onofrio Marcello's father; Marcello is at the outside no more than fifty.

He completes his inspection and strolls back down the avenue of cypress trees, nodding politely at the old fellow waiting patiently for his wife to finish paying her respects.

The Carabinieri are still checking the papers of people queuing for the Aliscafo and he thinks he spots Valeria among them. To avoid the policemen, Ric slips into the Corso Vittorio through a narrow alley to his right and strides up the cobbled street.

Halfway up the Corso a diminutive individual is sitting at a café.

There is nothing out of the ordinary in a man sitting alone; many of those loitering in the cafés sit by themselves and watch the world pass by. However, this man stands out from the many others. He is watching, though not in a casual or cursory fashion; his eyes are sharp and they move fast from one person to the next. He is judging those who pass him by, weighing them in his mind and committing their images to memory.

And, this man is not wearing the relaxed apparel of any local; for him there is no short-sleeved shirt fashioned from a material that resembles the kitchen curtains, no trousers that look as though long ago they lost touch with their corresponding suit jacket and no shoes that are slipped easily from one's feet at the door. This man is wearing a sombre grey suit, white shirt and funereal tie; his shoes are laced and polished. A grey Homburg sits on the table before him.

Yet what truly sets the man apart from the locals is that all the tables around him are vacant except for one, at which table sit two smartly turned out policemen. One of them is very tall and solidly built and neither of them are smoking or drinking. They wait, both attentive and apprehensive, like courtiers to a doge.

The man sees Ric come striding up the Corso and immediately picks him out to be a cat amongst pigeons.

Ric knows it is unwise to make eye contact with such an individual; his training has taught him to recognise such people and assume the pretence of ignorance.

However, his gaze is drawn to the man as if by some curious magnet and, once the connection has been established, Ric feels the only course left open to him is to acknowledge him. So he nods, politely.

The man inclines his head subtly. He doesn't nod outright. Evidently, he doesn't want those around him to know he has made Ric an exception to his rule.

29

Down in the Corta the day is drawing to a close. The square has tripped into shadow and the tourists have retired to prepare for evening.

Sandro is lurking in his usual café. Giuliana is hovering nearby. "Hey, Ric," he calls, "how is your boat?"

Ric swings by and pulls up a chair at the same table. "What are you, Sandro? Working for the CEKA?"

Giuliana appears as if by magic and Ric taps Sandro's beer bottle.

"No, my friend," the *escurzionista* replies frowning, "I'm not working for the secret police of the Duce. This is a small island and today I go to Porticello on my scooter. I pass by Canneto and see you and Maggiore in the café. So, naturally I think you have gone to find out about your boat. It is so, yes?"

Ric grins. "Just kidding, Sandro," he chuckles.

A Birra Messina appears. Giuliana lingers as she reaches over him and places it on the table; her perfume is all roses and she touches his shoulder as she stands back.

Sandro flinches.

"Yes, I know," Ric mutters.

"So, how is your boat?"

"Could be better. She needs a bit more than a passing dose of TLC."

"TLC? What is this? I don't know this." Sandro screws up his face, and, what with his doughy features and curly hair, he presents a curiously charming picture of dismay.

"Tender loving care. It's what all women need every now and then." Ric nods towards the waitress.

But Sandro has gone all po-faced, "This is not funny, my friend. If you put your fingers in this pizza, you must be sure to count them when you have finished eating." He shakes his hand as though to flick water off it.

"Sorry," Ric chuckles, "didn't mean to tread on your toes."

"No, my friend, I am serious. I like my toes as much as my fingers and I intend for them to be connected to my feet and my hands for a long time." Now it is his turn to nod and he does so towards the stony, pinch-faced owner, who is deep in conversation with a group of his acolytes at the back of the café.

"The wrong word can travel very fast in this place. You know, Gallese, a woman is like a Lamborghini: from being still one minute, she can accelerate to incredible speed and then be stopped very suddenly by an accident. This happens most often when the Lamborghini is in the hands of one who is not qualified to drive it." Sandro touches the corner of his right eye. "I would not want you to have an accident when you were a passenger in this car, eh?"

Ric laughs, which upsets his companion even further. "Sorry, Sandro, you are right on so many counts. I'm grateful for your advice and no little touched that you should go to the trouble of gifting it."

The *escurzionista* is embarrassed at such an explicit pronouncement of affection and colours instantly.

"Il Velaccino tells me I may be here for a couple of weeks," Ric says, "he tells me the Mara needs a fair bit of work."

"He would know this."

"I suppose he would," Ric replies. "He seems a pretty regular guy."

When Sandro doesn't follow this assessment of Marcello's character with a ringing endorsement, Ric is inclined to press further. "My Italian isn't up to much, I wonder if you might help me with a word I read today? I think I know what it means, but I'm not sure and wouldn't want to use it in case I offended someone."

"Sure! What is the word?"

"*Integerrimo*, if I've got the pronunciation correct."

Sandro thinks for a few seconds. "*Integerrimo*; it means... honest. When used to describe a man this way, you would say this man is a person of integrity."

Ric is pleased to learn his forebear, if indeed Antonio Sciacchitano is his forebear, was considered a man of integrity; an honest citizen. But the query serves his purpose.

"So would you describe Marcello Maggiore as a man of integrity?"

Sandro fixes him with a stern, questioning expression. "Integrity," he states, "is a commodity that can be measured in many different ways." He ponders his aphorism for a few seconds, fidgeting uncomfortably. "But for repairing a boat, I think you can rely on his integrity; that is all I can say."

Ric purses his lips and weighs up the *escurzionista's* judgement.

But something is rather obviously troubling Sandro; he looks about nervously.

Thinking that, perhaps, Sandro is nervous of talking about Marcello Maggiore in public, Ric suggests, "I've got a bottle of Caravaglio in the fridge, why don't we go and find a home for it?"

Sandro glances at him and sighs. "Yes, of course. Why not? This would be better."

Back at his *monolocale*, Ric throws together a plate of *antipasti* and uncorks the bottle. Though not short of a spare pound of flesh, Sandro tucks in to the *prosciutto* and tomatoes as though he hasn't eaten for a week.

"This is good wine, eh?" he mumbles between slurps.

"I see there's plenty of Carabinieri about," Ric says, casually.

"Yes, the Maddalena is still closed. They have the *medico legale* there. I think you call them forensic people, is that correct?"

"It is. They seem to be checking the identities of people taking the Aliscafo too."

"It is normal."

"I guess it's only natural what with Candela being such a bigshot."

Sandro looks up from his food and, as he chews, studies Ric. He swallows noisily and says, "I forget, you don't like the police. But yes, Candela's murder would upset many people."

"People to do with the new energy supply you said he was going to talk about; promising the people free electricity, that sort of thing?"

"Yes, that sort of thing. But also because it looks bad for the islands when a man of importance is murdered here," Sandro replies. "But it was not only the energy he promised everyone. In his speech he said that as well as the free electricity, he has put a group together to build a very large hotel at Porticello; a very large hotel: one thousand rooms, perhaps more. It would double the capacity for the island."

"That would be a good thing, wouldn't it?" Ric asks.

Sandro nods and then shakes his head: "Probably, but also possibly not."

"How come?" Ric remembers Valeria mentioning some plans to build a hotel and being fairly ambivalent about its benefits; something about the island losing its World Heritage Status.

"Candela said that this hotel would bring much work for the people. He said it would bring much money into the community; better schools, more transport, and so on." He scoffs as though Candela's idea was ridiculous.

"So, what's the downside?"

"The downside, as you put it, is that the island cannot support this. The tourist season is very short: three maybe four months. So, for the rest of the year it would be empty. There are not enough people here to staff a hotel of one thousand rooms; they would have to bring in many eastern Europeans to do the housework, the laundry, the waiting at tables, the kitchen; all this type of work. These eastern Europeans can be anyone: Romanians, Lithuanians, Croatians, all thieves and murderers. They would do more damage to the island than Barbarossa."

"I guess when you put it that way it doesn't sound so appealing."

"Also, they would upset the status quo. Not the pop group," he grins, "the ecology; this sort of thing. The Aeolian Islands may look like heaven with our clear blue waters, quiet beaches and quaint houses, but there is a balance to our society. It has become this way over many centuries, not overnight."

Ric recalls a similar conversation he had with Camille in Corsica. "But surely the island must have some kind of council which represents the people; some kind of planning committee?"

Sandro nods, "Yes, there is a planning committee. This idea of a big hotel has been tried before. It has always been turned down. But this new plan is so big the people who plan it cannot build it without first listening to certain people. It's not completely democratic, of course," he grins sheepishly. "You are on an island in the Sicilian Sea, if you know what I mean?"

"I think I do. You mean the Mafia?" Ric asks.

"Of a kind. But maybe it is more about where you think you exist in the food chain, eh? I told you, there is a balance to the society that certain people will not give up without a fight. Not all interests are the same, you know. It's not always about the money."

"Sure, Sandro, I get that. But if it's not about the money, who has so much to lose that they would do away with Candela? Isn't there anyone on the planning committee who carries enough clout to get a project of that size rejected?"

He nods as he slips the last tomato into his mouth. When he has swallowed it, he says, "Possibly, but also probably not. You know how the food chain works? The small dog is at the mercy of the big dog and the big dog is at the mercy of the bigger dog. Only," he pauses, working a morsel of food out from between his teeth with his tongue…

But Ric is inclined to think the *escurzionista* is avoiding speaking rather than paying attention to his dental hygiene: "Only what, Sandro?"

"Only…" he hesitates again, "mercy is like integrity; it comes with a price."

"So, what you're saying is that the dogs on the planning committee are not big enough to take on the big dogs in Palermo?"

Sandro bobbles his head from side to side again, "In a manner of speaking." He glances over at Ric as though he is beginning to dislike the route his questioning is taking. "You know, Ric, even small dogs can be vicious when left with no way out other than to fight."

"Yes, I know what you mean, Sandro. Believe me; I've seen enough of them. But what kind of people make up this planning committee: lawyers, judges, professionals?"

Sandro has cleared the plate of *antipasti* and the wine is finished. He wipes his hands on his grubby handkerchief and hauls himself to his feet, readying himself to leave. He looks strangely unsettled, as though he is late for an appointment. "All kinds of people," he says frowning, his fingers on the handle of the door. "People like Marcello Maggiore and his brother, Claudio."

30

At *passeggio* Ric decides to take a stroll out to see Valeria. There is more he needs to know about the man she calls the sailmaker and he feels he has exhausted his credit with Sandro.

The Maddalena is still closed, so he takes the steps up towards San Nicola. There is a late Mass taking place in the Santa Anna and apart from the echoes of the priest's solemnities and the tidal swell of murmured chorus from the congregation, the town is peaceful.

He passes by the house of Marcello in Capistello, there appears to be no one at home bar a dog sleeping on the veranda, and the sun is setting as he turns down the lane that leads to the Casa dei Sconosciuti.

Valeria is not in and he realises that perhaps it *was* her he had seen waiting for the Aliscafo.

As he walks back, he watches the sea cast off its soft imperial purple only to lay bare its stark obsidian veneer. There is little or no breeze and the clouds have long departed to the higher reaches of the mountains of Sicily, where they can rest more easily in the cooler atmosphere.

Mass is still in progress at the church and Ric is at a loose end. So he follows the Via Sant'Anna and turns down the Vico Cupido. Surprised that it is open so late, he stops off at the Pasticceria d'Ambra for *cannolicchio*.

He is, for some reason he cannot fathom, under the impression that he is being followed; the hairs on his forearms and the back of his neck bristle every now and again. But, standing outside the parlour eating his finger of ricotta filled pastry, he can see no proof that his concern is anything other than a self-conscious reaction to knowing the Beretta is now in the wrong hands.

Old Nino is sitting beneath San Bartolo, leaning on his stick. He is listening to an argument between two younger men, who now and then turn to Old Nino as if to seek his affirmation.

Ric sets himself carefully beside the old man, who tilts his head towards Ric to let him know he has recognised a newcomer on the low wall.

"*Buonasera*, Nino."

His face creases into a happy beam. "Ah, *buonasera, Ric. Cumu va?*"

"As it goes, Nino. You know how it is."

The old boy chuckles, "Yes, I do. It goes the way it always goes: some days our skies are blue; some days they are not. But forgive me a moment; I must settle a dispute between two young friends."

The two men arguing before Nino are both younger, but, Ric decides, that probably puts them in their late seventies. They wear pork-pie hats, striped, short-sleeved shirts, and their grey trousers are supported by thin braces. However, their clothing is not what is remarkable.

Nino holds up his slender palm as a signal he wants to speak, "*Per favore,*" he asks, gently, "*un'altra volta, per favore.*"

They turn to the old man. They are flabbergasted that he should interrupt their squabble. But when they see their referee has a visitor, they touch the rims of their hats and slope off like scolded dogs.

"Twins, eh? They come to me because they believe that as I cannot see them, their similarity will not confuse my judgement and therefore I will be able to understand the subtle differences upon which they argue."

The gentle hubbub of the Corta is broken only by the arrival of a smart *pulmino* from a luxury hotel. The occupants alight; their clothing far too *this season*, their tans too yellow for them to be anything other than tourists.

"You have found out something of this ancestor of yours?" Nino asks.

"Possibly. I found a gravestone up by the chapel wall. The inscription reads ANTONIO SCIACCHITANO and gives his date of passing as LUGLIO 1930. It says he was an INTEGERRIMO CITTADINO."

Nino sighs and repeats, "*Integerrimo...*" thinking for a moment, staring into the darkness before his eyes, remembering, calculating. He smiles, exposing his yellowed teeth, "This word, it means an honest man. Yes, it means honest. But, it also means something more. I remember the Americans have a saying, an expression, some slang for this word. They would say this of a man one could depend on. They would say this man was a *solid* citizen. That is the word: *solid*. It speaks well of your ancestor."

"Well, that's reassuring, Nino. Thank you."

"But the date you say: July 1930. This date," he stares once more into the distance, "this date, it is important..." The old man is silent for a while; his face impassive as he tries to recall the significance of it.

The lanterns in the Corta cast a gentle, muted glow over Old Nino as he wrestles with his memory.

Eventually, the corners of his mouth turn down and his expression changes to one of resignation. He shakes his head very slowly. "No, I am sorry. Tonight my recollections are dim. But there is a puzzle to this date and I must try to find the right pieces and put them together in the right order. I apologise, my friend, I will apply myself to the task. Come and see me another time. Or, when I recall, I will send for you."

Ric waits until he understands that Old Nino has closed his mind to the task of remembering. "Thanks for trying, Nino, I appreciate it. Don't lose too much sleep over it though; I'm sure I'll get to the bottom of it in good time."

"Sleep?" Old Nino repeats. "Sleep and memories: God may be the master of my sleep, but my memories he cannot rule."

They sit a while longer and watch the children play. Mothers and fathers gossip, debate and gesticulate at one another as though at any moment their disagreement will erupt into violence.

"How is Valeria? You have seen her?" the old man asks.

"Not today. I thought I caught a glimpse of her down by the pier, waiting for the Aliscafo. She is not at home. Perhaps she has gone to Milazzo."

Old Nino nods, thoughtfully. "Of course, I forget. Today is the day she goes to the hospital for her treatments."

"Treatments?"

But the old man is suddenly embarrassed: "Forgive me, I speak out of turn. On occasion my tongue lets me down. Forget I said this thing to you."

And with that, he holds out his hand for Ric to shake.

"*Ciao, Nino. E grazie.*"

"No, my friend," Nino replies, "it is I who should thank you. You force me to question my memory; in this way I recall many happy times."

He leaves the old man sitting beneath the bearded figure of the patron saint of the island and strolls across the Corta in the warm evening air.

Sandro is nowhere to be seen and Ric reasons it is probably because he is sleeping off the *antipasti*.

Giuliana is dawdling by the café. She shoots him a mischievous grin as he walks towards her. But, after the foolishness of the evening before, he decides it would be in his better interest not to encourage her, so he acknowledges her with a brief smile and walks on by. She pouts, playfully. Her uncle, the stern-faced café owner, barks at her and throws Ric a menacing glance.

161

The African women are sitting, toying with their children outside their shop halfway up the rise of the Garibaldi. They smile broadly as he steps between them. The narrow vico swallows him and it takes his eyes a moment to adjust to the darkness.

Ric turns left and right and comes upon the alley which leads along to the *monolocale* Marcello is so generously loaning him.

As he reaches the door, he is aware of a figure rounding the corner before him. The man has purpose and does not break his stride as he approaches.

Once again, Ric feels the hairs on his arms and his neck stand up and he hesitates before bending to retrieve his key from beneath the flower pot. He will have to turn side-on to the man to let him past, but there is something about his gait and poise that tells Ric he is not about to pass him by casually.

The man is only a couple of paces away when he draws something from his pocket and raises his arm to strike Ric.

Not having the room to square up and set his feet, Ric has to crouch to avoid the blow. The cosh comes down heavily on his left shoulder and knocks him off balance.

He tries to grab the man's arm, misses and the cosh comes down very swiftly a second time.

There is little else Ric can do but launch himself at his assailant. As he does so, he leads with the heel of his right palm and punches upwards towards the man's throat. He doesn't connect though; he merely catches him on the side of his neck. But the blow carries sufficient force to drive the man backwards and upwards, unbalancing him.

Ric follows on with another blow to the man's solar plexus, which does connect.

The man gasps, winded, and staggers back.

Inclined to maintain his advantage, Ric is about to slam his fist into the man's chest, when he is aware of footsteps behind him.

Knowing he is now trapped in the alley, he turns, grabbing the rubbish bin of the house opposite, and half throws, half pushes the bin at the approaching man's feet.

The second man stumbles over the garbage bin and falls heavily. But, in the breathing space, his original attacker has gathered himself and lands a heavy blow to Ric's kidneys.

The punch stings and stands him up. With nowhere to go and understanding that he must finish the brawl sooner or risk being worn down by fighting on two fronts, he kicks out at the inside of the first man's knee and, when he doubles, Ric clasps his hands and delivers him an upward cuff that smashes into the side of his head, bending him up over backwards.

The man behind Ric has regained his poise and throws himself forward, but rather than retreat, which is what the man expects him to do, Ric plants his feet and steps back to thrust his left elbow hard into the oncoming man's chest, using his right arm to drive home the weight of the jab.

The second attacker recoils and he too staggers back.

Ric, though, is not finished and knows he must press home his advantage before either of the men can recover. So he steps over the bin and delivers the fellow a short arm to his face and an uppercut to his jaw. The second man slides down awkwardly, reaching out to the wall of the alley in the vain hope of preventing himself from crashing to the ground.

Ric stands his ground now, turning to face the door of the *monolocale*, watching and waiting for the slightest movement that might tell him the men have not had sufficient.

They stagger to their feet, linger for a moment, deciding, then turn and run off in opposite directions down the vico.

Ric waits and listens: all he can hear is the thumping of his heart and the coldly laboured rasp of his breathing. His ribs are viciously sore and his shoulder feels as though it has parted company from his chest.

He hangs on to the wall until he can no longer hear their footsteps.

"Now," he coughs as he bends down very slowly to remove the key from beneath the flower pot, "let's try that again, shall we?"

31

For the second morning running Ric is woken by a noise from downstairs; someone is knocking on his door. But when he goes to haul himself out of bed, he is shot through with pain. His shoulder feels as though it is constructed with shards of glass and the cramps around his lower back are all but crippling.

There is another loud report from downstairs and he can hear a murmured conversation from the alley below his window.

Finally, he manages to lift his feet off the bed and struggle upright. As he does so, he hears a louder, more impatient rattling of the door.

Ric glances out into the vico: a policeman wearing a blue jacket and white cap stands beside a man sporting a grey hat. If the uniform isn't enough to convince Ric he is in some kind of trouble, the gun the policeman has holstered does.

"*Per favore, Signore,*" demands the *poliziotto*. "*Aprire la porta.*"

Ric climbs very gently into his clothes. The bruise above his shoulder is extremely tender and the discomfort around his ribs means he can move only gingerly. He wonders whether the arrival of the policemen is related to last night's scuffle.

The policeman bangs on his door once more.

"*Un momento,*" Ric shouts, in an effort to curb the policeman's enthusiasm.

When he eases the wooden door back, he is confronted by a uniformed giant and a suited dwarf. And while the *poliziotto* adopts the countenance of a man who doesn't like to be kept waiting, the dwarf next to him is all patience and virtue.

There is something about the shorter of the men that tells Ric he is not in any imminent, physical danger. Perhaps it is the way the man slouches a little; his lips sloping down in curious symmetry with his shoulders. Or perhaps it is his rather put-upon demeanour; an air which is very much at odds with his sharply-tailored suit, but one which suggests he'd really rather be elsewhere other than standing outside Ric's *monolocale*. Or perhaps it is the man's diminutive form, in as much that even if he does intend to threaten Ric with some form of harm, he is so vertically challenged that the giant beside him will have to lift him up if he is to reach Ric's nose. He is wearing a grey Homburg and funereal tie and he is the man Ric acknowledged in the Corso Vittorio the previous afternoon.

He stares and waits, but the little man isn't eager to explain or justify his presence.

Then the face recognition computer in his mind registers that he has seen Ric before. "Ah, so we already know each other. That is good."

"Well, if that's the case, I guess you'd better come in."

The pair of them do! The small, suited man removes his hat and takes a seat at the kitchen table; the taller of the two lingers by the door.

When the silence has continued for long enough, Ric walks to the sink at the back and examines his face in the mirror on the shelf. There is no doubt he looks a mess; the creases in his shirt match the furrows of his face and the plaster at his right temple has come off during the night, leaving a residue of dried blood on his forehead and cheek.

There is no doubt the man is the policeman Ric remembers

Sandro telling him about; the strange, little man who took charge in the moments after Candela's shooting. And as he washes and dries his face, Ric reaches the conclusion that the previous evening's ruckus is probably not worthy of such attention. "Do you mind me asking who you are?"

"No, not at all. I am Tommaso Talaia. Commissario Talaia to most people. Forgive my intrusion and for making myself known to you in such a brutal fashion so early in the morning."

He glances at his watch, "Well, perhaps not so early," and smiles, briefly. "But, as you probably know, people here have little else to occupy their time but idle talk and for the moment I would prefer it if we kept our conversation... let us say, discreet." He pauses and waits. "But now that I have introduced myself, let me ask you who you are."

Ric pauses to think, unsure how to answer and so says, "Just a guy doing a bit of sailing in a boat that isn't, for the moment, sea worthy."

The Commissioner smiles and asks, "May I see your passport?"

"Sure," he replies, and he reaches into the back pocket and puts the passport on the table.

Talaia sighs and sits forward, studying Ric's face, before reaching over. He deftly flicks open the passport and examines the photo page, taking his time.

There is little Ric can do but wait, "Coffee, Commissario?"

Talaia looks up, looks back at the photo and looks up again. He sighs as though the world is full of idiots and too much of his time is taken up in dealing with them.

Eventually, he sits back and smiles again, "Yes, please. That would be very acceptable." He turns to glance at his assistant who, in turn, vacates the room.

"I find it better to talk over a cup of coffee, don't you?" Talaia asks. "Although I never understood why the expression is that one uses a drink to break the ice; surely hot liquid can only melt ice, not break it? That would be more subtle, would it not?"

167

Ric fills the kettle and lights the stove. "Well, I'm sure you know how the British prefer to chat over a cup of something, Commissario."

He nods, "Oh, yes, I do," he studies the passport briefly once more, "Mr... Ross. Or may I call you Richard?"

"You can call me what you like, Commissario. It's your country."

"Mmm," he murmurs, "no, I don't think it is. When one looks closely at history, one is drawn to the conclusion that it is only a fool who believes his country really belongs to him. And Garibaldi was no different from the politicians of the modern day; he also was an opportunist." The Commissario pauses, thinking. "Oh, by the way, did you know, Garibaldi once worked in a candle factory on Staten Island in New York?"

"No," the kettle begins to boil, "I didn't know that." But the reference to candles is not lost on Ric.

"It is true," Talaia states with some certainty. "But then Garibaldi was born in France and went about his business all over the world before returning to finish the Risorgimento which, in real terms, Alighieri had started in the Middle Ages. You know, I find it interesting that Bonaparte had Italian parents and Garibaldi was born in France. It casts their true identity into doubt, don't you think? They remind me of the new-age of rugby players."

"In what way?"

"Oh, they choose their nationality by the country in whose team they believe they can exert most influence."

"I never looked at it that way," Ric replies as he pours out the coffee.

"Ah, you should," the Commissioner suggests. "You should. It is important to consider carefully when choosing both your nationality and your identity."

"Well, I'm probably past making a living as a sportsman, so what's there to choose? Anyway, I didn't think rugby was played down here in the south."

At this, Talaia smiles, sheepishly. "Yes, of course, you are right.

Although I am originally from Naples, but I have been working in the north for some years. They like their rugby in the north; it is very different to down here in the south. Like most places, the north is not without its corruptions, but it is perhaps not so... not so feudal." He pauses. "No, this is not the right word. *Per favore*, help me, please. What is the correct word for when things are shared only between the family and not outside. Do you know this word?"

"Incestuous?"

Talaia stares at the table top. "Yes," he says, hesitating, "in a way. But this implies a more physical relationship. I mean the blood that ties the families together. It is no matter; the word will come to me." He examines the passport again. "And this passport confirms what you say is true. You are, like me, over the hill as far as making a career out of sport is concerned." He pauses and sighs again. "I hope you will forgive me for saying this, Mr Ross—"

"Ric. Please call me Ric, Commissario, everyone does. There's no reason why you should be any different."

He nods, politely. "Well, that is kind of you to want to talk informally, but for now, let us keep this official. Forgive me for saying this, Mr Ross, but you look a little... corrupted." The Commissioner chuckles and indicates his own forehead.

"This?" Ric replies, fingering gently the wound above his right eye: "Boating injury: forgot to duck."

Commissioner Talaia smiles, "Yes, sailing can be a dangerous hobby. So, tell me, Ric, how long have you been here?"

Ric thinks, "Four, maybe five days; I forget exactly. Lipari seems to be such a timeless place."

"And what brings you to the Isle of Winds?"

Now it is Ric's turn to chuckle, "Pretty much what brings every sailboat to Lipari, Commissario: the wind."

"An ill wind, it would seem."

"How so?"

"Well," Talaia considers, "your boat has dealt you an injury and you have the misfortune to be living on the land. Most sailors, if you will forgive me for stating the obvious, stay on their sailboats."

"My yacht, the Mara, is at a yard in Canneto; a few mechanical repairs that require attention before I can continue my trip."

"Your trip to?"

"Oh, just taking some time-out; not going anywhere in particular; I thought maybe around the coast to the Adriatic. I don't know this part of the world well, so how better to get to know it than by sailing through it. There seem to be plenty of people with the same idea."

Talaia nods, knowingly. "It is true. This is a good way to get to know places." He sips his coffee and murmurs his appreciation before leaning forward across the table. "Let me ask you, Ric, where have you come from? Where were you before arriving here?"

"Sardinia: Cagliari the Costa Smeralda."

"And before that?"

"Corsica, where I bought the Mara. Seemed like a good idea at the time."

"Do you know many people here, Ric?"

"I've got to know a couple: the man who's fixing my yacht, a couple of people around town. Seem like a nice bunch to me. Why?"

Commissioner Talaia studies Ric for a few seconds before finishing his coffee and sitting back. "You know, Ric, a man was murdered here the evening before last?"

"Couldn't help but hear about it."

"You know, this man was an important man with, how would you say, political ambitions?"

"So I've heard."

"Naturally, when a politician comes to Lipari and is murdered, we, the police, take a special interest in those people who have recently appeared on the island."

"Naturally. But what you need to understand, Commissario, is that I wouldn't be here if it wasn't for the wind and the fact that my yacht needs repairs. And, I'm sure it won't have escaped your powers of deduction that if I did have anything to do with this politician's murder, I'd be long gone by now."

Talaia nods. "Yes, of course, that would be logical, Ric. But I have found during my many years as a detective, and particularly when dealing with criminals in this part of the world, that perpetrators of certain crimes are in the habit of hiding where most people can see them. It is a way they have of pretending to the authorities they could have nothing to do with their crimes." He considers his logic for a moment, before continuing. "That is unless they are the type of criminal who wants everyone to know what they are capable of; a form of self-advertisement, a desire for prestige."

"Mafia?"

"Precisely," he nods again. "You see, Ric, I am from Naples. In Naples we have the Camorra; they are nothing more than gangsters; sometimes sophisticated, sometimes not. In Calabria there are 'Ndrangheta, in Apulia – Sacra Corona Unita, and in Sicily it is a little crowded, with the Cosa Nostra and Stidda enjoying a form of mutual disrespect. They have many bad things in common and one of them is that they like to be known among the local communities for what they achieve through their violence. I believe, if you like, they seek a form of kudos through it. A strange form of public relations, I grant you, but nevertheless one that is effective in cementing their position, their status in the hierarchy of their profession."

There is the sharp white noise of a radio communication from beyond the front door. The *poliziotto* calls, "Commissario?"

"*Si*," Talaia replies, "*un momento.*" He turns his attention back to Ric. "However, on occasion, these organisations have been known to import professionals for their purposes, especially when their crimes are of a sensitive nature, politically. Signor Candela was perhaps a figure who would warrant such a strategy. So I must ask you where you were the evening he was murdered?"

"Curiously enough, Commissioner, I was out fishing."

Talaia raises an eyebrow and purses his lips. "Fishing?" he repeats, "Alone or with someone?"

"Signor Maggiore: the man who's fixing my yacht, which is in his yard and which is, as I've told you, in Canneto. And curiously, it was while fishing with Signor Maggiore that I received this injury to my forehead." And as he says it, the pains in his shoulder and ribs demand similar recognition. He shifts in his seat.

"I thought you said your injury was a sailing accident."

"I did. We were out in Signor Maggiore's boat fishing."

"And exactly where were you fishing?"

"About a mile, give or take, off the little bay at Portinente."

Talaia is studying Ric very closely. "That is particularly interesting."

"How so?"

"We understand that Signor Candela received a note summoning him to a meeting in a house in Piazza San Bartolo, where he was murdered. The house was unoccupied. We don't as yet know who he was meeting in this unoccupied property or why, but Piazza San Bartolo lies at the entrance to Via Maddalena and Via Maddalena, as you may by now be aware, leads to Portinente, where you were fishing with Signor Maggiore."

Ric stifles a chuckle. "And you think this is one too many coincidences?"

"Possibly."

"The curious irony of the situation you seem to want me to conform to, Commissario, is that Signor Maggiore and I were out fishing when we were run down by a large blue motor-boat seconds after we heard the gunshots from the shore. A boat both he and I believe was a La Polizia launch. I understand you arrived on the scene not long after Candela was murdered, so there is just a chance this is our third meeting, Commissioner, and you may be my best alibi."

The little man smiles. "That, too, would be something of a coincidence, would it not?"

"It would."

"And how did you meet this Signor Maggiore? Did you simply look him up in the *Pagine Bianche*?"

"No, I was introduced to him by a lady I met when I first arrived here."

"A lady?"

"La Signorina Vaccariello. She has a house on the Punta San Giuseppe."

"Ah, yes. I have heard of this lady."

The *poliziotto* knocks lightly once more.

"*Si, sto arrivando*," his boss calls. "Well, Mr Ross, if you don't mind I am going to retain your passport in order to help with my enquiries. And, if you don't mind me saying, your passport is in pretty bad shape. The image in this photograph here is so vague it could belong to my father; what did you do to it?"

"Beats me, Commissario, I guess I must have taken that fishing too."

"If you will forgive me for pointing out, Mr Ross, you need to take more care of your passport." Talaia takes his time to position his Homburg securely and at just the right angle off centre so that he can look at Ric without having to raise his head. "Oh, Mr Ross, I see your tap is dripping. *Ciao*."

32

The *escurzionista* is down in the Corta rounding up tourists. "Hey, Gallese. How goes it?"

"Okay, Sandro," Ric lies. "Tell me: what do you call those water taxis that take tourists up to the beaches?"

"*Taxi mare?*" His eyes light up: at last, he can live up to his expectations and supply Ric with something he needs. "Why? You want to go to see the sights for the day?"

"Figured I would. If I'm to be hostage to Il Velaccino's labours, I might as well play tourist for the day. Who should I ask?"

"Oh, many places," he scratches his head, "but cheapest and best is my friend Luciano. He will drive you to Canneto in his *pulmino* and from there you will take his *taxi mare* to any one of the Spiaggia della Papesca as far as Porticello."

"Where do I find him?"

"At the bottom of the Corso Vittorio, near the *alimentari*, there is a little box, a booth, with the sign *Spiaggie Luciano*. And—"

"I know how it goes, Sandro." Ric slaps him gently on his shoulder, "Don't worry, I'll tell him you sent me."

Of course, the girl at the ticket booth knows Sandro. She takes his money and directs him to a battered minibus parked on the down slope to the little harbour. A brace of tourists wait patiently in the shade of a wall.

After a few minutes, a middle-aged man wearing a seasoned tan and designer sunglasses waves them over to a dilapidated minibus. Beach towels cover the seats and the temperature inside the *pulmino* runs high enough to fry an egg.

They race around the Lunga in the direction of Monte Rosa, dodging and weaving through the pedestrians and scooters, and it is only when they are leaving the tunnel which opens into the bay at Canneto, that Ric thinks to ask the driver to let him out so that he can drop by Marcello's yard.

A hoist cranes over the stern of the Mara and Marcello and a second man, Salvo, are in the process of shackling the engine to lift it out from beneath the floor of the cockpit.

"*Buongiorno*," Marcello calls down. "As you can see, we are making progress."

Salvo salutes and grins.

Ric climbs the ladder up to the deck. "I came to see if I could lend a hand, but you look to have all the help you need."

The wiry Salvo, although he never says much if anything, grins again. He seems to understand what Ric is saying without, supposedly, speaking any English.

"Yes," Marcello replies, "with Salvo's assistance we will have the motor out by this afternoon and then we can begin to take it apart. I have ordered the new bearings and seal. Of course we will have to check the crankshaft; if it needs to be rebalanced, we can do this also. But," Marcello says, chewing on his cigar stub, "let us hope this will not be necessary."

They sit and discuss the likelihood of the extra work for a while.

Ric wonders how best to bring up the subject of the missing Beretta, but is again not sure how to do so without implying Marcello has taken it.

"You need something from me?" Marcello asks.

Apart from producing the Beretta and a certificate of

seaworthiness for the Mara, there isn't much anyone can do for Ric. "No, just something I've mislaid." He looks long and hard at Salvo, but the wiry individual simply grins back.

"What thing is this? You said this to me yesterday; that you were looking for something you have lost." Again Marcello's expression is deadpan.

Ric thinks to come clean and tell him about how he tied up to an old pier near the pumice mines and heard what sounded to him like a man being strangled, about how the Beretta he had stowed in the Mara has mysteriously disappeared and about how he has just been questioned by a Commissario of Police, a man who doesn't like coincidences. But, he decides not to. He is concerned that if he opens the can of worms he has been delivered, he will never get the lid back on.

Marcello smiles and says, "We are all looking for something, eh, my friend? Perhaps this is why you sail the Mara? Perhaps you are like Odisseo, looking for the way home? Well, we will soon have the Mara back in the water for you to continue your journey."

And at the mention of the way home, Ric is taken with the notion that, like Odisseo, disaster seems to be following him around and that just possibly he is trying to get away from home, not to it.

"No, Marcello, just something I left on the Mara which I can't seem to locate, that's all."

But in thinking of the events of the past few days and what his best course would be, Ric recalls again and all too clearly the screams from the shore the first morning he arrived in Lipari.

"Forget it, Marcello. I'm sure it'll turn up sooner or later. Are you sure you don't need a hand?"

"No, it is as I said: Salvo and I will have the engine out by this afternoon. Why don't you come back tomorrow; we will have had a chance to examine the motor more closely by then."

33

He walks along the dusty seafront into Canneto, passing the café he sat at the previous day with Marcello.

At the far end of the crescent beach, he locates a desk beneath an awning signed *Spiaggie Luciano*. The tanned individual who drove the bus recognises him, takes his ticket and they walk over to a white *barca*, beached at the breakwater. The hull of the *barca* is decorated with a succession of blue, curling wave crests. At the man's bidding, Ric climbs the stepped prow and sits on a bench by the helm.

The driver backs the water taxi noisily off the shingle breakwater, swings the boat round and steers it away up the coast. The aquamarine water shimmers under the sun and the breeze fostered by the boat's progress is a welcome relief from the heat of the village. Behind the slender strip of Canneto, Monte Sant'Angelo towers green and steep, and soon the pale pumice slopes of Monte Pilato come into view. Dotted in along the shoreline, old drying houses stand vacant, their slender brick chimneys pointing up at the sky like accusing fingers.

Five minutes later, the driver grins and points, "Pietra Liscia?"

Ric nods, recognising the gnarled iron stanchions of the dilapidated pier he tied up to the first night.

The *taxi mare* swings round, makes for the beach and the driver eases it onto the pumice breakwater, whereupon Ric alights, waving his thanks.

The driver points to his watch.

"*Due ore,*" Ric shouts, and the man nods, grins and reverses the little boat back out into the open water.

The dilapidated pier, a matchstick mess of twisted girders and stanchions, lies a hundred metres or so up the beach. A handful of sun-worshippers are gathered around a line of sunbeds in front of a beach bar fashioned out of blocks pilfered from the old buildings. The area at the far end around the warehouses seems deserted.

He stops by the bar to pick up a bottle of water. A fresh-faced youth serves him and thanks him enthusiastically when he refuses his change.

Ric trudges off up the beach, pausing every now and then to pick up a pumice pebble or smoothed fragment of obsidian.

The flat-roofed warehouses layer back up into the slope, their crude, grey stone block construction, blackened here and there by fire. They remind Ric of the bombed out homes and apartments he had the unfortunate duty to patrol through in the cities of southern Iraq. The tall, rectangular apertures contain no windows, which he assumes is to allow the breeze in to dry the pumice, and the small pocket-holes which would normally hold the butt-ends of joists are in most places empty.

Ric stands at the breakwater and looks back at the block houses behind him. It is as though the developer has run out of funds halfway through his project and given the place over to the ghosts of yesteryear.

The argument and screaming he heard seemed to come from higher up than beach level and the heavy, wooden door to the ground floor is tight shut. So he begins to climb up the uneven wall to the first level, testing each hand and foothold as he goes. In places, the stones set into the wall come away in his hands and he has to step back down and find an alternative route. As he climbs, Ric wonders whether the floor will be firm enough to support his weight.

Finally he gains enough height to enter through an arch.

Though the walls are as thick as his waist, his suspicions regarding the floors are confirmed when he notices that the wooden boards are holed in places and the exposed beams look unnervingly fragile. One corner of the first room is blackened by fire and rusting cans and broken bottles lie where tossed. However, apart from the detritus of a party long-finished, the room is empty but for a gecko hiding from the sun.

He tries to imagine the heat and dust the men, women and children must have had to endure as they carried lumps of carved pumice in and out and up and down the stairs. And he imagines Old Nino as a lad sliding down the pumice funnels to land with a great splash in the clear waters below.

Ric works his way methodically along the first floor terrace. Some of the windows are shuttered with metal plates and wire grills, and others have wood piled up against them.

When he is satisfied they are all empty, he throws some of the wood into a pile and climbs on top, up to the second stage.

The rooms here are empty too, so he climbs up onto the third and final stage. These rooms are open to the elements; their seaward-facing walls having collapsed many years before, their blocks and stones used to shore up other houses.

At the far end, a wooden door is set into the rock which forms the right-hand wall. The door handle is a single curve of rusted iron, but what catches his eye is that the handle is smooth, not flaked like the others.

Ric treads carefully, making sure to plant his feet on the beams and not the weathered planks between. The door is greyed and substantial, though splintered around the stile. The handle is worn smooth, suggesting it has had more than its fair share of recent use. But what is more unusual is that the door is fitted with a galvanised steel hasp and shackle, and secured with a heavy padlock.

Certain that he has found something which someone is trying to conceal, Ric crouches in the shadow of the wall and surveys the beach below him. The sunbathers down the way are swimming and lounging, and a hundred or so metres out a *taxi mare*, empty but for the pilot who stands at the helm, is chugging its languid course back to Canneto.

What he needs is some tool to help him prize the hasp off the wall; the padlock, he realises, he hasn't a chance of breaking open.

Ric picks a length of angle iron from amongst the rubbish in an adjacent room and forces it between the hasp and the door jamb. It loosens the hasp, but he has to lean all of his weight against it to prize it open, each time wedging the sliver of iron further down into the thin breach he has made.

Eventually the breach widens and the frame of the doorjamb starts to splinter. By leaning back and pulling on the fragment of iron he manages to heave the hasp off the jamb. It snaps off with a loud crack and he stumbles backwards onto the lumps of masonry, loose wood and dust.

Ric looks around, aware that the noise may have attracted the attention of the people down the beach. It hasn't: they are still swimming and busying themselves throwing pebbles and playing games.

The wooden door opens inwards to reveal a half-height chamber carved out of the rock face. Flies buzz at him as he steps inside. The air in the chamber is stale and fetid and reminds him of a similar odour from his past. He steps back outside to give the atmosphere a chance to clear.

He re-enters, crouches and sees the chamber is empty but for a pile of rubble heaped in the centre. And he is just about to turn to leave when he notices a fragment of grey material poking out from the bottom of the pile.

Ric bends down to examine the material and realises it is rounded, like the toecap of a shoe. He scuffs at it and sees that it is a shoe, pointing upwards out of the rubble. But when he picks up a couple of lumps of the rubble and moves them aside, he finds the shoe is still occupied by a foot and the foot is still attached to a leg, which is, he hesitates, attached to a body.

He backs away and stands up, forgetting that the ceiling is only inches above him and banging his head as he retreats out the door.

"Oh, Christ," he mutters, not so much at the pain as at the discovery.

For a few seconds Ric is stunned and not sure what to do next. Now that he understands what the smell means, he gags.

A cold fear invades his stomach and the sweat at his brow chills unpleasantly.

Ric scolds himself: if he was honest, it was what he had expected to find, not hoped, but expected. And it confirms his worst fear that what he'd heard that first morning was what he'd thought; all of which means, Candela is not the only person to have been murdered in the past few days. It also means that the Commissario Talaia has another coincidence to add to his already lengthening list.

There are two choices open to him: leave and forget he's found the body, or uncover the body and memorise the face of the man lying buried in the rubble. The second option isn't simply a case of macabre curiosity; it is more a case of whether it might help him later to know the man's identity.

Ric crouches again and crawls back into the chamber. Carefully, so as not to wake the dead, he removes the rubble from on top of the body. The work is unpleasant; insects and worms have wasted no time in feasting on the corpse. It is, or rather was, a man, dressed in jeans and a brown t-shirt with the name of the island stitched in yellow thread on the front: a man of medium height and average build, a bald man with a beard and the rictus grin of someone who has been strangled.

As he crouches, wiping the sweat from his eyes and committing the face of the corpse to memory, he hears the sound of a car pull up somewhere on the track just above his head.

Doors open and slam. The men talk in Italian. And they talk so fast Ric cannot understand what they are saying, except that he judges by their tone they are complaining about something or someone. The voices tail off as the men walk down the slope which winds between the derelict warehouses.

Ric crawls out of the chamber and drops to the floor, watching the beach below.

Two Carabinieri round the bend at the bottom of the track and stand for a moment, hands on hips, surveying the beach.

He can hear their voices; their moaning has developed into debate.

They turn and look directly up at the terrace of drying rooms.

Ric presses his head to the floor. A dark green snake slithers across in front of him not a hand's length from his eyes, but he cannot move.

The discussion between the two Carabinieri has now developed into a full-blown argument. Whatever it is they are at odds about concerns, in some way, the beach and the warehouses.

Ric risks a glance and realises by their gesticulating and their expressions that they are arguing about just how they are supposed to search the buildings: there are only two of them and, as always, they are dressed to the nines.

They part company and stump about at the base of the terrace until one of them points down the beach and they turn away towards the families at the far end.

Ric waits patiently as they walk off up the pebbled beach, still arguing. And while they are distracted, he slips as quietly as possible down the front of the building. In doing so he disturbs and fails to catch a couple of stones which tumble noisily away. But the Carabinieri are too busy to notice and the noise of their boots crunching on the pebbles probably drowns out any other sound. They continue walking.

He stows his clothes behind a rock and takes to the water to wash the dust from his skin. Ric strikes out down the long line of leaning stanchions and when he gets to the last of them, he clings to it, treading water, drawing breath.

The policemen are talking to the boy from the beach bar, so he waits. The sea is warm and oily and extraordinarily transparent; the bed of the sea a rippled carpet of alabaster and emerald.

Eventually, the policemen stroll back, traipse up the narrow track and drive away.

Ric swims ashore and lies down on a blanket of warm pumice. There is heat in the sun, but he feels chilled; the image of the body is printed hard in his mind.

An hour later he walks back down the beach. Luciano's *taxi mare* potters into the bay of smooth stones and the driver waves him aboard.

34

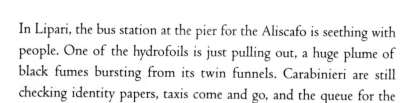

In Lipari, the bus station at the pier for the Aliscafo is seething with people. One of the hydrofoils is just pulling out, a huge plume of black fumes bursting from its twin funnels. Carabinieri are still checking identity papers, taxis come and go, and the queue for the petrol station snakes round the corner and up the hill by the cemetery wall.

Ric notices Valeria is making her way down the pier amidst the throng of arrivals. The bags she carries suggest she has been shopping for clothes.

When she stops at the *alimentari* at the bottom of the Corso, he walks over. "Hi, Valeria. You look particularly radiant this afternoon."

She turns as she is taking a brown paper bag full of grapes from the gravel-voiced woman behind the counter. "Hello, my young friend! It is so nice to see you." She smiles, studying him for a second. "I don't mean to be rude, but you look like a man who's making hard work of doing nothing. How is your face? How is the Mara?" She looks somehow younger; gone are the dark rings around her eyes and her skin glows.

"Could be worse; could be better." He fingers the abrasion at his temple. "Marcello and Salvo are taking the engine out today; should have the work done in a few days. Can I carry your bags for you?"

They stroll up the Corso together.

"It is hot here today. Messina was cooler," she says by way of conversation. The mood in the Corso is sleepy; people have finished lunch and are sipping espresso and limoncello in the shade.

"You've been shopping, I see."

"Yes," she grins, "a little retail therapy can be very restorative. What have you been up to that makes you look so..."

"That bad, huh?"

"Well, perhaps a little earthy. You look like a *becchino*."

"*Becchino*?"

"Yes, a man who digs graves."

Ric balks at her reference. He has not realised he looks so shabby. "Thank you for telling me, Valeria." He glances at her as they walk and realises how good she looks for her age. He wonders what treatments – as Old Nino put it – she is having that they can lend her such radiance.

As the Corso narrows at the top of the slope, he wishes her a good afternoon and thanks her again for putting him up that first night and for attending to his washing.

"Oh, Ric," she says as they are about to part, "if you have no other plans, do me the kindness of coming for dinner this evening: about eight?"

"Plans?" His shoulder and his ribs remind him it might be in his better interest to give the café in the Marina Corta a miss. "No, I have no other plans. Thank you for the offer, I'd be happy to: about eight, then. *Ciao*."

35

Sandro, camouflaged in a tatty straw hat, striped shirt and a pair of tennis shorts so tight they went out of fashion in the 80s, is tracking some victims up the Garibaldi towards the bottom of the Via del Concordato. When he sees them hesitate at the bottom of the broad steps, he pounces.

"Ah, my friends! It is good to see you." He spreads his long arms as though he has been searching for his goslings all day and is extremely relieved to find them. He points up towards the citadel. "This is the way up to the jewel of Lipari: the Cathedral of San Bartolo. These steps were built as part of the Spanish fortifications after the pirate Barbarossa ravaged the island in 1544…"

Ric waits across the road until the *escurzionista* has finished his turn at the pump and has handed out his flyers for the boat trip to Stromboli.

"Yes, tomorrow, just before midday, on the quay by the Chiesa delle Anime Purgatorio. Bring swimming costumes, cameras and a hat for the sun, oh, and something warm for the evening."

The gaggle of tourists – Empire shorts, long socks and sandals – nod, cluck their approval and set off up the steps.

"If the fat one makes it to the top without a heart attack," Sandro mutters as he crosses the cobbled street, "I will eat my hat."

"Looks as though you've had a go at it already," Ric points out.

Sandro removes his Panama and examines it. He grimaces, "You know, it is not wise to criticize a man's sense of dress, eh? You might offend someone and we Latin types are easily offended." He grins in case Ric should mistake his self-deprecation.

Ric chuckles, "It's a good hat, Sandro. It sends the right message; like you're doing alright, but not exactly creaming it. Do you have a minute?"

"For you, always, my friend."

Ric hates to think how the *escurzionista* must treat his enemies and supposes they must all be victims, just like the gaggle of goslings hauling themselves up the hill. He glances briefly up and down the street, but outside of a few tourists and the old women who sit outside their shops, hoping beyond hope for some business to break the monotony of their day, the cobbled street is empty.

Sandro begins to shepherd him towards the Marina Corta, "Come, let us go and take a Birra Messina in the Corta."

Ric, remembering the beating he was subjected to the evening before, holds fast and raises an eyebrow.

"Okay," says Sandro, a knowing look to his face, "I understand. Let us walk up the *città* too. Only a fool would walk up these steps in this heat and the Liparoti are not fools. Well, not all of them."

They turn in through the entrance to the Concordato. The steps, though broad and set several strides apart, are tall, as though they have been cut to suit coffin bearers. From the enormous flower pots set on each and every step, coconut palm fronds lean leaf-tips down, like mourners.

"What can I do for you that we need to be so secret?" Sandro asks, quietly.

"I need to know, strictly between you and me," Ric turns and looks hard at the *escurzionista*, wanting him to be in no doubt that he needs to trust him, "whether anyone has gone missing in the last few days; someone you would normally see about the place who isn't around?"

Sandro snorts, dismissively. "This is a small island, my friend. Everyone knows everyone and if someone is missing, word gets round pretty fast. But what do you know about this person? Is this a man or a woman we are talking about?"

"A man: medium height, medium weight."

He scoffs and replies, "This could be half the men in Lipari. Is there anything else you know about this man?"

"No, not much." Ric thinks hard, recalling the rictus grin on the face of the corpse. "Oh, he is bald and has a beard, a short beard. And he wears a brown t-shirt with the word *Lipari* stitched in yellow on the shirt chest."

Sandro scratches his head, "These shirts are available everywhere; they are common. But a beard, you say. Not so many people here have beards; it is the heat, it does not suit men to grow beards." He rubs at the stubble on his cheeks. "Yes, I know I have this, but it is because I am lazy and do not like to shave. A beard, eh? I will think for you. Anything else?"

"No, I didn't get a chance to look at the man for too long. If anyone comes to mind or if you hear of anyone missing, perhaps you'd let me know." Ric stares at him, holding his gaze: "But, between you and me, if you get my meaning?"

"Sure, my friend. I get your meaning." Sandro smiles; a look that holds promise, but not in so much quantity that Ric is adequately reassured. "Maybe you would answer a question for me, eh?"

"Fire away."

"I have heard it said that this policeman, the one who is making investigations into the murder of Girolamo Candela, came to see you this morning. Is it true?"

"Word does get about," Ric muses.

Sandro shrugs, "Yes, of course. It is as I said: this is a small island. When a Commissario from La Polizia comes to Lipari, a lantern is lighted and people whisper beneath it. And when this Commissario and one of La Polizia are seen coming out of your *monolocale*, this makes the flames of the lantern grow so bright that people no longer whisper; they talk openly. And now you ask me questions about a man with a beard who you say is missing. Whatever it is that you are up to, Gallese, I would tell you it is time for you to be careful."

"I think it may be too late for being careful, Sandro. But, thanks for the advice: I'll take it on board."

"No, I mean this," Sandro takes his arm to make sure he has Ric's full attention. "This type of policeman is not like the English Bobby; they are tricky, eh? They make their rules up as they go along."

Ric knows he has heard this before, something Valeria told him not long after he arrived, "they play by different rules".

He reaches for the *escurzionista's* hand and shakes it gently and slowly, but applying just enough pressure in his grip that his appreciation cannot be misconstrued. "Thanks, Sandro. I get the picture. I'll see you later," but adds as an afterthought, "my friend" and smiles warmly. Ric turns and strolls off down the steps towards the Garibaldi.

36

Valeria is at her stove when he arrives; the fragrance of capers and basil fill the air.

"Swordfish," she tells him as he hands her a bottle of Caravaglio. "Ah, my favourite wine! You learn fast, Ric. Thank you." She pulls an opener from a drawer and hands it to him.

There is much he needs to ask her, but he knows a frontal assault is only likely to make her suspicious.

"I see the injury to your face is healing well."

"It's getting there, thank you. The girl at the café did a good job."

Valeria is mixing pumpkin flowers with rocket, basil and mint. She chuckles, "This girl, Giuliana, she has eyes for you."

Ric reddens and busies himself opening the wine.

"It is better to be careful with this one," she says. "She is like the oleander the Berber call *oualilt;* a beautiful white, red and pink flower which looks good enough to eat, except that it is very poisonous. The smallest taste can provoke an irregular heartbeat and in some cases heart failure. It can make life very complicated when a girl like this has eyes for a man."

"So it would seem," he replies, flexing his shoulders and stretching his back.

Valeria frowns. "Oh, I see you have already got too close to this flower. Try to keep your distance; pretty though she is, Giuliana will be bad for your health."

"I hate to think." He pours the wine and hands her a glass.

"She comes from Rome, so she is not so shy of boys. And she is staying with her uncle, which means he will not permit any harm to come to her while she is in his care. Take my advice, stay away from her."

"Maybe someone should tell her that," he replies, remembering how Giuliana turned up outside his digs two nights before.

"There would be little point in saying this to her," Valeria suggests. "When a woman decides she wants a man, telling her she cannot have him only makes her want him more."

"You'll excuse me for saying, but that sounded like it came from one who knows." Ric sips his wine, watching her at the stove.

Valeria pauses as she cuts swordfish into small chunks. "Yes, perhaps."

"But, if you'll forgive me bringing age into the equation, she's a little young for me."

Valeria glances at him the way he imagines her glancing at a dancing partner who has trodden on her toes: "And what has age to do with passion?"

Though her tone is argumentative, Ric feels as though he has opened a door. "I guess you must have had quite a hard time avoiding the amorous attentions of all those movie stars?"

She glows briefly, but only briefly.

"How did you get into the movie business, Valeria?"

"Oh, as most in those days." She is peeling and de-seeding small tomatoes. "After the end of the war, during what people call the Italian Spring," she bridles, a shade theatrically, "like the Arabs and their Spring, eh? My friend, Rosaria entered a beauty pageant in our village. But she suffered from a blood disorder, Thalassemia which, because good food was hard to come by, was common in those days. The day before the pageant Rosaria was not well, so I took her place. I was too young really, but I won and the *Borgomastro* — the mayor — he

191

sent me to Palermo for a much grander pageant, which I won also; in this, there was much prestige for our village."

Valeria splashes white wine into the pan of frying swordfish; it sizzles and steams. "But in Palermo I was introduced to a talent scout from Rome; a very charismatic and powerful man. He knew Visconti, Gallone, De Sica, Rossellini, all the studio heads. He paid for me to go to the Accademia Nazionale, the acting school in Rome."

Ric is listening, casually, but he is also poring over a bookcase by the kitchen table: Benacqista, Varesi and Camilleri.

"You like Camilleri?" she asks when she looks up to check her conversation is holding his attention.

"Detective novels?"

Valeria beams, "Yes, Camilleri studied at the Nazionale too."

"Must have been a wild time," Ric says to encourage her to keep talking.

She pauses and leans against the wooden island of the kitchen, dreaming, "Yes, it was. But I was young and very naïve and I looked upon my benefactor as the father I never knew, until…"

"Until?" he asks.

The wine is boiling in the pan and she moves it to the side of the stove, dropping cherry tomatoes into it one by one.

"Until this man began to ask me to accompany other men to parties: political men, men of influence and importance, ambitious men with unusual and often unpleasant appetites. This type of man, I had not expected to meet. You know, it was not always easy to be a young hopeful in the world of cinema in Italy." She stirs the sauce in her pan, tasting and seasoning.

"Guess that's the movie business all over."

"Oh, don't think I was that naïve, Ric. I soon found out my favours were a currency which returned great dividends. But, too late I found out that this man who I had come to love – a man who I thought believed in my ability – also enjoyed the affection of many other women. Stupidly, I thought for him I was exclusive. One night I discovered I wasn't."

"That must have been a tough lesson?"

"Yes, it was." She forks macaroni into the pan with the sauce and the fish, stirring the contents and covering the pan with a lid. "One can break a bone and it will mend stronger than before; but a broken heart never mends."

"Amen to that," Ric whispers.

"Bring the plates and the cutlery, please," Valeria says, as she unties her apron.

They sit outside the little house and eat; the sharp flavour of the olives a contrast to the sweet tomatoes; the sauce and the soft chunks of swordfish a complement to the *al dente* macaroni. Away around the cliffs to their right, herring gulls wheel and glide and lament the passing of the day. An Aliscafo hurries across the bay.

Though the sun has slipped below the hills behind them, they are warm and the atmosphere is balmy. Tall anvils of thunderclouds are gathering above an early evening haze, which veils the Sicilian coast like the *hijabs* of the Muslim women in the Garibaldi.

"Yes," she says, "there will be a storm soon."

"You said you never knew your father. Was he killed in the war?"

"No," she replies, very casually. When she has finished her food, she pushes her plate away and sits back. "I never knew him because I never met him." Valeria glances at Ric to see if he reacts to her confession and when he doesn't, she carries on, "My mother would never speak about my father. By the time I was old enough to understand that the man my mother was married to was not my father, she had erased my true father from her memory."

"How did you find out, if that isn't a rude question?"

"Why, Ric? Does it matter?" she asks, permitting herself a wry amusement at his impertinence.

"I apologise."

"No, I am kidding." She smiles. "You know, the Pope, Alexander VI, fathered not only Lucrezia and Cesare Borgia, but also many other illegitimate children. The only shame in illegitimacy is the hypocrisy that defines it." Valeria shakes her head, dismissively, and as she does so her hair falls across her face. Ric is taken with thinking how beautiful she must have been in her youth.

"My mother," she continues as he lights one of her long, slim white cigarettes for her, "married a man in a town near Palermo. She ran away from home not only because of the humiliation of her pregnancy, but also because her priority would have been to find a husband who would support her and her child to be, me. My mother had three more children by him; they were all short and dark-skinned and ugly, so I soon realised he could not be my true father. He was not a bad man, though; a little narrow in his outlook perhaps, occasionally short-tempered, but in essence not an unkind man. It was better to have his name, Vaccariello, than no name at all."

"Valeria Vaccariello," Ric repeats, "seems a pretty catchy stage name to me."

"Yes, it worked well for me. But, as I told you, when I lost the part in Luchino's film to that young girl with the fierce eyes, I also lost the nerve to act; I could no longer find the self-assurance I needed to produce such good performances. Fortunately, my second husband had more money than I could burn and, after he died, I came here and found La Casa dei Sconosciuti. The first time I set eyes on this house, I knew I belonged here."

"And this is where you met Marcello and Salvo?"

"Yes, I have known Marcello since he was a boy. Salvo is some years older than him; he used to work for Marcello's father, Onofrio. Now he works for Marcello." Valeria chuckles, "But Salvo has had eyes for me ever since he saw me in an old movie they showed up in the amphitheatre in the citadel. He labours under the false impression I am some sort of screen goddess. If I ever need anything, Salvo supplies it: restorations for the house, a lift into town, he goes to the bank for me and comes to check on me during the winter storms."

"You place a good deal of trust in them."

This captures Valeria's attention and she stares at him as though he has just suggested her cooking is not up to scratch. "Of course, Ric, why would I not trust them?"

"I don't know," he replies, defensively. "It's just that I'm missing something from the boat."

When she begins to object to his inference, he holds up his hands to mollify her. "I know, I know. It sounds ridiculous, but I know I haven't mislaid it and only Marcello and Salvo have been on the boat without me being around."

But Valeria is visibly appalled at his suggestion, "Ric, they would not touch a man's possessions. Not even if they were of considerable value. This is not in their nature." She hesitates again, searching the table for a clue as to how to convince him of their virtue. "What is it you are missing, Ric? Tell me," she demands. "I will speak to Salvo, though I am not sure how to. It would be easier to ask him if his mother was a mule."

Ric colours with embarrassment. "You can see my problem, Valeria: if this is your reaction to my implying they've had something off the boat, I can only imagine theirs."

She exhales a long stream of grey smoke up towards the darkening sky. "This thing that you are missing, is it important; valuable?"

"In some ways. Or, rather, yes. It will be difficult to explain away if it gets into the wrong hands."

Valeria thinks for a moment longer and then fixes him with a challenging expression, "Tell me, Ric, what is this important thing you have lost, is it your passport?"

Avoiding her stare, Ric is reminded that Talaia has it.

"No, my passport is only too safe for the moment. What I am missing relates to another problem I encountered in Corsica."

37

Valeria grins knowingly, "A problem to do with Camille?"

"Long story," he cuts her off, watching her and trying to fathom why she should take the information in such a curiously casual manner.

"As you know, Ric, I have plenty of time for long stories. Try me? But, kindly fetch another bottle of wine from the fridge before you start; listening can be thirsty work."

While he fetches the wine, Valeria lights a small lantern and places it in the middle of the table.

Ric pours and sits down. "I spent last summer in Corsica, which is where I met Camille—"

"And Manou," she interrupts, delivering him yet another knowing smile.

"Yes, and Manou. And..."

"And...?" Valeria asks.

"And after that, I met with some trouble. Or rather Manou and Camille met with some trouble and I ended up getting caught in the middle of it."

"Trouble!" she says, shaking her head. "It follows some people around like bad perfume. Go on."

"Well, afterwards it seemed best I leave. Camille, as you know, sold me the Mara. Or, more accurately, he gave it to me." Ric pauses.

"I guess I never looked at it this way, but I suppose you could say it was a way of paying me for a service I'd rendered. The old fox might like to think of it in those terms, but I still can't get used to looking at it that way." He pauses again.

"Go on, Ric."

"When I left with the Mara, Camille presented me with a couple of passports the campers had left behind. He said that being the south of the island, the trouble would most likely go away in good time. They seem to have a way of burying the more uncomfortable aspects of the past over there."

Ric knows he has to keep the unpleasant details out of his explanation and right on cue his thigh twinges. "But, Camille suggested I use one of the passports over the winter in case the police in Corsica decided to take an interest in what had happened; in case they started looking for me. In the event, I didn't use them; it didn't feel right, pretending to be some other guy.

"The good news is I've still got the passports; the bad news is Camille gave me something else. And it's that something else which is now missing from the Mara."

Valeria lights another cigarette, mulls over what he has just told her and looks up, observing him the way a teacher might observe a child responsible for disturbing her classroom. "Why did you not throw these passports away when you had the chance?"

"Christ only knows," he replies.

She is quiet again for a moment before nodding her head, as though she has grasped some fine detail about his actions or rather his lack of them. "You did not throw them away because you are still running away from something and thought there might come a time when you needed them."

"Sure. From the police."

"No," she says, searching his face for a clue, "there is something more. Perhaps you are still running away, but not from something;

197

perhaps you are still running from someone. Not from Manou, from your wife. It is as Nino said: a weight which is too heavy to set down." Valeria stares at him, but not in the unyielding manner of an interrogator or with the inquisitive eyes of a gossip; more she gazes at him with the gentility and compassion of a priest.

When he does not reply, she reaches over and lays her hand on his forearm and squeezes it softly.

"I told you, Ric, I ran away from life when I understood I no longer possessed the energy to act. The camera would look at me and I would look back, but I felt the camera was looking right through me, as if I was made of glass. When this dreadful thing happens to an actor, the cinema makes an orphan of her; no one wants her."

Valeria bridles at a thought that has occurred to her and she hesitates, before saying, "This was the second time the world made an orphan of me, so I decided I would not risk being cast out a third time." She grins self-consciously and chews her lip. "I told you, Ric, this is why I came to Lipari, to La Casa dei Sconosciuti; to live among strangers who speak to me, but who can do me no harm."

He is very genuinely touched by her openness and feels minded to repay her generosity, but…

"But what, Ric?" Valeria urges. "But what?"

"But…" he replies, grimacing, wondering. "It all seems so simple and yet it isn't. You were there when I told Nino about how I was in Afghanistan, on my second tour of duty, and that it was while I was out there that my wife was killed in a car accident. If that wasn't bad enough, she had begged me not to go; she said she felt something awful was going to happen."

He glances at her in search of some encouragement.

Valeria's countenance is serious and questioning; the frown lines around her eyes indicating she is intent on hearing him out. "It is only natural that a woman should worry in this way. Please, Ric, go on."

"One morning, one of our patrols got into contact with the

Taleban and I was sent out with my men to help extract them. However, the initial contact turned out to be a feint to drag us into a larger fight and three of my men were killed. I sustained some injuries and was medevac'd out. While I was on the way back to the hospital, I had this incredible dream in which my wife was killed. It may have been the morphine – God knows they pumped me full of the stuff – or it may have been the shock of the injuries or some kind of post-traumatic stress from the engagement; nobody knows. All I do know is that exactly what I had seen in my dream turned out to be true; she had died."

Valeria pours more wine into his glass, as if to fuel his recollecting. "And after?"

"And afterwards… although I'm not sure there is such a thing as afterwards." He glances again at her in much the same way as she glanced at him only a few moments before. "Afterwards? Well, I'd lost my bearings, couldn't make any sense of any of it; I just wandered around in some sort of permanent blue funk. The shrinks said it was all perfectly natural; and it probably was. But eventually I realised I needed to find some kind of anchor; something solid I could relate to in order to get my bearings.

"During all of this, my father passed away and while I was sorting out his personal affects, I came across this old photograph of my great-grandfather in Foreign Legion uniform, standing beneath the gate to a garrison. Here." He shows her the photograph he has kept with him since the day he left home.

Valeria studies it in the dim light cast by the lantern. "And this is the man you think is Antonio Sciacchitano, your ancestor?"

"Yes. It's naturally a little faded. The man's features are indistinct because his face is in shadow, so it's not possible to see any facial resemblance. But it came to me one day that if I found out a little more about my own personal history, where I'd come from if you like, it might help me work out where I was and, with any luck, how to go forward."

"And this was when you met Camille?"

"In a roundabout way. I located the garrison in Bonifacio, on the southern tip of Corsica, but it's no longer in service. Camille, I met after that and Manou a little later."

"And there you met this trouble you speak of?"

"Yes." Ric sits back and folds his arms.

Valeria reads his body language and remains silent for a minute, pondering what he has told her.

There is no breeze and the Sicilian Sea before them reflects the polished obsidian of night. The cliffs to their right have surrendered the airy thermals which hold the *cavazza* aloft and the last hydrofoil of the day scurries away towards the mainland. Fishing boats, their navigation lights shining like fireflies, whine and dart to and fro in the darkness.

Her eyes glint in the light of the lantern and her cigarette glows red. "And now you think that whatever it is that you find here will provide you with the strength and the direction to continue?"

Ric assumes a melancholic expression. "Who knows? Maybe?" But then he remembers Commissario Talaia taking his real passport, "Maybe not?"

She stubs out her cigarette, drawing the evening to a close. "Let us hope Old Nino finds enough in his memory to help you, Ric."

"Which reminds me," he says, rising from his chair and collecting the dishes. "I spent yesterday afternoon looking around the cemetery and found a grave near the chapel house. The headstone suggests the occupant's name is Antonio Sciacchitano."

"That is interesting," Valeria replies, and after a moment's consideration, she begins to chuckle.

"Yes, isn't it?" But he realises from her amusement that there is something about his discovery he has missed. "What's so funny?"

Valeria laughs, loudly; a gay, melodious and unconstrained laugh.

"What?" he asks again, clearly mystified by her reaction to his news. And the greater his puzzlement, the louder she laughs.

Finally, when her laughter has subsided, she says, "Think about it, Ric," she tries to say as she surrenders to yet another fit of childish giggles. "How can this man be your great-grandfather from Britain if he is lying in a grave in Lipari?"

Even though, but for the gentle light thrown by the lantern, they are sitting in the dark, Ric reddens with embarrassment. He slaps his head as if to knock some sense into it. "Oh god, I didn't think of that."

"No, you didn't. But did the headstone say when this Antonio Sciacchitano was born; perhaps he was your great-great-grandfather?"

Ric recalls the image of the headstone, "Thought of that! But no, it didn't give his date of birth, only his date of passing, July 1930."

Valeria stops chuckling, "1930, you say?"

"That's how it read. I spoke to Old Nino last night; he seemed to think the date should mean something to him too, but his memory was a bit dull. Does it ring any bells with you?"

But instead of committing any more thought to it, Valeria gets to her feet and begins clearing their dishes. As she walks away, she says, "Only that 1930 is the year I was born."

38

Ric walks back around the small bay at Portinente, his arms above his head, trying to stretch the ache from his shoulder and his ribs. He is amazed how good Valeria looks for her eighty-plus years and understands why the little Salvo is so taken with her.

And then there is the fact that the headstone for the grave he has found suggests that his forebear, Antonio Sciacchitano, passed away in 1930. Without a birth date, he has no way of knowing how old the man was when he died or whether, perhaps, the man buried in the cemetery really is his relation. He finds the notion that he is trying to trace his own identity whilst at the same time hanging on to false passports, faintly amusing.

And with all these thoughts running around unchecked in his mind, he turns right at the town end of the bay and shortens his stride as he begins the short climb up beside the white-washed walls of the Hotel Rocce Azzurre, through the Maddalena.

The storms he and Valeria watched gathering over the coast of Sicily have not yet ventured out to the islands and the moon hangs like a lantern in the eastern sky, casting impenetrable shadows across the alleyway.

Towards the top of the rise he rounds the bend by the little maritime chapel and rests for a few seconds, realising he is not wise in walking by the piazza in which Candela was murdered two evenings before. But he is weary and his body counsels against the effort involved in turning back only to weave his way through the maze of little vicos that lead to his rooms.

Halfway up the Maddalena, the alley narrows and crowns once more before it begins its descent to the Corta. A television blares from behind a shuttered window and a cat slinks across his path before settling to observe his progress.

Debating whether it would be equally wise to venture in to the Corta after his welcome home committee of the evening before, he pauses by the entrance to the tiny Piazza San Bartolo.

The air in the piazza is cool and refreshing, and though it appears deserted, Ric is suddenly aware that he is standing at the entrance to a dead end and that if the two heavies from the evening before turn up, he has nowhere to run.

"Good evening, Mr Ross."

Ric spins round and plants his feet, readying.

A man steps out from the shadow of a balcony. If at first Ric doesn't recognise the man's voice, his height and the profile of his hat immediately give his identity away.

"Christ, Commissario! You'll give someone a heart attack."

"Oh, please forgive me for being so melodramatic."

Ric fights to control the surge of adrenalin fizzing through his limbs. "Well, excuse me for reacting so, but creeping about in the dark like that... what the hell are you doing?"

The policeman removes his hat and steps over, "Waiting and watching: patience and observation. Sadly, they are old habits which are now reduced in worth by modern technology." Talaia speaks softly as though he is wary of breaching the sepulchral tranquility of the piazza and in so doing disturbing the slumber of many ghosts.

He sighs, "Ah, these days, the new policeman is taught to rely on the efficiencies afforded him by forensic science and the conclusions

203

of his computer. I prefer the old ways: intuition, presentiment, deduction. Ah, I fear I may be considered by my contemporaries to be something of a relic, perhaps even a dinosaur."

Ric chuckles, nervously. "You'd do well to hide a dinosaur in this piazza."

"You know, Mr Ross, I have told you before about this house," he turns and gazes at the doorway of the house behind him; the moonlight lends the façade a cold and unforgiving aura. "This the house in which Edda Ciano lived after the war. It is difficult to imagine what it must have been like for Il Duce's daughter, Edda, to live in such humble surroundings, especially after the opulence afforded her by her father's exalted status. I wonder how she must have felt, being so despised for her privilege when, ultimately, she must have despised it herself for the sorrow it brought to her."

"And then some," Ric offers. "But don't tell me you're waiting patiently for her spirit to reappear, Commissario. I don't make you for a ghost hunter."

"No, Mr Ross, I am not interested in ghosts. Except..." he hesitates and turns back to face Ric. "Except, if it was possible, imagine how useful it would be if the dead were able to exchange information with us. Imagine what lasting peace we could offer them in return for such information."

"Isn't that what their Lord and Master *is* supposed to offer them when they finally get to meet him?"

Talaia allows Ric's suggestion to float in the cool air for a moment before replying, "So, you are not a man of God, Mr Ross. I have been suffering under the impression that all soldiers are simply the tools of God's labours. Are you the exception to this rule?"

Clearly, the Commissario has checked Ric's passport and his history. "First off, Commissario Talaia, I was a Royal Marine, not a soldier—"

"Oh, forgive my poor manners," he interrupts, with a heavy dose of sarcasm.

"And second," Ric allows his frustration to creep into his tone, "I've seen enough evidence of God's labours, as you put it, to last me a lifetime. I'm surprised you haven't." And again he realises that he is tarring the police detective with the same brush with which he tarred Bosquet in Corsica and cautions himself to adopt a more conciliatory attitude.

Judging by the silence that ensues, the Commissario is considering his response. The moonlight shines in his eyes, lending him a vaguely mischievous air.

"Oh, but I have, Signor Ross. I have seen more than my share of unpleasantness. But as a former soldier – forgive me again, I mean to say marine – you appear to me to be possessed of a moral conscience. This, I hope, sets you apart from those amongst our society who believe they can commit murder in the afternoon and go to Mass the next morning in the hope of obtaining absolution."

"Commissario, you'll excuse me for pointing out that your new Pope has outlawed membership of the Mafia; assuming that's who you are referring to."

The shorter man chuckles to himself. "Yes," he replies, "this presents an interesting... *indovinello*, a riddle, for the church to solve.

"Imagine a priest hears a confession in which a Mafioso admits to murder. What can he do? He cannot violate the Sacramental Seal of the confessional; the Holy Decree of 1862 dictates that he cannot abuse the confidence of the penitent in case it harms him. Of course, if the priest requests it, this penitent may give him permission to discuss the contents of his confession with a third party, but for obvious reasons this is unlikely.

"So, I ask again, what course of action is left open to the priest? By condemning the Mafioso, is our Pope removing the Sacramental Seal? No! Is our Pope permitting the priest a form of discretion to report the penitent for his crimes? No, again! The priest merely threatens to excommunicate the penitent if he does not renounce the path of evil. In which case, the penitent simply leaves, only to return to the confessional to unburden himself of his crimes the next time he commits them, and so on. It is a riddle, eh?"

"Not one for me to solve," Ric replies. "But if solving it keeps you up at night, don't count on getting any sleep soon."

The Commissario nods, knowingly. "Yes, it would if I did, but I don't, so it does not. As I told you, I was merely waiting and watching."

"For what? I mean for what or for whom are you waiting out here in the middle of the night?"

Talaia snorts, as if he finds it hard to believe Ric can ask such a naïve question. "You may not know it, but Signor Candela was murdered in the doorway to this house," he points at the door opposite, which Ric now notices is crossed with police tape.

"It is clear," Talaia continues, "that our killer possesses a sense of melodrama too; shooting Signor Candela in the entrance to the house of Edda Ciano, eh? I wonder if our murderer means us to understand something of his motive by luring his victim to such a location.

"Oh, forgive me again, I should have told you. We understand that shortly before his speech in the Piazza Mazzini, Signor Candela received a note inviting him to a meeting at this house. Against the advice of his security advisors, he came alone."

"I'd heard that."

Talaia straightens up, "Oh, yes?"

"Gossip, Commissioner: word on the street, in the cafés."

"Of course, yes, I see." He pauses. "But, I was thinking — something, as I have said, the modern policeman does not commit enough time to these days — if a man was possessed of such a desire for melodrama, perhaps he might be the sort of man who would relish returning to the scene of his perfectly executed crime."

"Perhaps," Ric interrupts, "it's your turn to forgive me, Commissario, but I think you've been reading too much Camilleri."

He lifts his hand and waggles a finger in denial, "No, but that is

206

not to say I do not enjoy the work of this Sicilian; a trifle overcomplicated at times, a little like trying to find one's way out of a Souk. But I suppose one must take into account that Camilleri is from Porto Empedocle near Agrigento, and Agrigento, as any educated man would know, is just across the water from Tunis. You like to read, Mr Ross?"

"Sure, but whoever shot Candela would have to be pretty stupid to return to the scene." And as Ric says what he is thinking, he realises in his next breath that that is exactly what the Commissario is thinking too.

"Whoa! Hold on, Commissioner. Just because I happen to take the shortest route from Portinente to the Corta, it doesn't mean to say I've dropped by for a quick gloat over Candela's corpse."

"Gloat?" Talaia repeats, stepping closer to Ric. "This is a word I do not know. What does it mean?"

"It means to glory in one's triumph."

"Ah, you read dictionaries. I see you are interested in the way people use language. For myself, I have always found it important to listen to what people do not say, as much as what they do say. This word, gloat, it is also an interesting word," Talaia repeats. "Its meaning – to glory in one's triumph – has a rather Roman feel to it. But, Mr Ross, you are here and here is where Signor Candela was shot. So you can see why I am, let us say, interested."

"More of your uncomfortable coincidences, Commissioner?"

"Exactly, Mr Ross! Exactly! And yet…" Talaia quiets, rubbing his cheek with his forefinger; appending his own gaudy punctuation to the melodrama of their meeting. "And yet, it is just possible the perpetrator of this crime would return to look for evidence he has left behind."

"I guessed there must be a good reason why you wanted to discuss apostolic conundrums at midnight in the Piazza San Bartolo, rather than at *passeggio* in the Marina Corta like everyone else."

Talaia chuckles, "Yes, there is, Mr Ross. There is." The Commissario takes a small evidence bag from his pocket. The moonlight silvers on the clear plastic sac and inside it appear to be three small, bronzed metal cylinders.

"Bullet casings?"

"They are, Signor Ross. And they are most likely to be the casings from the rounds that were responsible for Signor Candela's death. They were found near to Signor Candela's body and one does not need the eyesight of an owl to know that he was shot from extremely close range. Would it interest you to know what calibre of gun they are from?"

"Not particularly, but if you think it's important, please go ahead."

"At first glance, a 9 millimetre of some sort; possibly an old semi-automatic pistol; the sort that was much in evidence during the Second Great War."

"I guess," Ric suggests, "there must be a lot of old ordnance left over around this neck of the woods."

"Yes, Signor Ross, there is much that still hangs over us from the two Great Wars." He pauses. "Now, I think we have spoken enough for one evening. If we have to speak again, which I have a feeling we will, I must say again how important it is for us to speak when it is not so easy for others to take an interest in what we might be speaking about; word on the street, in the cafés, as you so rightly say. You know how it is, eh? I notice you don't carry a cellphone."

"Don't have much call for one, if you'll excuse the pun."

"Ah," Talaia sighs. "I know what you mean by this."

"You do, huh?"

"Yes, of course. Cellphones are a constant interruption to our thought and relaxation. How can a man think or relax if his phone rings and people know where he is all the time?"

Ric knows what the policeman is getting at: cellphone tracking by multilateration of radio signals and GPS. "I'm sure if I need you, I'll find you, Commissario."

"I am sure you will, Mr Ross. The police station is not far from your current residence. It is on the Via Marconi Guglielmo, but you will see me around the town. *Buonanotte*, Signor Ross."

"*Buonanotte*, Commissario."

39

The Marina Corta is peaceful. The late-closing cafés play host to a few *escurzionisti* parting with the last of their day's wages.

Sandro is sitting in his usual haunt, Giuliana is absent and her guardian lends Ric another of his menacing stares as he strolls beneath the statue of San Bartolo. The citadel looms over the fishing boats like a monumental night-watchman: the little ships will be safe for as long as San Bartolo can keep his eyes open.

The clothes and knick-knack shops on the Garibaldi are long closed and the Muslim women lean out of their second-floor windows to watch him pass beneath.

He holds back for a moment, thinking he could take the little alley; it is the shortest route home. But having just made the same mistake – a mistake which led him to bump into the Commissario in the Maddalena – he decides the safer route would be less direct, and he knows that once he leaves the brightly lit Garibaldi, he will be consigned to the impenetrable gloom of the *vicolos* which lead to his room.

The breeze has picked up and the sign above the *farmacia* tells him the temperature has dropped to the low twenties. Even though the narrow corridor of stars still shine clear and bright high above his head, he knows the storms will have departed their perch above the mountains of the mainland and will be making their way towards the islands.

Ric isn't certain, but he thinks he can hear someone following him.

Halfway up the rise of the Garibaldi, Ric pauses to glance in through the darkened windows of a trattoria. The awnings are rolled back and the chairs and tables cleared and stacked inside. The sound of footsteps from behind him ceases, so he moves on a few paces and turns the corner into the Maurolico and again immediately left into the confines of the little Vico Selinunte, which lead back down the slope.

But the entrance to the poky little vico is exposed by the light thrown by the neon sign of the pharmacy, so he treads softly ten paces and slips into a doorway.

Making himself as slim as possible so that his profile does not show against the light stuccoed walls, he waits.

Whoever it is that is following him is also waiting and listening before entering the cramped alley.

Eventually the figure begins walking down towards him.

Ric cannot judge the size of his stalker because the lack of light lends the other man a similar advantage. And it strikes him that his stalker might just be Giuliana, coming once more to force her charms on him. He breathes gently and waits; for the second time in an hour a tide of adrenalin surges through his form.

But, it isn't a girl; it is a man who breathes heavily and, like Ric, pauses to listen now and then.

As he nears Ric, he halts again and looks over his shoulder.

While he is distracted, Ric steps down and as the man turns to face forward again, Ric traps his left hand around the man's throat, squeezes it hard and lifts the man violently off his feet up against the opposite wall.

"Listen to me, whoever you are," he hisses, "I don't like being followed so..." Something about the man's hair and the way it hangs down around his neck is familiar to Ric.

The man gurgles as he tries to speak through gritted teeth, but he doesn't resist.

Ric loosens his grip, but keeps the man pinned up against the wall so that his feet do not quite touch the ground.

The man tries again to speak and this time manages to whisper, "Gallese... wait... it is me... Sandro."

Ric runs his right hand down the man's shoulder and realises by their slope that the figure he has hold of can only be one man, Sandro. He relaxes his hand around the *escurzionista's* throat, eases him back down to his feet and releases him.

"What the bloody hell are doing, following me around like this? You'll get yourself hurt," Ric hisses.

Sandro doubles and gags and clutches at his throat. "What are you trying to do, Gallese, kill me?"

"Jesus, Sandro, a simple hello would have done well enough."

But Sandro is wheezing and spluttering.

Chevrons of light appear on Sandro's anguished face: the neighbours are awake.

"Come on, you idiot," Ric murmurs as he pulls his hapless night-stalker down the vico.

Sandro coughs and splutters as they twist and turn through the warren back to Ric's room.

They pause at the last corner and Ric realises his charge is making so much noise that anyone else hiding in the darkened alley would likely as not have heard them coming and legged it.

He pours a glass of water from the sink. "Sorry to have been so rough on you, my friend." He passes the dejected figure the only olive branch available to him.

"Gallese... next time," he gags as he drinks, "I get into a disagreement with my mother," he drinks again, "make sure you are near me, eh? I think you are a match for her."

Ric chuckles in admiration at Sandro's humour.

"Do you have anything stronger?" he asks, blinking and thrusting his glass across the table. Sandro rubs at his neck, as if to remind his assailant of the disrespect he has done him and therefore why he warrants a stronger drink.

"Sure," Ric replies and gets up to liberate a bottle of wine from the fridge.

When he opens the bottle, the pop of the cork causes the *escurzionista* to flinch.

"Okay, Sandro, I'll ask again. What the hell are you doing following me home?"

He looks up from beneath his curtain of curly black hair, his expression way past miserable.

"Did you not refuse to have a beer with me the last time we met because you wanted to talk in private? Well," he raises his arms in appeal, "this is my idea of private. So I come to your house to talk, rather than talk in the café where we can be seen, and you beat the shit out of me. I say this for you, Gallese; you have a funny way of showing your appreciation."

"I said I'm sorry, Sandro. But bumping into people in the dark twice in one night is apt to make me a little tense."

Sandro eyebrows disappear up into his mop of hair, "Twice? Who else have you met this night?"

"Never mind all that. What have you come to tell me that makes you so eager to go stealing about like a thief?"

Sandro sits upright and purses his lips at Ric's inference. "Not nice," he says. "If you ask me questions about things I notice, you have to be nice. You have been nice with Sandro so far, why now so insulting?"

Ric understands that the *escurzionista* wants a little love while he thinks he is being screwed. "You're right, my friend." He smiles a patronising but slightly camp smile and reaches across the table to stroke Sandro's arm lightly, "I'm really sorry. What can I do to make it better?"

Sandro withdraws his arm quickly. "Hey, don't joke about this kind of stuff. The President of Sicily may be gay, but this is not my way."

"Okay, okay! Look, I'm sorry I was a little harsh on you. What have you found out?"

Now that Sandro believes he has the upper hand he demonstrates his new-found status by taking his time; he finishes his glass of wine and refills it without asking.

Ric grins, but not so much that his companion might mistake his look for amusement. "Come on, Sandro, enough games. I haven't got all night."

Sandro straightens up in his chair, leans forward over the table and whispers, "The policeman, the little man I told you about who orders everyone about after Candela is shot, he is not La Polizia from Milazzo; he is from the north and he is the Chief Commissario of a new taskforce investigating corruption in politics."

"Investigating Mafia?"

"No, not necessarily Mafia. People are saying he is investigating many politicians in Palermo, Catania, Messina and Bagheria..."

"Please, wait a minute, my friend." Ric holds up his hand to interrupt Sandro's inventory of Sicilian towns and cities. Do you mean he was investigating Candela?"

Sandro nods, his expression one of disbelief that Ric can be so stupid, "Of course. Candela began his political career in Bagheria before he bought his ticket to the Palazzo dei Normanni in Palermo."

"Bagheria," Ric repeats, as he stares at the table and tries to remember if he has heard of the town before.

"But," Sandro carries on, "this policeman is investigating all of them." He hunches his shoulders even closer to his head and spreads his arm in appeal, "Hey, Gallese, just because they are centre-left and they call themselves Democrats doesn't mean they are any less corrupt than the centre-right party who call themselves the People of Freedom, eh?" Sandro pauses and scratches his mop of black hair.

"I guess not," Ric replies. "So, tell me about him. What do you know about Candela?"

"Oh, the usual. He was a young *comunista*; campaigned for shorter working hours, better working conditions, better pensions. He became a labour man, then a union representative, and finally a socialist councilman. It is the way they climb the tree of politics; and, let me tell you, they don't mind if they tread on the heads and hands of others on their way up, eh?"

"Sounds like a pleasant enough guy," Ric adds with requisite sarcasm.

"Sure," Sandro nods. "Like most. They start out with nothing, like all good communists, eh?" he bridles. "They earn a little bit money for themselves and soon enough they learn it is easier to take the money from another man's wages rather than have to work for it with their own hands, so they become union men. The next year they learn they don't want to mix with all these ignorant, dirty people, so they get work with the council and get to wear a suit that hasn't already seen a hundred funerals. A few years later, they are wearing Armani, sitting in a nice office with a view over the Palazzo Reale. You see how it goes?"

Sandro is pleased with his monologue and deems his efforts worthy of another glass of wine. Once he has drained half of it, he continues, "Then, of course, they put the little woman in a villa out of town, the children go to school in Bologna and the politician has a mistress in a fancy apartment near the Teatro Massimo; all very expensive. They spend much time in Brussels eating and drinking, but one day a man who knew a friend of his brother's asks this politician to help him get permission to build a small factory in Catania, or perhaps the politician knows how to dispose of certain Carbon Credits from Romania, or set up a ghost company which moves fuel from one country to another to avoid paying duty. It is the only way they can afford such a style of life.

"Pah! They are all the same." Sandro shrugs as if someone has just thrown a lice-ridden jacket over his shoulders.

"And Candela?" Ric asks, "Is he any different?"

"Why should he be? I told you, they are all the same." The *escurzionista* thinks. "Ah, I remember one thing, or maybe it was more than one, I don't know."

Ric reaches across the table and pours the rest of the bottle into his companion's glass.

Sandro smiles appreciatively and sips. "Mmm, you know, I remember talk from some years ago... The current President of Sicily, Rosario Crocetta, is from Gela near Agrigento. When he tried to run for the office of Mayor in 2002, the Mafia fix the election against him. The next year, *Tribunali Amministrativi Regionali* finds out about this fix and reverses the result. Crocetta is instated and the Mafia, because they don't like this insult to their authority, bring in a Lithuanian to assassinate him. The Lithuanian fails." He holds his palms up in surrender. "They try to silence Crocetta again in 2008 and again in 2010, but they are not so good at their work."

Ric is none the wiser. "So the President leads a charmed life!"

Sandro shakes his head, slowly. "Gallese, you go too fast; this is Sicily we are talking about, not one of those black and white London gangster movies which is over when the eye blinks." He drains his glass.

"The last time the Mafia try in 2010, La Polizia are suspicious that someone in the *Assemblea Regionale* is supplying the Mafia with information about Crocetta's movements."

"And you think Candela was involved?"

"Mmm, it's very possible. Candela was elected to the assembly in 2008."

Ric chuckles, "But that's a bit like suggesting anyone who joined the U.S. Senate from 1963 onwards was in on John F. Kennedy's assassination."

Sandro nods and grins, "Well, most of them were, weren't they?"

"But you think that's why Commissario Talaia was shadowing Candela?"

At this, Sandro sits bolt upright, eyebrows raised, "You know this man, the Commissario?"

Ric remains silent. If he has been seen with Talaia, a lie would only make life worse for him.

But Sandro is suspicious, "You know his name?" he asks again.

"Guess I must have heard it in the café."

But, Sandro isn't sold. He studies Ric, eyes wide. "So is it true, this Commissario did come to see you yesterday morning?" He pauses, thinking something over. "I tell you this Gallese. Sometimes I think you know much that I don't, and Sandro likes to know everything."

"Another glass of wine?" Ric offers, getting to his feet. "I'm really sorry about your neck. I hope the bruise around your throat doesn't keep you from sleeping."

Sandro is beginning to look decidedly nervous, glancing about the room as though in mentioning the Commissario Ric has intoned the devil. He stands abruptly, leaves his wine glass unfinished and turns for the door, "Yes, I hope it will not stop me from sleeping." And, as he is about to shut the door behind him, Sandro hesitates, "Gallese, you ask me to find out if there is any person missing: a man of medium height, weight, short brown hair and brown t-shirt with the island name stitched here." He indicates his heart.

"I did."

"This description fits many people and many people come and go on the Aliscafo everyday—"

"But," Ric interrupts, "I thought you said not many men here have beards—"

"And this t-shirt," Sandro comes back quickly, "as I have said, is very common. I know of no one like this who is missing right now. *Ciao.*"

Ric watches the black mop of curls slope off into the darkness of the alley, aware that Sandro may have been about to tell him who was missing, but because of his meeting with the Commissario, he no longer trusts him.

40

The next morning Ric wakes to a head full with questions. He is at a loss as to what to do about the detective, Talaia, the missing Beretta, the Mara, Marcello, Valeria and lastly Sandro, whose toast he has very evidently browned.

In not being straight with Sandro, he has abused the *escurzionista's* confidence and pricked the masculinity with which his self-respect is so delicately intertwined. Ric is painfully aware that even if Sandro does know who around town is missing, he is now unlikely to pass the information along.

Expecting an early morning visit from the policeman, Ric wastes no time in getting downstairs and preparing for the day.

On cue, there is a knock at his door.

But it isn't the diminutive Commissario who stands outside, it is the short, gentle faced Ariana, the young girl who cares for Old Nino.

"*Per favore,*" she says, blushing and handing him a note.

Before he has a chance to read it, she turns to go.

The handwriting is raw and child-like, and the scrawl reads, *Per favore visitare Nino oggi.*

By the time he understands the brief message, Ariana has turned the corner.

Sandro is on station, handing out leaflets at the bottom of the

Corso Vittorio. He ignores Ric when he enters first the *giornalaio* to buy a map and second the *supermercato* for a bottle of water.

Ric takes the bus out to Canneto, asking the driver to let him off just through the tunnel.

The Cantiere Nautico Maggiore is deserted but for the dog, which lunges at him, barking wildly.

Marcello is making progress: the engine of the Mara sits naked and disassembled on a bench beneath a lean-to, its innards exposed for all to see. He studies the various organs for a while, picking up the pistons, the rings and the crank, and examining them for signs of wear.

What he has come for, though, are his walking boots.

The Mara looks naked and embarrassed, stood up on her blocks, no screw at her stern and a gaping void in the floor of the cockpit. He checks the stow-hole just in case some angel of mercy has decided to take pity on him and return the Beretta. But, San Bartolo is watching over others elsewhere and the gun has not reappeared.

Once he has slipped on the boots, Ric takes a moment in the shade to pore over a relief map he has bought. The simplest way to get out to Old Nino's is to take the bus, but he fancies a day away from inquisitive glances and idle talk.

He pats Mara's hull. "Get well soon, please."

From Marcello's yard the road winds in a series of tight hairpins up to the little village of Pirrera, where he stops to drink water.

Low white houses, their square walls white-washed in lime and volcanic sand, their round pillars and perfect arches supporting first floor terraces, their pergolas graced with bougainvillea and grape vines, stand dotted about the hillside as though God has shaken a handful of dice and dropped them haphazardly about the hill. Colourful mosaics decorate tiled steps up to wrought iron gates, behind which stonewall benches sit vacant beside equally vacant, dome-shaped bread ovens. A wrinkled old man watches him pass and raises his hand. And whenever Ric looks up at the blue heavens, a buzzard circles lazily on the thermals, tracking his progress.

At the back of the village, Ric studies the map before turning up the dusty track to Colle Sant'Elmo. Higher up the slope, the path steepens and he can feel the sun at his back. Tree heath and broom line the track, and imperial crows hop about, nervous of and inquisitive at his passing.

The better part of an hour later he reaches the summit of Sant'Elmo and pauses to take in the view: Vulcano to the south, its flattened ashen dome rising from the sea like a vast mollusc, and Salina to the north-west, its rich slopes shining like polished greenstone. Ric drinks the last of the water in his backpack. The buzzard still circles high above him, watching and waiting.

Old Nino's house lies between Sant'Elmo and the coast in the direction of Salina. The map tells him he can follow the road up to Monte Chirica and cut down towards Castellaro or head across country to the settlement at Quattropani and hope to pick up the track to Old Nino's which he took with Valeria.

As he walks, he remembers Valeria telling him about the two deportees who escaped from the citadel and hid in the hills until their hunger got the better of them. Apart from the small red berries of the occasional wild strawberry bush and the odd stunted chestnut, Ric sees nothing in the maquis that might sustain a man for long.

An hour and a half later and cooled by the breeze blowing in from the purple sea, Ric rounds the curve in the track and comes upon the bald ridge which sweeps down towards the small white dome of the Chiesa Vecchia.

He pushes back the gate. It grates noisily on its hinges. He knocks on the door.

"Yes, I am here. Please come," the old man calls from his terrace.

"*Salve*, Nino," Ric greets him.

"*Salve*, Ric. I am glad you got my note. I was afraid that young girl would forget to deliver it. Thank you for coming. Please," he raises his arm and invites Ric to sit.

They shake; the old man feeling rather than squeezing Ric's outstretched hand.

Nino inclines his head towards his guest, "The sweat is cool on your palm; you did not take the bus, eh?"

"No, I needed some exercise."

"Also, you wanted to get to know the island. Did you come by Monte Sant'Angelo or Pianoconte?"

"Pirrera and the Colle Sant'Elmo."

"Ah, you came by Poggio dei Funghi, the hill of mushrooms below Cugno di Mandra. It was beautiful, no? I used to pick the mushrooms for my mother; she made good *zuppa* from them. Perhaps you are a little early for them; they are better after the late summer rain."

Old Nino stares through his sunglasses in the direction of Salina. Wind squalls darken, dance and whirl across the purple sea which separates the islands, and small, white-sailed yachts pitch and yaw. An Aliscafo sprints towards Santa Marina like a busy water-boatman.

"There is a bottle of *legbi* on the kitchen table," Nino says. "And bring two glasses and some cool water from the fridge. Also, Ariana has left us a plate of *prosciutto* and *pomodori* and *melanzane*. Bring it also."

Ric sets the glasses of palm wine and the *prosciutto* on the table, trying his best to set the tray before the old man in exactly the same way the young girl Ariana had that first time he visited.

"Please, eat. We will talk when our stomachs are silent."

The tomatoes are soft and juicy, the dry-cured ham sweet and the aubergine bake rich and sumptuous. Ric notices how deft and delicate the blind man is with his hands.

When they have finished, they lean back and allow a few minutes for their food to settle.

"Now we can hear ourselves talk without fear of interruption from our hunger," Nino promises.

"You've remembered something about the date I mentioned?" Ric asks.

"Perhaps." Judging by the slight tilt of his head, Nino is trawling his memory. He waits for a moment before continuing, "If I recall rightly, you said you found a grave for a respected individual who went by the name of Antonio Sciacchitano and that the date of death on his headstone reads that he passed in July of 1930?"

"Correct, Nino."

"I have been thinking about this time when I was ten years old."

Ric thinks quickly.

Nino pauses. "Ah, yes. You are impressed I am still here at ninety-three years. I am not sure why, but it is only of importance to me. Now, where was I?

"Ah, I have it. In those days I lived with my family in Canneto. My father was a fisherman and my mother, and my brothers and sisters and I, worked the *pomice*. The summer days were long and dusty and hot, and the winters were always difficult. We would leave very early every day to walk to the warehouses at the beach of smooth stones. There we would pass the days grading and drying the *pomice*. The work was hard, but La Cava was not a bad employer; we had a roof over our heads and, what with the fish my father caught, we were fed better than most."

Nino's throat dries as he talks and he coughs as he tries to raise the saliva in his mouth.

Ric passes him a glass of water.

"As you can imagine, I could not wait to gain enough years to leave my mother's side and go with my father on his fishing boat. But the first night I was to go with him — and I believe this is why I remember the time so clearly — a man and a young woman came to our house and my father took me to one side and told me I would have to wait for another evening before I was to go fishing with him.

"I was very upset. I cried and shouted at him that he was a liar for breaking his promise to me, that I would never believe what he told me ever again and that I would rather work in the warehouse than take to the sea with him.

"My father should have hit me I was so disrespectful to him. But he did not. I remember him looking down at me with tears in his eyes and begging me to forgive him; telling me he would prefer not to be leaving me behind, but that he had important business to attend to and that even though the sea was not rough, it would be too dangerous for me to go with him."

Nino wets his whistle a second time and follows his water with a sip of his palm wine.

"Ric, think of how I felt? I knew the other boys would believe he had not allowed me to go with him because he thought I was not capable of doing the hard night's work of a fisherman. Sure, it was not easy, but most of my friends had been fishing with their father's since they were nine or younger. I knew why he did not take me before, because he wanted me to look after my mother during the day and at night I would be too tired. But he had promised me that on my tenth birthday, I would go with him. So, I cried and beat the door to our house and shouted at him as he walked away to the beach.

"Now, you may know that at this time we had many political people living here in Lipari."

"Political deportees, exiles."

"Si, *deportati*. They were very poor individuals; some had money, but not all of them. My father would sell them fish when they could afford it, but to others he gave the fish if they promised to pay him later.

"One night, three of these deportees tried to escape. It had been done successfully a year or so before."

"Valeria told me," Ric interrupts. "Nitti, Lussu and Roselli."

"Yes, those were the gentlemen. Valeria does well to remember their names. Three more tried to escape by the same method; a fast boat was to come and take them to Tunis. I can't remember their names. Ah, Drago was one."

"Farinelli and Tamboia were the others, or so Valeria said," Ric offers.

"Yes, of course she is right. Farinelli and Tamboia were the others. But the plans of their escape were passed to the Fascists and they were intercepted and shot, along with the people who came to liberate them. This night on which they were killed in the bay at Punta San Giuseppe, was two nights before my father was supposed to take me fishing for the first time. It was a coincidence, no?"

Ric glances at the old man and sees the lines of blue veins standing proud on his slender hands and forearms.

"Oh, don't be surprised that I remember so much. Eighty-three years ago is simple; last week is not so easy, eh?"

"But why is this so important to me, Nino?"

"All in good time, young man. One door leads to another; this is how it must be."

Nino scratches at a red mark on his neck and Ric is minded to pull his hand away just as Valeria had done. But he doesn't. Instead he refills Nino's glass with more *legbi* and passes it to his hand.

"Thank you." He wipes a dribble of wine away from the corner of his mouth. "The night my father would not take me fishing, he did so for two reasons. The first was that the Carabinieri had told everyone that if they were caught out in the water this night, their boats would be confiscated: they were patrolling in their launches with powerful lamps.

"The second was that a man came to our door and begged my father to smuggle him and a young woman to Baarìa in Sicily. He said that he did not expect my father to take him because if he was caught, he would probably be shot. All this I did not know until my mother, seeing that I was inconsolable at the wrong my father had done me, decided to tell me during the night. She did not want me to hate this mild-mannered, hard-working man who was my father. But other than that, all I knew was that these two were not *deportati*. My mother would not tell me who they were or why it was that they were fugitives.

"Of course, I understood then that my father was a hero, even if I felt a little aggrieved that I missed out on the opportunity to be the same." Nino quiets for a minute and sips his wine, staring out into the sea as if he can still see his father's fishing boat dodging the line squalls racing through the Canale di Salina.

"Did your father return from his trip?"

"He did. But he was gone for three days and the Carabinieri were our constant visitors through that time. When eventually he returned, they questioned him and he told them a story about his engine having a problem and how he had to wait in the islands over there while it was mended." He points towards the horizon where Ric can just make out the hazy profiles of the little twins, Filicudi and Alicudi.

"What is most important, though, is that many years later my father told me that the man he took across to Sicily that night was Antonio Sciacchitano, the man whose grave contains no corpse."

41

Ric feels a little dizzy. Perhaps it is the heat or the palm wine, or perhaps it is that he feels cheated. He isn't sure which. But he is also taken with the idea that every time he thinks he is getting close to finding out about his forebears, instead of being content with the information he receives, he is left with the impression that there are yet more questions he needs to find answers to.

"Well, Nino," he says after this new piece of news has been allowed sufficient time to sink in, "that is a tale and a half. So, you mean to tell me that I've come all this way to find an empty grave?"

The old man grins, mischievously. "It would seem that way, my young friend. For eighty years that grave has been empty and no one has thought to question why."

Ric knows he is being led, but is more than happy to be if by doing so he will be afforded more information. He smiles, perfectly sure that the old man can feel him do so.

"So, why, Nino? Why has Antonio Sciacchitano's grave sat empty all these years?"

"Mmm, I will tell you. And I can tell you this now because all the players in this opera are all long passed and it can no longer put anyone in danger. But first, a little coffee, which you will have to make. Oh, and bring some of the biscuits, please. That girl is more careful with her rations than a field kitchen."

As Ric gets up to begin clearing the table, Nino reaches out and grasps his forearm. The old man does this so speedily and accurately that Ric is wont to question his lack of sight. He waits.

"My friend, Ariana only allows me one teaspoon of coffee in the *caffettiera*. Perhaps, as she is not here, we can spoil ourselves and have two each." He touches briefly the rim of his dark glasses and whispers, "What the eye does not see; the head will not worry over, eh?" He chuckles.

"Seems like a good idea to me, Nino."

When Ric returns with the tray of coffee and biscuits, Nino has fallen asleep, so he places the tray as gently as he can on the table. The old man's posture suggests he is still awake; his head is upright, his back is straight and his arms are folded across his chest. But there is tranquility and serenity to his form and Ric wonders for a moment if he might, like the players in his opera, have passed on.

"This is why I need the coffee," Nino says, very suddenly. "The mind is tempted to sleep and I would rather it stayed awake. That way I know I am still alive. Now, where were we?"

"The empty grave?"

"Ah, yes. *Una tomba senza cadavere*," he repeats. "An unusual occurrence, a grave without a corpse. Of course, one finds many graves without names, but a grave with a name and yet without a corpse is most unusual."

Old Nino sips his coffee and nods, "Mm, that is better. So how do we come to have an empty grave in our cemetery, eh? Firstly, I am too old to remember all the funerals I have attended. When you get to my age, you have seen so many they all blend into one unhappy procession; few of them are remarkable. But my father told me this man, Sciacchitano, learned from a conversation he had overheard in a café in Canneto that the three *deportati* – Drago, Farinelli and Tamboia – were betrayed to the Carabinieri. At that time, one of the principles involved in the arrangement of the escape was Vincenzo Maggiore, Marcello Maggiore's grandfather. I believe you know Marcello."

"I do. He's fixing my boat."

"My father told me that when Vincenzo heard these men had been betrayed, he sent Antonio Sciacchitano to Punta San Giuseppe to warn them. Alas, he arrived too late and the men were killed in the ambush the Carabinieri had set for them. On his way back through the town, Tonio was stopped by a patrol and questioned as to what he was doing out so late. With no excuse and soaking wet after his futile attempt to warn the unfortunate *deportati*, he was arrested. However, Sant'Agata was watching over him: a bribe was paid and he was permitted to escape. And this was when he came to my father and begged him to spirit him and his companion away to the mountains, to Sicilia."

"That still doesn't tell me why he's not in his casket in the cemetery."

"Patience, my friend, patience! When the *Commendatore* found out Tonio had escaped, he went completely *pazzo*. The Carabinieri searched the island as if they had been told the treasure of San Bartolo would be theirs to keep if only they could find it.

"Tonio hid in the *pomice* warehouse at Pietra Liscia until the noise had died down, at which time my father took him to Baarìa. However, the *Commendatore* did not allow the Carabinieri to let the matter drop. He proclaimed that Tonio would wish he were dead rather than suffer the tortures they would inflict upon him when they found him. This gave Vincenzo Maggiore the idea of making the *Commendatore* think Tonio was actually dead. He persuaded the… the… *pubblico ufficiale che indaga i casa di morte sospetta*, I don't know this word…"

"The coroner?"

"Sì, the coroner. He persuaded the coroner to provide a death certificate and so a funeral was held. The whole town turned out; the procession was as long as the Corso Vittorio and the coffin without a body was buried in the cemetery. In fact, there were so many people that the *Commendatore*, who was also by chance a highly superstitious man, feared a riot like the one in 1926 when the people of Lipari protested against the criminals who were sent here. This he could not afford for fear of being disgraced, so he allowed the funeral to take place without interference."

Ric chuckles, "He wasn't much of a one for the job, was he?"

"No," Old Nino replies. "Many of the Fascists were more concerned with keeping their positions than they were with doing their work correctly. For us, this was a blessing."

"So my great-grandfather – if he is my great-grandfather and not a figment of someone's fertile imagination – left Lipari for Baarìa and never came back?"

"How could he? He was dead! Oh, there are others here with the name Sciacchitano, but they are not of the same family and you will find families of this name throughout the south of Italy and, no doubt, some in America too."

"And after the war? He didn't return after the war?"

Old Nino turns to face Ric as if reading his expression, "The war was not finished until fifteen years later and by that time there was even less reason to come back. *Pomice* and *zolfo* were being mined more economically in the Americas, there was no tourist trade to speak of and there was so much poverty that anyone with a gram of ability departed for greener fields. And besides, Tonio was not a fool; he would have understood he would not have been safe in Baarìa. It would have been better for him to leave Sicilia for good. Probably, he went to Tunis or perhaps on a boat to France."

Ric thinks, "Perhaps even to Britain?"

"Yes, perhaps even to Britain. After the war, many went to work as agricultural labourers." Old Nino turns his face back towards the strait between the islands. "Many went and have never returned; I, of course, could not."

In an attempt to lift the old man from his maudlin, Ric offers, "Your father was a brave man, Nino, in much the same way as you were; you both answered the call when it came."

He nods his wizened head very slowly. A slender line of tears trickles from beneath his dark glasses. He wipes his nose with a handkerchief. "It is true. Even though I have no sight, I can see my father in front of me as if it were yesterday." He pauses. "Now it must be time for you to find your excitement elsewhere. An old man has only so much energy for this kind of recollection and now that I have brought my memories back into my mind, I would like to be left alone with them."

"Sure, Nino, I understand. It goes without saying how much I appreciate all the time and effort you've committed to remembering what happened. Is there anything I can do for you before I go?"

The old man smiles a little mischievously. "If you would be kind enough to replace the *legbi* where you found it and wash these glasses, it will make Ariana's return all the more agreeable, thank you."

Ric does as he is asked, wondering, while he is washing and drying, how he will ever find out whether or not he is related to the courageous Antonio Sciacchitano.

Outside, Old Nino has regained his upright posture, suggesting he may have gone to sleep.

The wind is strengthening, white caps litter the purple sea below the point and Ric wonders if he should cover the old man with a rug. He watches and realises that if he ever makes it to such a venerable age, he would like to be left sitting on a stonewall seat, in the shade of a pergola, fanned by the sea breeze and before such a fair view; especially if that view was exactly the same as the last time he'd seen it, nearly sixty years before.

As he leaves, he recalls the old man saying that Tonio Sciacchitano had brought a young woman with him to his father's house that night, and he wonders about the woman and whether she, too, made the journey in the fishing boat to Baarìa.

42

Ric walks back over the ridge into Quattropani. While he sits at the side of the road, waiting for the bus, he chews over the information Nino has supplied him. It is comforting to learn that his supposed forebear was a solid citizen, if that is an adequate description of a man who gives up his existence for the good of others. However, it also leaves him feeling a shade flat. There is no doubt, with the odd shove from Camille and Valeria and Old Nino, that he has climbed several ladders in order to learn about Antonio Sciacchitano. But, the idea of treading the streets of Baarìa – wherever on the Sicilian coast Baarìa might be – to press the locals to remember some fugitive from eighty-odd years before, seems to slide him right back down the snake to square one. He might as well be back in the marine cemetery of the Bosco, in the walled citadel of Bonifacio in Corsica, asking the gravediggers if they know of a grave marked Ross.

He laughs out loud at the thought that when he'd plucked up the courage to ask the gravediggers that very question, they had directed him down the steep hill to the municipal office in the town below. And when, eventually, he'd enquired at the counter in the municipal office, they'd told him he would find the answers to his questions up in the cemetery.

The irony is that it isn't the marine cemetery in Bonifacio that has provided him with answers; it is the cemetery in Lipari.

The bus, when it eventually pitches up, is huge, roomy and air-conditioned, and looks completely out of place against the backdrop of rustic houses.

Back in town, the Carabinieri are still checking the identity papers of those hoping to leave Lipari on the early evening Aliscafo, but they appear more concerned with making polite conversation and flirting with the girls than executing their duties.

Ric stops off at the *alimentari* for provisions and strolls up the Corso Vittorio. The flamboyant waiter at La Precchia – where he'd breakfasted before going out to see Old Nino with Valeria – is laughing with Giuliana. She stops and frowns when she sees Ric, and then whispers to the waiter, who straightens and watches as Ric walks on up the street.

After dropping off the provisions and changing out of his boots, he walks through the cool vicos down to the Corta. The square around the small harbour is quiet, the cafés almost deserted. Sandro is absent, there is no sign of Marcello and even the Purgatorio lacks its usual, venerable congregation. So he strolls over to the Casa dei Sconosciuti to tell Valeria what Old Nino has remembered.

Police tape still cordons off the Piazza San Bartolo and the Maddalena is narrowed by a stream of people, both locals and tourists, walking back towards the Corta. They are laughing and joking as though they have recently enjoyed the company of a stand-up comedian. There is, perhaps, a festival taking place in the small bay of Portinente.

When he turns the corner by the fisherman's chapel above the bay, he realises the attraction: a police launch is moored off the beach and there are frogmen in the water.

Ric has to ease his path through the throng of spectators gathered at the foot of the slope. The residents of the Rocce Azzure are leaning from their balconies and the terrace is crowded with onlookers. The paraphernalia of sub-acqua gear litters the pebble beach and policemen shoo children away and strut this way and that with the earnest intention of stewards at a football match.

The solitary and diminutive figure of Commissario Talaia stands, as far from the crowd as he can without actually getting his feet wet, observing the action. Two teams of divers wallow like confused porpoises in the shallows.

"*Attenzione! Medusa!*" A voice calls out.

A diver looks up, distracted, and laughter ripples through the crowd.

"Attention! Jellyfeesh!" someone responds from the terrace of the hotel.

The crowd cheer with undisguised contempt.

The police ignore the taunting.

Valeria is watching from the stone wall of a cottage garden and Marcello is deep in conversation with a covey of locals.

Ric makes his way over to them and, as he does so, he briefly makes eye contact with Talaia. The policeman does not acknowledge him.

"What's all the fuss about, Marcello?"

On seeing Ric, several of those around Marcello turn their attentions to the floor and move away as if Ric has gained the status of a social pariah.

Il Velaccino turns, smiles and then returns his gaze to the frogmen. "If I was one of those contestants from a game show, I would say they are looking for the keys to the *Schiavettoni*. Oh, sorry, of course, I mean a kind of heavy iron handcuffs the *Fascisti* used to use. But, if you ask me for an educated guess, I would say this is the kind of thing they do when they are searching for evidence. Already today, they have searched the houses and the sewers in the Maddalena. It is very possible they are looking for the weapon which was responsible for Girolamo Candela's murder?

"But what kind of fool," he adds, aside, "would shoot a man and then throw the gun into the sea not three hundred metres from the scene of his crime?"

"Beats me, Marcello. How's the Mara coming along?"

"You should know, Ric. You were there this morning."

The facetious tone he employs, unsettles Ric. "Sure, I needed a couple of things off the boat. I didn't think you'd mind."

Marcello grunts, "She's your boat," and adds below his breath, "and for the time being she is not going anywhere."

They watch in silence, although the speculation as to what the police frogmen are searching for provokes a constant hubbub of conversation.

Marcello glances at Ric again. "Did you get what you wanted from the Mara this morning, or are you like the police, still looking for what it is that you have lost?" he asks. His tone suggests he would like Ric to have asked permission before he let himself into the boatyard.

But Ric is not taken with Marcello's pique and feels inclined to harden his response, "Thank you, yes: my boots. If it's all the same to you, I needed them for the hike over to Old Nino's. Turns out he's remembered a good deal about the guy I think might be my great-grandfather."

"Oh, yes?" But still Marcello's concentration is focused on the action off the beach.

"Yes. It seems he might have known your grandfather, Vincenzo."

At this, Marcello tears his gaze from the water and turns to look at Ric. His expression, though, is one of discomfort, as though Ric has just nudged him in his ribs. "And precisely what nonsense did the old fool come up with this time? He is quite mad, you know?"

Not wanting to land Nino fairly and squarely in Marcello's bad books for digging up a Maggiore family skeleton... Ric chuckles.

"What is so funny?"

"Nothing," he replies, thinking of skeletons not being where others believe they should be.

Marcello glances at him and raises an eyebrow, "Let us talk after the Circus Maximus has completed the production. I think this promises to become more amusing, eh?"

One of the divers suddenly stands up. He cuts a faintly farcical figure in his red dry-suit and breathing apparatus, the sea water only just clearing his knees.

He removes his regulator and calls to the beach.

A second diver, who looks curiously naked without his bottle, mask and flippers, trudges noisily about the shingle, searching for something. One of the uniformed *poliziotti* approaches a child at the front of the crowd and asks to borrow his long-handled net. The child is reluctant at first and clutches it tight to his chest. But after some very theatrical pleading from the *poliziotto* and well supported by the gentle encouragement of the boy's parents, he very begrudgingly hands over his net.

The *poliziotto*, aware of his now crucial contribution to the investigation, struts proudly down to the water's edge. He holds the net out towards the diver, but he is a couple of metres short of reaching him and does not want to get his feet wet. They stand, staring at each other for a few seconds.

"*Continua,*" someone shouts and the crowd roar.

"*Vai! Vai!*" the crowd begin to chant in unison.

The diver stands his ground; the *poliziotto*, the same. And the longer the stalemate continues, the louder the chanting grows.

"*Vai! Vai!*"

But they stand and wait each other out. And as though egged on by a conductor, the volume of encouragement swells until it deafens.

"*Vai! Vai!*"

But the diver and the *poliziotto* are anchored in despair; neither will surrender his position for fear of very publicly surrendering his ego along with it. They stare, helplessly at each other, each one waiting for the other to concede.

"*Vai! Vai!*"

Commissario Talaia shouts, although his words are lost in the racket from the multitude. The *poliziotto* looks briefly down at his polished shoes. He hesitates, shrugs his shoulders and resigns himself to wading into the water. But as he gets to within a couple of metres of the diver, he stumbles and falls flat on his face.

The diver, reaching out to try to grab the net, falls too, and the pair of them flounder and thrash in the sea like two children engaged in a water fight.

The multitudes are beside themselves, guffawing, slapping their thighs and creasing up double in amusement.

Commissario Talaia raises his hands to his face and turns away, not wanting to witness the farce a moment longer.

Eventually, the saturated *poliziotto* leaps up and staggers like a drunk back to the beach. The diver, though, takes a while to regain his balance and composure, and when he has replaced his regulator, he sinks slowly back down, child's net in hand, his embarrassment concealed behind his face mask.

"*Vanno a pesca!*" a wag calls from the perfect anonymity of the crowd.

The onlookers laugh hysterically.

"They go feeshing," the man on the terrace responds.

However, this final appreciation of the circus clowns is tinged with a degree of nervous anticipation as the diver is evidently trying to find his original mark.

"*Opera buffa*, eh?" Marcello growls, sucking his teeth.

The diver's shoulders roll and his arms and elbows pump as he tries to shovel into his net whatever it is that he has found on the seabed.

After a minute, the crowd grows restless for more entertainment. "*Vai! Vai! Vai!*" they begin to chant again, quietly at first and then louder and louder until they are very suddenly interrupted by the diver, who stands up and holds his net aloft.

At first, all they notice is the white bikini bra hanging from the end of his net.

The crowd begins to laugh hysterically until as one, they realise there is something else weighing down the little boy's fishing net.

The laughter dies away gradually and they quiet, unable to laugh as they crane their necks to get a better view of his catch.

It is a gun: a pistol. And from where Ric is standing, he can see it is the Beretta.

43

Nobody moves and nobody breathes. They stand and stare, open-mouthed at the diver, as he examines the gun dangling in the mesh of the child's net.

Ric tries to remember if he wiped the gun clean the last time he touched it. He knows he dare not move. The very last thing he can do is to look over at Talaia. It is precisely how he feels driven to react and he can feel the Commissario's eyes boring a hole in the side of his face, but he knows he would give himself away as surely as if he put his hand up and shouted, "That's mine, thank you."

The diver wades to the beach and hands the net to the soaking *poliziotto*, who, now that there is something of significance in the net, is far more enthusiastic about his part in what was, until a few moments before, a gentle comedy.

A man whistles and a collective groan is thrown up by the crowd; it is as if the balloon of their tensions has burst and the air is escaping in one long, relieving breath. Most turn away to discuss the find, the hubbub of their analysis growing with each added opinion; others press forward wanting a closer look at the gun which is, beyond any reasonable doubt as far as they are concerned, the weapon used to kill Candela.

Marcello folds his arms over his chest as though his mind, too, is made up. "So, now all they have to do is find who this gun belongs to."

"Looks that way," Ric replies, focusing his attention on the gun and in so doing avoiding Talaia's gaze.

"Everyone likes the circus; the adults more than the children, eh?" Marcello mutters.

Valeria is no longer standing on top of the wall which overlooks the beach and the crowd begins to drift away as the evening shade draws a curtain on the spectacle.

"Now," Marcello produces a stubby cigar from his shirt pocket, lights it and puffs away until he produces a cloud of smoke sufficiently noxious to disperse the crowd around them, "what were we discussing before these clowns began their very entertaining performance? Ah, yes, you were asking after the Mara and at the same time telling me Old Nino provided you with some information about this ancestor of yours. Well, my friend, there is good news and bad news."

"Marcello, you said the Mara isn't going anywhere for the moment. With the engine out and stripped back, that's pretty obvious. So, what's the bad news? Are the parts a problem?"

Marcello puffs and removes the cigar from his mouth. "No, it is not parts; these I have managed to get from suppliers in Milazzo. This is good news."

"Then there is another problem?"

"Yes, a bigger problem than putting the Mara's engine back together."

Ric tears his eyes away from the blue shirts inspecting the Beretta and turns to face Marcello. "Okay, let's have it?" he asks, wracking his brain for some other malady the Mara is suffering from that could be worse than a broken engine.

Marcello puffs, removes the cigar and picks a flake of tobacco from his tongue. "You see this little cockerel on the beach. The one wearing the suit and hat," he waves his cigar in the general direction of Commissario Talaia who, curiously, shows little interest in the stir created by the appearance of the gun.

"He comes to my place this afternoon. He introduces himself: his name is Talaia, Commissario Talaia. He is calm and polite, but dangerous, like the *tracina* fish; you call them weevers. They look harmless until you tread on them and then..." He winces and waggles his foot. "He is not like normal policemen, who one can often persuade to see a certain point of view, if you get what I mean by this? No, this man works for everyone and yet for no one; *Guardia Finanza, Polizia di Stato, Direzione Nazionale Anti-Mafia*. But he is accountable to only one politician, the *Ministero dell'Interno*, which means that he has great powers. His kind do not have to ask permission before they act and sometimes they act in ways that are questionable."

"Large brief for such a small man."

"Yes," Marcello smiles a hapless, slightly envious smile, "he will have a judge in his pocket; a judge who will provide him with a warrant for whatever he needs, whenever he asks."

"I get the picture."

"*Bene*, because when he speaks, a wise man listens. The Commissario comes to my place. He searches the Mara. He finds a little locker beneath your bed. In this locker, he finds a plastic bag with money and two passports. He tells me that he expects to find something else, but he is not surprised to find the passports. Next, he tells me he would prefer to eliminate you from his enquiries, but he can no longer believe what I have told him about you and me fishing when Candela was shot."

"So now I'm the chief suspect in Candela's murder."

He shakes his head, "I did not say this. I said he tells me he would *prefer* to eliminate you from his enquiries; I did not say he thinks you are the *chief suspect*. Finally, he tells me the Mara will not be put back in the sea without his permission; *completa autorizzazione* was what he said. And that, my friend, means he has not *yet* eliminated you from his enquiries."

Ric is hardly surprised at the news and doesn't feel the need to show it either. He tries to summon a smile, but it will not come to him. "Well, Marcello, if I'm a suspect and I can't account for my whereabouts at the time Candela was shot because I was out fishing with you, then neither can you account for your whereabouts because you were out fishing with me. So that makes you a suspect as much as me, even though the only people who we know for sure can't have shot Candela are the two of us."

Marcello grunts, "Yes, this thought has occurred to the little cockerel. It would appear we are both in the same boat, so to speak."

"It does, doesn't it?" Ric replies, frowning. "The only difference is that I don't have a motive for shooting Candela, where as you may."

The cigar twitches in his mouth. "And what could I gain from Candela's death, eh? Tell me this, if you are so intelligent." Marcello's tone is heavily laced with menace.

Ric grins, "It's hard to imagine, him being a politician from Palermo and you being a... well, I guess you are the best yacht repairer in the islands."

Marcello bristles at Ric's rather oblique compliment.

"But I understand, from what I've been told of his speech in the Mazzini, Candela promised the people of Lipari increasing prosperity: free electricity, improved schooling, free transport and other benefits. I gather he even promised to build a colossal hotel up at Porticello; a thousand rooms – he said."

"So? It's like you said, Ric, it is none of my business."

Ric sniggers, impolitely, "Oh, pull the other one, Marcello. A thousand bed hotel would mean heavy money and heavy money brings with it heavy characters, more than a few of whom would be unable to resist flexing their muscles around the island. Why would you want a load of new kids on the block when you and your cronies have got the whole place wrapped up tight?" Ric is goading Marcello, and judging by the glacial hardening of the shorter man's expression, his strategy is bearing fruit.

"Even an uneducated soul like me knows you and your brother are on the planning committee. If Candela was half the politician I think he needed to be to get to where he was, I'm sure he would have figured to pay you both off in order to get planning consent."

At this, Marcello rounds on him. "What do you know of this?" he spits. "How do you know about our business? And what gives you the right to interfere in what we do? You are nothing but a piece of driftwood washed up on our beach. Your kind washes through these islands every week. I tell you this, Ric, I like you and, because I like La Strega, I let you have the *monolocale.* But don't put a price on our friendship, eh?" Marcello's mask of loathing leaves Ric under no illusion he has overstepped the mark.

"Listen, my friend," Ric soothes, "please don't think I'm not grateful for what you've done for me and what you are doing for the Mara. I meant no disrespect, but—"

"Then this is a strange type of respect coming from an Englishman."

"I'm Welsh, but that's by the bye. What I was trying to tell you is that you've got motive for wanting Candela out of the way and I haven't. And if I can figure that out, it's a racing certainty the little cockerel can too."

"Perhaps someone has paid you to shoot Candela?" Marcello spits in return.

"Don't be an arse, Marcello. If I'd wanted to do away with Candela, I'd have seen to it and been off the island before you could have said Christopher Columbus."

"He was from Genoa," Marcello grunts, but his temper is cooling.

"You know what I mean," Ric replies, swallowing his frustration. "Anyway, if the Mafia wanted him dead, why waste him here, in this island; why not in Sicily or on one of his trips to Rome or Brussels?"

Marcello chews his cigar and exhales a stream of smoke at a bystander who is trying his best to listen in on their conversation.

The man moves away, sharply.

"Okay, you have a point. But it is interesting that you talk of Brussels and business trips. We are to understand that this little cockerel has the two passports – British passports – he has found on the Mara." He grins once more and raises his eyebrows in mock surprise. "I hope you have yours safe."

"Sure," Ric lies.

"It is only that I was intending to ask you," he pauses to assemble his words, "what it is that you were looking for when you came to the yard yesterday? Was it these passports, or was it something else?"

Ric smiles, "The passports were part of what I was looking for."

"Then I am sure whatever else it is that you have lost will turn up. Everything is somewhere, eh?" He nudges Ric gently in his ribs and winks at him. "Now, what did that old fool Nino tell you?"

"Oh," he drags his reply out, "he spun me a yarn about Vincenzo Maggiore, your grandfather, trying to help some deportees escape from Devil's Island in the 1930s."

Marcello nods. "This is possible. The Maggiore family has never been Fascist."

"It turns out that on this occasion the deportees were betrayed to the Carabinieri. He went on to tell me that your grandfather sent my great-grandfather, Antonio Sciacchitano, to warn the deportees, but that he got to them too late. Unfortunately they were ambushed and killed by the Carabinieri. Sciacchitano was picked up by a patrol later that night and Old Nino's father had to spirit him off the island. He told me Vincenzo organised a mock funeral to convince the authorities my great-grandfather was dead. Old Nino reckons there is no corpse in Sciacchitano's grave."

"Mm," Marcello mutters, "I told you he was mad. That old fool has nothing better to do with his time than picture the sailboats in the Canale di Salina and make up ridiculous stories. It is all that is left to him, his imagination."

"So you think it's likely to be a shade fanciful?"

Marcello coughs, clears his throat and spits, "It is a nice story. Believe it if you will. Now, if you will excuse me, I must go. I would say we will meet for a beer in the Corta at *passeggio*, but maybe it would be better if the little cockerel does not see us together."

But as Ric is reminded of Talaia, he turns his attention to the beach only to see the diminutive Commissario watching them.

"It might be a bit late for that, Marcello."

44

By the time Ric arrives at La Casa dei Sconosciuti, Valeria is sitting out on her patio, gazing out to sea. She doesn't turn towards him when he walks over; instead she sips from her glass and says, "You make enough noise for an army, Ric. Why don't you make yourself a drink and freshen mine while you are there?"

He mixes them both *Aperol Spritz*, careful to pour it the way she likes it: Aperol over ice before adding the Prosecco and soda.

"I saw you talking to Il Velaccino," she remarks, casually. "Did you ask him if he has taken what you have lost?"

"No, I didn't need to."

"You have found it?"

"In a manner of speaking."

At this, she turns and studies him. "You have no need to speak in riddles, Ric. If you do not want to tell me who has found it, I am not bothered to know." Her tone is a shade offhand, as if he has annoyed her by refusing to confirm something she has no doubt already guessed. She stubs out her cigarette, sips her *Spritz* and puts down her glass. "Ric, you should know that the police have been here asking questions about you."

"Why am I not surprised?" he replies.

"It suggests they think you have some involvement in Candela's murder."

"What did they want to know?"

"Oh, the usual: how long have I known you, how do I know you and what sort of person are you? That kind of thing."

"What did you tell them?" he asks, watching for the slightest change in her expression which might suggest she is not being straight with him.

"I told them the truth. I said you are a friend of Camille's and that you are searching for your family history; that is all. But, this Commissario Talaia is no fool. He is not the kind to ask questions he does not already know the answers to." Valeria pauses. "He asked me if I knew of any reason why you would want Candela dead or if it was possible that you were the kind of man who would be hired to commit a murder."

"And?"

"And I told him that, as far as I was concerned, I could see no reason why you would want any part in this business. I hope you don't mind, but I told him about your wife and what happened to her while you were in Afghanistan. I hoped by doing so, he would see that you have no motive."

"What was his reaction to that?"

"He said, "Every man has motive; to find it is simply a question of understanding the man". As I have just said, this kind of policeman is not a fool."

"Thank you for being so direct with him. Let's hope he's got the message."

"But," Valeria replies sharply, "he also told me he has found the passports you told me about; the passports that are not yours..."

"Yes, I know. They are a bit difficult to explain away. The Commissario came to see me yesterday morning. And last night he was hanging around the Maddalena. I guess he was waiting to see if anyone was going to return to the scene of the crime. We had quite a talk, apostolic conundrums mostly. He likes to talk around the houses, does the Commissario."

"So what do you think will happen?"

"Well, I would imagine he'll find who the passports belong to and where the owners lost them; then, he'll check where and when I became the owner of the Mara and put two and two together." He thinks for a moment, before pointing out, "I'm beginning to get the most unpleasant feeling I'm being fitted up for Candela's murder."

"Forgive me for saying, Ric, the next thing you know the police will be saying it is your gun they have found."

And again Ric struggles to remember whether or not he wiped the gun clean after that morning at Porticello.

Noticing his discomfort, she attempts to pour oil on his troubled water, "Oh, Ric, why would anyone want to drag you into this mess? There must be a queue of suspects as long as the Aqua Claudia Viaduct for that particular crime. Girolamo Candela may have promised Lipari much, but most people disliked him enough not to concern themselves with who killed him. We should be grateful some public spirited citizen has done us this kindness."

"I didn't realise he was that unpopular."

"He was a politician. As I have told you, they are all unpopular."

"Sure, I remember you saying. But just how unpopular was he? I understand some people believe he was in on the attempts to assassinate the President of Sicily."

Valeria drags on her cigarette and thinks in silence for a few seconds. "He may have been; who knows? All I know is he was once a good communist and now he is no longer."

"What about Candela promising this brave new dawn, this great hotel and the free power, doesn't that count in his favour? Or do you think he's ruffled enough local feathers for someone to want to shoot him?"

"Yes, why not?" she replies, as though it would be a perfectly natural event. "People have been killed for far less. But to get this hotel built, whoever is behind it would need very deep pockets. There would be many mouths to feed along the way."

"How many?"

Valeria chuckles, a long, hopeless, inevitable chuckle, as though Ric is a child who, having just walked in through the school gate, has asked how long it will be before he can go home.

"To begin with, there is a succession of governing committees, all of whom think they should have a louder voice than the next. They cast their watchful eyes over the Aeolian Islands like Aeolus himself. There are the Ministries of Environment, Cultural Heritage and Foreign Affairs. Below these last two sits the UNESCO Commission for Italy and, after that, the regional committees, provincial committees, and even the consortium for ecological development. Of course, this is before you have climbed your way past the President of Sicily and the office for small islands, which answers directly to him."

"Sounds like quite an extended family."

She laughs, "Yes, it would be a long and very costly meal. These *professori, ingenieri, avvocati* and *dottori* are known for their appetites, and the only thing they like more than their food is the sound of their own voices. In Italy, nothing is simple; everything must be discussed. You are more likely to die of old age before a judge will sentence you to death. And obtaining planning permission can take even longer.

"But first, you would have to eat breakfast with the urban committee here in Lipari and most of the members of the urban committee have too much invested in this island to want to see someone else move in on their... what do the American gangsters call it? Their turf? The last time planning permission was requested was 2007, when some developers asked to build seven hotels on Lipari and one on Vulcano. They were laughed off the island."

"Is Marcello on the urban committee?"

She glances at him again, clearly puzzled by where he is taking their conversation, "Yes."

"And his brother?"

"Yes, his brother too."

"What's his brother's name?"

"Claudio. Why?"

"No great reason," Ric shrugs. "It's just that I see Marcello about the town all the time, but I've never seen or met his brother."

Valeria frowns and replies, "There is no reason why you should see Claudio; he is the little brother. He is not capable in the same way as Marcello. Claudio has a *negozio di ferramenta* in Canneto."

"When you say not capable, what do you mean?"

"What I mean is he stands in his brother's shadow. He is not an alpha male; Claudio is not built like a bull, not like his brother. He is what some would call the *piccolo della cucciolata*."

Ric searches the floor for a translation and then fastens on it, "The runt of the litter?"

"Yes, that is the right expression: the runt of the litter. If you have seen him, you would know him. Claudio is unusual, he has more hair on his face than on his head."

45

"Oh," she says, studying the combination of surprise and horror etched in his expression, "so you have seen him."

After a few seconds during which Ric recalls the body buried beneath the rubble in the padlocked room of the pumice warehouse, he replies quietly, "I may have, yes."

"Then you would not have forgotten his face."

"No," Ric replies; an image of Claudio's awful rictus grin leaps into his mind, "I guess I wouldn't. You said he has a *negozio di ferramenta* in Canneto; a hardware store."

"Yes, for building supplies and this kind of thing. Most of the building materials that come to the island are brought over by Marcello and his brother. Claudio only has a small shop, but it is a fairly exclusive business; what you might call a monopoly on the supply of construction materials."

"What's he like? I mean, I understand what you say about him being different to Marcello, but is he a popular guy like his brother?"

Valeria considers his question and decides, "In some ways. He is not married, so people assume he is gay. There is still some homophobia here, despite what others will tell you. But, they are right. When Claudio is not to be found in his shop, he is in Palermo. He goes to a club there: Exit, I think it is called. I have always found Claudio to be pleasant and polite. But then, most people are this way with me. After all, when one reaches a certain age one becomes venerated like the statue of San Bartolo, which, I am sure, is why the old people congregate there at *passeggio*."

"Does he get on well with his brother?" Ric asks, careful to employ the present tense.

"As far as I know, yes. But he has a difficult – no, one would say tempestuous – relationship with his father, which is probably why he was not present at the funeral on the day you arrived. His father was not one for modern attitudes, particularly when it comes to single men, so Claudio saw him only occasionally."

"Must have been awkward for him to stay away from the funeral," Ric remarks.

"Yes, I gather it has caused some argument within the family. But Claudio is a very sensitive creature and I am told he went to the mountains rather than risk causing a scene at the service and after in the cemetery." She pauses. "Of course, Marcello did not understand his brother's behaviour."

Only, Ric knows Claudio was never going to make it to his father's funeral; he was too busy waiting for his own; one which may never be held. And he wonders if Marcello had anything to do with his brother's death. His reaction could be what Commissario Talaia described as hiding in plain sight.

"Marcello's father was Onofrio?" he asks.

"Yes. Onofrio. He could be a very unforgiving man. They say he was one of the last of the *Vecchi Signori*: the old men, a senior figure."

"A godfather?"

Valeria laughs, "No, not in the sense of being the boss of a crime family. Onofrio was well respected and one who, like a magistrate, would provide judgements others would abide by. Life was Onofrio's way or…"

"The highway?"

"Yes, although I was going to say Aliscafo." She thinks, wondering how best to capture the spirit of the man. "There were times when Onofrio could be brutal when passing sentence. Those he judged against could be told to leave the island; those he looked upon kindly, could expect charity. Nobody ever questioned his authority."

"Is Marcello now the same?"

"Perhaps," Valeria replies, a shade solemnly. "We will see." She reaches over and lights the small lantern on the table.

"Did Onofrio die of natural causes? The date on his casket plaque suggested he was quite an age."

"I understand he fell. He lived on his own in a house up in Pirrera; the maid found him out on the terrace the next day. The house was open and nothing was missing, so the police were not suspicious. When the doctors examined him, they could not tell if he had died from a haemorrhage or from the blow to his head when he fell."

"There were a good number of mourners in his funeral cortège," Ric remarks, thinking out loud of the long procession in the Corso Vittorio.

"It is as I said; he was respected."

"I didn't see you amongst the crowd."

"No," she shakes her head, "I stay away from funerals; the cortège only ever leads to journey's end and that is a journey I would rather live without making. Cemeteries remind me of how little time I have left."

Ric is at a loss as to how to respond. The sadness in her tone and the inevitability of her assertion leave him temporarily winded. Slowly, he hauls his thoughts back on track. "Is Old Nino a *Vecchio Signori*, like Onofrio?"

"Yes, in a way, but he is not a man of such influence. The *Vecchi Signori* were men of power and influence. They controlled as much by the strength of their character as by their wisdom."

"Antonio Sciacchitano's headstone reads that he was *integerrimo*. Would that have made him one of the old gentlemen like Onofrio?"

"No," she replies, "I hate to burst your bubble, but being one of the *Vecchi Signori* means being something considerably more than being a *cittadino integerrimo.*"

Ric is lightly crestfallen, "But Old Nino told me that if you described someone as *integerrimo*, you thought of them as solid."

"And he was correct in telling you this. There must be worse ways of being remembered other than by being solid. He was solid?" she repeats, dreamily. "I wonder what made him solid. You have seen Nino since yesterday?"

"Yes, this morning, his girl Ariana passed me a note in which Nino had written that he wanted to see me. I walked over the hill and had lunch with him. He told me an extraordinary tale about how his father spirited Antonio Sciacchitano away to Baarìa, in Sicily, after he had become mixed up in the escape attempt of the three deportees. You told me the story, if you remember, about Drago, Tamboia and Farinelli, and about how they were killed trying to escape. He seems to think there is no corpse in the grave belonging to Sciacchitano; seems to think the whole thing was set up by Vincenzo Maggiore to fool the authorities into thinking Sciacchitano was dead."

Although the sun has now set, Ric can make out her expression from the light cast by the small lantern and the glow of her cigarette when she draws on it. Valeria is looking at him very intently.

"Baarìa, Nino said?" she asks. "Are you sure he said Baarìa?"

"Yes. Why?"

"Because Baarìa is what they used to call the land that runs down to the sea. And Baarìa is the old name for what is now called Bagheria. And Bagheria is where I was born." The wavering emotion in her voice betrays the nostalgia his naming the town has provoked. Her tone is both soft and sad, and almost lilting, giving the impression it is floating in from the obsidian sea before them.

"And," she begins slowly, "this escape I told you of? It took place in 1930, which is the same year in which I was born?" Valeria lets the question hang in the cool evening air; it is not a question she intends for him to answer.

Ric waits for her to draw open the curtain of her thoughts and says, "Valeria, when I looked around the cemetery a couple of days ago — when I found Antonio Sciacchitano's grave — I came across the Maggiore mausoleum. I suppose I looked around it because you'd introduced me to Marcello and I just happened to be in the Corso Vittorio when his father's cortège passed by. You've never seen it?"

"No," she replies from the shadows, "I told you, I stay away from cemeteries. I am inclined to cross myself, ask for forgiveness and walk on by; nothing more. Only God will persuade me into a cemetery. Only *He* has that much power. Why?"

"Antonio Sciacchitano's grave — the one Nino thinks is empty — tells us he died in July of 1930. But there is also a casket plaque in the Maggiore mausoleum which suggests that a member of their family, Katarina Maggiore, died that same month, on the 18th. I was intrigued by the coincidence."

He takes a generous sip of wine and pictures the casket plaque below Vincenzo's and beside Onofrio's. And he remembers Nino saying that Vincenzo Maggiore was involved in arranging the botched escape of the deportees. Ric hesitates as the opaque images before his eyes become clearer: a frightened man and a petrified girl, standing before an old fisherman, wringing their hands, begging him to take them away from Devil's Island. And Ric is not absolutely sure, if Valeria does provide him with the answer to his next question that he expects, whether he should prise open the casket of her past. But he cannot help himself.

"What was you mother's name, Valeria?"

She sighs very slowly and hangs her head in her hands before mumbling softly, "Katarina."

46

The silence is broken only by the cry of a herring gull. To Valeria, it must sound as though the soul of her mother is lamenting the island she deserted in her youth.

Valeria shifts uneasily in her seat and replies a shade angrily, "This is far too much information for an old woman to contemplate in one evening, Ric."

"I can imagine."

"But what are you saying by this?" she responds, with more than a hint of incredulity. "Are you saying that your great-grandfather ran away with my mother? That perhaps you and I are in some way related? Because, if you are, I would say you have spent too much time with Nino and that the idle fascinations of an old blind man are, like some ridiculous hallucinogenic drug, stimulating your imagination. We don't even know for sure if this Antonio Sciacchitano is related to you. Perhaps Camille has sold you the first half of a story, only for Nino to supply you with the second?"

Ric is not sure how to answer. On the one hand he knows full well the information Camille has given him is, at best, tenuous and as for Nino, he has no idea whether he can rely on the visions of a man who sees only through his mind's eye. "I can't argue with that."

Valeria is clearly considering the implications of what he has just told her. "If this is true, then this would mean Marcello is my cousin.

And," she adds with a curious, almost condescending dose of disdain, "this means that this Antonio would have been more than a simple travelling companion for my mother; it means he would have been her lover."

"I take your point," he replies, a little wounded by her arrogance. "But what if your mother was pregnant? Wouldn't that have been sufficient motivation for her to run away?"

"Ric, there is no way a man of Vincenzo's standing would allow his daughter to consort with a man who was little more than a manual labourer. The Maggiore family were respected; they had standing. A daughter who would bear a child out of marriage would have brought disgrace to their house." She pauses to think. "Of course, she would run away. At that time, it was not unheard of for a father to disown his daughter if she was pregnant outside of marriage. I told you, hypocrisy knew no bounds back then."

"Which means?"

Valeria lights a cigarette. Ric is certain she is buying time to think.

She smokes in silence for a full minute before carrying on, "All of which means that either there is a possibility that I am Marcello's cousin, in which case there are two graves in the cemetery which lie empty, or Katarina Maggiore died of perfectly natural causes in the same month Sciacchitano fled from the island and therefore my mother is no relation of hers. It is as complicated or as simple as that."

"Which option would you prefer?" Ric asks, trying to lighten the mood.

He doesn't so much see Valeria straighten up in her seat, as feel her do it.

She grinds the stub of her cigarette into the ashtray. "Ric, you think this is some kind of humorous discovery you have made, eh?"

But before he can extend any kind of olive branch for what she perceives to be his inappropriate levity, she carries on, "Well, it is not.

Because even though this happened more than eighty years ago, it does not lose its significance. It is the kind of scandal that can ruin a family and bring down a house, particularly one as reputable and influential as the house of Maggiore."

Ric's embarrassment warms the air between them, "I apologise, Valeria, I didn't mean to be flippant. I thought you would be pleased to know this woman might have been your mother. You said the other day you never knew your father; I thought this might help you track him down."

"You think he would be still alive? He would have to be older than Nino," she scoffs.

In the face of her indignation and out of respect for her years, Ric feels there is little else he can do but retreat. "I apologise, Valeria. I didn't understand the affect this information would have. Please don't think I knew where this conversation was going; I had no idea Baarìa was the same place as Bagheria. I suppose Nino uses the old name out of habit."

She is silent again, smouldering at him across the table. And if the stars aren't enough, Ric is sure her wrath contains sufficient energy to illuminate the darkest of shadows.

"Please, tell me, what can I do to atone for such a misjudgement?" He waits and watches her hide behind the redoubt of her silence.

Valeria's eyes glow in the light of the lantern and slowly the searing heat of her displeasure dissipates, allowing the cool of evening to disperse the cloud which has blown up between them.

"Ric," she leans forward, resting her chin on her hands and gazes at him, "you are a young and very attractive man. If I was but thirty years younger, I would take you to my bed and make you the gift of my body. Sadly, this is no longer a gift any man would welcome, and with good reason. However, women have other ways of persuading men to do their bidding. So, let me appeal to you as the mother I would like to have been. This information you have uncovered; let us keep it between ourselves. Please, let it be our secret. If it is true that Antonio Sciacchitano was your great-grandfather, then you have found another piece to the jigsaw of your heritage. After all, this knowledge affects no one other than you. But as far as the idea that I am related to Il Velaccino goes, this knowledge will affect many others, not least an old lady who would rather remember her life as she has known it, not how others will interpret it. Please, Ric, swear to me that you will not speak to anyone of this?

"Swear this to me as though I was your own mother."

47

Ric wakes in the bedroom of his *monolocale*. His head is thick, his muscles ache and the rhythmic drip of the kitchen tap reminds him it was an Italian who invented Chinese water torture, not an Oriental. He feels exhausted, as though he has passed the night swimming against a rip tide of emotion.

He avoided the Maddalena on his way home in case the little Commissario was watching and waiting for him at the corner of the Piazza San Bartolo. On leaving the Casa dei Sconosciuti, he decided the policeman was probably already running short of blank pages in his notebook of coincidences, so he took the winding road past San Nicola rather than the shorter route through Portinente. If he was followed, he neither noticed nor cared.

This morning his, or rather Marcello's, *monolocale* seems smaller than at any time since his first night. The walls threaten to box him in and when he opens the shutters and looks out into the narrow alley, the margin of blue sky running above and between the eves of the terraced houses appears much thinner than before. He feels as though he could reach out and touch the balcony opposite only to find out it is not real.

Ric is aware that, so far, he has been woken by first Valeria, then the curious little policeman and more recently Nino's maid, Ariana. He wonders who is yet to come to disrupt his morning.

But no one disturbs the peace of the vico. Women go about their washing and pensioners, legs bowed from the years of malnutrition in their youth, hobble unhurriedly down to the Corso Vittorio to exchange gossip with the fishmonger at his *Ape*.

Ric knows it is only a matter of time before Commissario Talaia comes looking for him; the thought provokes a hollow, painfully impotent anticipation deep in the pit of his stomach. If the passports don't have his prints on them, there's a chance the Beretta will. Someone, and all the fingers would seem to point towards Marcello, has stolen it with the express intention of shooting Candela with it and laying the blame at his door.

But Ric knows it can't have been Marcello, as the cigar-chewing, bull of a man was out fishing with him: they both heard the shots. But Ric also reckons Marcello is not naive enough to have committed the crime himself. Clearly, he is a big enough fish to have employed someone else to do his dirty work. Perhaps the wiry Salvo is his man or, perhaps, one of the men who roughed him up?

The only logical conclusion can be that he is being set up to take a fall. It must be why Marcello has been so generous in loaning him the room; it must be why Marcello took him fishing on that particular night, to ensure his alibi would be, at best, questionable; and it explains when the Beretta was stolen and why Marcello was so ready and willing to take the Mara out of the water.

Ric sits on the edge of his bed and weighs his options. They are simple: front up to Commissario Talaia about the gun and the passports, sit around and wait for the situation to spiral even further out of control, or get up and go out and force others to show their hand. The first risks his annihilation at the hands of the Sicilian justice system: he recalls what Valeria said, "You are likely to die of old age before a judge will sentence you to death." The second is tantamount to surrender and he knows that would leave too unpalatable an after-taste. But the third will at least afford him some comfort in the knowledge that he is trying to fight his way out of a cul-de-sac someone else appears hell-bent on backing him into.

He shakes his head and rubs his face in frustration. All he knows for certain is that, with the Mara as good as impounded, there is nothing he can do to hasten his departure; that Valeria is very possibly related to Marcello; and that Marcello's brother, Claudio, lies dead in the dust of the deserted pumice warehouse at Pietra Liscia. Perhaps, he wonders as he tries to climb into a shirt and jeans without troubling his shoulder, it is a more muscular approach to solving the problem that is required.

He locks the door carefully behind him, considers taking the key with him rather than leaving it beneath the pot where others can get to it, but realises that apart from the few Euros in his pocket, he has nothing left worth stealing.

The brioche from the *pasticceria* and the sharp air of morning go some way to improving his mood as he strolls down the Via Roma to the Corta.

Sandro is plying his trade, but when he spots Ric he looks away and pretends he hasn't seen him.

Giuliana, too, tries her best to pretend the same, but she doesn't make such a convincing job of it.

Ric walks over to the café and pulls out a chair.

The pinch-faced owner, sitting at the back, mutters something to Giuliana before she has no choice other than to serve Ric.

"*Salve, Ric,*" she greets, nervously.

"*Buongiorno, Giuliana, un caffè espresso, per favore.*"

She hesitates, before replying, "*Scusate, Ric, siamo chiusi.*"

Ric makes a play of looking round at the few tourists taking their breakfast and repeats, "*Un caffè espresso, per favore, Giuliana. Grazie.*"

She hesitates again, glancing to look for guidance from the owner.

Giuliana turns her back so that the owner cannot read her lips.

"*Ric, per favore,*" she pleads. Her half-hearted attempt at a smile touches a nerve in him; if she had her way, there is no doubt Giuliana would bring his coffee right away, but he would be doing her a considerable favour if he would leave without further fuss.

But Ric is not to be got rid of quite so easily. He pushes back his chair, stands up and looks past Giuliana and fixes the owner with an uncompromising glare.

The owner stares back, impassively.

"I'll take a coffee, please," Ric states more than asks.

The eye contact between them is direct and provocative; the man's face a picture of contempt. Eventually, the owner shifts his gaze back to the nervous girl and nods very slowly.

"*Grazie, Giuliana.*" Ric sits back down.

When she returns, she places the espresso before him and he notices her hand is shaking.

"*Molto gentile,*" he says softly.

The harbour is peaceful; fishermen are cleaning down their smacks and a few tourists are craning their necks to look up at the citadel looming over the square. Sandro sneaks a look at him every now and then.

Ric finishes his coffee and attracts Giuliana's attention, "*Il Conto, per favore?*"

She sidles up to his table, but does not remove her hands from her apron. "Today, the coffee is free," she whispers.

"*Grazie, Giuliana. Buona giornata.*" He stands up and looks over at the owner, who is still seated at the back, smoking a cigarette.

Ric nods. The owner inclines his head a fraction, but does not offer any kind of smile.

Before he walks up out of the square, he calls across to the *escurzionista* who persists in pretending he is not watching Ric, "Hey, Sandro, thought I'd pop up to Canneto, I need a couple of things for the boat and I gather there's a good *negozio di ferramenta* Marcello's brother runs. See you later."

The Garibaldi, too, is peaceful; a handful of tourists browse the knick-knacks on display and measure themselves against t-shirts and skirts. When he acknowledges them, the dark-skinned women grin, exposing their super-white teeth. In the Corso Vittorio the shopkeepers are laying out their wares: ceramic dishes decorated with images of blazing suns, fist-sized sculpted effigies of Roman gods, and postcard racks and newspaper stands. Valeria is absent.

The Carabinieri have given up their identity checks amongst the crowd on the pier; whoever they were looking for is long gone. An Aliscafo has just tied up; those passengers disembarking fight their way through those jostling to be first on to secure a seat.

The bus to Canneto takes no more than a few minutes and when it grinds noisily to a halt on the front, Ric takes a seat in the café he was introduced to by Marcello a couple of days before. If the portly waiter remembers him, he does not show it; the sorry-looking hound ignores him.

When his coffee arrives, Ric asks the location of the *negozio di ferramenta Maggiore*. The waiter waves him away along the front.

To the south the small desalination plant is overshadowed by the twin summits of Monte Rosa and, breaking the horizon to the north east, the cone-shaped volcano of Stromboli coughs a single plume of white smoke. Lazy dust devils dance up the road, each one burst by scooters that weave, whine and buzz, and clouds of exhaust gas issue from the grocery truck, forcing shopkeepers to cover their mouths.

The village which fronts the crescent bay holds one road up, along the front, and one road back a few houses behind. He locates the *Ferramenta Maggiore* on the corner at the northern end, where the two roads meet.

From the outside it looks exactly as he expects. Brooms, brushes, acro jacks, props and assorted scaffolding lean like tall, thin men waiting for a bus. There is a yard down the side where men in brick-dusted vests and shorts are loading an *Ape* with sand and cement.

Ric wanders inside; the air-conditioning chills and a radio blares a lively phone-in. A woman is busy burying her face in a fashion magazine.

"*Claudio Maggiore, per favore?*" he asks her.

She drags herself away from the magazine and tips her horn-rimmed spectacles back up her nose, "*No, non è qui.*" She waits for a reply.

"*Più tardi?* Will he be in later?"

"*No, non vieni oggi.*" She doesn't really look at him; she just looks vaguely in his direction, hoping he will be going soon.

"*Domani?*"

She shrugs, "*No, è in vacanza.*"

"Of course," he mutters beneath his breath, "a very long holiday."

It occurs to her to slide a notepad and pen across the counter to him, "*Vuole lasciare un messaggio, eh?*"

"*No, grazie,*" he replies and turns to leave.

Just as he gets to the door, a black saloon car pulls up outside. The wiry Salvo is driving, but it is Marcello who gets out. He does not realise Ric is watching him and his body language suggests he is agitated. But when he gets to the door and sees Ric, he calms.

Ric walks over and holds the door open for him to enter.

"*Buongiorno,* Ric," he says, scowling. "You want something from the shop? First, you come to my yard without telling me. Now you come to my shop. If you need something, you must tell me and I get it for you."

"Hi, Marcello. You look a little flustered; not trouble with the Mara, I hope? How's she doing?"

Marcello flicks the butt-end of his cigar into the gutter. "No, no problem with the Mara; she is in reasonable shape. Her motor will be fixed by tomorrow afternoon; the propeller shaft the next day. But I cannot put her back in the water until the little cockerel comes to me and gives me permission. You know this, eh? Now, what brings you to my store?"

265

"Oh, I was reading about the new desalination plant and it set me to think that I needed to do something about that dripping tap in the kitchen back at the house. Didn't feel right letting that tap drip all day, what with water being so short in the high season. And, seeing as you've been so generous in letting me stay in the house while you're fixing the Mara, I thought I'd repay your kindness by fixing the tap."

Marcello grunts, "There is a *ferramenta* in the Corso Vittorio. Why come to Canneto?"

Ric smiles. "Didn't think about it until I was sitting in the café round the corner. Valeria said your brother had a *ferramenta* here and the waiter at the café told me where it was; thought I'd pick up some tape while I remembered."

He grunts again, "If you want some tape, I will give it to you." He pushes past Ric and waves for him to follow. "But you will need a wrench; this I can give you also."

Marcello walks up to the counter and barks at the girl, who quickly slides her magazine below the counter.

She skulks away to the back of the shop and returns with a roll of pipe repair tape and an adjustable wrench, both of which she hands over to Ric.

"*Grazie,*" he says to the girl. "Thank you, Marcello. Nice place your brother has here; must be a good business. I don't think I've met your brother," he lies, "I gather he's on holiday."

Marcello straightens, but disregards Ric's mention of his brother. "Okay, now I am going back. You want a lift?"

"Thanks for the offer, but haven't you got business here or were you just calling by?"

Marcello doesn't appreciate the inference that he has arrived merely to check up on what Ric is up to, "You think you know what I am doing better than I do?"

"That's not what I meant, Marcello. I simply thought that, bumping into you like this, I may have distracted you from what you were doing; that's all. Wouldn't want to get the blame for getting in the way of important business." He studies the bull of a man, looking to see whether he shares any facial resemblance with Valeria and wondering if there is the slightest chance the man might be her cousin.

Marcello, realising he is being studied, eyes Ric back suspiciously. "No, you will not get in my way; important or not. Now, I have to be going. I ask again, do you want a lift?"

"No thanks," Ric replies. "I might take a walk on up to Porticello; see what's about. Explore the old warehouses and pumice mines. Old Nino was telling me about them; they sound fascinating. You could hide an army up there."

And Ric is not certain, but he thinks he sees a hardening of Marcello's expression when he mentions the warehouses.

"Well, be careful in those places; the floors and ceilings are broken and you can fall and hurt yourself. They are not safe and many people have been injured when their curiosity is not contained." He squares up a bit, his posture perhaps a little aggressive. But he reconsiders for a second, pouting. "And there is nothing to see. Even the ghosts have lost interest in such places. Okay, I must go." He reaches across the counter and takes a plastic bag, which he hands to Ric. "Put this wrench in the bag. You are too clean to be *idraulico* and walking around with this in your hands will make people think you are looking to do someone harm." He glares at him and ushers him to the door. "Be careful, eh, Ric! *Ciao.*"

Marcello throws the girl a stern glance, turns and marches out of the shop.

As Marcello's car speeds away up the street, the girl frowns at Ric, mystified as to what has just passed between the two men.

48

The wrench is heavy in his hand and lends Ric a certain comfort. He doesn't need to go up to Pietra Liscia to know what is already hidden there, so he walks down to the front, where he orders a beer in a beachfront café and waits for the bus.

Once back in Lipari, he strolls up the Corso Vittorio. The benevolent godfather of the citadel watches over a tall, short-haired dog, its long tongue lolling as it patrols the cobbled street like an unofficial traffic warden. It pauses briefly by each of the pavement cafés to observe the customers and then, when it is doubly satisfied there are no new faces who might throw it a morsel, the leggy mongrel snaps at a fly and strolls on.

The peace of the Corso is broken by the buzz from a helicopter, which flashes across the rooftops and settles somewhere at the back of the town. In spite of the midday heat, the air in the vicos is cool. Nobody, as far as he can tell, is following him.

He bends to retrieve the key from beneath the pot, but it is not where he left it.

Ric turns quickly, but both ends of the vico are silent and deserted. Gripping the wrench in his right hand, he turns the handle and eases the door open, stepping back in case whoever it is inside rushes at him.

Nothing and no one stirs. He pulls the door back a little further, pauses, then steps inside.

Seated at his kitchen table is Commissario Talaia. He is wearing a blindingly bright white shirt and the jacket of his dark suit hangs over the back of his chair, suggesting he has been waiting a while. There is an old leather briefcase by his seat and he has a notebook open before him.

"Ah, Signor Ross, I was hoping you would not be too long. Please excuse this strangely clandestine method by which we meet, but I needed to have a talk with you." He glances at the wrench: "You were expecting less agreeable company?"

"Strangely, as you put it, Commissario, I wasn't expecting any company. But when I find my key is missing, I'm never quite sure who's going to be here when I walk in."

The Commissario picks his Homburg from the table and flicks a speck of dust from its rim. "The key? Yes, I apologise for taking it upon myself to make use of it. To stand around looking like I am about to burgle your rooms would, very naturally, make a policeman feel uncomfortable. Why don't you come and sit down; this is, after all, your table?"

Ric removes the wrench and the roll of tape from the bag and lays them on the washboard by the sink. He picks a cup off the rack, fills it with water and drinks.

"I see your tap is still dripping," Talaia remarks. "Has not anyone told you that even though this island is surrounded by water, the people here value water as much as they value their insularity?"

Ric holds up the wrench, waves it and raises his eyebrows.

"Oh, yes, I see; stupid of me," Talaia replies.

Ric sits, slowly. "Can I get you a glass of wine or a beer, Commissario Mr Talaia?"

The offer elicits a warm genial smile from the little man. "Unofficially, I can see no reason why I should refuse your offer; a cold beer would be most welcome. But, sadly, officially I cannot."

"A plate of *antipasti*?"

Talaia grins. "Such hospitality is truly most welcome, but if I drank wine and ate *antipasti* with everyone I interviewed, I would be obese as well as short and to be short is perhaps enough of a challenge, so no. But, thank you."

"Coffee, then?"

The little Commissioner shrugs, "Please."

Ric makes the coffee and sets it before them. "Last evening I was walking back from a friend's house, but, rather than take the Maddalena and have you think I was stopping by the Piazza San Bartolo for a gloat, I walked round by San Nicola. I hope you didn't wait too long?"

Talaia shakes his head and tut-tuts, playfully, "This word gloat: I like it, I really do. It is so expressive. I must try it when next I meet with enough success to justify myself such a bourgeois reward. But last night I was not in Lipari, I was in Palermo finding out some more information about Signor Candela and what he has been doing before he came here."

"Did you find out what you wanted to know?" Ric asks.

He wobbles his head and purses his lips. "That is for me to know, one might say."

"So to what do I owe the pleasure?"

"Well, Signor Ross—"

"Look, Commissioner, if we are going to keep meeting like this, perhaps you ought to call me Ric."

Talaia raises a small slender hand, "Okay, why not? Please call me Maso, except in company; then perhaps it would be better to be formal."

"Works for me, Maso. You obviously want some information from me, what would you like to know?"

"Please, refresh my memory about where you were the evening Signor Candela was shot." He takes a pen from his jacket pocket, flattens a page of his notebook and expects.

"As I think I told you, I was out fishing for squid with Marcello

Maggiore. And, as you already know because he tells me you have been to see him and unofficially impounded the Mara, he has my boat in his yard at Canneto. In these parts they seem to know him as Il Velaccino."

"Ah, yes, the sailmaker," Talaia replies, writing the name in his book, "I have heard people talk of him by this name. I don't understand why they refer to him in this way, especially when his business interests extend far beyond those of the average sailmaker, do you?"

"Beats me, Maso! Perhaps he just likes making sails."

Talaia sips his coffee, winces and reaches across the table for the sugar. "So, Ric, tell me, you went fishing with Signor Maggiore?"

"As I said, we went fishing, we caught some *totani* and got run down by a big blue boat that wasn't showing any navigation lights." Ric lowers his head towards Talaia and fixes him with a knowing look. "I was knocked overboard," he makes to tap at his forehead, "and Signor Maggiore's boat was sinking so he couldn't hang around to pick me up. I swam ashore from about a mile out, walked to the Corta, drank a couple of *grappa* and that's the end of it." Ric spreads his arms, "Simple as that."

The policeman sips and mulls over the flavour of the coffee. He purses his lips and then smacks them quietly: "Not bad, Signor Ross."

"My alibi or the coffee?"

"Both, except the coffee, it is plain to see, is in the cup." He pauses and wipes his mouth on his handkerchief. "Fortunately for you, your alibi has been verified by this man they call Il Velaccino."

"Funny that, I had a feeling it might not be."

Talaia is surprised and writes this down, "Why wouldn't he?"

"Not sure; just a feeling in my bones."

"At this time, we have no reason to doubt Signor Maggiore. But it is interesting to me that you have your doubts. Are you not living in a *monolocale* that is the property of Signor Maggiore?"

"Mm, I am."

"Then why would you doubt his generosity?"

Ric thinks for a moment and changes tack. "There's an *escurzionista* who hangs around down in the Corta, goes by the name of Sandro; don't know his surname; long, curly hair, sloping shoulders. I saw him on the same evening before I met Maggiore at Portinente. He might speak for me."

"He might," Talaia replies. "However, it is the time between your meeting with this *escurzionista* and your return to the Corta that interests me."

Ric grins a shade haplessly, "About the same time Candela was shot?"

"For certain, Ric."

"Well, Maggiore and I heard the shots from out in the water, and that was seconds before we were run down. I'd have done well to swim ashore, do for Candela and get down to the Corta in such a short time, but I suppose if Marcello Maggiore vouches for me, you'll just have to take his word for it or..."

"Or what?" Talaia asks.

"I don't know; that's up to you, Commissario. If you think Candela gave me this cut when I shot him, you've probably no alternative but to view me as a suspect."

"I wish it was so simple, Ric. One of our local policemen remembers seeing a man — a man who answers your description — at the bottom of the Maddalena. He recalls the man was soaking wet and that he had an injury to his face."

"I told you, I'd just swum ashore. I don't suppose he noticed the welts from the jellyfish stings on my arms too? They were that painful I'd have traded them for a shot at Candela." He offers his forearms for the policeman to inspect; the welts, though no longer raised, are still clearly visible.

Talaia nods and jots this point down, "Yes, I believe they can be very unpleasant."

Ric looks up sharply, "It's that simple, Commissario. That's the length and breadth of it."

"You know this Signor Maggiore well? Do you think you can trust him?" Talaia asks.

"I don't know him well enough *to* trust him, if that's what you mean? He's been extremely generous in allowing me to stay in his *monolocale* and he seems to know what he's doing when it comes to the Mara. As yet, I see no reason why not to trust him. But as I've told you already, I was introduced to him by the lady I met when I first arrived."

"Ah, yes," Talaia looks up, as if seeing the frescoes on the ceiling of the Sistine Chapel for the first time, "I spoke with her, La Signorina Vaccariello. A remarkable actress; so senior in her years and yet still so very beautiful. This lady... I understand some of the people think she is a witch. They call her La Strega; a curious name for one so elegant and refined. There is a film, La Strega in Amore: the Witch in Love," he says, lifting a finger to his lips and tapping them slowly in thought. "I think the book is by a different name. Ah, yes, I have it. The book is Aura, written by Fuentes. And, if I remember correctly, it is about an old woman with a very beautiful daughter, and at the end of the book they turn out to be the same person; quite alarming, but also strangely erotic."

Ric chuckles, "Commissario Talaia, you really are a mine of useless information. Are you suggesting Valeria sheds a few years by the light of the silvery moon?"

"If only one could have that opportunity," Talaia suggests, wistfully. But, he remembers he is supposed to be concentrating and frowns. "This woman told me you have your own reasons for coming to Lipari. And please," Talaia winces, "please don't give me any of that *stronzate* – sorry, I mean bullshit – about Aeolus blowing you this way; I have heard this once too often."

Ric sighs and chuckles. "I came here to find out about my great-grandfather. His name might have been Sciacchitano. A fellow I met in Corsica told me there was a possibility he came from here."

Talaia raises his thin eyebrows. "Ah, I understand; *uno che cerca*, you are one of those. Yes, we have many who come to Sicily to search."

"Search?"

"Yes, you search for your *avi*, your ancestors. You are looking for a history; a convenient history, perhaps. There has been much emigration from these islands; so now, it is a common pastime for people to return to search for their *avi*."

"A convenient history?"

Talaia grins. "Yes, a convenient history. The human race likes to know what it is that makes them the way they are, and understanding their ancestors provides them with an excuse for their often poor behaviour."

"You're quite the sociologist, Maso. And there I was lingering under the misapprehension you were a dinosaur."

The little man shrugs and pouts, "Oh, human nature is constructed with many delicate balances. Tell me, Ric, this woman, how do you come to know her?"

"I was given her name by a friend in Corsica. He provided me with the information about my forebear and suggested I look her up. La Signorina Vaccariello has, like Signor Maggiore, been very helpful."

"*Bene*, it all fits very well then. And yesterday afternoon, when we searched the bay at Portinente, both Il Velaccino and La Strega were present, as were you also. Do you have a nickname, Ric?"

"Haven't been here long enough to earn that kind of respect and don't intend to be here much longer. That is, once you've released the Mara. Why?"

Talaia shrugs, "I don't know. Il Velaccino, La Strega, it would make more poetic sense if you were known by a stage name. Perhaps you are Leporello, who does Don Giovanni's bidding. But then, no: Il Velaccino is not what one would imagine for Don Giovanni, he is not so suave perhaps. And as for La Strega...? Although I think Mozart intended for us to view his opera more as *buffa* than *seria*..."

Ric grins, "Talking of *opera buffa*; that was a pretty good show you put on yesterday afternoon."

Talaia sucks his teeth and moans, "Mm, I agree, it was. But this was, I think, more *buffa* than we need if the Liparoti are to take us seriously, which brings me on to why I am here."

"Which is?"

"This gun. Or, more accurately, this Beretta which has been recovered from the shallow waters of the bay at Portinente." Talaia waits and watches.

Ric has to think quickly: playing first one to blink will condemn him, as Talaia will reason by his lack of response that he has something to hide. Leaping without looking, though, is equally dangerous.

"What about it?" he asks.

Commissario Tommaso Talaia smiles, "Yes indeed, what about this gun. Tell me, Ric, have you seen this Beretta before?"

"Maso," Ric leans forward and rests his forearms on the table, "look, I'm sure you've checked out my passport, so you will know that what I've told you is true; namely that I was in the Royal Marines. I am also sure that by now you will have found out that I completed tours of Iraq and Afghanistan. I've seen enough guns to last me a lifetime."

This time, Talaia doesn't smile, he grins in appreciation, "That is an excellent answer, Ric. But I am not talking about guns in general; I am talking about this particular pistol, this Beretta."

"But, that's precisely what I am saying, Maso. I watch a man in a monkey suit pull a gun out of the water at thirty yards and you ask me if I've seen it before?" Ric tries not to overplay his incredulity; he doesn't want Talaia to mistake his sarcasm for cynicism.

The little cockerel sighs, suggesting he has heard it all before. "Okay, okay! Ric, let me ask you if you own a Beretta?"

"No, Maso, I don't." Strictly speaking the Beretta still belongs to the Corsican, although Ric is aware that the rule of possession being nine-tenths of the law is likely to be just as valid in Sicily as it is anywhere else.

"You are not going to make this easy for me, are you, Ric?" He takes another sip of his coffee.

"Come on, Maso, work it out," Ric fixes the policeman with a deadpan expression, "if I found I was missing a pistol, I'd go directly to the police station to report it, like every other solid citizen."

Talaia chokes, coughs and a spray of coffee issues from his nostrils. "Excuse me; I think, perhaps, you are joking." He wipes his nose and blows it very loudly for one so small.

Ric grins, "I am."

"So British," Talaia mumbles through blowing his nose once more, "to joke when the outlook is so gloomy."

"Bleak," Ric corrects.

At this, Talaia rests his pen and pauses. His eyes seem almost black, like the obsidian Ric has seen for sale outside the diver's shop, and his face is pale and lined from a lifetime of taking notes. "Okay, bleak. I thank you for correcting my poor English."

"Strangely enough, Maso, I was thinking your English is unusually good. Where did you learn it?"

"Oh, in school, watching movies, listening to music, like everyone. I have found it pays to speak other languages; most people like to communicate and I have found other police forces provide information more willingly if you remove the barrier of language." He pauses, thinking.

"I speak French also," Talaia adds. "In fact I spoke it yesterday to an acquaintance of mine in the *Gendarmerie* in Ajaccio. You know where this is?"

"Sure, Corsica. If you remember, I told you it's where I bought the Mara."

The policeman sits back and stares at the ceiling for a second. "Yes, of course. Ah, I remember this now. Thank you for reminding me. Interesting place Corsica; another island, like Lipari but not so small.

"You know I searched the Mara? I am sure Signor Maggiore will have told you."

"He did. He said you'd found two passports and some money. As to knowing them…"

"Yes," Talaia waves Ric's objection aside, "quite a significant amount of money. Well, it happens that both of these passports belong to men, Englishmen, who were on holiday in the same *departement* of Corsica. It was where they lost them; near Porto Vecchio. Are you familiar with this part of Corsica, Ric?"

"You know I am, Maso. You would have checked out the papers for the boat when you searched it at Maggiore's yard yesterday morning."

The policeman's dark eyes light up. "And here, if you will excuse me for reintroducing my theory of coincidence, I have found that you bought your boat at approximately the same time as these two passports went missing."

"What can I say, Maso? Buy one boat, get two passports?"

Talaia frowns and purses his lips, "Now is not the time to be joking, Ric. You have told me that the evening Girolamo Candela was shot you were first fishing, then swimming in the sea off Portinente where this Beretta was found. If I find your fingerprints on this Beretta or, come to think of it, these passports, you will be in grave trouble. Our government, with its sensitivity to terrorism, has granted me great powers. If I feel it is necessary, I can speak with a *magistrato* and he will immediately give me permission to have you locked up for a long time, even before you come to trial. Do I make myself clear?"

"Loud and clear, Maso."

"*Bene!* I was hoping you would be an intelligent man." The little inspector appears to have grown taller in his chair. "Also, if you are sufficiently intelligent to understand, this Beretta which has been found, it has been sent to Messina, where it will be examined for fingerprints and, if possible, matched for the casings and the bullets which have been removed from Signor Candela's corpse."

"That's a lot of ifs, Maso."

Commissario Talaia glowers at him; his eyes almost disappearing beneath his furrowed brow. "But, Ric, the way things are going, I think it is highly probable that one or more of these coincidences will tell me who shot Girolamo Candela."

The silence perches on the table like a bird of prey.

"More coffee, Maso?" Ric asks, as much to drive the bird away as to divert the policeman's stare.

"No, but thank you." Talaia stands; he is almost as tall standing as he was sitting. He slides his notebook and pen into the breast pocket of his jacket and then puts the jacket on. "I am waiting for the forensic information about this pistol and I should have it by tomorrow morning. Please come to the police station. You know where it is?"

"On the Via Marconi?"

"Exactly. On the Via Marconi. Please be present at the police station at ten o'clock. If you do not come, I will immediately issue a warrant for your arrest. In the time between, do not even consider leaving the island," he glares across the table at Ric, "no matter who tells you it would be better for you. Do I again make myself clear?"

"Sure."

Commissario Tommaso Talaia sighs, picks up his briefcase and turns for the door. But in true detective style, he pauses as he pushes the door open and glances back, "Oh, by the way, Ric, you really should fix that tap." He steps out into the shady vico.

49

Ric is inclined to take the policeman's advice. He's tried needling Marcello, but that hasn't worked. And he can see no alternative other than to sit and wait until Talaia has the reports he's waiting on, by which time it will probably be too late to avoid arrest. As far as he can see, he might as well fix the bloody tap; that way, at least he will have gained some small sense of achievement for his labours.

Fortunately, there is a turn valve under the sink to stop the water supply to the tap, but unfortunately the headgear nut is seized solid and he skins his knuckles when the wrench slips off it.

"That's why everyone else has given up on trying to fix it," he mutters as he wraps a cloth around his bleeding hand.

The rest of the afternoon threatens to pass as slowly as the tap drips, so rather than suffer the torture of it, Ric decides to walk down to the Corso Vittorio.

Just as he is closing the door, he is distracted by a noise behind him. He whirls round expecting to be set upon.

An old lady steps out of the *monolocale* opposite and they bump into each other.

"*Scusi,*" he offers.

The old woman is garbed in trademark black. Her ankles are thick; her grey hair tied back in a bun.

"*Permesso,*" she says, trying to squeeze past him in the narrow alley.

Ric breathes in and flattens himself against the wall.

Once she is past, the old woman turns and eyes him suspiciously. "*Ora mi scusi ma...*" she says.

"Sure, grandma. Excuse me too?"

With no particular place to go and to avoid having to wait behind the old lady until she gets to the end of the alley, Ric takes the opposite direction up towards the Garibaldi.

At each corner he pauses and looks back to see if he is being followed. It would make sense for the little inspector to have him watched in case he decided to get off the island. But then, Talaia has his passport and the Mara is going nowhere, so what would be the point? Unless of course he is the hired gun Talaia suspects him to be, in which case common sense dictates he would have run by now.

The African women greet him politely as he emerges from the shade of the vico and the patron of the trattoria on the corner of the Maurolico seems intent on monitoring his every step as he pauses at the breach in the fortress walls. Ric starts up the broad steps of the Concordato which lead to the citadel.

Walking with purpose, he is warm and short of breath by the time he reaches the top. Ric halts before the cathedral and pretends to take an interest in the archaeological excavations below the apron. He glances back down the way he has come and sees a man making his way up towards him. The man wears sunglasses, blue chinos and a white short-sleeved shirt. He might be a tourist – he is consulting a map and talking on his cellphone – but he might not be. When he realises Ric is watching him, he stops and turns away.

Whilst the man is turned, Ric jogs up the last of the steep steps and strides over to the tall grey doors which lead into the Cattedrale San Bartolomeo.

The Baroque façade is almost South American in style, with a tall bell-tower at one corner and a statue of San Bartolo presiding over the entrance. The air inside is almost cold. Two lines of dark-wood pews grace the chequered-tile floor of the nave and tall marble and granite arches support a rib-vaulted ceiling, decorated with frescoes of San Bartolo, Saint Francis and The Immaculate Conception. Tourists stand and point and refer to their guides, and widows sit alone to censure the past and contemplate the future.

Ric slips to his right and waits.

The man he has seen outside steps into the cathedral. He crosses himself, nods towards the apse and looks round. He is middle-aged and olive-skinned, and when he notices Ric lingering, he looks away again and wanders off down the far aisle towards the silver effigy of San Bartolo.

In front of Ric is a portal, in the centre of which stands an alabaster baptismal font filled with small fragments of obsidian; a note beside it asks for one euro to contribute towards the cathedral's upkeep. Behind the font stands an arched, heavy wooden door.

He lifts the latch and pulls the door open. When he steps through, he finds himself in an L-shaped Norman Cloister, the vaulted ceiling of which is bland and much lower than that of the cathedral.

Too late, he realises there is no way out of the cloister other than the way he had come in. He turns to walk out, but as he does so the door opens towards him.

Ric squares up ready to confront the man who is following him—

But it is Marcello who appears. He glances behind him and closes the door.

"Hey, Ric, you are taking in a little culture, eh?" Out of respect for his surroundings, Marcello has dispensed with his cigar and in consequence appears almost naked.

"It doesn't hurt," Ric replies.

The bullish Liparotan has lost the harassed look of earlier and smiles and, also unusually, offers his hand for Ric to shake. There is no doubting Marcello's strength; his grip is unyielding.

When they turn to begin walking along the cloister, Ric says, "Popped up for confession or did your man tell you I was here?"

Marcello pouts and raises an eyebrow in conciliation, "Oh, he told me."

Ric is oddly reassured that Marcello does not feel the need to lie. "You like our cathedral?"

"Sure," Ric replies, "though I'm not much of a one for architecture. It seems a bit of a jumble."

"Yes, for sure it is. You know, of course, that San Bartolo was one of the twelve apostles? In the book of John, Jesus recognised him as being a man in whom he saw no deceit."

"*Integerrimo?*" Ric interrupts.

Marcello considers, "Yes, perhaps; a man of great integrity. Jesus told Bartolo he would see the heavens open before him, and he would see the angels of God ascending with the Son of Man; this is what you see painted on the ceiling of the cathedral. Unfortunately for him, Bartolo went to the Caucasus to spread the word of the Bible and the people there were not ready for what he was trying to teach them. They flayed him until he had no flesh left on his body. This is why he is the patron saint of *conciatori*; tanners, I think you call them. It was a cruel business. But then, the Caucasus is a barbaric place even now."

Ric thinks of the Armenian he met in Corsica.

As they stroll between the fluted, bare-stone columns lining the courtyard, Ric is taken with the feeling that the Liparotan is about to deliver him a lecture on the virtues of the saints.

"But…" Marcello continues, clearly pondering on what he has just said, "while I think of this, I think it is important to remember that Sant'Agata of Sicily had her breasts cut off because she preferred God to sex. So maybe we should not think the Caucasians so barbaric, in case we risk condemning ourselves."

"Sounds fair to me, Marcello."

"What I am getting at, Ric, is that a man lives and dies by what he believes. Some people believe what they believe so deeply it costs them their lives. I am sure you must have met people like this. You believe one thing, they believe the opposite, and it finishes with you having no alternative other than to take their life before they take yours."

Ric winces, as much for Marcello's benefit as his. "Fair, but you make it sound rather formulaic."

Marcello halts and steps in front of him, "But it is, Ric. It is a kind of formula. San Bartolo surrendered his life for what he believed. He refused to renounce his beliefs and paid the ultimate price. He invented the formula for integrity."

"I think he might have got the formula from his Lord and Master, don't you?"

Marcello shrugs, "Possibly, I suppose so. But San Bartolo taught us all a great lesson in how important it is to be this way."

"Okay, so Saint Bartholomew and my great grandfather, Antonio Sciacchitano, were men of integrity. I'm grateful to you for pointing that out."

"No," Marcello replies, turning back and walking on, "this is not what I am saying; although it is, of course, true." He quiets for a couple of strides as he loads himself up for whatever it is that he has come to ask Ric.

"Today you came to the *ferramenta* in Canneto and ask to speak with my brother, why was this?"

Ric is quick to reply, "I told you, Marcello, like I told you this morning: I was sitting in the café and remembered I wanted to fix the tap. Valeria said your brother had a hardware store in Canneto, so I thought I'd drop by and pick up the kit to mend it, which, by the way, I haven't been able to because the head nut's rusted on." He holds up his skinned knuckles in evidence.

"But you ask personally for my brother."

"Sure, why wouldn't I? Doesn't everyone tell you it's important to say who sent you? Even the *escurzionista* tells me that every time I go near a café or a restaurant I should say who recommended me to them. I'm not sure what you're getting at here, Marcello. Is there a problem with my meeting your brother?"

He turns again and studies Ric for a few seconds. He is trying to make up his mind as to whether Ric is holding back on him. Eventually he decides, "No, there is no problem. My brother went to Palermo last week. He goes often; I think he has a lady friend there. He is not due back until next week."

"Well, when he does come back, perhaps he can send someone over to fix that tap. I'm damned if I can."

"Sure, I will see to it."

They reach the end of the cloister and turn back.

"Ric," Marcello begins again, "I must ask you if you have been talking with this Commissario of police who is making himself very busy?"

There is little point in lying. If Marcello has had him followed to the cathedral, he will know Talaia has been to the *monolocale*: "Late this morning. I found him sitting at the kitchen table when I got back from Canneto. No *please*, no *thank you*; he simply used the key I'd left under the flowerpot outside."

Marcello shrugs, "It is what everyone does. What did the little cockerel ask you about?"

"Everything and nothing," Ric replies and then stares at a carving of birds feeding from a vessel. "Or better make that everyone and no one; much of the same stuff he asked about the first time he questioned me. He said you'd vouched for my whereabouts the evening of Candela's murder. He asked me how I'd come to meet you and Valeria, and asked about the passports. He asked me very directly if they were mine. Eventually he got round to asking me if – no, make that he implied – the pistol they fished out of the shallows at Portinente is mine too. Just before he left…" And Ric is about to tell Marcello that he is to report to the police station in the morning, but he holds back.

But the barrel-chested Liparotan is intrigued and again is watching him carefully. "Yes? Before he left he said… what?"

"He asked me if I thought I could trust you." Now the tables are turned and he has Marcello on the back foot. Now it is Ric's turn to watch for any sign that he might be lying.

"How did you answer, Ric? What did you say?"

"I told him you've been very helpful with repairing the Mara and very generous in allowing me to stay in your *monolocale*. I told him I saw no reason why I should not trust you. He also suggested your business interests were very extensive for the average *velaccino*."

"And you replied how?"

"I told him you liked making sails."

Marcello shrugs and shakes his head, "The world is a strange and sad place, eh? Why is it that people cannot appreciate the art in something as beautiful as a sail?"

Ric squares up in front of Marcello and looks him straight in the eye, "But can I trust you?"

At first he looks vaguely offended, but after a moment he softens, "Yes, of course, Ric. It is as I have said; San Bartolo has taught us that if you do not possess integrity, you possess nothing.

"You know, you have a hospital in London named after our Saint; St Bartholomew's, or Bart's I think is the name you would recognise. A *buffone* to the court of King Henry…"

"A court jester?"

"*Si*, a *buffone* called Rahere; he went to Rome on a pilgrimage. Unfortunately, he became unwell and rested here on Lipari. While he was here, San Bartolo came to him in a vision and instructed him to build a hospital in London. When he was recovered, he returned to London and built not only a hospital, but also a monastery. I believe he is buried there. It's a nice story, eh?"

Ric steps back, unconvinced. "Are you saying it's time for me to leave?"

"Perhaps."

"Commissario Talaia thought it would be a bad idea if I did."

Marcello is surprised, "He said this?"

"He did."

"This is interesting."

They arrive back at the heavy wooden door which leads into the cathedral.

Marcello is thinking. He pushes back the door, but then closes it again. "There is something here I do not understand, Ric. Once they check this pistol they have found, and if it proves to be the pistol that was used to shoot Candela, they will know who murdered him." He glances at Ric. "But I think this little cockerel already knows who has done this, so why has he not acted? That is the more important question." He pauses by the door. "I think our little Commissario is after something more. What, I don't know; but I will give it much thought.

"Now I must go," he says, holding out his hand for Ric to shake. "But before you leave the cathedral, be sure to have a look at the silver statue of San Bartolo. It would not be right to have walked all the way up here and leave without seeing it." He opens the door, "*Ciao*, Ric, and be careful. They will be watching you, eh?"

Ric grins back, "You and them both, Marcello!"

50

"*Salve, Nino!*"

The old man sits, leaning on his stick, and cocks his head a little to the left. To most, he looks as though he is politely acknowledging the greeting of one who knows him. But he is not; rather Old Nino is turning his head so that he can hear better the direction from which the greeting has come. He frowns momentarily, his face gaunt, his mottled skin stretched lean over his cheeks and jaw. Gradually, his expression changes to one of appreciation, "*Buonasera, Ric.* Come. Sit beside an old man and tell him of the adventures of your day."

The evening air in the Marina Corta is cooler than of late and clouds, like the wisps of grey hair on Old Nino's head, dull the sky. San Bartolo stands high on his pedestal, waiting to address an audience deaf to his teaching.

Ric takes a perch on the low wall.

"Can't say I've had much of a day, Nino. I've just been hanging around waiting for Il Velaccino to fix the Mara."

In truth, he thinks, his day has proved less than exciting. After his talk with Marcello, Ric sat for a while before the silver effigy of San Bartolo in the cathedral. He found the statue curiously pagan in style; a silver-gilt, bearded figure wearing a gold crown, a palm leaf in one hand and dagger in the other; the bunched muscles of a flayed torso in stark relief to the opulence of the jewelled sash draped around his shoulders.

San Bartolo's expression stayed with Ric as he walked the broad steps of the Concordato back down to the town; an old town made new by the vagaries of the internet, but an old town still dressed in the clothes of yesteryear.

What both Talaia and Marcello have said bothers him. The Commissario is obviously convinced that the Beretta will turn out to wear his prints. And Marcello is right; the policeman is after something more significant than merely bringing Candela's murderer to book. If not, then there is no reason why he would have left Ric free to walk the *vicolos* of the *città bassa*. He could simply lock Ric up and wait for the results rather than risk the possibility that he will find a way off the island. And then there is Marcello's less than subtle reference to the court jester, Rahere, leaving the island and returning to London; an encouragement which Talaia seemed to know was coming.

Ric scratches his head. "I feel like one of those deportees you told me about, Nino: a hostage to Devil's Island. I guess they must have felt the same, cooped up on a lump of lava with no chance of reprieve. No wonder some of them died trying to escape."

Nino sits impassive behind his dark glasses. Slowly, he turns down the corners of his mouth and tips his head forward, as though what the younger man says is true, but there is nothing to be done about it now.

"No, this was a time of great perversity. A man could be imprisoned simply for speaking to the same people he had been speaking to all his life."

They sit in easy silence; Ric watching, Nino listening. Boys who are nearly men skitter to and fro on their bicycles, showing off to girls who studiously ignore them; plump women slap their thighs and explode into fits of giggles at some reported indiscretion; and the thin metallic chimes from the campanile of the San Giuseppe strike eight times.

"I have been committing much thought to our talk of yesterday," Nino croaks, then clears his throat. "There is some more detail I have remembered."

"I'm all ears, Nino, if you'll pardon the expression."

Nino sniggers. "You will have to be young man. But this is more about eyes than ears; a subject, as you can imagine, which is close to my heart. Do you know the story of Santa Lucia of Syracuse?"

"No, I don't. Marcello told me about Sant'Agata having her breasts cut off: it all sounded pretty heathen."

"It was," Nino replies. "And it is true, eh? Jesus Christ has a good deal to answer for. But a few years after Sant'Agata was tortured to death, there comes a girl, Lucia. She was born to a wealthy family in Syracuse, though, sadly, her father passed on when she was young. Her mother became unwell, so the mother and daughter made the pilgrimage to the tomb of Sant'Agata in Catania in the hope that the mother would be cured. While they were there, the daughter was visited by Sant'Agata, who told her that her mother would be cured if Lucia gave her soul to God. Lucia, of course, agreed. The mother was cured of her illness and Lucia was so grateful to the Saint that she gave all her wealth to the poor. This enraged her mother, who in the meantime had found a husband for her." Nino silences, his throat too dry for him to carry on.

Young Ariana is watching them from down the way. She strolls over to them and hands the old man a bottle of water. "*Grazie, Ariana. Grazie.*" He sips.

"Now this is where the story has many different endings. One story tells how with no money, the fiancé refused to marry her and reported her vision to the Romans, who then put out her eyes because she would not turn them from God.

"But, another story tells how Lucia's fiancé was so handsome she refused to look at him in case *he* turned her eyes from God. In order to preserve her faith, Lucia put out her own eyes and cast them into the sea. This is where the legend of the eye of Santa Lucia comes from, although many people have their own opinions as to what actually happened to Santa Lucia of Syracuse."

"Forgive me, Nino, but what has Santa Lucia got to do with Antonio Sciacchitano?"

Nino taps Ric gently on the knee. "In good time," he chides. "Do you know the sea shell they call L'Oeil de Sainte Lucie?"

"I've seen it in Corsica," Ric replies, trying to remember the significance of it. "They call it the Eye of the Virgin or Venus. It's a small curved shell with a spiral in it, mostly white, but sometimes red. They believe it brings good luck. Although, rather like the different versions of Santa Lucia's story, there are those who believe it is the evil eye."

"Yes, you are right. The eye of envy," Nino states, pleased with his pupil. "They say that people who have this blood mark are occupied by a bad spirit who brings only confusion to their lives. The bird of prey has this eye too; the bird that is the evil spirit returned."

Ric feels the hair on the back of his neck rise and a sharp chill creeps up his spine.

Even though he knows the old man is blind, Old Nino turns his head as if to look directly at him. "My young friend, what I have remembered is that on his forehead, above his right eye, Antonio Sciacchitano wore the blood mark of Santa Lucia."

51

To Ric, it is as though a cold breeze is rippling through the Marina Corta, freezing the frame of activity; boys dismount their bicycles and look up, girls stop fussing over their charges and the old women cease their gabbling and stare to watch the sky.

Old Nino sniffs the air, "Mm, the clouds are driving the humidity before them. It will be warm this night, but there will be a storm at dawn. In the deserts of the south, the relatives of the Arab women in the Garibaldi are restless. The Scirocco is stirring."

Of course, Ric knows that birthmarks are not hereditary and that they are nothing more than a simple irregularity, like a mole. Yet the significance of the strawberry mark above his right eye is profound. Manou had convinced him of as much in Corsica and she had tried and failed to rid him of it with her magic.

"Nino," Ric says, but then his voice leaves him and he is unsure how best to proceed. The old man will doubtless think him nuts, if he mentions it, but the coincidence of his sharing such a mark with Antonio Sciacchitano is too extraordinary not to.

"Yes, my young friend? You are troubled by something, what is it?"

"Nino, I have a similar mark above my right eye."

What remains of Nino's eyebrows arch in surprise, "This is the truth you speak? If you are making fun of me, remember it is wicked to play such tricks on a man without sight."

"It's not a joke; my sense of humour doesn't run that far. I have a strawberry mark just above my right eye. I've had it as long as I can remember." Ric hesitates, "But these things are not handed down from one generation to the next; neither my father, nor my grandfather had such birthmarks." Ric pulls the photograph of his great-grandfather out of his pocket and examines it, just as he has done a hundred times before. But the light lent him by the street lantern is soft and insects dance around it, reducing its glow still further. The photograph is faded and grainy and creased, and he cannot make out the facial features of the man wearing the uniform of the Foreign Legion because he too stands in shadow.

Nino grows agitated; he grips his walking stick so tight his knuckles take on the pallor of San Bartolo's pedestal. "But Ric, to deny the possibility of this is to deny the legend of Santa Lucia in the same way that the unbelievers denied her belief and for that reason put her to death. You cannot do this," he says loudly. Others sitting around them stop their talking and look round at the man who has upset Old Nino. The twins in their pork-pie hats and striped shirts are standing close by, they stare menacingly at Ric.

He musters a diluted smile for them and they resume their chatter.

"Sorry, Nino, I didn't appreciate the offense my scepticism would cause."

His knuckles relax and a half-smile assumes his lips. "That is okay, Ric. We sometimes forget the world has moved on while we have been sitting still. But be careful to whom you say such things; there are many who would put your eyes out for not believing in our blessed saint."

"Thanks, Nino. Once more, I have to apologise for being so casual with my observations."

He taps Ric on the knee again. "That is okay, okay," he insists. "In many ways I am honoured to meet the relative of Antonio Sciacchitano, *un uomo integerrimo*. It is important to remember that like the eye of Santa Lucia, integrity runs in the blood."

At the mention of integrity, Ric sits up a fraction straighter. It is the second time today he has heard the word integrity and the recurrence of it spooks him.

"Now," Nino says, "if you will excuse me, I must sit in judgement of the twins. No doubt there is some matter they have been squabbling over which requires my resolution."

Ric is embarrassed at taking up so much of the old man's time and feels as though all the eyes of *passeggio* are upon him. He stands and rests his hand softly on the bony shoulder of the *magistrato di Marina Corta.* "Thank you, Nino. Again, I am heavily indebted to your memory."

"*Ciao*, my young friend." He pats Ric's hand and smiles beneath his thick, black glasses. "Again, it is I who should thank you for shepherding me down so many overgrown paths."

As soon as Ric moves away, the curious twins rush to sit down and bombard the old man with the details of their latest dispute.

The Corta is beginning to empty. Mothers gather their offspring, like fishermen drawing in their nets. Giuliana flashes him a smile as bright as any from the cameras of the tourists, who busy themselves arranging and rearranging the vivid cocktails on their tables with which they pose for a record of their holiday.

Sandro is lurking on the fringes of the café at the foot of the Garibaldi. As Ric walks past, the *escurzionista* hisses to attract his attention.

When Ric looks over at him, Sandro points to his right and touches the corner of his eye as if to warn him of a threat.

It is the same man Ric noticed following him up the Concordato earlier in the afternoon. The man wouldn't look so conspicuous but for the fact that the *gazzetta* he is reading is upside down.

Ric chuckles to himself and gives Sandro the thumbs up. But the *escurzionista* shies away, clearly not wanting to risk being seen to fraternise with him.

52

He turns on the bedside light and lies staring at the ceiling, waiting for what he does not know. His room is hot and stuffy, and his body creaks and rebels every time he tries to find a comfortable position. Eventually, he tires of his restlessness, gets to his feet, pads downstairs and puts his shoes on. He feels nauseous, but reconciles that his feeling is understandable given the awkward situation he finds himself in.

He opens the front door, peers out into the alleyway and pauses to listen. The vico is even warmer than his room, and the air is dry and dusty. He waits for a full minute before closing the door silently behind him.

Tonight, there are no cats prowling in search of overfilled dustbins, they are safely tucked up away from the coming rain, and the wireless of the old lady opposite is, for once, hushed.

When he is certain he can hear no sound beyond the thumping of his heart, he steps down. The high cloud he observed while sitting and talking with Old Nino has thickened and now blankets the sky, locking the stars out and the heat in.

There is no longer any doubt in his mind that it is Marcello who has taken the gun from the Mara. But, what bothers him most is the timing of events. Why would someone throw the Beretta into the water at Portinente, other than because Ric just happened to have been abandoned out in the water nearby?

Now that Sandro will not speak directly to him and Marcello is given only to deliver lectures on the value of integrity, he has no one else to talk to but Valeria. She is the only person who might have an idea of what is going on.

He weighs up which is the best route for him to take out towards the Punta San Giuseppe: the Maddalena is narrow and he knows that once he is in it, there is no escape from it. He decides that up around the back of the town through San Nicola is the safer route and so turns right.

He walks slowly and carefully, minding the dustbins and flowerpots, and is a couple of paces from the corner, when he hears a shuffling of feet.

"*Buonasera signore*," says a figure in the darkness.

In the gloom of the vico, Ric can just about make out a man's profile. He is tall, very tall and very broad, and he wears a peaked cap.

"Signor Ross, *resti dov'è*," the figure orders. "*Ritorni alla casa, per favore.*"

Ric cannot make out the man's face, but knows he has little alternative other than to do exactly as the officer says.

That he is under house arrest is all too obvious. Now there is nothing he can do until he meets the little detective in the morning.

Back in his room, he cannot settle. The tap drips. He washes his face and lies down on the small sofa. He feels dirty. His shirt is stuck to his back and though he knows he would be better off upstairs in bed, he is too weary to take a shower, let alone climb the narrow stairs. Soon, his fatigue overwhelms him and he succumbs to an uneasy sleep.

During the night, Aeolus stills the winds of the Levante in the east and conjures the warm Scirocco from the deserts of Africa.

Ric lies half awake, listening to the God of Winds howl his encouragement as he unleashes his storm against the island. It is as though the small fry of Lipari have born Aeolus some great offence and he designs to wash them clean of their misdemeanour. The shutters rattle and the gutters overflow, the rainwater gushing and slapping down against the flagstones in the passage outside.

He feels vaguely sorry for the tall *poliziotto* standing sentry outside and briefly considers asking him in.

But his dreams consume him. They are, like Aeolus' thunder and lightning, violent and vivid, and ceramic masks, like those he has seen in the shop window in the Corso, dance in the shadows. The beautiful Minerva fears for a future she has foreseen; Bacchus carouses, he has no cares; the elderly Neptune warns him of dangers to come; the two-faced Janus watches to see which choice he will make; and last in line Vulcan, who busies himself lighting the flame in which Ric is to burn. They file on and off the stage of his nightmare, delivering their oratory like actors in a tragedy. And, at the close of their performance, the players gather before him and remove their masks to reveal their true identity: first Valeria, then Sandro, Nino and Marcello, and finally Maso Talaia.

When, eventually, the grey light of dawn creeps along the alley, the rain is still falling hard and Ric comes to the conclusion that he is even more confused and weary than when he lay down. He gets up and makes his way down to the Corso Vittorio; the sentinel outside his door has been washed away by the rain.

53

Commissario Talaia is waiting in a back office of the police station on the Via Marconi. The room is bare but for a couple of grey filing cabinets, a desk and chairs, and a small electronic terminal about the size of a large credit card reader. The window behind the desk is barred.

"Very punctual, Signor Ross, thank you. Please sit."

The tall, broad-shouldered *poliziotto*, the one standing guard on the early shift outside his rooms, is in attendance. His uniform is creased and crumpled. He pulls a chair out from the desk.

Ric, though, is also soaked. Outside, the clouds hang low and grey, and issue a steady stream of rain. "Don't thank me, Commissario," he replies, as he runs his hands through his hair and shakes the water off his fingers. "The waiter at La Precchia wears a watch, I don't."

"Oh, don't you need to know the time for navigation? For when you use a sextant? I noticed you have one on the Mara. She doesn't seem to me to be the kind of sailing boat for more modern conveniences. It is a wonder you managed to find your way to Lipari."

Ric grins, "I told you, Commissario, I was just blown..."

"By the winds. Yes, and very amusing this over-used cliché is too. To think, Aeolus blows the voyager this way only for Il Faro del Mediterraneo to scare him to death when he arrives."

"I know the story," Ric chuckles.

On the desk before the little inspector are three passports. He picks up Ric's. "So, clearly this is your passport, Signor Ross. The photograph shows this strange birthmark on your forehead." He taps his right temple. "And now that your fishing injury has healed it is plain to see you are this man."

Talaia places Ric's passport on the table between them, but not so close to him that it is intended for him to take it. The Commissario picks up the two other British passports.

"These two are, just as clearly, not your passports. These we will return to the appropriate authorities. Exactly how they come to be lying on the desk of this police station in Lipari is a mystery. We have had them examined, dusted for prints, but they would appear to be clean almost to the point of sterile, which is, to me, not such a mystery." He drops the passports on his side of the table and taps them rhythmically.

"What is a mystery, as I have told you, is that these passports were reported missing from Porto Vecchio in Corsica not long before you became the owner of the Mara, which suggests you were *at* or, at the very least, *near* this location. Through further enquiries, it has come to my attention that at about this time you were declared a person of interest by the local Gendarmerie. My friend in Ajaccio, the *Commissaire de Police Judiciaire*, also tells me that a number of deaths occurred very close to where this boat was registered and in a similar time frame."

"I–" Ric begins.

Talaia leans forward and waggles a finger at him. "No," he interrupts, "now, I talk and you listen. Later, you talk and I listen." He sits back.

"One of the few benefits of being a member state of the European Union is that extradition is now a fairly simple business. Do I make myself clear, Signor Ross?"

"As ever, Commissario Talaia. And I get the feeling that if it wasn't such a simple business, there's more than half a chance I'd wash up on a beach in Corsica at exactly the spot your counterpart chose to take his breakfast."

The little man grins. His pencil-line eyebrows slope down at the same angle as his lips, lending his face the aspect of a road sign amused at the deceptive bends along its route.

"Before we come to the matter of the pistol, let us have coffee." He looks up at the uniformed poliziotto, "*Paolo, due caffè, per favore.*" The tall Paolo steps out.

"The issue of the pistol we can look at in one of two ways. It is a little like the chicken and the egg, which some like to think of as a paradox and others a dilemma." Talaia's expression collapses from amused to serious. "The fact that the pistol must have come first before Candela's shooting is not in doubt. But what is in doubt is who came first, Signor Ross or the Beretta?"

Ric smiles reluctantly and asks, "So which one am I, Maso, the chicken or the egg?"

The little Commissario frowns and replies, "Please, not Maso in front of my officers, only Commissario Talaia. The fact that I find you engaging as a personality is not relevant to my enquiries." He pouts in apology.

The door opens and officer Paolo walks back in with two cups of coffee.

"Possibly the correct way to approach this is on a historical basis. First, this pistol is a 9mm Beretta Model '34 Corto, marked with the letters RE and the date of its manufacture in Roman numerals. These markings tell us that this Beretta was produced in 1939 for the Regio Esercito, the Royal Italian Army. But, there were so many made that unless it was registered to an individual, which I think is highly unlikely, the serial number is of no consequence.

"All this tells us, though, is that the Beretta is older than both you and me. So, let us state, for the moment, that the pistol came first. But…" he holds up his finger to emphasise his point, "but, did the pistol come to Lipari first, before you, Signor Ross? Or did you come to Lipari with or before the pistol? That is both the paradox and our dilemma."

Talaia leans forward, sips his coffee and winces. He frowns at officer Paolo.

"Second, what we do know for certain, because we have examined the gun and matched it with the bullets removed from the unfortunate Girolamo Candela, is that this was definitely the gun that was used to kill him.

"And then we have to take into account the coincidence that you were enjoying a swim in the sea at Portinente at about the same time Signor Candela was murdered. And Portinente, as we know, is the location from which the gun was recovered."

The coffee is bitter. Ric sits back and folds his arms across his chest. "The Beretta isn't mine, Commissario. I've told you that already."

Talaia waves away his objection. "Yes, yes, of course. And the chair I am sitting in does not belong to me, but it is mine until I vacate it; if you see what I am getting at.

"What our forensic department has been able to establish is that the Beretta contains only one fingerprint, or more accurately a partial thumbprint, and that the gun was contaminated with oil, an oil with which, it seems, the assassin attempted to wipe the gun clean before throwing it into the sea. Our brilliant," Talaia briefly sucks his teeth and glances at Ric, "scientists have not, as yet, identified the exact type of oil, other than that it is not the usual oil one would use to lubricate or clean the workings of the pistol. But, they assure me they will be able to identify it given time."

"Plenty of engine oil on the Mara, Commissario," Ric says.

Talaia pouts, "Yes, thank you, it had occurred to me. So, in order to eliminate you from our enquiries, Signor Ross, we will now take your fingerprints and see if they match the partial print on the Beretta." He nods at Officer Paolo, who steps forward and passes the fingerprint scanner to Ric.

"*Con permesso,*" Paolo says, bending down and taking hold of Ric's right hand. "*Il pollice, per favore.*" He holds his own thumb up so that Ric is in no doubt which of his digits he is supposed to place on the reader.

"Sure," Ric replies, not inclined to resist Officer Paolo's extremely firm and yet surprisingly gentle grip.

The *poliziotto* twists Ric's hand so that his thumb is uppermost and presses it down against the screen of the device. He holds it steady, counts five seconds and then releases Ric's hand. Paolo stares down at the reader, but it offers no noticeable return. He shrugs, examines the device a little more closely and then breathes deeply and exhales. The gentle giant presses the ON button and stands back.

Talaia does not react; he merely sits, leaning forward on his elbows, waiting patiently.

Officer Paolo says, "*Un'altra volta, per favore?*"

"*Naturalmente,*" Ric replies, careful not to allow humour into his response in case he embarrasses the big man.

They repeat the procedure. The device chirps to let them know the print has been read. Paolo let's go of Ric's hand. "*Grazie,*" he says.

"*Prego,*" Ric replies.

Officer Paolo picks up the terminal and presses a sequence of buttons as though he is dialling a telephone number. He waits. The device chirps once more. "*È fatto,*" he says, standing up, proudly.

"*Bene!*" Talaia encourages. "*Ora aspettiamo, eh?* Now we wait."

"*Sì, Commissario.*" Officer Paolo stands back, even more pleased now that his superior has acknowledged him in front of their chief suspect.

The little detective smiles, perhaps a shade patronisingly. "Signor

Ross," he begins, but then thinks better of what he is about to say and looks up at his uniformed associate. "*Ci lasci in pace, per favore, un momento, Paolo?*"

The big man frowns.

Talaia dismisses him: "*Per favore, Paolo? Passa al di fuori. Sarò a posto.*"

Officer Paolo leaves.

"A good policeman," the Commissario says by way of excuse, "though I am afraid he, like many, does not follow his instincts. He believes the evidence provides us with the conclusion that you are not to be trusted, which is why he was reluctant to leave me alone in this room with you. However, we will see."

"Thank you for the vote of confidence, Maso."

"Oh, don't thank me, Ric. The weight of evidence may appear to be against you, although I must point out that at this precise moment much of the evidence is what a court would describe as circumstantial. But, there are too many questions to which I cannot find the answers.

"Again, firstly, the Beretta. While Berettas may be perfectly usable handguns, they are rarely the instrument of a professional assassin." Talaia pauses, thinking. "No, that is not quite accurate; Mahatma Ghandi's assassin used one. But, they are, if you like, the kind of pistol one puts in a drawer and forgets about. It is doubtful that a contemporary assassin would rely on such a weapon.

"Secondly, as I have said before, why assassinate Candela here in the Piazza San Bartolo? Why not do this in Palermo or on one of his many visits to Rome, where he would be a much easier target?

"Thirdly, what possible connection do you have with Candela? And, fourthly, what message could you have delivered to Candela that would have compelled him to meet you in the Piazza San Bartolo? This last point causes me much concern.

"Then, of course, there is the question of why Signor Maggiore should confirm your alibi at the risk of implicating himself. This also gives me much cause for thought."

There is a knock at the door.

"*Avanti*," Talaia calls, loudly.

Officer Paolo strides in. He places a sheet of paper before the little Commissario.

"*Grazie, Paolo*," Talaia picks it up and reads it. He rests his head against his right hand and rubs his lower lip with his index finger. He glances at Ric, reads through it once more, and then puts it face down beside his Homburg.

Officer Paolo seems to have grown in stature and the rain flays the window, reminding Ric of San Bartolo's fate.

Commissario Talaia studies the surface of the desk, as though he is waiting for a genie to swell up out of it and solve the riddle of Candela's murder.

"*Questo è tutto!*" He sits back and immediately see-saws forward again. "*Ei-yaei-yaei*," he mutters.

"What's the news?" Ric asks as innocently as his humour allows. His shirt is still wet on his back and a drop of water drips from his hair.

"This partial print we have found on the pistol," Talaia taps the report in front of him, "it matches yours."

54

Of course, Ric knew what Talaia was going to say. He knew what the results of the fingerprint test would show the moment the detective told him the Beretta had been wiped clean but for one partial print.

"And I was hoping this situation would not get much worse for you, Signor Ross."

"Thank you for your... sympathy, if I read you correctly, Commissario. But you and I both know there's no way I did for Candela."

The detective shrugs. "This," he taps the report again, "would suggest otherwise. And this makes me sad: I was beginning to like you. But you could have made this so much easier for yourself, if you had told me when I asked you yesterday if the gun was yours."

Ric thins his lips and replies, "It wasn't and it isn't. It just happened to turn up on the Mara. I should have filed it in a couple of hundred fathoms. Don't know why I didn't."

Talaia inclines his head. "Oh, this is understandable. I think it is impossible for a soldier – pardon, a fighting man – to throw away his weapon. It is against his nature. This, I will grant you."

"You're too understanding," Ric replies, with deserved sarcasm. "But the Beretta stayed on the boat until it was taken out of the water. I found it was missing when I went to Maggiore's yard. Didn't you tell me a few minutes ago that the chair you are sitting in is yours until you vacate it?"

He nods, "Yes, but you know very well what I meant when I said this. And even though this pistol is not in your possession at this moment; it has your fingerprint on it, which tells me that it *was* in your possession and that is how it came to be here."

"Okay, you're right, Commissario. The Beretta was on the Mara when I arrived; it was left on the boat by someone who thought I might need it. For what reason, I don't know. But maybe that's a story for later. However, sometime between my arrival in Lipari and the boat ending up in Maggiore's yard, someone removed it and used it to shoot Candela."

Talaia scoffs, "And you expect me to believe Candela's killer removed the pistol from your yacht in order to implicate you?"

"It explains why the pistol was wiped clean except for one of my fingerprints."

"It would, but, if you will permit me, this theory stretches the imagination too far. How did this person know that your print was still on the pistol after he had wiped it clean?"

Pellets of rain slap against the window behind the detective.

"I don't know; maybe they hedged their bets."

Talaia looks up at Officer Paolo and nods at Ric. The tall poliziotto steps forward.

"Hang on a minute, Commissario, you know as well as I do that I've no motive for shooting Candela."

"It is true. But..." he pauses, considering. "So, what you are suggesting is that Signor Maggiore Marcello removed the pistol from your yacht and used it to shoot Girolamo Candela?"

"No, Commissario, he can't have shot Candela. Maggiore was out in the ocean fishing with me. I can verify his alibi in the same way he has verified mine—"

"Which makes this a conspiracy between the two of you," he interrupts, pouting and raising his eyebrows. "If you remember, I asked you if you trusted Signor Maggiore."

"And, if I remember rightly, I told you I had no reason not to. Now, though, I'm not so sure."

"Because you think it must be Signor Maggiore who stole the pistol from your yacht?" Talaia's tone and expression suggest he is leading his suspect down a path he has been expecting him to take all along.

"Or one of his men," Ric replies, thinking of the wiry Salvo. "I know Maggiore didn't shoot Candela, but that doesn't rule out the possibility one of his men did it."

"No," Talaia agrees, "it most definitely does not, Signor Ross. However, I have made many checks on Signor Maggiore and though he may be the acquaintance of some less than desirable members of the wider community, I find it hard to believe he would be stupid enough to commit, or even commission, this sort of action."

"You mean he's not part of the Mafia? I thought everyone was in some way."

The Commissario groans, leans forward on his forearms and interlaces his fingers, putting his thumbs together as though he is imitating a church spire on the roof of his fingers.

"Signor Ross, we have spoken about the Mafia. I was hoping to have educated you as to how many strands of this insular organisation exist. But what you have singularly failed to appreciate is that the Mafia is only a natural extension of the way society is constructed here. There are many families, associations and even corporations — call them what you will — who conduct themselves perfectly peacefully and yet they adhere to the same unspoken laws as those of the criminal gangs. These laws are a complex sociological construct which has evolved over many centuries. The concept of the Godfather has been made real and popular for us by writers like Puzo and film-makers like Coppola, or, come to think of it, even by some opera composers. What I am not saying is that these larger than life characters do not exist, because sadly they do. But, what I am saying is that their origins lie in a feudal system where one man, by his own nature, has the power to impose himself over others."

Ric interrupts, "And Marcello Maggiore is one such character?"

"In some ways, yes. But what I am talking about is a society founded on respect. Each man has respect for the other, but individual strengths and weaknesses produce a society in which one man generates more respect than the next. Also, this respect is handed down from one generation to the next, from one *Vecchio Signori* to the next, and so the respect becomes, quite literally, inherent; it is not questioned."

Talaia's lecture on the laws of the Sicilian jungle confuses Ric. It knocks him off balance for a while. For if the Commissario does not suspect Maggiore for having some part in Candela's murder, Ric cannot think who else might have killed him.

The little detective smiles, evidently pleased that he is ahead of Ric. "Signor Ross, in my opinion Signor Maggiore has too much to lose to be involved in Candela's assassination. He is neither a big enough, nor a small enough fish for such a crime."

Ric is fast running out of ideas and is puzzled as to why Talaia should want to lend Maggiore such a ringing endorsement. "What about his brother? I understand Marcello Maggiore had a brother," he offers. "Is he big enough to fry?"

"Yes and no," Talaia replies. "This Claudio, I have not met him, but I am led to believe he walks in his brother's shadow; he has not the same spine as Signor Maggiore. However, my counterparts in Palermo, who have been investigating Girolamo Candela, have discovered correspondence between Claudio and the deceased."

"What sort of correspondence?"

The detective chews Ric's question over for a couple of seconds before replying, "For the moment, let us not concern ourselves with the communications between these two individuals. They are in all probability irrelevant to our enquiries."

Ric notes his reluctance to explain the connection further.

Talaia blinks and frowns, "You said *had*, Signor Ross. If I recall correctly, you said Signor Maggiore Marcello *had* a brother. What did you mean by this?"

Though Ric knows the news will mean a whole load of trouble for Marcello, he has no option left other than to give it up: "What I mean, Commissario, is that Claudio Maggiore, like his pen-friend, Girolamo Candela, is dead."

55

The news knocks the wind out of Talaia's sails. "But I am informed his yacht is moored in the Villa Igiea, in Palermo. My officers tell me the port authority record shows that he arrived a week ago. He was seen in Palermo."

"His yacht may be there, Commissario, but I can assure you he isn't."

Talaia sits up and glares at him. "How do you know this, Signor Ross?"

"Because, Commissario, Claudio Maggiore is lying dead in a pumice warehouse near Porticello. I heard someone kill him a week ago."

"You heard someone kill him?" Talaia mocks. "Was it a very loud gunshot?"

Ric expects him to be sceptical, so he holds his peace.

"Signor Ross, I heard San Bartolo's effigy is made of silver, but I'm not about to try and lift it to find out if it is true." He chuckles, "Although I believe the Germans found this out when they tried to steal it." Then he, too, waits and watches.

When, eventually, the detective realises Ric is being serious, he sighs. "*Va bene*, tell me."

Ric relates the curious episode of his arrival at Lipari: how he tied up to the bent and rusted stanchion of the old wharf; how he sat in the mist and listened to a man plead for his life; and how, when his explanations, excuses and apologies had all been taken into account, the man was strangled. When he's finished, he too sits back once more and folds his arms.

Talaia smirks, clearly believing Ric is being over-imaginative in his story telling. "You know," he says, "it is strange the tricks a mind can play on a man when he is fatigued. You say you heard voices? Did you recognise either of them? Was, perhaps, San Bartolo one of them?"

"Not that I recall, no."

"Then how do you know if it was Claudio Maggiore who was being killed?"

"Because I've seen his dead body."

"Oh, I see," Talaia replies, dragging out his response to suggest he doesn't see, at all. "You have not only heard this man being murdered, you have also seen his corpse." He holds up his hands in surrender and looks up at Officer Paolo as if waiting for his confirmation that the story is too far-fetched to carry even the slightest ring of truth. He looks back, "Okay, Signor Ross, if you have seen Signor Maggiore's corpse, where exactly is it?"

"Buried under a pile of rubble in the old La Cava warehouse at Pietra Liscia."

"Spiaggia di Pietra Liscia," Talaia repeats. He quiets for a moment and turns his attention to the surface of the desk. "The beach of smooth stones, you say? It sounds like a nice place. Do you know where this beach is?"

"Of course! It's the last beach up the coast before Porticello."

"I see; the last beach before Porticello?"

"Yes."

Commissario Talaia smirks, briefly, and then stiffens. He blinks and rubs his eyes. "And does this killing of Signor Maggiore Claudio have any connection with this Beretta?"

"No, I had the gun on the Mara at that time. It was the last time I saw it. Listening to Claudio's screams prompted me to retrieve it from the locker in case I was next. In the end I didn't need it, so I replaced it. I probably put the Beretta down grip first, which is why it would have had my thumbprint near the muzzle."

"Okay, Signor Ross," Talaia decides, "I truly give up. I must say this was not what I expected; another corpse. Now I have two to deal with."

Ric chuckles a little nervously and says, pretty much to himself, "At least they'll make up for the two empty graves in the cemetery."

Talaia looks up sharply, "Empty graves? What empty graves?"

"Long story, Commissario."

"Aren't they all? So, what we do from here is we have to go to Pietra Liscia to see for ourselves the body of Maggiore Claudio." He turns in his seat and stares out the window for a few seconds: "Come to the sunny Aeolian islands," he mutters. "*Paolo, sai qual è la Spiaggia Pietra Liscia?*"

"*Si, Commissario.*"

"*Va bene. Prendi l'auto, per favore.*"

The tall officer leaves the room.

To Ric he says, "Come, we will go find your corpse, if he hasn't already drowned."

56

Before they leave, Talaia makes a couple of phone-calls while Ric waits in the entrance hall.

Officer Paolo drives them. Commissario and Ric sit in the back.

The island looks oddly sad in the rain; it is as though the tears from the sky are being shed in apology for the bother the clouds are causing the people. The bus station is deserted and the pier for the Aliscafo looks forlorn without its usual, colourful crowd.

"Tell me about Girolamo Candela, Commissario. Was he popular?"

Talaia pouts, "Oh, popular enough to be elected."

"Valeria Vaccariello told me he used to be a good communist," Ric says, trying to jog the policeman along.

"They were all good communists at one time, but The Party lost ground after the war. In Sicily, the Christian Democrats became too close to the Mafia and in return for being allowed a free hand, the Mafia would assassinate socialists and communists, insisting they were fighting against the influence of the Soviet Union. It became very difficult for the communists."

"And Candela?"

"Candela was different. He was intelligent with the company he kept. He benefitted from the financial backing of many celebrities in the seventies and eighties: writers, musicians, film-makers; many of them communists who supported his ultra-left wing views." He silences as they drive through the tunnel to Canneto.

The wipers scrape against the momentarily dry windscreen and as they exit down the hill a torrent rages through the gulley beside the road.

"*Paolo, non così in fretta, per favore,*" Talaia pleads.

"*Sì, Commissario.*"

"But," Ric carries on, "La Signorina Vaccariello told me he was no longer a good communist. What did she mean by that?"

Talaia shrugs, "Oh, like most people who cannot see a way ahead, he changed direction. The *Partito Comunista Italiano* became the *Partito Democratico della Sinistra* and many of the members, including Candela, became socialists; their concentrated views were, over time, watered down. As a hard-line *comunista*, it was unlikely that a relatively small-time politician like Candela would become a minister in the Sicilian Parliament, but by falling in with the Democrats and the Socialists he moved further to the right. He became what we call *assessore*, then *sottosegretario*. This is first an assessor, a councillor if you like, and later a secretary for the President. He enjoyed increasing power. And as his power grew and he grew closer to the right, the left-wing celebrities who had been funding his electoral campaigns began to question his political fidelity. With his funding reduced, so he looked for other sources and some of these were very dubious. It is these sources which are my concern and the concern of many of my fellow investigators."

The car twists up the tight turns out of Canneto. The rain still falls in stair rods and out to sea the Mare Siculum is a commotion of white and grey.

"I understand the Maggiore family were anti-fascist," Ric states. "Is there a chance they used to bankroll Candela?"

Talaia waves his suggestion away. "We have no proof of it if they did. I am not sure they have ever had sufficient money to bankroll a politician. Look," he points out the window at the barren landscape of pumice scree at Monte Pilato up ahead, "in 2002 there were only forty people left to work the mines, these days you don't get rich from this kind of commercial enterprise; maybe eighty or ninety years ago, yes, but not now."

"You said Claudio Maggiore had been in correspondence with Candela. What were they up to?"

"That is for me to know," Talaia replies, curtly.

"Was it about the new hotel Candela had been talking about?"

"Perhaps."

"Claudio Maggiore was on the urban council, wasn't he?"

Talaia glances at Ric out of the corner of his eye. "So I am led to believe."

"Is it true what they say," Ric asks, "that this new hotel planned for Porticello is supposed to have a thousand rooms?"

The Commissario doesn't answer in words; he shifts in his seat. "Porticello," he repeats. But the way Talaia repeats the name implies that it is of some greater significance than simply being the sight of the planned development.

"Sure, Porticello," Ric adds. "That's where it's supposed to be built, right?"

"Yes, Porticello," Talaia sighs. "But the first part is to be built on the site of the old La Cava warehouse at Pietra Liscia."

Ric is stunned. He turns to look at the Commissario, who simply stares out of his window.

Officer Paolo drives on through the unrelenting rain; his two passengers each marshalling similar thoughts. Above, the dirty-white mountain of pumice towers over them; below, the grey ocean dissolves in the gloom.

"You think the Maggiore family sold out to Candela?" Ric asks, knowing full well that is the only conclusion to be drawn.

"Possibly," Talaia grunts. "But even if they have, there would be no guarantee that this hotel would ever be built. There would still be many mouths to feed before he could think of applying for permission."

It was what Valeria had said, "Many mouths to feed". "It's the next track right," Ric states.

The Commissario exhales loudly, "Ah, I'm sure Paolo knows where he is going; he grew up in Lipari before going to the academy in Spoleto."

Officer Paolo does indeed know the track and he knows enough not to attempt the steep track in the heavy rain. The pumice dust has turned to mud and whilst they might make it down to the beach, there is little chance they would make it back up.

Commissario Talaia shrugs on a raincoat, but otherwise seems oblivious to the rain and the mess the mud will make of his suit and shoes. Officer Paolo, though, is still sodden from his overnight vigil. Ric hardly cares; he is more concerned about the consequences of showing Talaia Claudio Maggiore's body.

The three of them trudge down the winding track.

Though the wind is blowing the rain horizontally across the slender, pebbled beach, the lad at the beach bar leaves the cosy confines of his post to wave and watch them.

"It's up there," Ric points to the third floor of the derelict warehouse.

Talaia glances at Paolo and nods for him to follow Ric.

The two of them make their way gingerly up the side of the building, Ric showing the tall poliziotto where to put his feet and where to take hand-holds. The rain spits in their eyes and the pumice blocks are treacherously slimy.

A couple of times, Officer Paolo cups his hands and hoists Ric up to the next floor and he returns the favour with a helping hand up. They reach the third floor and walk to the far end, careful to place their feet squarely on the exposed beams.

The wooden door set into the rock is still in place, but it hangs slightly ajar.

He turns to Officer Paolo and indicates his head: "*Attenzione, eh?*"

"*Si,*" he replies and crouches.

Ric eases the door back and inches inside. He motions Officer Paolo to follow. The grey clouds cast a dim light and his eyes take a moment to adjust. The room seems crowded and even darker with the two of them in it, but it takes Ric only a couple of seconds to see that Claudio Maggiore is no longer in residence.

57

From the third floor of the old warehouse, the diminutive Commissario looks even smaller and by the time Ric and Officer Paolo have climbed back down, he is soaked through and in poor humour. He glowers at Ric. "*Paolo,*" he grumbles, indicating the hill behind them, "*eh?*"

"*Si, Commissario.*" The tall *poliziotto* draws his pistol and cocks it.

"Oh, come off it Maso," Ric says, shaking his head. "You seriously think I've got you up here on a wild goose chase? All this way? In this bloody weather?"

Talaia dips his head and a trickle of water spills off his Homburg. "I'm not sure what to think, Signor Ross." He raises his eyebrows, nods at Officer Paolo and inclines his head towards Ric.

"*Si, Commissario.*"

"I'm not about to make a bolt for it either," Ric states.

"No?" Talaia replies. "But if any more fanciful notions should come to your mind, Paolo here will hinder your flight by putting a round in your leg. Do you understand?"

"Sure! But that won't be necessary, Commissario. I've got as much to lose as any of us; more probably."

The walk back up the hill is hard work and takes them much longer than the walk down. The rain whips at their heels and the mud and sludge from the saturated pumice makes the going slippery. Talaia's short legs struggle against those of his taller companions.

The windows of the car steam up and Officer Paolo has to wipe the screen continually to keep sight of the twisting road.

"So, where do we go from here?" Ric asks.

"Why don't you tell me, Signor Ross? All of my sources inform me that Maggiore Claudio is in Palermo. You are the only one who seems to think he is dead."

"Not think; know. I told you, Maso, Claudio was in that room, dead as a post two days ago. The marks on his neck and the look on his face were consistent with him being strangled, exactly as I heard him being strangled the morning I arrived."

Talaia's expression is one of only mild interest. "I am Commissario Talaia, not Maso, Signor Ross. I think the time for such informality is over." He pouts for a second, "You know the look on a man's face when he has been strangled?"

"Unfortunately, I do. To see it once is enough; it's not something one forgets." The faces of the dead parade in front of him, like ghouls in a house of horrors. Ric blots them out, trying to concentrate. "Now I haven't the first clue why anyone would want to kill him. Perhaps it's to do with this hotel, perhaps there's something else entirely, I don't know. I understand he was gay; might that have something to do with it?"

"I doubt it very much," Talaia murmurs. "Isola di Lipari might well be a World Heritage Site, but the attitudes of the people are no longer so out-of-date."

"Is it possible Candela thought he was going to meet Claudio Maggiore in the Piazza San Bartolo the evening he was murdered?"

"Signor Ross, I am surprised you can make such a suggestion. If Maggiore Claudio is dead, how could he hope to have enjoyed a rendezvous with Girolamo Candela?"

"Was Candela gay?"

"Not according to my sources."

"Then it has got to be something to do with this planned development," Ric reasons.

"I told you before, there is little to no chance of this construction ever happening; too many—"

"Mouths to feed, I know. Then there has to be something else going on; something we're not looking at."

"Looking at!" Talaia repeats, burying himself in the collar of his jacket. "Looking at! It may have escaped your notice, Signor Ross, but at this point we have only one body, that of Girolamo Candela. For this crime we also have a weapon and a chief suspect whose fingerprint is on this weapon. This is fact; inescapable fact. Also, at this point we possess no evidence that Maggiore Claudio is dead; no body. We only have the testimony of the man whose print appears on the gun which we know was used to murder the man whose body we do have. Until, therefore, I have the body of Maggiore Claudio, I must assume that he is alive and well and busy sampling the delights of Palermo.

"You know, Signor Ross, I mentioned before that though the islands are a World Heritage Site, the people are no longer backwards in their outlook. Well, there are many myths and legends concerning the ghosts of those exiled to Lipari, and it is believed that if you walk over the Poggio dei Funghi you have a good chance of meeting many of the former, long-departed residents of the island: everyone from Fulvia Plautilla, the wife of Caracalla, to Massimo Farinelli, one of Il Duce's greater antagonists. Perhaps it was one of those you came across in your fatigue."

"Farinelli?" Ric repeats. "I've heard that name before somewhere."

"Massimo Farinelli?"

"Yes, someone told me he was killed here while trying to escape."

The Commissario is surprised, "You have heard of him."

"Sure, there's an old guy I've been talking to. He's been trying to help me trace my great-grandfather. It turns out my great-grandfather, Antonio Sciacchitano, tried to warn Farinelli that he had been betrayed. This old guy – Old Nino they call him – remembered his father had smuggled my great-grandfather over to Sicily in his fishing boat. Saved his life or so it would seem."

"It was a bad time," Talaia adds, nodding thoughtfully. "Farinelli was a very important man. He had many good political connections with the Americans. If he had lived, who knows what he might have been able to achieve."

The rain slashes against the screen and waves crash against the shallow beach before them. Officer Paolo has to slow the car as they descend the tight turns into Canneto.

"How come you know so much about him, Commissario?" Ric asks.

"Oh, before I became a policeman I studied history. It pays to understand history when so much of the past is continually dragged into the present; particularly in Italy.

"Massimo Farinelli, though much younger than Matteotti, was a very outspoken critic of Il Duce and he was fortunate not to suffer the same fate. Although, if I remember correctly, he was equally fortunate not to suffer a similar fate at the hands of one of his many girlfriend's fathers. He was quite the Lothario, the Casanova; a roué of note, one might say. He was almost as successful at seducing young women as he was at furthering his political career. When news of his death was published in the papers, there followed an outpouring of grief which eclipsed even that of Valentino."

"What did he look like, Maso? I mean, was he tall or short, thin or fat, or was he dark-haired or what?"

"Farinelli was tall, very tall, and blond and strong. He was one of the Arditi, the daring ones. If you were to put together the perfect curriculum vitae for seducing women, he would have ticked all the boxes."

Ric is quiet for a moment. He is thinking of the characters he has met since his arrival, the faces of whom came to him in his dream-filled sleep. He considers telling Talaia the story Old Nino has told him, but figures that the little detective is unlikely to buy it now that he has been dragged up to the beach at Pietra Liscia in search of a corpse which has got up and walked.

"Commissario?" he asks. "What's going to happen when we get back to the police station? Are you going to charge me for Candela's murder?"

Talaia stares out the window at the torrents of rain threatening to drown the village. He sighs as though he has the weight of the world on his shoulders. "I am not sure, Signor Ross. So far you have not been truthful with me. The fact that you did not tell me the pistol was yours when I asked you, leads me to suspect there is more that you are keeping from me. Perhaps only a fool would not put you behind bars until we have completed our investigation. Your association with Maggiore Marcello and the alibi you both insist on trying to sell me makes me uncomfortable.

"But I think keeping you here on the island is not wise for now. Perhaps a short period of reflection in one of our cells in Messina is what is required."

"I had a nasty feeling you were going to say that."

"Oh, yes. Why?" Talaia glances at Ric.

"Because if you send me off the island, there's not much chance you are going to complete your investigation. Obviously there's got to be some connection between Candela and whoever murdered him. Surely, if you find the connection, getting to his murderer will be the easy part."

"Of course."

"In which case, can you do both of us a favour and ask Officer Paolo to take us over to Quattropani? There are a couple of questions I need to ask Old Nino. I'm not certain it will help the pieces of your jigsaw fall into place, but it might give us a clue as to whether they are part of the puzzle."

Talaia glances at him once more; his right eyebrow is raised in question, "Do you seriously expect me to take you sightseeing when you have already destroyed my shoes?"

"Oh, don't worry, Commissario. I'll try not to get your shoes any dirtier than they are. And, if you're lucky, there might just be the reward of a glass of palm wine when we get there."

"You drink that stuff?" Talaia asks, astonished. "They say it makes you blind."

Ric laughs, nervously, "Oh, Commissario, you've no idea."

The little detective studies him for a minute. "I must say the promise of palm wine as opposed to the promise of a corpse is far more attractive." He groans and rubs his face in exasperation, "Okay! As long as I don't have to drink the *legbi*, I suppose this detour won't hurt. I doubt whether the Aliscafo will be running and there is no chance they will send a helicopter in these conditions. It looks like we are both going to have to spend one more night here. Please inform Officer Paolo where you would like to go."

"Nino lives above Quattropani," Ric offers.

"*Cafarella Nino, vicino Chiesa Vecchia. Lo so,*" Officer Paolo replies.

58

"But this man must be nearly one hundred years old," Talaia remarks, as the car pulls up.

Ariana answers the door. At first she is pleased to see Ric, but when she realises he has *poliziotti* with him, the pleasure shrinks from her smile.

"*Signor Ric, buon pomeriggio.*"

"*Mi dispiace disturbarla, Ariana.*"

"*Sì, per favore, entrate.*" They follow her through to the living area.

Nino is reading, in Braille. Enveloped in the sofa, he looks even smaller than the Commissario and the gloom of the leaden sky lends his skin a leukaemic pallor. "Come in, Ric. So good of you to come and see an old man who has nothing to do with his time. Oh, you are not alone; you have brought friends?"

"Yes, Nino, I have brought Commissario Talaia and Officer Paolo with me; I hope we're not interrupting."

"No, not at all. You are a welcome diversion from Dante Alighieri, and like most of the dead poets, he will wait." He cocks his head, "Ariana, bring some wine, please. Officer Paolo, you say? Is this Favolaro Paolo, the son of Augusta, who lives in San Calogero?"

The tall *poliziotto* steps forward and leans down to offer his hand.

Old Nino feels for it, "Ah, such large hands! You are tall, Paolo, eh? You were tall as a child. Your mother used to worry that you were growing so fast your bones would be weak. They are not; I am glad."

Officer Paolo steps back, grinning, obviously embarrassed but no little proud that he has been greeted before his boss.

"And this Commissario? For what reason do I merit the visit of an Inspector of Police?"

Ariana takes the Commissario's coat, hangs it in the corner and disappears to the kitchen.

"*Vossia benedica, signore*," Talaia begins, politely. "We apologise for calling unannounced, but Signor Ross has some questions he would like to ask you."

"Questions, eh? He is always asking questions, Commissario. That is why he has come to Lipari; he is looking for his holy grail. Please, sit."

Ariana returns with a tray of wine and glasses.

Nino smiles and spreads his hands as though he can see the drinks he is offering his visitors. "*Legbi*, Commissario. Can I persuade you to take a glass with an old man?"

Talaia scowls, but replies, "Sir, if I can avoid it without offending your hospitality, I would prefer to."

"Ah," Nino says, his face lighting up with amusement, "a wise policeman and an honest one too; such a rarity. Naturally I am not offended. There will be more for me and good palm wine is, like a straightforward policeman, hard to find. Ariana, coffee for the inspector. Ric?"

"I'll take a glass, thank you, Nino," Ric interrupts. "I don't know about the others, but I need it."

As is the custom, they drink and make small talk for a while.

"Now," Nino says, satisfied that custom has been observed, "what can I do for you?" Even though he cannot see him, Nino looks towards Talaia.

"*Signore, allora—*"

Nino lifts his hand to interrupt, "In English if you don't mind, Commissario? We have a British guest; let us grant him the honour of speaking in his tongue."

Talaia scowls briefly, but then, forgetting Nino is blind, grants the old man a strained smile, "Of course. Signor Ross thinks you may be able to help us with some detail of history."

"Please?"

The Commissario clears his throat and, hoping that Old Nino is now ready, begins, "He has told me that it is possible you knew his great-grandfather, Antonio Sciacchitano, and of how the night three political deportees made their escape, he tried to warn them that they were betrayed. I am not sure what relevance the details of a failed escape can be to my investigations, but it cannot hurt to find out if there is a historical connection. Perhaps you would do us the kindness of relating the story once more?"

Judging by the way he looks up sharply and frowns, Old Nino is not taking an instant liking to the little detective, "This is not a story, Commissario. A story suggests an imaginary event, a fiction. These things he has told you actually happened. This is the truth, not a story!"

Talaia winces, "*Chiedo scusa, Signor Cafarella.*"

Over the next hour, Old Nino repeats his account of the events from that night over eighty years before. Like any proficient raconteur, he is prone to embellish whenever the scene will allow for it and he glosses over some of the detail which might not stand up to the scrutiny of a more cynical audience. And whenever the old man strays from the path, Ric does his best to stifle a grin. But he tries not to reduce the impact of Old Nino's account by diverting Commissario Talaia's attention away from the notes he is taking. Every now and then, he glances at Ric out of the corner of his eye, as if to suggest he is finding some of the account hard to swallow. And when the old man gets to the part about both Antonio and Ric sharing the same birthmark, he coughs and splutters out loud and immediately apologises. Yet, other than this mild outburst of incredulity, he keeps his observations to himself and treats the old man with the respect his years demand.

Nino raises his hands in appeal, "So you see Commissario, amazing as it sounds, the grave of Antonio Sciacchitano contains no corpse."

Talaia allows the old man's conclusion to hang for a moment before stating, "*Con permesso, Signore*, there is only one way to find out if this story, *scusi*, this version of historical events, is reliable; and that would be to exhume the body of Antonio Sciacchitano. Do either of you," this time he raises both eyebrows towards Ric, "have any idea of the legal issues involved in obtaining permission for this?"

"No," Ric answers for both of them. "We haven't got that far yet."

Talaia shakes his head, "There is a saying in Italian, *non svegliare il can che dorme*, which if I am right in thinking translates as do not wake up the dog who sleeps. Do you know what is meant by this?"

"Naturally, Commissario," Ric replies. "But if you will permit me, I think you're getting a little ahead of me. There are a number of reasons I've asked you to come here and so far you've only heard half of what I want you to hear."

"Nino," Ric turns his attention to the old man, "you've told us that Antonio Sciacchitano came to your house and pleaded with your father to take him and a young woman to Baarìa."

"Si, he took Tonio and a young woman."

"And it's the girl who interests me as much as Sciacchitano. Who was she, Nino? Who was the girl your father took to Baarìa that night?"

He inclines his head, his dark glasses masking his thoughts. Gradually, the old man grows animated, as if he is remembering where he has hidden the *legbi* from Ariana.

"Ah, that is it! It was Katarina Maggiore of course: Vincenzo's daughter. I remember now; she was Vincenzo's daughter, Katarina. She was," he pauses searching for the right words, "enjoying a liaison with Massimo Farinelli. They had been seen together at *passeggio*.

326

"Much later, the rumour going around the *città* was that it was Vincenzo who had betrayed Farinelli to the *Fascisti*. Vincenzo found out that Katarina was with child and he was outraged that a man with such a questionable reputation would take advantage of his daughter, particularly when Vincenzo was doing so much to help him escape."

Ric interrupts, "But you told me that Vincenzo sent Tonio Sciacchitano to warn Farinelli that he had been betrayed. Why would Vincenzo do that?"

Old Nino looks up, as if the conclusion of the tale is written on the ceiling: "Because Katarina begged her father to rescue him. She told her father she would surrender herself to the sea if he did not halt the progression of his plans."

"Katarina was pregnant with Farinelli's child," Ric repeats for Talaia's benefit.

"Yes, it was so. Sadly, Tonio Sciacchitano was too late to warn the deportees and, as we know, Farinelli and the others were killed."

"And afterwards," Ric adds, "Vincenzo sent his daughter away?"

"No. Katarina could not forgive her father for being complicit in the murder of her child's father, so she ran away. She came with Tonio to ask my father's help."

Commissario Talaia, having held his peace, remarks, "I am not sure what this has to do with our investigations, Signor. Perhaps we have bothered you for no reason."

"Hold on Maso," Ric says, reaching over and urging the little detective to sit back down. "Give me a couple more minutes, please?"

Talaia demurs, but reluctantly.

"Nino," Ric turns back to the old man, "what you are suggesting is that Katarina Maggiore's body does not rest in the Maggiore mausoleum, which means there is more than one empty grave in the cemetery?"

"Yes, that is true. After much searching, the family assumed that Katarina was overcome by her grief and that she had, as she had said she would, thrown herself into the sea. Her body was never found and the funeral was purely ceremonial. It was very sad, very solemn; a girl had died of a broken heart which would never be mended. At the time of the funeral, I did not know my father had spirited her away to Baarìa with Tonio Sciacchitano. It was only much later that my mother explained this to me and told me I was never to tell anyone. She knew if Vincenzo ever found out my father had taken Katarina to Baarìa, Vincenzo would kill him."

"And this was in July of 1930?"

"About then, yes."

"Nino, do you know where Valeria Vaccariello was born?"

"No."

"Or when?"

"Such things are not polite to ask."

"Or what her mother's Christian name was?"

Nino thinks and begins to understand the direction Ric is taking in the line of his questioning. "No, I don't believe we have ever discussed her mother. However," Nino looks so directly at Ric, it is disconcerting, "I am sure you are about to answer all three of your own questions."

"You're right, Nino, I am. Valeria was born in Baarìa, in late 1930 and her mother's Christian name was Katarina. The man she knew as her father was a man her mother married in order to provide her child with a family name."

The old man's brow furrows in astonishment. "It is so? Really? She told you this?"

"Yes," Ric replies, "but you, also, you told me in a round about way. I spent an afternoon in the cemetery and put two and two together. After that, I told her. Leastways I put it to her and the rest of the facts just seemed to fit in around it."

Old Nino sits back in his chair and cups his hands to his face.

The Commissario is, however, still none the wiser. Ric glances at him, encouraging him to be patient.

When Nino has arranged all the information into some semblance of order, he drops his hands and stares out of the window in the direction of Salina. His expression suggests that he can see it standing tall and proud and green. The clouds and driving rain prevent Ric, Maso Talaia and Officer Paolo from seeing the island across the Canale di Salina, but Nino suffers no such restrictions.

"If this is true," he says, "Valeria is not only Farinelli's daughter, but she is also Marcello's cousin."

59

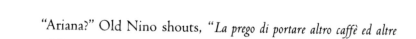

"Ariana?" Old Nino shouts, "*La prego di portare altro caffè ed altre nacatuli.*"

"*Si, subito,*" floats the reply from the kitchen.

"*Apetta un minuto, per favore,*" Talaia pleads.

"You would prefer wine, Commissario?"

"*Non,* that's not what I mean. What I mean is, you have already been very hospitable, Signor Cafarella, but as interesting as it is for me to hear that between you, you have solved the riddle of Signor Ross' and La Signorina Vaccariello's complicated ancestry, I am still none the wiser regarding what relevance this has to my investigation into Girolamo Candela's murder. And the day, as we can all see…" he indicates the fading light, "Oh pardon, that was insensitive of me. But the day is drawing to a close and I have other business to attend to, thank you."

"But, you are a policeman," Nino replies, his tone dismissive. "Surely you have not forsaken the art of looking and listening? Please, I urge you to be patient and let us see where this road takes us."

Talaia is noticeably piqued at having the merits of his own virtues thrust upon him, but once again he demurs, "*Per rispetto, signore. Vi prego di continuare.*"

"*Grazie, Commissario.*" Nino smiles, but with his dark glasses, liver-spotted complexion and his yellowed teeth, his expression comes across more as maniacal leer than smile.

"*Bene, Ric.* This is very interesting that Farinelli Massimo was very possibly Valeria's father; it would explain why she is so earnest in her politics."

"It does, Nino. Commissario, didn't you tell me Candela started out as an ultra left-wing candidate in Palermo?"

Talaia nods, "You are correct, I did. He stood in Palermo, even though he began his political career in Bagheria; the town which used to be called Baarìa and the town in which, as you have just told me, La Signorina Vaccariello was born. But Candela Girolamo was much younger than La Signorina Vaccariello; to suggest there has been a recent relationship between them is, frankly, preposterous."

"I agree," Ric confirms. "But if I remember rightly, you said Candela received a lot of funding from left-wing celebrities, movie stars, writers and the like."

"He did. We know this," the Commissario replies, tersely.

"Do you know if he ever received any funds from Valeria Vaccariello?"

"No, not that we know of."

"Or her husband?"

"Again," Talaia replies, very obviously tiring of being treated like a witness for the defence, "not that we know of."

Nino raises his hand, wishing to be heard: "Gentlemen, what you have singularly failed to take into account is that Vaccariello is her stage name."

"I mean no disrespect, Nino, but it is the name of the man her mother married," Ric adds.

"Yes, yes," Nino agrees, impatiently, "but, more importantly, this was her stage name. She was married twice; both of her husband's names were different from this. If she had made any political donations, they would in all probability have been made in the name of either of her husbands. Do either of you know what their names were?"

Commissioner Talaia shrugs. He looks to Ric, who shakes his head and looks to Old Nino. And it is clear from the bewildered look on the blind man's face that he doesn't have the first clue either.

Ric trawls his mind for something Valeria said when they were talking about Candela. He snaps his fingers, "I remember Valeria telling me Candela was "once a good communist and now he is no longer". I thought she meant he was no longer a good communist because he was, by that time, dead. I also remember asking her if he'd ruffled enough feathers for someone to want to shoot him."

Talaia is now paying far more attention. "And what was her response?"

"If I remember rightly, she said people had been killed for less. However, it wasn't so much what she said, as the way she said it. She was very casual about it, as though it would have been perfectly natural for someone to shoot him; like it would make no difference to her."

Old Nino sniggers into the back of his hand, "Oh, Ric, we are forgetting..." and he continues to snigger until he can control himself no longer and bursts out laughing.

"What, Nino. What am I forgetting?"

"Oh, Ric, we are such fools. If Valeria told me my sight would return, I would believe her." He roars with laughter, so much so that Ariana comes from the kitchen to see what all the fuss is about.

Talaia looks across at Ric and shrugs again, and they wait until the old man steps down off the cloud of his amusement.

"Okay, Signor Cafarella, we appreciate that we are not seeing, sorry, grasping something that appears obvious to you, But—"

Old Nino raises his stick-like arm and offers his surrender, "No, I apologise, Commissario. I am not laughing at you; I am laughing at us."

Ric and the Commissario frown in ignorance.

"For what," Nino continues, "is Valeria, if she is not an actress?"

The only sound is the howl of the gale across the terrace and the belts of rain whipping against the window.

Talaia scratches his head, examines his hat as though it has let him down in some way, and sighs. The curl of his lips suggests he has sampled a food which offends him.

"No! I simply refuse to entertain the idea that a woman of La Signorina Vaccariello's age can lure a man like Candela to a deserted alley and shoot him dead. This proposition is surely the product of a fertile imagination. No wonder Signor Cafarella was laughing. What possible bait could this woman offer that it would attract Candela, alone and late at night, to the Piazza San Bartolo?"

"Money, Commissario," Nino replies. "What else? Like the *totani* drawn to the *ontreto* by the flashing light only to impale themselves on the hooks, the promise of a woman's money would draw most politicians to their death. And if she had donated to Candela's cause before, there would be all the more reason for him to answer her call."

"Okay, okay," Talaia says, waving his hand as though swatting a fly, "I cannot deny your theory has the air of plausibility about it, but as to whether it is...? It sounds to me as though we are fitting the horse to the blanket, and not the blanket to the horse, which is how it should work. I still find it hard to believe that La Signorina Vaccariello would steal the gun from Signor Ross' boat and shoot a man in cold blood. No," he decides. "There are times when a policeman would like to follow the road of convenience; after all, it makes life easier in the long run. But, there are also times when he must follow the trail of hard evidence and not allow himself to be distracted from his path by the fantastic imaginings of an old man and his primary suspect."

At this, Nino perks up, "Ah, Ric, is it true? Are you the Commissario's prime suspect?"

"Looks that way."

Talaia stands up. "We have Signor Ross' fingerprint on the gun used to shoot Signor Candela."

"Was it your gun?" Old Nino asks.

"The Commissario seems to be under the impression the gun arrived here on the Mara, with me." But as he says this, Ric notices Talaia throw Officer Paolo a knowing look.

"Signor Cafarella," Talaia steps over to the old man and bends respectfully, "we have taken up too much of your time and I must return to Lipari. I am grateful for your sharing your thoughts with us."

Nino looks up, "Commissario, your presence has filled the void of a rainy afternoon and it is I who should thank you for going to the trouble of listening to the ramblings of an old man. I hope I have been of some service to you. But," he pauses, "there are times when a man who has lost his sight recognises more than those who see all that is there before them. I must tell you that Tonio Sciacchitano was, as it says on his grave, *un uomo integerrimo*. He provided a great service to a community suffering at the hands of the *Fascisti*. For this he paid the price of not only having to leave the island of his birth, but also of giving up the name of his family. You will appreciate how difficult this must have been for him. This *uomo*, Signor Ross," he points in the direction of Ric, "is made of the same material as his forebear. I doubt that he is a murderer. He is, in my opinion, also *un uomo integerrimo*."

Even though he knows the old man cannot see him, Talaia clearly believes that his smile will put the old man at ease, "Thank you, Signor Cafarella. Please rest assured I will take your reference for his character into account. *Arrivederla, Signore.*"

Ric reaches out for the old man's hand. It feels slight and brittle. "*Ciao, Nino,*" he says, "*e mille grazie.*"

"*Ciao, Ric. Buona fortuna, eh.*"

Salina disappears into a bank of low cloud as they drive back down through Quattropani. The atmosphere in the car is strained and Talaia fidgets, inspecting his hat as though the tall tales it has been subjected to have in some way wilted it. A large coach lumbers round a corner at them, leaving Officer Paolo no alternative other than to slam the car against the uneven kerb.

"*Scusi, Commissario,*" he says.

But Talaia ignores his apology, "I must congratulate you, Signor Ross. This was an interesting diversion listening to Cafarella Nino entertain us with his stories. There is much I have to look into and it will take others some time to assemble the information I need. Remember I am still waiting for the results of more tests on your Beretta."

"My Beretta?" Ric repeats, glancing at the detective. "If I was a betting man, I'd put a lot of money on the pistol, or my Beretta as you insist on calling it, not having my prints on it. But I guess we'll have to wait to find that out."

Talaia simply raises an eyebrow and pouts as if it's all the same to him.

"What's next, Commissario? Slap me in irons and beat a confession out of me?"

"Oh, how very medieval, Signor Ross: *Schiavettoni* and a Saint Antony?" he chuckles.

"*Schiavettoni?* I've heard that word before."

"Yes, these *Schiavettoni* were iron handcuffs which were tightened with a heavy screw. They were extremely painful to wear. Each of the political deportees who came here in the twenties and thirties would have worn these while in transit." He wags his finger to emphasise his point. "And each of these handcuffs would have been locked to a chain and this chain would have been attached to three other prisoners. These chains were so heavy, the prisoners found it almost impossible to stand up and walk carrying this weight."

"And a Saint Antony?"

"You know," he sucks his cheek, remembering, "most of the prison warders of this period were either from Sicily, Calabria or Sardinia. They did not exactly understand a convention of human rights and, not unnaturally for men from poor backgrounds and with little education, they viewed politicians from the north as privileged fools. If they took the slightest dislike to one, they would take him to solitary confinement, throw a piece of carpet over his head and beat him senseless, often leaving him to drown in a pool of his own blood. He could, of course, not complain to the Prison Superintendent because, with his head covered, he could not identify his assailants. It is extraordinary to imagine such medieval practices were employed as recently as eighty years ago.

"I have often wondered why it was called a Saint Antony, though. Perhaps it is because Saint Antony of Padua is the patron saint of finding things," he turns and appeals to Ric. "Eh? You could never find out who was responsible for your assault." He thinks for a moment, before adding, "Or perhaps I am confusing him with Saint Antony of Egypt who was continually being beaten by the devil. After listening to the old man proclaim Antonio Sciacchitano's many virtues, I am surprised he was not proclaimed Saint Antony of Canneto."

"You think Old Nino is a diversion?"

"No, Signor Ross, you are missing my point. The point is, or rather the points are that one: we no longer beat confessions out of suspects. And two: there is no point in putting you in irons with the weather as it is. No one is going anywhere until this storm lifts. So, you are at this time as much a prisoner to this island as the political deportees who were confined here in the time of Il Duce. You are going nowhere fast. Do I make myself clear?"

"You sure do, Commissario. But where does that leave us with Claudio Maggiore?"

"Where does that leave us? It leaves us without a body and therefore without a crime to investigate. That is precisely where it leaves us, Signor Ross."

They drive on in silence, the only noise the slapping of the windscreen wipers and the gentle humming of the engine, which magnifies to a reverberating boom as they pass through the tunnel back into town.

"I suppose you'll be going on to see La Signorina Vaccariello?" Ric suggests.

Talaia blinks and shakes his head as though the world is full of idiots. "Signor Ross, do you think I am that stupid?" he asks. "First I must establish a reason for going to see her. If you think I am about to arrest an old lady on suspicion of murder on the grounds of an elaborate preparation cooked up by an old blind chef and his *secondo posto della cucina*, then you have another think coming."

"Then I guess you'll be wanting me to accompany you to the station?"

Talaia shrugs: "What good would it do me to lock you up and feed you at the taxpayer's expense, eh? No, I think for the moment you can look after yourself better than we can. And besides, you would do well to remember that the *città* sees all that goes on down in the town. That is always the way it has been."

Ric looks at the little detective and frowns. "Next thing you'll be telling me the walls have ears, Commissario."

"Oh yes, my friend; the *città* hears everything too."

"In that case, Commissario, ask Officer Paolo to drop me off behind the sports stadium. I'd rather no one saw me being dropped off by a police car; wouldn't want to get any of the tongues wagging. I'll walk the rest of the way into town."

Talaia is amazed, "In this weather?"

"Sure! But don't think I didn't appreciate the ride."

"*Paolo, fermati qui per favore.*"

The car slows and halts, and Ric gets out. He is in no hurry to close the door, holding it open so that rain spatters the inside of the car causing the little detective to inch away from him.

"And I'm sorry to have led you on such a wild goose chase,

Commissario. I'll try and come up with a body next time round. *Ciao*, Officer Paolo. Thanks for the ride."

60

Down in the *città bassa* the wind whistles through the alleys and the rain lashes at the windows. Awnings are furled, tables and chairs stacked inside, and doors shut fast. Even the vegetable stall at the *alimentari* has been packed away and the gravel-voiced proprietor stands staring out from the dim confines of her shop, grumbling at Aeolus for yet another afternoon's lost trade.

As he passes La Precchia, Ric first hears then spots Sandro playing cards with three other redundant *escurzionisti*. The colourful array of picture cards laid spread out on the table matches their colourful language.

Ric is soaked through, but finds the rain curiously comforting; it is warm, it holds no menace.

He is up past the Piazzetta when he hears someone shout after him.

"Hey, Gallese, wait for a moment."

Ric turns. It is Sandro.

The *escurzionista* hurries after him, grabs him by the arm and leads him into the narrow vico Tindaris, where they are sheltered from the rain.

"I thought you weren't talking to me, Sandro."

"Talking, my friend? No, I am talking to you. Why should I not be talking to you? We are friends, eh?"

"Sure, Sandro. If we are friends, what can I do for you?"

"For me?" He wipes the excess of rain from his curly hair and peers up at Ric. "I know you always think I want something from you, Gallese, but this time it is what I can do for you."

"Surprise me."

Sandro looks about, nervously. "I am told that this policeman, Commissario Talaia, has been to visit you at your house again. I ask you the other day if it is true and you did not answer me straight. Now I am told he did."

Ric does not need to reply.

"This is not good, my friend. When policemen like this take an interest in you, the people round here will not look kindly on you. I want to tell you to be careful. There are many who think you are helping the police; this makes you a very unattractive person."

Ric smiles, "I think I know what you mean by this, Sandro, but I don't think it's got anything to do with my looks."

Sandro frowns.

Ric puts a fatherly arm around the sloping shoulders of his harbinger of doom. "Don't worry about it. I've already come to the conclusion that whatever I do I'm going to upset someone. Doesn't seem to be much I can do about it. But, thanks for the warning. I'll keep my eyes peeled and my ears pinned back," he says, thinking of what Talaia has just said about the citadel having eyes and ears.

Sandro is offended and the furrows on his forehead deepen. "This is not funny my friend. Why do you always have to make a joke of what I tell you? What I say, you know it is for your own good. If you know better, then—"

"No, I don't know better," Ric interrupts, adopting a more serious tone and expression. "Listen Sandro, I am very grateful to you for your concern; really I am. If you've got any suggestions as to how I'm supposed to get out of the mess I'm in, then I'd like to hear them."

"Er, no. I don't think I can be of any use to you..."

"What? In case you end up with the same Saint Antony I'm being touted for?"

"Saint Antony? What is this?"

"Oh, never mind. What I mean is I appreciate you putting yourself at risk to warn me. Thank you."

Sandro smiles a shade sheepishly. "Okay! You are welcome. You know, I like you, Gallese. I would hate for you to have any trouble. Why don't we go back to your place and play Scopa." He digs in his pocket, "See, I have my cards."

"Nice idea, Sandro, but I need to pay La Strega a visit before the evening closes in."

"La Strega? But today is Wednesday," Sandro says, dismayed. "She will be at the 'ospital in Messina."

"Saturday today, I think you'll find."

"Oh, yes, I have my days wrong. It is always difficult to tell which day it is when it is raining."

"Tell me, Sandro, Valeria doesn't like people to know about her going to the hospital, how is it that you know?"

"Oh, my friend Angelo. With the taxi. He picks her up from Milazzo and takes her to Messina. Crazy thing this: when she goes in to the hospital, she looks like she is about to die and when she comes out she looks like she will live forever. Must be some magic, eh?"

"Must be," Ric agrees.

"You sure you don't want play Scopa? I teach you."

"No thanks, Sandro. As I said, I appreciate the offer, but another time."

"Okay, okay. Another time, yes, perhaps. *Ciao*, Gallese. Be careful, eh? Don't go looking for any trouble. *Ciao*."

"As if I need to look for it," Ric mutters. He stands and watches Sandro dodge the puddles as he scurries back down the Corso Vittorio.

The wind rushes as Ric hesitates at the entrance to the vicos which lead him back to the *monolocale*. He knows he ought to change, but figures he'll be just as wet by the time he reaches La Casa dei Sconosciuti, whatever he's wearing.

61

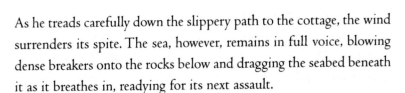

As he treads carefully down the slippery path to the cottage, the wind surrenders its spite. The sea, however, remains in full voice, blowing dense breakers onto the rocks below and dragging the seabed beneath it as it breathes in, readying for its next assault.

It takes Valeria a while to get to the door and when she pulls it back, she shades her face with her hand.

Valeria lets him stand, dripping in the rain for a few seconds before opening the door wider and stepping back to allow him in. "I am not at my best, Ric, and I was not expecting visitors so late in the evening. You will have to excuse my appearance."

"Only if you'll excuse mine," he replies.

When she turns round to face him, Valeria drops her hand away from her face. Her complexion is mottled with brown and white patches, and the skin around her eyes is so lacking in pigment that it assumes the pale hue of the alabaster walls of the mausolea in the cemetery.

"Yes," she says, "this is how a woman looks when youth deserts her."

Ric is embarrassed. He has walked in on the movie star pre-makeup and searches for a response that will alleviate her awkwardness. Sadly, nothing appropriate comes to his rescue.

"There's a bottle of Amaro Averna on the sideboard, Ric. Be a good fellow and pour us both a good measure. I'll be back in a minute."

He pours two generous measures and sits at the kitchen table. His thoughts are punctuated by the thump of the waves as they crash against the stone wall outside.

Valeria comes out of the bathroom. Her headband gone and hair brushed back, she works hand cream into her long, elegant fingers as she sits down opposite him. She has concealed the flesh around her eyes behind large, oval sunglasses.

"So, to what or to whom do I owe your presence, Ric? Please don't think I am not pleased to see you, but a woman of my age likes a little warning so she can at least soften some of the lines time has sought to engrave in her countenance."

"I apologise for arriving unannounced and uninvited. I thought that I would stop by and see if you were alright. That's a pretty unpleasant storm."

Her eyes flash a brief defiance. "Thank you, Ric. I am grateful for your attention, but I can assure you the storms of April are far less forgiving. This gale will blow through before midnight." She raises her glass, "To your good health," she says.

"And yours," he replies. The chestnut brown liqueur is sweet and yet bitter with herbs.

"I like a glass before bed; it is a digestive and helps me sleep. But tell me, how has your day been, Ric? Touched though I am that you have come to enquire after my health, I think there may be other reasons which have brought you to my door on such a rainy evening. Have you found out any more about your relation, Antonio Sciacchitano?"

"Some," he replies a little enigmatically.

"How exciting, Ric!" Valeria smiles and leans forward in anticipation. "Tell me, please. On such a dull day as this, good news is always welcome."

Ric tightens his mouth and wonders, "Trouble is, I'm not sure whether this kind of news will be welcome. Somebody said something the other day about letting sleeping dogs lie. You know the saying."

"Of course, but unless they are dead, all sleeping dogs wake eventually. So, what have you found out? What extravagant tale has Old Nino come up with this time?"

"I asked him if he could remember any more about the night his father smuggled your mother and Antonio Sciacchitano to Baarìa, and he did. He remembered that the girl's name was Katarina Maggiore and that she was running away because she was pregnant. He also recalled his mother telling him that Vincenzo Maggiore had betrayed the three deportees to the Fascists, because one of them had been having an affair with Katarina. Finally, and perhaps most importantly, he remembered who it was Katarina Maggiore had been seeing."

The smile falls from her lips and is replaced by a thin crease of abject indifference.

Whatever reaction he had expected from her, whether eager expectation or nervous dread, Ric is confused. Then Old Nino's voice leaps into his head: "For what is Valeria, if she is not an actress."

"Christ, Valeria, you've known all along."

But Valeria maintains her indifference, as though waiting for the director to shout "Cut". She reaches for her pack of long white cigarettes, passes Ric her lighter, and waits.

He reaches over and lights her cigarette, holding her gaze as he does so, "That's why you don't want me to tell Marcello. You don't want him to know you're cousins, because if he did, he'd know how much of a grudge you have to bear against the Maggiore family."

Again, her expression holds firm.

"Unless of course Marcello knows as well and the two of you want to keep Massimo Farinelli's skeleton permanently locked away in the Maggiore closet? What is this, some kind of code of silence you've been sworn to; a kind of filial Omertà about a wrong that can never be righted because it's already written in stone up in the cemetery; an episode in the family scrap book made all the more unpalatable because your grandfather was responsible for your father's murder?"

He is inclined to shout to ram home the weight of his disbelief, but he speaks as softly as the wind and the crashing of the waves permit.

"Is that why you live out here in this haunted old house? Are you waiting for your father's ghost to walk out of the water and forgive the Maggiore family, your family, its sins?"

When Valeria doesn't respond to his gentle taunt, Ric sits back. He isn't sure whether she is leading him on with her silence or whether her silence is meant to suggest she thinks him impertinent for poking his nose into her affairs.

"There's something I'm missing here, isn't there Valeria; something I'm not seeing?"

Still, nothing; she simply sits and smokes and sips her drink.

Ric studies the swirling grain in the surface of the wooden kitchen table: "It's got to have something to do with Girolamo Candela, hasn't it? Somehow he's tied up in this thing with you and Marcello. But how? I don't see the connection."

At last, Valeria leans forward to tap the ash from her cigarette. "There is nothing more to see, Ric. As we say, what you cannot see does not concern you."

"Concern me?" he replies, as though she's just prodded him with a skewer. And now Ric feels it is time to release all the uncertainty and frustration which has built up in him over of the past few days. He knows Valeria is fragile and may not withstand the rage of his pent-up emotion, but he cannot hold it back any longer.

"Right at this moment, Valeria, what I cannot see concerns me a hell of a lot," he growls. "I've got a policeman threatening to lock me up because he's got a body in his morgue which he thinks I put there. He's got a gun which he believes to be mine, because it's got my fingerprint on it. And, the only people who I can be sure know I didn't shoot Girolamo Candela are Marcello and whoever shot him.

"Now, either Marcello lifted the gun from my boat or your chum Salvo did. I get the feeling it doesn't much matter which of them did it, because they seem to be playing for the same team. That is," Ric pauses and wonders if he isn't about to make an even bigger fool out of himself, "unless you stole it, Valeria."

He waits.

She watches.

Perhaps it is the actress without her makeup, the mottled skin around her grey eyes, or the way her thin, scrawny arms project from her voluminous towelling robe. Perhaps, he thinks, it is both: but she looks to him small and vulnerable and, peculiarly for a woman in her eighties, so strangely childlike. Yet, however hard he tries to provoke her, he cannot seem to draw a response from her. Valeria is like a beautiful oyster, closed tight-shut to defend her pearl. And Ric knows that if he cannot prise it from her, he is lost.

Ric wonders what kind of illness she has that her trips to the hospital can rejuvenate her so. "What type of blood cancer do you have, Valeria?"

She drags on her cigarette and lowers her eyes. "Does it matter?"

"Sometimes," he replies.

She smiles a brief, hopeless smile. "The curious part of it is that it is not the dying I am frightened of; it is more the invasion of my body that troubles me.

"You see, Ric, I have always believed that a person is free to do with their body as they please. When I was young, there were times when I used my body in an infelicitous way; let us say to achieve my own ends. However, in later years, when one's body is no longer such... such a marketable asset, one is prone to rely on it for more basic functions, such as walking or talking. But this illness? It is like sharing your heart with a stranger who you do not love and who you cannot be rid of. This illness has reminded me of everything I hate in this world."

For the want of any more comforting reply, Ric says, "I'm sorry to hear that, Valeria."

"Don't be," she replies, her tone hardening. "I have no need of your sympathy and neither do I want it."

He is tempted to ask what she does want, but—

"When the doctors told me I have not long to live, my reaction was probably very typical. At first, I refused to believe this could be happening to me. For a few months I even denied the possibility that it *could* be happening to me. This illness is surely something that happens to other people, not me. Later, when I realised the affect it was having on my body – my tiredness, my loss of weight, other things – I grew angry at the world for all the wrongs it has done me. And it was at that time I began to wonder, to hope, that if I made some of these wrongs right, then perhaps God would release me from this curse.

"Of course, he would not; I knew this. But the idea that I could make something right for those who were no longer capable of doing so: this idea was irresistible."

"You mean your father, Massimo Farinelli?"

"Yes, among others," she replies, dreaming. "But in many ways what happened to my father he brought upon himself. Vincenzo Maggiore's reaction to finding out his daughter – my mother – was pregnant was, given the period, understandable. I can hate him for it, like I can hate Marcello for being his grandson; for being a Maggiore. And yet, I am a Maggiore too, so to hate Marcello would mean I would have to hate a part of myself also. In this, there would have been only more confusion."

"Forgive me for interrupting, Valeria, but does Marcello know about Massimo Farinelli being your father and about Vincenzo's part in his death?"

She quiets for a moment before replying, "I don't know, Ric. Can any truth be found in a rumour that was started so many years ago? Can one know for sure that Vincenzo Maggiore betrayed my father and his companions to the *Fascisti*? Any one of a number of people could have betrayed them; and for so many different reasons: the snitches, the informers, they were everywhere. People were starving; they had little to hope for and the Carabinieri were not averse to beating confessions out of suspects when they believed they had information that would be of use. To lay the blame for this betrayal at the door of a man who believed fervently in the *Resistenza*, is to disrespect him. Few would have been brave enough to question his integrity. Who knows? This rumour was probably started by the *Fascisti* to undermine his position in the community."

She thinks for a minute in silence; a silence Ric is not inclined to intrude.

"My mother told me this story in the days before she died. She also told me that the Maggiore family were *una famiglia di integrità* – a family of integrity, *integerrimo* if you like, like the inscription on Antonio Sciacchitano's grave. My mother wanted to believe her father would never have betrayed Farinelli and the others, but she could not. However, she told me she ran away because she did not want to bring shame on the house of Maggiore. She told me it was her duty as a daughter to run away like this.

"She carried the knowledge of this secret throughout her life; it weighed heavily in her heart and I sometimes wonder if it was the effort of bearing it that led her to an early grave. On her deathbed, she made me swear never to tell anyone about this.

"As to whether Marcello knows, I am not sure. We are very similar and find ourselves drawn together. He recognises this in the same way I do. Probably, it is why he looks after me. Marcello and I have talked about our attraction for each other, but I have never told him the truth. Sometimes it is better to let the sleeping dog lie."

"So where does Girolamo Candela come into this equation?" Ric asks, hoping that now that she has started talking, she will continue.

"Candela? Oh yes, Girolamo Candela."

"Only I heard he started out in Bagheria, or Baarìa as Old Nino still calls it."

"Who told you this? Nino would not have known this."

"No, he didn't. I heard it from one of the *escurzionisti* down in the Corta. He told me the Commissario, Talaia, was investigating a number of politicians, Candela being one of them. He said Candela had started out in Bagheria before moving on to Palermo."

"It is true," she says, lighting another cigarette, "I knew him when he was a young activist in the local communist party. I did not think he was like the others. He had principles and ideals. He had charisma and a burning desire to rescue the common people from the privations their poverty inflicted upon them." As she talks, Valeria grows increasingly animated, her eyes begin to glow with a hot energy and she sits up straighter, demanding his full attention.

To cool the ardour of her political fires, Ric interrupts, "I gather Candela courted the intellectual crowd. Someone told me that was where the funds for his campaigning came from."

Valeria exhales a long stream of smoke at the ceiling, "Yes, he was politically shrewd right from the start: he knew which of the intelligentsia to suck up to. That was something else which drew me to him, his perfectly amoral immorality. The writers, the directors, the actors, they all thought Girolamo Candela the perfect standard bearer for the red flag. He came from a poor background, so he was not one of those rich kids passing through the tunnels of their political adolescence. He was sufficiently unsophisticated for the cognoscenti to find him engaging and he was ruthless in his quest for campaign funds."

"Did you donate?"

Valeria pouts, as though he should know better than to ask, "My first husband was a studio producer; he donated. In fact he donated so much that the studio fell into bankruptcy and he committed suicide." She quiets.

"Because of the bankruptcy?"

"No, because even though I was much older than him, I had an

350

affair with Girolamo Candela and my husband found out. The bankruptcy may have encouraged him to draw his sword, but my infidelity forced him to fall upon it."

Now Valeria is back watching him again, waiting either for his sanction or his censure.

"Is that why you changed your mind about Candela?" Ric asks. "The last time we spoke about him I remember you weren't exactly enamoured of him."

She teases her thumbnail with her teeth, as if she is trying to make up her mind about how best to answer.

"No," Valeria replies. "And yes. Perhaps this was a part of it, although I could hardly lay the blame for my infidelity at Girolamo's door. It was, in the first place, my idea: I seduced him, not the other way round. Remember, Ric," she smiles, a salacious, lustful smile, a turning of her head and the raising of her eyebrow, "my best years may have been behind me, but youth will never lose its appetite for certain fruits. A precocious young man he may have been, but I knew what I wanted from a political Adonis like Girolamo.

"Oh, don't look so disapproving, Ric. You British can be such prudes."

"Sorry to disappoint, Valeria, but you read me all wrong. I'm trying to figure out what else he did that turned you against him?"

Valeria frowns, playfully, "Ric, this constant need for answers is most unbecoming in you. Can't a woman simply fall out of love with a man?"

Ric shakes his head slowly, without losing eye contact with her, "Not far enough to want to murder him, no."

She laughs, sitting back and roaring with an abandon he would not have imagined. But her laughter is not attractive; she cackles like a witch, her tone thin and sharply pitched.

"You think I shot Girolamo Candela? You must be out of your mind, Ric. Women of my years don't exact vengeance on disenchanted lovers."

"You weren't home when I dragged myself out of the sea the evening Candela was shot," Ric states. "So what did you want from him? Were you going to ask him to return all the money you had donated to his cause?"

"I don't need that kind of money, Ric. As I have already told you, my second husband had more money than sense."

"And so, it would seem, did you by that time. Or were you still donating to Girolamo's campaign coffers at that time?"

"No," she shouts, her voice seething with protest. "After that, I never gave the *bastardo* any more money."

"After what, Valeria? After what?" he whispers. "What did he do to you that made you hate him?"

She stares him down the way he imagines she will stare down her God when he admonishes her for her sins. Her poise suggests she is defiant and stubborn and not to be bullied, and yet Ric is still suspicious of her motive. Somewhere deep in the locked vaults of her past he feels there is a darker secret waiting to emerge. Valeria is consumed by a resentment and guilt she will not permit herself to recognise.

"After what?" he asks again.

Finally, her face crumbles and her previously belligerent pose wilts, like a delicate flower surrendering to the needle-chills of autumn. She rests her head in her hands and whispers, "After I got rid of his child."

But for the waves beating the shoreline beyond the walls of the little cottage, the silence is deafening and extends until it is disturbed only by Valeria's weeping.

"I am sorry, Ric. This episode in my life, I have never told a soul of this before. It has always been too painful to recall."

"No one?"

"I said, not a soul. After my first husband's suicide, I could not bear to have the baby. The child would have been too much of a reminder of the consequences of my infidelity."

"Your husband knew?"

Valeria nods. "He could not deal with the shame and, after he died, I could not come to terms with what I had done to him. I went to Girolamo and told him we were very suited politically. I told him being married to the daughter of Massimo Farinelli would open many doors for him and that we, with our new child, would be good together. But, as San Bartolo is my witness, he just laughed and walked away. As he walked he said the world would not take him seriously if he had to campaign in the company of yesterday's actress, a woman old enough to be his mother and a woman with a child some thought belonged to her dead husband.

"I found a doctor in the backstreets of Naples and paid him a handsome price for his silence. It was so much easier back then."

She dries her eyes. "It was only later, when my mother told me how she had run away to Baarìa and married a man to save me from being born illegitimate, that I understood exactly what I had done. I had killed my child, something my mother would not do. She left me with no place to hide from my conscience."

Ric fills her glass and pushes it towards her. She looks, now, even more reduced and though he feels oddly rewarded for listening to her confession, he feels guilty that he has had no other alternative than to extract such painful memories from her.

"So you sent Candela a letter asking him to meet you in the Maddalena near where Edda Ciano lived. Your sense of theatre should have forewarned him, but I don't suppose he could have refused, knowing what had gone on between you. You were the only person on the island who had the power to lure him away from his bodyguards."

"I did not kill him," she protests.

"Valeria, face it, you took the gun from the Mara and shot Candela," he both accuses and pleads. "What beats me is why you threw the gun in the sea at Portinente. Without it, Commissario Talaia

353

would not have connected me to Candela's murder and without it my guess is you probably wouldn't have killed Candela. In which case, I must wear some of the blame."

She looks up and tries to smile at him, but her tears have swept away her defiant veneer in much the same way as the salt-water smoothes the stones of the beach.

"No," Valeria whispers, "you must believe me, I did not kill him."

Ric looks deep into her cold grey eyes and remembers what Camille wrote in his letter and what Nino pointed out to him and Talaia not a couple of hours before; that Valeria is, or was, an actress.

"That night," she begins, "when I heard his speech up in the Mazzini, I learned the difference between man and god. You see, Ric, if you place all your faith in one man, it is inevitable that you will be disappointed. They are, after all, only flesh and blood and therefore prone to weakness. God, on the other hand, is not made of flesh and blood: we construct him in our minds and make him as perfect as we want him to be. We, on the other hand, are imperfect. We only have ourselves to blame." Her voice cracks and dries; she sips her Averna.

"I hated Girolamo Candela for how he treated me and I swore I would never forgive him. But, after some water had passed under the bridge, I found I was prepared to forgive him in a small way. Why? Because I believed in his dreams and his aspirations for those who could not afford to feed their children.

"I had heard the stories about how he had moved to the Socialists and how he was getting money from the Mafia, but I ignored these stories, hoping he would never change his ideology. So when I listened to that speech about the brave new world in which the people of Lipari would be bribed like Judas to allow this hotel to be built, I realised Girolamo had ransomed his soul, just like all the others. This was when I made up my mind that I had to tell him I would go to the papers with my story. If it was going to be the last thing I could do before I die, I wanted to have the satisfaction of going to my grave knowing that I had destroyed his political career. I thought that in the same way I had rid the world of his child, I would rid the world of his ambition.

"You see, Ric, Girolamo Candela had already destroyed my life once and by coming here and building this hotel, he would destroy the only life I have left: this island, the family I should have belonged to and the father I never knew. To preserve all this, I had to destroy him."

"You said Candela knew your father's identity?"

Valeria looks down at the floor; a child accused of talking out of turn. "Yes. In those days I was both romantic and naive; this was a very poor combination in my character. I should never have told him; I have regretted it ever since."

Ric sits and watches Valeria. He finds himself swimming in a sea of conflicting emotions, unsure as to whether he should reach out in consolation or scold her for her stupidity.

"So what are you going to do, Ric?"

"About what?"

"About this situation I have caused for you?"

"I don't know," he replies. "If the gun really does have my prints on it, then I'm done for."

Valeria looks horrified. She reaches out and touches his arm, "No, Ric. It would be better for you to leave."

"Funny, Marcello said something like that."

She rests her head against her fist and grimaces, "Would it be better that I go to this Commissario Talaia and tell him it was me and not you." She is Garbo and Bergman both rolled into one: she would give herself up for him, for his cause, for...

Ric smiles, "A noble offer, Valeria, thank you. But that would only confuse him even more. Imagine what a feast the press would make of this sordid tale. Imagine the shame you would bring to the Maggiore family? Would it be worth that much?"

355

She shakes her head. "The papers don't need to know about my connection with the Maggiore family and," she frowns, "I have only a few months left to live. A failed actress who once enjoyed a brief liaison with a dead politician? Hah, they are not likely to condemn me to life in the Ucciardone for that," Valeria scoffs. "I am sure Commissario Talaia will be only too happy to finish with the case of who killed Girolamo Candela."

"If only it was that simple."

He thinks to mention the killing of Claudio Maggiore, but thinks better of it when he remembers the argument he overheard was between two men. And though he now thinks Valeria may possess the requisite hatred for murder, he doesn't reckon she'd be up for strangling a man and burying his body beneath a pile of rubble.

"So I ask again, Ric, what will you do?"

"I don't know, Valeria, what do you want me to do? Tell you that you were wrong to lure Candela to the Piazza San Bartolo simply to threaten to expose him? Tell you it wasn't your fault that someone else was waiting to shoot him? Absolve you of your sin?"

"No, Ric," she shakes her head, her wavy hair flowing around her, "absolution is not yours to grant. The time for *la resa dei conti* will come soon enough and only God has the wisdom to decide whether I am worthy of absolution." She is calmer now that she is ready to depart her confessional. "But, Ric, what happens now is up to you to decide."

62

Aeolus grows bored with the vicissitudes of the islanders and casts his eyes northwards. Naples, a crowded crucible of discontent slumbering in the shadow of Vesuvius, will provide greater amusement for his capricious energies. He has vented his frustrations upon the steep flanks of the *città* and once more the cathedral of San Bartolo has withstood his assault.

In the Via Maddalena, the residents have bolted their doors and shuttered their windows, and the Marina Corta is deserted when Ric strolls back through it to his *monolocale*. Like Aeolus, his thoughts are taken with the constant changes in his fortune and he can see no way out of his maze of alternatives. Tonight though, he does not care if he is being followed through the narrow alleys. Whether it is Aeolus, Marcello or Commissario Talaia who is watching him, Ric is too tired to care.

Once inside the front room, he drops onto the small sofa and falls deeply asleep.

63

Something is wrong. Something is seriously wrong. He cannot breathe.

Ric is drowning. He is deep in the water, in the dark, surrounded by thrashing *totani*, diving down and down and down. He must get away from the screaming propeller of the launch before it can carve a channel through his skull. His chest tightens and he begins to struggle for air. He is deep and knows it because the sea is always cold when one is down so deep. He is very deep now, too deep and has not allowed himself enough time to swim back up to the surface before his lungs burst and the sea floods in. Ric has made the same mistake once before. How could he be so foolish as to make it again? He stops, suspends in the cool water for a split second, then turns and makes for the surface, his legs kicking wildly like an electric frog. He can't hold out. He–

"Ric?" murmurs a voice from the darkness.

He opens his eyes: the room is black and someone has their hand over his mouth.

It is the sailmaker. "*Per favore, sta 'zitto, eh?* Don't move for a moment." Slowly, he lifts his hand away from Ric's mouth.

"How the hell did you get in here?" Ric mutters under his breath.

"You forget, my friend, this is my house."

"You and I need to talk–"

"*Sta 'zitto*, Ric. Be calm," Marcello's breath is hot against Ric's cheek. "We will talk, but now is not the time. We must leave. Get up and follow me."

"Give me one good reason why I should trust you, Marcello?" Ric manages to restrain himself from shouting, but cannot keep the anger from his tone.

"A good reason?" Marcello replies, as though he is toying with several ideas and isn't sure which will best suit his purpose. "Okay, how about if I leave you here, you will either be arrested at sun rise or dead by sunset. Is that good enough? Or are you as dumb as Talaia obviously thinks you are?"

Ric scoffs, but softly, "And if I come with you, how do I know I'll be any better off?"

"You would trust the little Commissario before me? He is Candela's man and Candela is dead. If I had wanted you dead, you would already be so," he hesitates, "and the only way out of here is through the vico." He waits. "Okay, stay here, you fool."

For a couple of seconds Ric wrestles with his visitor's uncomfortable logic. "Well, when you put it like that..."

"Bring what you have," Marcello whispers as he stands.

"I have nothing. Talaia has my passport."

"Then bring nothing. We will be quicker."

"Okay, but there is a policeman outside and probably another at the far end of the alley."

"It is true," Marcello murmurs, "the big *poliziotto* is there, but he is sleeping."

And it is very possibly the first truth he has been told all day: Officer Paolo is present at the corner of the alley, but he is sprawled unconscious, his arms and legs crooked and limp.

They step deftly to avoid disturbing him. Ric starts to voice his concern, but Marcello hisses at him to keep quiet.

Like thieves, they wind their way through the narrow *vicolos* of the *città bassa.* The storm has passed over and the moon and stars shine bright, painting the alleyways in a canvas of sharp contrasts; silver and black flashing over their shoulders as they dash and dodge and duck and dive from one doorway to the next.

A couple of times, Ric stumbles into his guide, so he hangs a pace off Marcello's back and tries to keep in step.

Marcello holds up his hand as he slows and stops.

Cigarette smoke hangs in the night air.

Two policemen are loitering in the curve of the Via Roma; they are chatting, their voices pitched low.

Marcello turns, raises his finger to his lips, steals across the cobbled street and is gone, swallowed by the shadows.

Ric realises that he only has to step straight out into the street and give himself up to the policemen to make life simple. The idea of putting himself in further danger seems stupid; that is, if he prefers to trust Talaia.

He can't make out Marcello's profile at the foot of the steps opposite, but he can feel him. An arm extends into the light as he waves, impatient for Ric to follow.

One of the policemen bends to light a cigarette. Ric knows it is his best chance to get across the street unseen as the flaring light will momentarily blind the two officers. But again, he hesitates: if Talaia believes there is any likelihood of the Beretta being his gun, then surely he would have locked him up in a cell by now? There is too much that doesn't make sense.

Ric slips as quietly as he can across the street.

Marcello pulls him up the steps, muttering beneath his breath as though tiring of his charge's doubts.

They slink between the plane trees in the Franza and scurry through the shadows of the Sant'Anna, paying particular attention to their footfall, as the sound of each stone they trip over or kick echoes louder than a gunshot.

It is way past midnight and the town, like those tucked up in bed, is sighing. Away up on Monte Gallina a baby wails and from the flats behind Diana a couple argue as if the lives of their children depend on the outcome of their dispute.

Ric would like to know where they are going, but he has to hurry to keep up with Marcello. Each time he slows and Ric arrives at his shoulder, the sailmaker darts off into a doorway or the shadow cast by a balcony.

The Maddalena, through which Ric walked not a couple of hours before, is cool and peaceful. They relax a little now that they are further from the Corta. At the bottom, where the alley opens onto the little shingle beach beside the Hotel Rocce Azzurre, Marcello stops and listens. Beyond the lapping of the water, the occasional shriek of a *cavazza* from the cliffs beyond the Punta and the solemn moaning of a fishing smack way out in the darkness, there is no noise that warrants their attention.

"We go to La Casa dei Sconosciuti," Marcello murmurs. "Salvo meets us there with my boat. But we must walk at the water; it is too dangerous by road."

So they slip across the back of the beach, being careful not to disturb the pebbles, and wade through the shallows beneath the wall which runs along the back of the small bay.

The steep road up past the Carasco is lit, but by keeping to the hillside they make it up and over into the next bay without incident. But as they stroll down the zigzag path towards Valeria's little house, they hear the shrill blowing of a whistle from somewhere back in the town.

Marcello halts briefly, "Now we must hurry. They have changed the watch and found our sleeping policeman."

The path is unlit and they stumble as they make haste on the uneven track.

Valeria is waiting for them. Even in the dark, her long hair seems to shimmer like a hundred individual strands of light. "Ric, are you okay?"

Marcello continues on to the slipway and Ric stops to reply, "If someone was to tell me what was going on, I'd feel a whole lot better."

She surprises him by reaching out and taking his arm. Valeria pulls him close, her lips against his ear. She whispers, "I have not told him about our conversation this evening. If you must, then know you have my blessing. But if you can keep my secret, our secret, then... This night it is better you go with Marcello and Salvo. You can trust them! You must trust them."

"Do I have a better alternative?" Ric can smell the citrus and the vanilla and the lime of her perfume and he is reminded of the old blind man, Nino, and how he recognised Valeria by her fragrance.

"For now? No."

The boat which ghosts in out of the night is not the delicate skiff of Ric and Marcello's aborted fishing trip. It is sleek and stylish; a twelve metre *motoscafo* with a forward cabin. The pilot coasts it into the slipway with all the assurance of a man who knows exactly where Homer's coffin mushrooms up from the seabed.

They clamber aboard, Valeria waves and the sleek motorboat burbles and sweeps slowly out of the small bay below Capistello. In the glow from the instruments of the control panel Ric can make out the pilot's face; it is Salvo.

Marcello takes up his station to the left of the cockpit; his expression hard and uncompromising, his eyes dark and concealed like the night and the sea before them. He pulls a cigar out of his shirt pocket and chews thoughtfully on it as Salvo eases up the throttle.

"What the hell is going on, Marcello?" Ric asks. "Where are we going?"

"Vulcano," he replies, pointing towards the south. "You will be safe there."

"Safe from whom? From the police? From Talaia?"

"And other people."

"Other people? What other people?"

"Ric, we have found out that Candela's people have sent a man to kill you. Whoever it is that is coming would have been here this afternoon, but because of the storm the Aliscafo has not been running, so he or they will probably arrive in the morning. It is no longer safe for you to be in Lipari."

"Wouldn't I be safer in the police station with Talaia?"

"You think so, eh? You think you can trust this Commissario? My friend, wake up! You are in Sicily."

But Ric is not convinced, "You may have forgotten, Marcello, but the last time I got on a boat with you I ended up having to swim ashore. You left me out in the water. How the hell do you expect me to believe the same won't happen again?"

"No, Ric, I think not. As I said, I sent a boat to look for you. How was I to know you would swim to the shore and not wait? My people did not leave you to the fishes; they searched until they heard you were safe. And you know I had to get back in a hurry. You know my boat was sinking. You saw the damage." Marcello glances at Ric as though he expects him to understand. "When I heard the shots, I knew it was Candela; there was a rumour going round the *città bassa* that someone was going to kill him. I needed to find out what was going on. The collision with the police boat was bad luck, bad timing, nothing more."

"Talaia's convinced I had something to do with Candela's murder. He says my prints are on the pistol and he has the passports off the Mara."

Salvo eases the throttle back and the *motoscafo* slows; the swell from the backwash lifting them, lowering them and then lifting them again. "What gun is this, Ric? Why do you have false papers and a gun? Are you running from someone? Are you a criminal?"

"No, not running. I had a little trouble in Corsica." Ric's right thigh pains him and he rubs at the scar. "The passports were given to me in case I needed them; it seemed a good idea at the time."

"And the gun?" Marcello asks, raising an eyebrow in concern. "Why do you carry a gun with you? Are you an assassin?"

Ric scoffs loudly, "I'd have to have been a magician to shoot Candela when I was a mile out in the ocean, with you. If I didn't know better it would look to me as though you planned for me to be out of the way so I had no alibi. It wouldn't look that way to Talaia though."

"I told you, Ric, Talaia cannot be trusted. He is *Palermitano* – from Palermo. The police there cannot be trusted; they are always ambitious for power. Candela was going to run for mayor in Palermo. If he was elected, he could have done much for Talaia."

"Then explain why he seemed to know from the start that I was mixed up in Candela's murder."

"This is simple, my friend. After the shooting he would have asked the Carabinieri if anyone unusual had recently come to the island. Normally the Carabinieri would not walk across the vico to spit on a Commissario of La Polizia from Palermo, even if he was dead. But this man, Talaia, has much authority in Palermo, Milazzo and Messina. They cannot afford to ignore him. This is how it works. From the Carabinieri he would have found out about you, Ric, and he would have found out where you were staying; that was easy enough, eh? The Carabinieri are not always as blind or as deaf as we would like. And you told him the Mara was in my place, so he comes to Canneto to search her."

Salvo works the helm and the throttle, guiding the craft between the peaks and troughs. The bald cone of the volcano across the Bocche di Vulcano blacks out the stars and once they clear Punta della Crapazza, the southern point of Lipari, the water chops up rough; the current running out of the Mare Siculum beating into the current coming on from the western Mediterranean. In their battle to overcome each other, the obsidian sea is the loser.

"So why would Talaia want to pin Candela's murder on me?"

Marcello shrugs: "*Ambizione*, I told you; he is an ambitious man. It is possible he doesn't care who killed Candela: dead men do no favours, eh? But he would certainly care about being seen to catch the killer; this would be a good profit for him."

"But what if the gun doesn't have my prints on it?"

Marcello wrests his gaze from dark waters before them and stares hard at Ric. "What difference will it make? He has your gun. We have a saying, a tailor does not make a man for the clothes, but when he does not have sufficient cloth..."

He ushers Ric to the stern and they sit down on the cushioned seats at the transom. Though the motorboat is pitching and yawing through the waves, Ric realises that rather than heading for Vulcano, Salvo is now steering the *motoscafo* around in wide circles.

Marcello lights his cigar with an old Zippo lighter and puffs away for a few seconds. He examines the end of his cigar and, happy it is properly lit, says, "Ric, yesterday I asked you why you came to the *ferramenta* and asked to see my brother—"

"I—"

"No, *un momento*, Ric. Two days ago, you were seen at Pietra Liscia in the old warehouse of La Cava. I don't know what you were doing there, but today you went with the Commissario to the same place. I think it would be better if you told me why. What were you looking for?"

"Your brother, Claudio."

"Why?"

"Because the day I arrived here in Lipari I tied up to the old pier and heard an argument between two men. It ended in screaming and it sounded to me like one of the men murdered the other. I asked an *escurzionista* if anyone notable on the island had gone missing. He didn't know at first, so I went to the old warehouse to see if I could find a body."

"And did you, find a body?"

"Yes, buried beneath some rubble in a room cut out of the hillside."

"Did you recognise this man?"

"Not until I described him to the *escurzionista*. He seemed to think the man was your brother."

"*Puddaciaru!*" Marcello spits.

Ric flinches.

The barrel-chested Liparotan sits and stares at Ric, his eyes burning like the glow from his cigar. "He was my half-brother, not that this makes much difference. Tell me, why did you take this Commissario Talaia to the pumice warehouse?"

"Because I found myself between a rock and hard place and had to make a decision. Talaia was going to lock me up; the body was my only bargaining chip. But your brother's body has been removed. I guess your kid up at the beach bar saw me when I went up there, told you and you realised I must have gone there for some reason."

Marcello sighs and exhales a great cloud of cigar smoke, which swirls about his face. "Yes, you led me to my brother's body and I had to have Claudio moved. If Talaia had seen it, he would have made life difficult."

Ric is taken aback by the man's casual attitude.

"You think I killed my brother?"

"I'd like to think not, Marcello. I heard the man who strangled Claudio call him "*Puddaciaru*" just before he killed him. But he didn't say it the way you just said it."

He nods. "Yes, it may be true. Claudio was *puddaciaru*. You know what this word means?"

"Talkative."

He nods again. "Yes, talkative. But there are different kinds of talkative; one is trivial talk, the other is to talk when you are not supposed to. This is what my brother did; he talked when he was not supposed to."

"Seems a pretty hefty fine," Ric interrupts.

Marcello leans forward, his forearms on his knees. He glances at Ric as though asking for his patience and understanding. "My brother was close to Girolamo Candela. They were planning this new hotel for Porticello. I found out that this *bastardo* had persuaded my brother to offer others money if they would vote against me at the planning committee. Fortunately for me, these people repeated this to me. In this way, my brother was talkative.

"But, there is another, more important reason why Claudio's time had come. The morning you arrived at Casa dei Sconosciuti, you came to town and sat at La Precchia in the Corso Vittorio. You were there when the funeral procession of my father passed by. I saw you and I know you saw me. Claudio, of course, was not present." Marcello sighs and smokes, no doubt dwelling on an unpalatable truth.

"Claudio was younger than me. He was the child of my father's second marriage and not the same as the rest of my family. My father helped him; he set Claudio up with the *ferramenta*. But Claudio was lazy; he took drugs and made friends with many bad people, so I had to manage the business most of the time. Claudio was going to Palermo often to satisfy his social appetite and this was where he met Girolamo Candela. Two weeks ago, my brother told my father of this plan to build the hotel. He, my father, went into a rage and said he would take everything away from Claudio and tell the people that he was no longer the son of Onofrio Maggiore. They argued and they fought. My father was old, but he was very strong; even stronger when angry. He beat Claudio and Claudio knocked him down. My father hit his head and died during the night. I know this because Claudio was so upset and consumed by his guilt that he told me the whole story the next day. At first, I did not know what to do. My father could be a hard man to answer to and I have no doubt that Claudio did not intend to kill him.

"I found out later that Claudio had run away with his boat to

367

Palermo. I also learned that he went to see Candela who helped him drown his sorrows and provided him with a shoulder to cry on. Unfortunately, he told Candela what had happened. He should not have done this, for this kind of happening is not to be spoken about."

"Omertà?"

"Yes, in a way. This Omertà can be interpreted in many ways; one of them is that we do not need the police to help us sort out what happened between Claudio and my father. This kind of happening we sort out ourselves, quietly, among the family. But this problem with Claudio and Candela left me in a very difficult position. If I did nothing, I would place myself below Candela, because he would know things about my family which would give him an advantage over me. I could not stand and do nothing. You, Ric, must understand that this is how it is."

"I seem to have heard that story before," Ric says, thinking of how Valeria could not live with Candela knowing about her father. Somehow it all appeared to start and finish with Girolamo Candela. "So Claudio came back to have it out with you?"

He shakes his head. "No, I telephoned Claudio that he was to come home for the funeral. He refused, so I sent Salvo to bring him back. The night before the funeral Claudio disappeared and the rest you know."

"Why are you telling me this, Marcello? Surely the less I know the better."

He removes his cigar, examines the glowing end and throws it over the side. "Perhaps yes; perhaps no. Now, there are only three people who know what happened to Claudio: you and me and whoever killed Claudio."

"So the fact that I know someone murdered your brother binds me to you?" Ric asks, both offended and astonished.

"No," Marcello replies. "First of all, we are not absolutely sure who killed Claudio; although we have an idea. Second, the fact that you heard the man speak means you are the only person who can identify him."

"So what have you done with your brother's body, Marcello?"

"His corpse, you mean?"

"Yes, of course, his corpse," Ric replies, angrily.

"You are sitting on it."

64

Ric stands up; an involuntary reflex born of revulsion as much as a mark of respect for the dead. He looks down in wonder at Marcello and knows his wonder is not of the kind found in San Bartolo's expression on the ceiling of the cathedral.

"Is that what this boat trip is about, Marcello? Burial detail?"

"Yes and no, Ric. Salvo and I can manage this without you, but the opportunity comes, so we make use of it. But it is more important to get you away from Lipari to a place of safety. Go and take the helm from Salvo while we attend to Claudio."

The wiry Salvo stands back, allowing Ric into the pilot seat. He is deferential and solemn, and nods his approval when he understands Ric is competent at the helm.

Salvo and Marcello lift the cushions and open the locker beneath the seats.

Claudio's corpse is wrapped in sailcloth, sewn neatly up the centre, and judging by the grunting and groaning as they lift it out of the locker, weighed down with rocks. They teeter at the side of the *motoscafo* before swinging the corpse once, twice and then a final time over the side.

Ric is still unsure as to whether or not he can trust Marcello. He looks around the cabin for some weapon that might help him avoid Claudio's fate. However, aside from a box of fishing tackle in the corner, there is nothing.

The breeze and the motion of the boat snatch the few words Marcello offers after his brother and both he and Salvo cross themselves in the traditional fashion. As they pay Claudio their last respects, Ric picks an *ontreto* from the box and slips it into his pocket.

"I don't like to bury him like this," Marcello moans, once he is back in the cockpit, "but the sea is two to five hundred metres here. It is better that no one will ever find Claudio, even if it means no one will be present at his grave to mourn him in the way a man should be mourned. I hope San Bartolo will forgive me."

Salvo takes the helm again, speeds up and steers the *motoscafo* towards the small peninsula of Vulcanello. Once they have passed the lights of the Punta Samossà the sea is calmer and the odour of rotten eggs hangs heavily on the air.

"I don't buy this, Marcello," Ric shouts. "Someone stole my Beretta from the Mara and used it to kill Candela. The only person who could have done this was either you, Salvo or Valeria. I found out this evening that Valeria lured him to the Piazza San Bartolo the night he was shot; she admitted that much. However, in my experience, eighty-year-old ladies don't go around shooting ex-lovers in shady alleys late at night. You may call her a witch, but I doubt she'd know how to use a gun. All of which means she got him into the alley and your Salvo, here, shot him with my gun, the three of you hoping the police would pin it on me."

Marcello glares at him. "If I had intended for you to be blamed, would I have confirmed to the Commissario that you were out fishing with me when it happened?"

Ric fingers the *ontreto* in his pocket. The spines are sharp and dig into his thigh. He tenses and readies for the assault he is expecting: "Not unless you were also intending for me to join your brother out here to sleep with the fish. That way, Commissario Talaia could lay the blame at my door and wrap up his case."

But instead of Marcello and Salvo throwing him overboard, the burly Liparotan runs his hands through his hair and sits down, exasperated. "You question my integrity, Ric. This I do not like. Perhaps you are tired. I would prefer to believe this for now, because if I do not, the only course left after your disrespect *is* for me to throw you over the side. You can swim; I know this. But the waters here are treacherous and many have perished trying to swim between the islands."

Marcello sighs and pulls out another cigar. The flame of his lighter illuminates his face for a second. His expression is stark and brooding.

"Let us think about what we already know for sure. You heard this man who killed Claudio speak the word *puddaciaru*. But, there is another way you can identify him. He might have something which belonged to Claudio; a *cornicieddu*. It is a charm; a small silver charm shaped like a little horn with a curve. Someone gave Claudio this *talismano* because he was superstitious; he never went anywhere without it. He used to wear this charm on a silver chain around his neck. We searched very carefully the place where he was left at Pietra Liscia, but we could not find it."

Ric leaves Marcello hanging for a moment before turning and asking in a disbelieving tone, "And that's how we're supposed to recognise this man other than by his voice, by this charm?"

"That, yes; by this charm, his voice and by his name. But you are the only man who heard him speak. Ric, we have found out that Claudio and Girolamo Candela met each other in a club, in Palermo. This club, Exit, is frequented by men who prefer each other's company to that of women. We also understand Claudio was introduced to Candela at this club by a man whose name is Francesco Ferro. We are told this man has not been seen in Palermo since Claudio disappeared; he may still be here in the islands. We are looking for him and if we find him, it is possible you will help us identify him."

Ric recalls Valeria mentioning Claudio patronising a club in Palermo. "You seriously think I'd be better off hiding out in Vulcano rather than handing myself in to Talaia?"

"Yes, I do, Ric. If Palermo has sent someone to kill you, you are not safe with the police, especially if they, too, think you shot Girolamo Candela."

When they approach the low isthmus at the harbour of the Porto di Levante, Salvo throttles back and weaves the *motoscafo* between the many sailing boats at anchor. Lanterns spaced at regular intervals project perfectly round pools of light along a wooden dock, leading Ric to believe they have arrived at a prison camp. When the boat's motor quiets, the relentless beat of club music booms and froths from a beach beyond the trees; if it is a prison camp, it is the first he has ever heard of with an entertainment facility. A stern-faced, thickset man wearing overalls appears out of the shadows and helps tie up.

The odour of sulphur lays thick upon his tongue. Ric coughs.

"*Solfatara! Solfo!* You cannot get away from the smell here," Marcello mutters. "Now, we take the *pulmino*."

Salvo stays with the boat and Ric follows Marcello along the dock. A minibus is waiting; they get in. Beyond a brief nod between Marcello and the driver, there is no conversation; evidently the driver knows who they are and where they need to go. Sitting in the back, Ric is very suddenly aware of his tiredness; his limbs ache, his ribs still pain him from his dust-up in the vico and his head seems hell-bent on reminding him of the glancing blow the hull of the fishing boat dealt him. He isn't sure what time it is or whether it matters, but the night seems to be extending far beyond its normal duration.

The minibus winds its way up a slight slope into woodland and, after a couple of minutes, pulls up before a pair of ornate but rusty wrought-iron gates.

An old man ghosts out of the shadows. He steps over to the side of the minibus, checks to see who is inside and, once he is satisfied, walks back to open the gates.

The drive up is steep and after a succession of long, dogleg curves they halt at a collection of low, white-washed buildings.

Ric gets out, stretches and looks around. Here and there amongst the trees he notices several, single-storey holiday chalets and down the hill a small stage sits vacant before rows of empty chairs.

Marcello waves him to follow and they walk through a gated arch in the wall.

If the rusty gates backed by a sheet of brown paper lend the property a rather drab and dilapidated aspect, Ric is not prepared for what confronts him next.

The courtyard resembles the terrace of a five-star hotel: tables, chairs and umbrellas are set out on a marble patio surrounding an infinity pool, one side of which is flanked by a long beach-style bar. On the far side plush lounge chairs and coffee tables sit beneath a cinema screen.

Marcello, hands on hips, grins. "Not bad to relax, eh?" he asks.

A young, unsmiling man, wearing a white majordomo's uniform, appears next to them; his skin is coffee-coloured and his features smooth and vaguely effeminate. He nods politely and waits.

Marcello turns to Ric, "You can stay here for a few days until the storm in Lipari blows over. These people are no friends to the police. Kasim will take you to one of the little houses. It has been a long night and there is not much darkness left. Get some rest. Now, I must go back and I will see you sometime tomorrow."

"Don't you ever sleep?" Ric asks him.

"The sailmaker never sleeps," he replies, stretching his arms above his head, "he is always watching the sky; watching and waiting for Aeolus to grant him the gift of his winds so that his sails may be filled. *Ciao,* Ric."

As he turns to walk out, Marcello hesitates and turns back, "Oh, Ric, a word of advice. There are people here who it would be best not to talk to. There are no mobile telephones and the fewer the people who know this place exists, the better. It is, one might say, off limits to ordinary people. Perhaps it is best for you to remember what I have said to you about *puddaciari,* eh?"

65

When he wakes, Ric has no idea how long he has slept or where he is. The room is pitch-black and there is no clock on the bedside table. He stumbles about in the dark until he finds the living room curtains and draws them.

Soft sunlight floods in through glassed patio doors.

His clothes smell of sulphur and when he picks them up they feel coarse with wind salt from the previous night's travel. A cupboard reveals shirts and trousers in various sizes, and a selection of swimming briefs and shorts. A fancy DeLonghi Nespresso machine sits on the sideboard and the fridge is stocked with bottles of mineral water.

He shivers; it is as though they knew he was coming.

The glass doors slide open onto a neat patio with a table, chairs and an umbrella. Lemon, lime, olive and chestnut trees dapple sunlight on the forest floor and girdle the chalet in a corset of brown and green. There are no books or magazines on the table and there is little to do but make a cup of coffee, bathe in the deep silence and reflect.

That Ric has, for the moment, no other choice than to trust Marcello is obvious. But how far he trusts him is another matter.

If the Liparotan had wanted to dispose of him all it would have taken was for the two of them to throw him overboard in the straits between the islands; in the maelstrom of currents it would have been nigh-on impossible to survive. And besides, Marcello's right-hand man, Salvo, though wiry and possessed of all the benign charm of a rural vicar, is clearly his enforcer. The way Marcello said he'd sent Salvo to bring Claudio back from Palermo, told Ric all he needed to know about the little guy. To have tried to take Salvo on out in the darkness of open water would have been unwise and that was to discount the raw physicality of his boss.

The choice of who to trust lies between the barrel-chested sailmaker and the diminutive detective, neither of whom Ric knows well enough.

So far, Marcello has been true to his every word. He's confirmed very readily to Talaia that Ric was out fishing with him at the time Candela was shot, he's lent Ric his *monolocale* and attended to the Mara's repairs without demanding any money. What Ric cannot fathom, though, is what motivates Marcello's profound openness and generosity. The bullish Liparotan is so casually frank with him, it unnerves him.

Since his arrival, nearly all those he has met have been only too happy to accept him, take him into their homes and treat him as a member of the family. All of them, Valeria, Sandro, Old Nino and Marcello appear to possess a streak of integrity a mile wide. And, as he thinks of the most appropriate word which describes their straightforwardness, he realises that all of them at some time have used the word integrity when describing each other. Valeria described the Maggiore family as *un famiglia di integrità* and Old Nino the same. Even the inscription on the grave of Antonio Sciacchitano indicates he was *un uomo integerrimo*, regardless of whether his bones lie in the grave or not. Ric is surrounded by people of integrity, but he knows all too well from Corsica that integrity is measured in actions, not words.

Commissario Talaia, however, is not such a known commodity.

That he is playing some form of long game is self-evident. If he had simply wanted a neck to tie a noose around, he would have read

Ric his rights, banged him up in a police cell and hauled him off the island at the first opportunity. But there is something about the little cockerel, as Marcello insists on calling him, which draws Ric to him. He is a thinker, the antithesis of the obsequious Bosquet, the policeman he tangled with in Corsica. But, Ric is guarded to think, that doesn't make Talaia any less of a liability.

If he is honest with himself, and he sees no reason why he should not be seeing as everyone else apart from Talaia seems to be, he hasn't got the first clue who to trust. He can't even be sure there is a contract out on him or if he is safe strolling about this curious camp. The only thing he can be sure of is that someone murdered Claudio Maggiore and Girolamo Candela, and it wasn't him.

Having gone round in a perfect circle, Ric closes the door behind him and strolls down to the courtyard, a hundred metres or so down the slope.

The encampment is peaceful and the mood docile, like that of an old people's home. And apart from the insects chattering away in the scrub, the quiet is broken only by distant samba rhythms down the way. A couple sit out on the patio of their chalet, reading the papers; they don't acknowledge him.

At the pool, a group of men sit around a table playing Scopa. They mock in unflattering terms each others game-play and moan when their opponents capture a coveted card. Half a dozen others sit in couples, observing their own space as if enveloped in a quarantine zone; the men, suntanned, heavyset, with shining bald pates and dark glasses, ignore their women, who are mostly pale-skinned, slender and bored, their bikinis more supermarket than Milan.

Ric looks around and notices there is one man who sits alone and apart from the rest. He pulls out a seat at the table between the bar and the man, and measures his surroundings against his hazy impressions of the night before.

At first glance the infinity pool lends the beach-style bar an air of opulence. But, like the women perching close to their partners, the two are not perfectly matched. The marble-tiled courtyard gives way in places to unfinished concrete and beyond the pool's edge the gardens peter out to rough scrub and, further on, forest. Whoever has put the place together has a Monfortino palate, but a Moscato wallet.

Kasim appears at his table. "*Vuoi bere? Mangiare?*"

"*Grazie, Kasim. Per favore, una Birra Messina.*"

The beer arrives accompanied by a menu, which reminds Ric he hasn't eaten a square meal in over twenty-four hours. "*Per favore, Kasim, delle sarde.*"

"*Alla Catanese Palermitana o Messinese?*" he asks.

Not realising there is a choice, Ric replies, "*Catanese.*"

The man sitting alone at the adjacent table turns and says, "You should have chosen the *Sarde a Beccaficu alla Palermitana*, they are better."

Ric adjusts his chair so that he can address the man without twisting his tender torso. "If I'd known the difference, I might. Perhaps you'd enlighten me?"

His face is familiar, but from where Ric cannot recall. The man is tall and lean of build and sits straight-backed. His skin is saddle-brown and his shoulder-length, wavy black hair is combed straight back over his head to curl around the collar of his sky-blue linen shirt. He wears wrap-around sunglasses and a vaguely conceited expression, as though he would prefer not to be associated or confused with those other, bald, muscular beefs seated around the pool.

"The *Beccaficu* alla *Palermitana* is baked with capers and raisins and pine nuts," he offers. "*Alla Catanese*, the sardines are marinated in vinegar and deep fried; the flavour is all cooked out. Messinese is okay, but cheese with sardines, eh? I ask you?"

"Thanks, I'll remember for next time." He goes to turn away, but thinks again, "It's that obvious, is it? My not being Italian."

The man chuckles, "Yes, it's that obvious. You have significantly more hair and better manners than most of the others here.

"Which tells everyone I'm not French or German?"

"A lucky guess, eh? A Frenchman would have taken more time to choose his food and a German would not have chosen a dish that is named after a small bird that pecks at figs; *Beccaficu* is not enough food for a German. I am Ciccio." He holds out his hand. His fingers are slender and manicured; his grip, though, only a fraction off intimidating.

"Ric," he replies. "Nice place they've got here."

"Just passing through, Ric?"

"A couple of days."

"Where are you from?"

"Oh, here and there. Much the same as you, I expect." But it is the way the man who calls himself Ciccio sits that brings to mind where Ric has seen him before. He is the same man Ric noticed in the *barca* which passed close by him the day he arrived in Lipari.

Ciccio raises his head and curls his lip, "What do you mean by that?"

"Well, Ciccio, most of the time I'm either on my way to somewhere or on my way back from somewhere else. But right now I'm sitting in a chair beside a pool, looking forward to a cold beer and something to eat."

"The beer here is not good," Ciccio states, holding up his dark brown bottle of Birra Messina. "They," he nods at the table where the men are playing Scopa, "drink this because they think it is the beer of their birthplace. Let me tell you, Ric, this beer no longer comes from Messina; it is no longer made by *Siciliani*. Now, it is owned by Heineken and brewed in Massafra, in Puglia," he speaks the name of the town as though he has experienced some unpleasantness in it. "The only true Sicilian beer is Birra del Sole; it carries the Trinacria, the Sicilian flag: the head of Medusa with the three legs and ears of wheat?"

"I know it."

"I tell you, my friend, the beer here is only for the pigs!" He nods in the direction of the card players.

"You know your beer then, Ciccio," Ric suggests.

"Enough to know what tastes good and what does not." He leans over towards Ric and waves him closer as if to impart some great secret, "There is a little brewery," he whispers, "a *microbirrificio*, you know what I mean by this? I forget the name. It is on the Via Cavour in Palermo. It makes great beer, but don't tell these *viddani*. These peasants will only tell others and then the place will be full of their ugly friends."

Ric tries to imagine exactly how much uglier than these *viddani* their friends could be.

"You don't know Palermo, Ric?"

"No," he replies, "it's not one of those places I've been to. Maybe I'll get the chance one of these days." He recalls what Marcello has told him about Claudio, Candela and the club called Exit, and realises that Ciccio is the only man around the pool who isn't partnered by a female. He is surely the grain amongst the chaff; his nose is straight, his face unscarred and his teeth white.

He sits back, still upright, very possibly content that his new friend doesn't know Sicily's capital and is therefore a man apart from those around him.

Noticing this, Ric asks, "You know Palermo well?"

"Sure, I know Palermo well; certainly better than any of these pigs."

"Good place to enjoy a little fun?" Ric asks.

"Sure. It depends on what kind of fun you are looking for, but most of what a man would want is available."

Kasim interrupts their conversation and places a plate of breaded sardines and a basket of *focaccia* with olives before Ric.

"I told you, my friend, you should have asked for the *Palermitana*," Ciccio reminds him and, looking over at Ric's plate, he tugs Kasim's sleeve. "*Tesoro,*" he whispers, "*Capunata.*" A brief, intimate look passes between the two of them.

"Thanks," Ric replies. "I'll remember your advice for next time. You want to join me?" Ric starts to eat.

"Eh," Ciccio says, getting up out of his chair, "why not? A man who eats alone, eats too fast and gets a bad stomach. I know this; I have eaten alone too many times." He hauls himself out of his chair and pulls it over to Ric's table. His sky-blue linen shirt is open to his waist, revealing a thick growth of chest hair. "What kind of entertainment would you be looking for, my friend?" His expression, concealed as it is behind his wrap-around sunglasses, Ric cannot read, but his tone is unsettlingly licentious.

"Well," he replies, rubbing his ear and trying his best to look self-conscious, "everything, really. I like bars, restaurants and clubs. A friend of mine told me about a club..." he hesitates, "it might not be the kind of place everyone likes... Exit, I think it was called. Do you know it?"

Kasim reappears with a plate of aubergines, onions and tomato. This time, he doesn't linger for any appreciation.

"Sure, I know it. It is in the Piazza San Francesco di Paola; a good place for those who prefer things a little different, a little exotic." Ciccio grins, tucking into his food.

"My friend," Ric begins, tentatively, "told me it's where the arts crowd hang out, you know, intellectuals, politicians, that sort."

Ciccio bridles. He cuts a morsel of aubergine into a neatly symmetrical portion, forks it delicately into his mouth and closes his eyes to savour the flavour. He waits until he has swallowed before replying, "Yes, of course, it can be. Now that our President, Rosario Crocetta, is open about his sexuality, places like Exit are more acceptable. It doesn't make him any more popular, though. You know, when he was mayor in Gela, he almost put Stidda out of business; no one could collect their *pizzo.*"

"*Pizzo?*" Ric repeats.

"Yes, *pizzo*," Ciccio repeats, a lecturer amazed that his pupil can be such a dimwit. He places his fork carefully at the edge of his plate and rubs his thumb and index finger together: "*Pizzo*, the beak that needs wetting, the money others make from making sure your business is not bothered. Do you not have this in Britain?"

Ric chuckles and nods, "Of course we do, but in Britain *pizzo* is charged by the council, not the Mafia."

This concept of official *pizzo* is anathema to one such as Ciccio. He juggles it around in his head before replying, "Mm, if it isn't one type of tax, then surely it is another, eh? What can we do?"

"The poor man's burden," Ric adds.

The two sit and eat and watch the women who wait on their men the way a bitch waits in the presence of her master.

Ciccio eats only half of his meal before pushing his plate away. He sits back and closes his eyes for a moment before asking, "Do you mind if I smoke while you are still eating?"

"It's a free country," Ric replies.

"As long as you pay your *pizzo*," Ciccio suggests. He smokes and studies Ric from across the table. When he has reached a conclusion of sorts he says, "It is said," he hesitates, lowering his voice, "it is said that the police suspect a foreigner of the killing of this politician who was shot in Lipari. Have you heard this, Ric?"

He remembers what Marcello told him regarding not trusting those he meets, so he looks up from his plate and delivers the Sicilian a stern, uncompromising expression; one designed to leave him no doubt that Ric has much to hide and doesn't appreciate his line of questioning. It is, he reasons, the reaction Ciccio would expect.

Ric pauses and is about to return to his food, when he reconsiders, looks back and says, "No, I hadn't heard that, Ciccio. What nationality do they think the foreigner is this time, another Lithuanian?"

Ciccio grins. "No, English."

"Counts me out then, I'm Welsh." Ric delivers the Sicilian a stark glance, which spawns an anxious silence while he works his way through the plate of sardines.

Ciccio sits, quietly smoking his cigarette, still studying and assessing. He stubs his cigarette end into the ashtray, smiles and lifts the blanket of silence: "No, I am mistaken. This man they are looking for is not English; he is *Gallese*, like you, eh?"

He waits and watches for Ric's reaction to his less than subtle accusation. Judging by his smirk, Ciccio is both amused and no little pleased that he has now joined all the dots in his puzzle.

Ric offers him as serious and deadpan an expression as he can muster, then, "What's it to you, Ciccio?"

"To me? Nothing," he replies, shrugging his shoulders and holding up his hands in mock surrender. "Nothing except that someone should have shot that snake Candela long ago. It was as much as he deserved. No, I am mistaken. It was probably not as much, come to think of it; he deserved worse."

"Except that I didn't shoot him," Ric states.

"Of course you did not my friend. Of course you did not. And I am King Ferdinand III." Ciccio laughs, as much at his own joke as at Ric's. But gradually, his amusement wanes and his serious, game-face returns. "Wait a minute, my friend; this is why you asked me about the club in Palermo, no?" He leans forwards. "You know that Girolamo Candela was often seen in this place and you wanted to know if I knew this place also."

Ciccio frowns in thought and then appears very suddenly enlightened. "*Gallese*, you are playing some kind of trick with me. Be careful, eh? Francesco Ferro is not so amused when people play tricks with him." His lip curls again and he glares so hard, Ric can feel the heat through Ciccio's dark glasses. "I tell you, *Gallese*, I met you only five minutes before and already you make me nervous, and when I am nervous I do not react so kindly to people who ask questions."

Ric, though, is equal to Ciccio's stare. "A moment ago, you were the one asking all the questions." He hadn't known there was the chance the man in front of him was going to turn out to be Francesco Ferro; Ric had only been fishing for information. But, now that he has given up his name, Ric knows for certain Ferro is the reason why Marcello has spirited him through the night to Vulcano.

Anger wells up through his core and threatens to overwhelm him. Marcello has set him up. His hands begin to tremble and he is sure his face must be reddening with embarrassment that Marcello can take him for such an easy ride. But why? That is the question which suddenly creeps under his shirt like an army of ants. If Marcello knew Ferro was here, at this curious encampment, why not just stroll in and have it out with him?

Ric looks around and wonders if he has been billeted in some kind of Mafia convalescent home; a retreat or safe-house where no one can be touched.

"Oh, cut the crap, Ciccio," he murmurs, tetchily, his expression matching that of the man opposite him. "Everyone knows you and Candela were more than just friends. You and Candela and Claudio Maggiore all tucked up in your love nest in Palermo, cooking up dishes no one round here wants to eat." Ric smiles, "You ought to know that since Candela was shot, you've been the favourite topic of conversation at *passeggio* in the Corta."

Ciccio glares at Ric for a second and then looks around the patio. The card players are too interested in their game to bother with what is going down between the two of them. The other couples sit, like stone statues sunning themselves, while Kasim stands polishing glasses behind the bar.

"*Puddaciaru!*" Ciccio spits.

Ric waits until the man's venom has dried on the marble floor. "*Puddaciaru?*" he repeats, recognising the word he heard during the quarrel between the two men that night he was tied up to the jetty at Pietra Liscia.

"I've heard that quaint expression before, Ciccio. I gather it has two meanings. A friend of mine explained it to me. He said *puddaciaru* are either people who have not enough to do with their hands, so they exercise their mouths, or they are people who don't know when to remain silent, so they speak out of turn.

"Is that what Claudio Maggiore did, Ciccio? Did Claudio speak out of turn? Is that why Girolamo Candela sent you over to Lipari before his grand presentation?"

Ciccio stiffens in his seat. His face reddens and he clenches his fists. But he looks around once more and realises that he cannot go across the table at Ric with so many witnesses present. His lips twitch and he bares his teeth.

Ric watches him very closely and continues, "My guess is that when Candela found out how Marcello Maggiore had sent his man over to Palermo to bring Claudio back for his father's funeral, he got jumpy that Claudio might spill the beans to his brother about how you and Candela were trying to bribe the others on the planning committee to vote for the new hotel up at Porticello.

"Candela sent you over to persuade Claudio to keep quiet and you took him up to the beach at Pietra Liscia to talk some sense in to him. You couldn't do it at his place, because too many people had come into town for his father's funeral. But when Claudio told you he'd already spoken to his brother, you knew the game was up and you decided you had no alternative but to silence him and bury his body in the warehouse. You knew Claudio's boat was in Palermo and you hoped that people would come to the conclusion he'd gone back there to mourn his father's death in private. Afterwards, while most of Lipari was preparing for Onofrio's funeral, you paid one of the fishermen to take you over to Vulcano, thinking that as there was no body, no one would know a crime had been committed and therefore no one would be looking for you.

"What you didn't reckon on was that the police were onto

Candela's game and that nothing goes on here without the right people knowing about it. Lipari is a small island, Ciccio. You've spent so much time in Palermo, you've forgotten that."

Ric pauses, but he isn't finished. "But someone tipped the police off about Candela bribing the planning committee and they came here to arrest him. They left it until after his big speech up in the Piazza Mazzini because they wanted to look good. They like a bit of *opera seria* when they can get it and they wanted the best publicity they could get for their money."

Ciccio fidgets uncomfortably, as though he has fallen victim to one of the many feral cats which wander the Maddalena at night.

"What you, and they, didn't bargain for was someone shooting Candela. The police wouldn't normally get so annoyed; after all, Girolamo was just another cheap *politico* from Palermo. But whoever shot Candela emptied the theatre on their curtain raiser, so they locked down the island. You didn't panic though; you thought you'd just lie low here until the noise dies down. Out of all of this, you were going to be the only winner. With both Candela and Claudio Maggiore out of the picture, there's nothing to link you to either of them, which means you'll get away clean."

Ciccio is now squirming in his seat; his facial muscles twitch and draw tight over his cheeks. "*Fituso!*" he snarls. "*Ed a chi la racconterai questa frottola*, eh? You think anyone will believe your fairy tale?"

Ric leans as far across the table as he can without getting up. "It doesn't matter whether you believe me," he whispers, "but there's a little cockerel of a Commissario in Lipari who won't fall asleep when I read him your bedtime story. You see, Ciccio, I heard you use the word *puddaciaru* once before. It was late the first night I arrived at Pietra Liscia and you were talking to Claudio. And as if that isn't enough, I heard Claudio Maggiore call you by your name just before you strangled the life out of him."

66

Ciccio draws all the bitterness he can muster from his black soul and marshals it into one damning gaze at his accuser. It is a look Ric has seen in too many men before; it tells him his quarry knows he has nowhere left to run and so he will fight until only one of them is left to carry on.

But the menacing Sicilian is not foolish enough to start with Ric now. There are too many other slap-headed, muscle-bound oafs lounging at the poolside bar; men, Ric understands, who are no strangers to violence. And whilst there is no question Ciccio could do him harm, it is more than likely, Ric hopes, that those present would overwhelm Ciccio before he could silence Ric.

Or so Ciccio decides. His shoulders relax, his muscles slacken and he leans back in his chair, grinning confidently.

"You are either a brave man or a fool to think you can provoke me so easily," he says. "But if you are, as people are saying, the man who was hired to assassinate Girolamo Candela, then clearly this type of work is your business. If this is true, then I would have to be a fool to permit you to provoke me. So, perhaps we should put what separates us to one side and relax and enjoy the moment."

"You think it's that simple, Ciccio?"

"Sure, why not?" he replies, shrugging. "This accusation you make about me and Girolamo and Claudio is pure fiction. Of course I was acquainted with Girolamo, who wasn't? He was known and admired as much for his appetite for power as he was for his hunger for the company of both men and women. And you forget, Ric, you are in Italy and even Benito Mussolini started life a socialist. And, like Candela, Il Duce enjoyed a hunger for the company of many mistresses. It is doubtful, though, that he shared with Girolamo such a passion for variety."

He lights a cigarette and looks towards the bar to order more beer. "So," he waves his cigarette with all the aloof conceit of a Cardinal waving to his devotees, "there is little evidence that Girolamo and I enjoyed anything more than a passing acquaintance. As to Claudio? I met him in Palermo, in Exit, as you so rightly suggested. He was a confused young man."

"I'm not sure I want to listen to you read Claudio's obituary, Ciccio," Ric interrupts.

"No," he cuts back, acidly, "I am sure a man of your cold temperament has little time for obituaries. Isn't that what an assassin needs to complete his assignments; a detached view of his victims? You are perfect for this. You even possess the evil eye," he points at the strawberry mark on Ric's forehead, "the *malocchio* as we call it. The Corsicans call it *l'oeil de Sainte Lucie*, the Arabs *ayn al-has d*, and the Jews believe a man with the evil eye takes pleasure in the suffering of others. But for Sicilians, with the head of Medusa the Gorgon on our flag, we know it is the eye that turns those who see it to stone."

"We call it a birthmark, Ciccio," Ric replies. "We don't put much store by it." But, as he says it, Ciccio has reminded him of Manou and he wishes he was back in Corsica with her.

Ciccio reaches into his pocket and pulls out a trinket. It is a horn-shaped silver charm and he juggles it between his fingers.

Although he has seen nothing like it before, Ric recognises it instantly. It is the *cuorniceddu* Marcello said Claudio always wore on a chain around his neck.

Not wanting Ciccio to know he has recognised it, he looks away, but does so too late.

"Let me tell you about Claudio, Ric. This poor, gentle young man was never going to measure up to his brother. Sure," he nods, "you would be right in thinking certain attitudes have changed. But his father, Onofrio, was one of a generation who refuse to adopt a more modern understanding of a man's preferences. This haunted Claudio so much he wanted to tear down the world that did not understand him. I introduced him to Girolamo one evening in Palermo; they became friends, or perhaps more, who knows? Girolamo, because of his position in the Palazzo dei Normanni, knew about the possibility of the geothermal electricity coming to the islands and Claudio understood what this could do for his people; people who he considered to be anchored to their past. Between them, they formulated a plan to build this grand hotel.

"At first, there was nothing disagreeable about either their plan or their relationship. It was only later, when Claudio began to harbour second thoughts about the bad effect the plan would have on the island and his family, that he..."

"Allowed his conscience to get the better of him?" Ric adds.

"Yes," Ciccio nods, appreciating Ric's choice of words, "Claudio would like the way you put it. It is most appropriate."

"I get the feeling conscience is in pretty short supply round here, Ciccio."

"And you would not be wrong, Ric. You would not be wrong. But you must understand that Claudio both loved and hated his father because the old man accepted and rejected him with the same breath. This provided him with a burden he found too heavy to bear. To understand this way of being, you must first live it. And it is a strange truth, but the further south one travels through Italy, the heavier grows this type of burden."

Kasim appears with two more bottles of beer, sets them on the table and scuttles back to the bar.

Ric reaches for the bottle and takes a long pull at it. The pungent odour of sulphur seeping from the fumaroles of the volcano coats the atmosphere.

"I'd toast your health, Ciccio, but I wouldn't mean it."

"Please, Ric, do not concern yourself with such formality." The Sicilian raises his bottle, grins a shade cynically and salutes Ric. "If you cannot drink to my health because you think I had something to do with Claudio's death, and if I cannot drink to yours because you will not return the courtesy, then let us drink to our own, eh? Perhaps we are like Claudio. Perhaps you and I also love and hate our lives. This way, we can at least lay down our burdens and rest for a time. *Cin cin*, Ric! *Cin cin!*"

Ric takes another sip of his beer. Watching Ciccio fondle the lucky charm is making him nauseous. But if the Sicilian prefers to believe he shot Candela, he is inclined to let him. As smooth as he appears, Ciccio revolts Ric, not simply because he is so shameless, but also because of his unpalatable logic. What concerns Ric more though is what Marcello is expecting him to do with the knowledge that the man now sitting before him murdered Claudio.

Cosseted like an exclusive refugee in the peculiar oasis of villains that is the camp, Ric has no way of getting the information to Marcello until he comes for him, and the day is nearly done. He has no cellphone and neither do any of the others sitting round the pool. He thinks to ask Kasim if he can use the office phone, but isn't convinced, having seen the way Ciccio looks at Kasim, that he can trust the young waiter. And then there is perhaps the most important point: he doesn't know Marcello's number. The idea of walking into town and taking the first Aliscafo out of the islands appeals, but Ric figures the sentry at the gate is probably posted to keep those in the camp from getting out as much as unwelcome visitors from getting in, and now that Talaia knows he has skipped, it is likely the harbours are being watched. There is little else he can do but wait it out.

He attracts Kasim's attention, "*Il conto, per favore?*" he asks.

The waiter simply shakes his head and turns away.

Ciccio chuckles: "So British of you! Very charming! There is no money changing hands here; the bill, the reckoning or whatever you are comfortable calling it, is to be paid at the end of your stay."

"Free lunches make me nervous," Ric replies, getting to his feet and glancing at the lucky charm one last time. "But outside of that, I've had enough excitement for one day. Enjoy the rest of your evening."

Ciccio stands, "*Ciao*, Ric. It has been very interesting to meet you. Later, perhaps." He offers his hand.

Knowing it is the hand that killed Claudio Maggiore, Ric ignores it. "Yeah, sure, *ciao*, Ciccio," he says and walks out.

The card players are settled in for the duration and none of the couples take the slightest notice of his leaving. But as he walks away, he can feel the Sicilian watching him and Ric knows there will be a time when Ciccio comes for him.

67

The bed in his chalet proves far too welcoming and, once he has locked the door, checked the windows are locked and taken a large kitchen knife out of the drawer and placed it by his bed, Ric lies down and waits for the arms of Hypnos to embrace him. Distant disco music drifts on the sulfurated air, but the slightest scratch of a beetle or the scraping of a bird jerks him rudely awake. Hypnos, the God of Sleep, is plying his trade elsewhere tonight and it is his sons, Morpheus, Phobetor and Phantasos, who come to lead him to a world of uneasy dreams.

This time the players wear no masks. They are no longer trying to deceive him; the time for deception is passed: Valeria is calling him in from the water and Marcello is urging him to hurry. Sandro is whispering words of warning and Old Nino offers him a glass of palm wine. The beautiful Giuliana is waiting outside his room, a room in which the little Commissario sits.

Ric wakes. It is night and the disco music has quieted. With the windows shut, it is unbearably hot in the room and the sheets are soaked with his sweat. There is a knock at the door.

He grabs the kitchen knife off the bedside table and clumsily feels his way to the door.

"Who is it?"

"*Signor Ric, Kasim. Telefono per voi.*"

Ric thinks quickly and decides it is not unreasonable to assume that it is Marcello who needs to speak to him. He dresses quickly, knowing he can't turn the light on in case he is framed against it when he opens the door.

"*Un momento, per favore, Kasim,*" he replies. But instead of opening the door, he crosses the room and slips out through the sliding doors onto the patio.

The stars are out in force and he has no trouble finding his way quickly and quietly round the side.

Kasim, still dressed in his majordomo's whites, is standing patiently outside his door. There is nobody with him.

"Hey, Kasim," Ric calls softly.

The young man jumps and turns to face him. He is wide-eyed at the sight of the knife.

"*Scusa, Kasim. Chi è?*"

He shrugs, "*Non lo so, Signor Ric.*"

"Okay, let's go." Ric slips the knife in his back pocket and they walk down the lighted path towards the pool area. He watches the trees either side for the smallest movement.

"*È tutto a posto, Kasim?*"

Kasim keeps his head down, studying the path, "*Sì, signore.* Everything is okay."

The light in the office is on and the phone is lying out of its cradle.

Ciccio, wearing a dark grey suit and black shirt as if ready for a Saturday night dance, is standing by the desk.

"Sorry to disturb your sleeping, Ric," he greets, smiling, "but it is time for us to leave." His face looks thinner without his wrap-around sunglasses and the gun in his right hand lends him a pathetic, if threatening demeanour.

Ric studies the gun for a second, a semi-automatic fitted with a silencer. He throws Kasim a dull look, but notices the young man has a slight abrasion to his cheek. He lays his hand on Kasim's shoulder and winces in sympathy. Not knowing the Italian, he tries to make up for his ignorance by employing a conciliatory tone, "I'm sorry Kasim, you shouldn't have to put up with that kind of treatment on my behalf."

Kasim tries to smile, though the mere thinning of his lips obviously pains him. "*Non importa, Signor Ric.*"

"Was that necessary?" Ric asks Ciccio.

He bridles, considering, "I am afraid it was. Young Kasim was reluctant to wake you. He required some encouragement."

Ric squares up to the Sicilian, "Well, now you've got what you want, you can leave him out of this."

Ciccio shrugs and grins, keeping the gun trained on Ric. "Sure, no problem. Young Kasim is staying here, but you, Ric, are coming with me."

"Why not get it over with here? Now?"

"If I had wanted you dead, I would have shot you when you were walking down the path. But I think it would be better for you to come with me."

"Where are we going, Ciccio?"

"Oh, for a short walk." He waves the gun towards the door. "Now, Ric you walk in front of me and I will tell you where to go."

"And if I don't?"

"Then you will leave me no alternative other than to shoot you now… you and our young friend here. And, unless I am very much mistaken, you'd rather not go to your grave with Kasim's blood on your conscience."

"Conscience, Ciccio?" Ric replies, acidly. "Like I said earlier, that's a commodity you don't appear to possess."

"Enough talking," Ciccio growls, "start walking."

Ric turns slowly and starts towards the door. As he does so, he is aware of movement behind him. He glances back just as Ciccio slams

394

the butt of the pistol into the side of Kasim's head. The young man moans, clutches his face and slides unconscious to the floor.

"You arsehole, Ciccio," Ric mutters.

"Save your breath," he replies, raising his pistol. "I didn't enjoy that any more than our young friend here, but I cannot have him raising the alarm. We have a way to go and we have to be at the other side of the island by dawn. Now move."

"Why don't you take one of the cars parked out the front?"

Ciccio shoots Ric a threatening glance. "Because, my friend, there is a police launch at the harbour and there is only one road that joins Vulcanello with Vulcano. There is no way of knowing if they are looking for you or me, but I suspect they are looking for both of us and I have no intention of advertising our journey."

They walk down the winding drive to the gate; Ric a couple of paces ahead of the shepherding Ciccio.

The gatekeeper is asleep on his chair in a pool of light cast by a tall street lamp. Insects buzz and flutter in and out of the glow. He stirs when he hears them approach and is naturally surprised to see two men taking a stroll in the small hours of the morning. But, not thinking there is any danger, he hauls himself off his seat and stretches his limbs as he waits for them to reach him.

"Move to the left and then stand completely still," Ciccio murmurs.

Ric is not minded to either move or reply. He knows he has to keep testing his captor.

"*Gallese*, let me remind you if there is any trouble here, I will shoot you and this old man. Understand?" The menace in his voice suggests Ciccio will be as good as his word.

Ric nods and walks over to the left-hand side of the gate.

"*Buonasera*," the gatekeeper grumbles, irritated that someone should interrupt his dozing. "*Che stai facendo a quest'ora?*"

But instead of replying to the old boy's greeting, Ciccio simply

395

walks straight up to him, pulls the gun out from his waistband and slugs the man.

He staggers back, raising his hands in protest.

Ciccio ignores his protest and delivers him a second blow which fells him on the spot.

"You don't take any prisoners do you, Ciccio."

He waves the gun at Ric, "I don't have time for detail. Open the gate and when we are through, close it and make it look how it is now."

Ric unlocks the gate as Ciccio drags the gatekeeper's body out of the light.

"Now, we walk down the hill and through the village. If anyone comes, you will leave the talking to me. And please, Ric, don't make me tell you again. If there is any trouble I will deal with you first. No one is going to hear you die, eh?" He jabs the end of the silencer into Ric's ribs. "Tell me you understand what I am saying."

Ric hesitates in his stride, "Save it, Ciccio. You've got your message across. But one thing..."

"What is it you want to know?" he sneers. "I would have thought the situation was perfectly clear to a man of your intelligence."

"No," Ric changes his mind, "make that two things." They continue walking down the slope towards the village and the harbour. "First off, you have me all wrong. I didn't shoot, or assassinate as you like to call it, Girolamo Candela. I think I know who did, but if I told you, you wouldn't believe me. And second, doesn't your God frown on your methods? Or will a trip to confession gain you your absolution?"

"Shut up, Ric," he snaps back. "They are irrelevant to me; both God and Girolamo Candela." He points the gun directly at Ric's ribs. "Now, it would be better for you if you don't talk until we are the other side of the harbour. Move!"

The road leads them down across the narrow isthmus which joins

Vulcanello to its larger sister. They ghost past the sulphur pools and the raised terrace of Stevenson's Cantine, and Ciccio steers them away from the harbour, taking a path that twists and turns between vacant shops and shuttered houses. They can hear people talking down at the quay, but other than that the village is peacefully asleep.

Somewhere over near the harbour a car starts.

Ciccio steps up behind Ric, grabs his arm and pulls him into a doorway.

Ric can feel the cold muzzle of the pistol poking into his ribs, the man's breath against his neck.

"Be careful," Ciccio murmurs as he jabs the pistol in a little deeper.

A police car rounds the corner; its headlights sweep the wall beside them, lengthening the shadows. Ciccio tenses, but the car proceeds at a casual pace up the road to their right. When the noise from its engine eventually fades, he yanks Ric back out into the road and thrusts him forward.

At times, Ric wonders if he wouldn't be better off making a run for it into the shadows, so he watches and waits for the right opportunity. But whenever he sees a chance, Ciccio seems to sense it too and closes up behind him.

After twenty minutes, they are through the town and stealing up the long straight road, which rises along the foot of the volcano before curving up and round towards the southern tip of the island. Once out of the village, they lack the protection of the shadows and though the moon has long since set in the south eastern sky, the canopy of stars lights their way as though they are strolling in daylight. Low white walls front the road, and thorn-edged agave and dwarf fan palms stand proud above the sourfig and bougainvillea crowding the gardens of single terrace houses.

"What's up ahead that's got you all fired up to get there by dawn, Ciccio?"

The slender Sicilian is beginning to find the rise of the slope hard going. He pauses to draw breath before answering, "A man is coming with a *motoscafo*. I have to meet him at Punta della Sciarra del Monte, below Monte Lentia; there is a track most of the way. By the time the police have had their breakfast I will be back in Palermo and you, my friend, can tell them your ridiculous fiction about Claudio. That is, if they can be bothered to listen to you. Do you really think they care what goes on out here in these little islands?"

Ric walks on for a minute before halting and turning round to face the labouring Francesco. "Listen to me, Ciccio, Marcello Maggiore has his brother's body, I know it. He recovered it from Pietra Liscia. My guess is that's why he brought me over to Vulcanello; to flush you out. He knows you killed Claudio and slipped out of Lipari. What makes you think Palermo will be safe for you after this? You know damn well he'll find you and you know damn well what he'll do to you when he does. Wouldn't you be better off handing yourself in?"

"Marcello Maggiore," he replies and spits. "He may be a man of influence around here, but in Palermo? I don't think his friends are any grander than my friends. Lipari may be his town, but Palermo is mine. Now shut your mouth and keep walking."

The road climbs straight and steady. To their right the houses give way to scrub and to their left the flanks of the *forgia vecchia* soar away up to the great crater of the Fossa.

"Up ahead, fifty metres," Ciccio puffs, "there is a turning to the right. We take this and at the end there is a path that will lead us round Monte Lentia to the little village. When—"

A scraping brushing noise from the undergrowth startles them. Ciccio spins on his heels, loses his balance and staggers back into the broom that lines the road.

Ric, though, darts across the road in the direction the sound came from. He charges through the broom into the scrub beyond and runs straight into a goat.

It is difficult to tell who is the more shocked, the goat or Ric, as both are instantly winded. Fortunately Ric has missed its short, sharp horns and has clattered right into the centre of its long back, which softens the impact. But the collision causes him to fall over the top of the goat in the manner of a vault gone hideously wrong.

The bell at the animal's neck clanks loudly and the goat bleats in dismay, but Ric has no time for apologies. He scrambles to his feet and takes off up the slope.

The slope is steep and the lava crumbles under his feet. He steps up and slides back, and the going is painfully slow. Grasping at bits of broom, tufts of hard grass and anything that will support him, he scrabbles and grapples and scrapes and crawls up the steepening gradient.

Very quickly he understands that his progress is slower than it need be; if he turns to his right he can traverse the slope. He slows his breathing, calms and quiets. He crouches behind a fern, takes the kitchen knife from his pocket and grips it, blade down.

His view down to the road is clear, the night is so bright that the stars throw countless shadows around him. He waits, listening, but all he can hear is the goat's bell clanking as it saunters away from their unscheduled meeting.

There is no sign of Ciccio and Ric wonders whether he might have cut and run for his rendezvous with the boat; a sensible man would have. He weighs up his options: stay where he is until dawn and risk being caught by Ciccio when he breaks cover, or break cover while he still has an advantage lent him by the shadows.

Ric looks to his right; there is cover, but the flank of the volcano grows steeper and is cut by rainwater gullies, some of which deepen into ravines. His only way out is either up or to his right; a course that will eventually lead him to rejoin the road.

He waits, holding his breath and listening. When even the bell of the goat has rung its last, he sets off along the slope. The going is tough, not so much in making progress, rather than in making progress quietly, as each footfall dislodges lumps of rock and lava, which roll until coming to rest against pockets of broom.

After half an hour, the undergrowth gives way to an open area staked with signs. It is the car park at the foot of the zigzag path up to the Gran Cratere of the Fossa.

Ric waits and watches, but nothing moves.

He creeps out from his hiding place onto the loose lava sand at the edge of the car park.

"What took you so long?" Ciccio asks with a heavy dose of sarcasm. The voice comes from not more than a couple of yards away. He steps out from the shelter of the shadows, his pistol glinting in the starlight.

Ric shrugs and quips, "That goat had a lot to get off its chest."

Ciccio chuckles, "You know, Ric, you may just be telling me the truth. Either you are out of practice or you really are not the assassin I've taken you for. There was no other place for you to go but here." He raises his arm and points the pistol very directly at Ric's head. "Now come with me. We haven't much time; dawn is only half an hour away and it will take us that long to get beyond Monte Lentia. But first, give me the knife you have in your right hand."

"What knife?"

Ciccio cocks the pistol, "Now!"

Ric throws the knife at Ciccio's feet. But the sun will not be long in waking to chase the shadows from Vulcano and so rid Ric of any chance of escape. He knows he has to play for as much time as he can draw.

"There's still something bothering me, Ciccio."

"Shut up, Ric. Get moving."

"No, hang on a minute. We're not running from the Fascists now. This isn't 1930. Christ knows, Ciccio, it was difficult enough getting off the island eighty years ago, think how much harder it'll be now. The police will see your boat coming for miles. They'll pick it up on

400

the radar, wait until you're on board and then close in on you. You'll have nowhere to run when they stop you out in the water."

Ciccio snarls, "You think my friends will bring *taxi mare*? They are used to outrunning the police; they will not catch us. Now stop talking and move before I run out of what little charity I have left. Go on, move," he hisses, cocking his pistol again.

Ric feels inclined to put his hands on his head and slope off like a prisoner of war, but he can gauge the impatience in his guard's voice and knows he's pushed the man about as far as he can.

"Okay, Ciccio, I give in. Let's go."

They walk down to the road and pause before crossing. When Ric gets to the middle, he hesitates. He can hear a car. He waits, turning to his left.

"Get moving, you fool!" Ciccio snaps.

But Ric holds his ground. The flash of the car's headlights sweep the hillside of Monte Lentia, like the beam of a lighthouse.

They stand and watch, transfixed. The road curves a couple of hundred metres beyond them to the south. And as they watch, the headlights appear and approach at speed.

The air is strangely cool and Ric turns and looks to the east. A slender yellow glow fringes the horizon.

"Move, Ric, or I will shoot you."

Ciccio steps back and pulls Ric out of the road. He drags his prisoner back into the car park and in frustration slashes him over the head with his pistol.

Ric covers his head in self-defence and crouches down.

The car slows and stops. Two policemen get out and start walking towards the car park.

While Ciccio watches them, thinking he has for the moment subdued his hostage, Ric bolts. He is hoping that even though the pistol is silenced, the Sicilian will not risk giving their position away by using it.

The sand and gravel are soft and the running is hard work. He starts up the hill until he comes across a path which climbs away to his right. The track alternates between hard lava and scree, and he stumbles often as he scrambles up the slope as fast as he can.

Ciccio is coming after him. Ric can hear his laboured breathing and his heavy footfall, but he knows he is younger and fitter than his pursuer and that the odds of making it up out of sight before the light betrays him are in his favour. The scree beneath his feet is loose and he feels as though he is running on quick sand; working hard but getting little return for his effort. The only comfort is that if Ciccio is making similarly heavy weather of the going, Ric might build up a slender lead.

When the path draws level with the summit of Monte Lentia away across the shallow valley, Ric risks a pause to look back. The crown of the sun has burst the horizon and he can see Lipari across the Bocche di Vulcano and beyond it the island of Salina.

The black shirted Ciccio is fifty metres below him, hustling up the slope; the two policemen a further hundred metres or so behind him.

Ric gasps and drags great draughts of air deep into his lungs. The smell of the sulphur from the crater is strong, the taste thick and acidly metallic on his tongue. Without knowing where he is going, except up to the rim of the crater and therefore away from the danger, he sets off again.

The path bends sharply and the drop beside it is precipitous. Deep, ridged gullies cut down the lava face and across the path, and in places the track has been washed clean away. A second sharp bend reveals an open flank up to the rim of the crater.

He can't see Ciccio because he is concealed by the bend and the slope, but Ric knows he will be helplessly exposed once he starts the final climb. His pace has slowed to little more than a jog as he tries to conserve both his breath and his energy for the final climb. He looks back down. There is no choice but to carry on. He breathes deep and attacks the slope in short, regular steps.

Ten minutes later, he reaches the rim of the crater. Expecting to find some relief in the form of cover, Ric is disappointed. What faces him is a barren landscape of brown shale broken only by lumps of yellow and white magma. The crater of the volcano is vast, almost a kilometre across and the steep sides descend into a lagoon of pale grey lava overlaid with wisps of steam. The path splits into two; one tracing a southerly ridge up to the summit, the other a slight descent round to a concrete hut, beyond which clouds of yellow and white gas issue from the slopes either side.

Ric glances back down and watches Ciccio making his way up towards him. Not knowing whether the path upwards to the summit will leave him at a dead end, he jogs away down the slope towards the hut.

The pungent odour of sulphur dries his throat and forces him to gag and spit as he shambles along the path. The sun is clear above the eastern sea now and the ground beneath his feet begins to heat through his shoes.

Sadly, though the hut is solid and square, its metal door is locked shut.

Ciccio clears the rim; he has reached the fork in the path. He hesitates and seeing that Ric has not opted for the route up to the summit, he starts over towards the hut.

Ric looks around for some place to hide, but there is nothing that will afford him any kind of shelter. His only hope is that the clouds of yellow and white sulphur gas seeping from the fissures around the rim will obscure his flight. But the gas that swirls around them is noxious and when he jogs through it, it blinds him. He loses his footing and falls, and in putting his hands out to soften his landing, he burns his palms. He gets to his feet, but finds he is criminally dizzy. The acrid stench coats his lungs and sears his nostrils. His eyes water, he begins to cough uncontrollably. He retches.

Ric staggers away, not realising he is moving closer to the centre of the field of fumaroles. How long he is wandering around in a daze for, he doesn't know. He can hear a voice. Someone is calling him and he can't think who it might be. Knowing he will suffocate if he stays where he is, he starts to walk in the direction of the voice.

"It is difficult to imagine what could be worse," Ciccio says from no more than ten paces in front of him, "drowning in the fluid that is filling your lungs or being shot. Personally I would prefer a quick end; pulmonary oedema, so people say, is very painful and really makes no sense."

Even if he possessed the wherewithal to reply, Ric isn't sure he would choose to. All he can think of to say is, "You killed Claudio, Ciccio. You killed him, stole his lucky charm and buried him in an unmarked grave. You have no heart."

Ciccio grins, his demonic expression wreathed in the vapours of the underworld. In his sober suit and suntan, he looks the perfect executioner; the Mafioso stepped out for an early morning murder.

"You are right, Ric. I killed the poor young man. He was such a delicate flower, so sensitive; too sensitive for his ambition. But, you are absolutely wrong when you say I stole this?" He puts his hand in his pocket and pulls out the *cuorniceddu*.

"This worthless piece of shit?" He throws it at Ric's feet. "I gave it to him for his birthday ten years ago; it was mine in the first place. And what would be the profit in him taking it to the next world? There is no room for superstition in the afterlife, Ric. It is a shame though; he would have needed his *cuorniceddu* in the company of a man like you; a man who wears the *malocchio*. It's a shame you never got to meet him. Perhaps you will soon."

Ric rubs his eyes in an attempt to gain some focus. He reaches into his pocket for his handkerchief, but all he finds is the *ontreto* he picked up off the floor of Marcello's boat; he grips it, nervously, pricking his fingers on the sharp spines. Ric is now way beyond angry that he should find himself in such a desolate place, standing before a man with murder in his heart. He is tired and frustrated that his search for his roots should lead him to such an end. But most of all he regrets doubting Marcello, even if the burly Liparotan has set him up to flush Francesco Ferro from his hiding place.

"You know, Ric," Ciccio continues in a triumphant tone, "this is a fitting place for you to die. People say the Fossa is the gateway to the underworld. They say Vulcan, the God of Fire, makes his furnaces here in the entrance to hell."

Ciccio raises the gun, cocks it and aims.

"You forget, Ciccio, I have met Claudio. Only because of you, I met him too late to save his life."

As a cloud of sulphur gas drifts between them, Ric summons all the latent fury his frustrations have put at his disposal, draws the *ontreto* from his pocket and flings it at Ciccio.

The squid-jag hits him in the face and the umbrella of hooks stick into the soft flesh at his eyebrow. He screams and reels back beneath the blow. As he does so, a cloud of gas shoots from a fissure at his feet and envelopes him.

Ric lurches away swiftly to his right, but he stumbles over a rock and falls. The ground burns his hands a he heaves himself upright and starts running. But, he trips again, half-falls and staggers. He is running blind across the slope, hoping beyond hope that he will soon clear the field of fumaroles.

At last his vision clears and the air thins. He falls, gets back up and gulps in as much of the clean air as he can manage.

He looks round to see where Ciccio is, but again, he is standing right in front of him.

The Sicilian is clutching his face, the *ontreto* still hanging limply from his eyebrow, obscuring his sight. Blood pours down his cheek and he is trying to staunch the flow of it with his left hand whilst at the same time aiming the pistol with his right.

Ric lunges at him and knocks him down. He grabs Ciccio's wrist and tries to wrest the gun from his hand. But Ciccio pulls away. He half stands and staggers, and drags Ric back towards the belching fumaroles.

The ground scalds them as they land struggling, wrestling, punching and kicking.

Ric grabs at Ciccio's wrist once more and manages to get a grip on it. His face is inches from Ciccio's. The terror of knowing only one of them can survive is written large in his eyes.

"A fitting place, you said, Ciccio," he shouts. "Well perhaps it's time for you to go to hell."

Instead of trying to pull the gun from his hand, Ric pushes it away, but holds on and forces Ciccio's hand into the yellow crusted fissure of a fumarole.

He screams and tries to let go of the gun, but Ric forces his arm further into the crack and, after hanging on for as long as the immense heat allows, he releases his grip. Ric rolls away and stumbles and lurches until he is upright.

Ciccio is on his knees, clutching his cauterised hand, screaming. His perfect black suit is sullied by the yellow sulphur and his expression suggests he is horrified it could be so.

Ric steps back, gasps and steps immediately forward again. He kicks Ciccio as hard as he can in the side of his head.

Francesco Ferro falls back, rolls and collapses onto his front. And as he collapses, so his head drops into the crystalline cleft of a crack in the earth's surface. A geyser of yellow-white gas, like the ink which shoots from the octopus, spews from the fumarole directly into his face.

Ciccio jerks, twitches like a demented Sicilian puppet and stills.

Epilogue

It is late afternoon and Ric is sitting in the café La Precchia, halfway down the Corso Vittorio. Couples are strolling and watching. Young girls giggle and blush in the presence of boys, and younger girls push prams and scold dolls.

Commissario Tommaso Talaia sits opposite him, his Homburg the centre piece of the table.

"Did I mention to you the reflections of Giambattista Basile in his novel *Il Corvo, The Raven?*"

"Not that I recall," Ric replies.

The little cockerel smiles, "Of course. Perhaps I did not; so much water has passed through the Straits of Messina since that time that I…"

The music of brass instruments, flutes and drums drifts down the cobbled street. The waiter asks, politely of course, if they would mind transferring to a table on the pavement. They do so, immediately if unhurriedly.

The shopkeepers of the Corso Vittorio Emanuele are closing up, shepherding their staff out into the street, and a boy on a scooter is shooed away down a side alley.

First in the column filing down the Corso are the dozen or so musicians of the band; their blue uniforms pressed, their shoes shined. They are playing a Sicilian funeral march. Ric has heard the solemn and foreboding score before, but cannot recall when or where. It is, he decides, appropriately vainglorious.

Maso Talaia glances up at the blue sky and sucks his teeth, loudly.

Ric smiles back. Sure, the march is a shade theatrical, but he reminds himself that in her time La Strega had been something of an actress and, therefore, a little theatre is not to be denied.

The pavements are not as crowded as they were the day Ric arrived and witnessed the funeral cortège of Onofrio Maggiore, but there are still a healthy number who have gathered to pay their respects to the old lady of La Casa dei Sconosciuti.

Behind the band comes the old, green three-wheeled *Ape*, weighed down by a host of brightly-coloured bouquets.

The clergy precede the shiny black hearse bearing La Strega's casket. The coffin is plain in design but, like the old *Ape*, it too is draped in a cascade of many colourful flowers.

Behind the hearse the mourners are led by the barrel-chested sailmaker, his head held high, his eyes cast down. And immediately behind Marcello file the members of his extended family and friends.

Marcello had asked Ric to accompany him at the head of the procession, but in reply Ric had demurred, saying that only those who knew her well were entitled to make up the cortège.

As he passes them, Il Velaccino looks over, bows and nods his head. In turn, Ric and the little Commissario repay the compliment.

Old Nino leans on the arm of Ariana. His progress is stilted and his black suit, dark glasses, wizened features and thin white hair lend him a godfatherly air. Even Sandro has done his best to smarten up.

Once the procession has passed down the Corso and the music has faded away, they retake their seats and the street returns to normal.

Ric is warmed by his memories of Valeria. On his return from his night on Vulcano, he'd gone to La Casa dei Sconosciuti to look for her. When he could not find her, he informed Marcello, who sent a fisherman out to search the shore to the south. The cries of the herring gulls soon led the fisherman to the emerald waters below the cliffs beyond the Punta San Giuseppe.

"For a funeral march, it is perhaps a little melodramatic, no?" Talaia suggests, sighing.

Ric smiles again. The perfect irony that Valeria should consign herself to a fate which her mother was believed to have suffered does not escape him. It saddens him, but in that he decides there is also an element of theatre; a tragedy which, just possibly, completes the circle of Valeria's life.

Talaia is, evidently, thinking something similar. "Did you know that she was unwell?" he asks.

"I did," Ric replies.

"Such a shame! She was an extraordinary woman, so..."

"Full of life?"

The little Commissario raises his eyebrow and pouts, "I was going to say righteous in her beliefs. Citizens of good faith are few and far between these days. *Bona fides*: a dying breed."

Ric sips his coffee. "I hear she left a note."

"Oh, yes," Talaia fiddles with his hat, "very precise instructions regarding her funeral arrangements, which is why we have to sit here and endure La Sollevazione Di Cristo. Most people associate this noise," he curls his lip, "with the Misteri di Trapani, the Procession of Passion at the end of Holy Week. Trapani, as I am sure you know, lies on the very western tip of Sicily. Your Strega asked for this march to be played as she passed by La Precchia for the last time." Maso chuckles: "Ah, even in death she is the perfect drama queen!"

"Much else?"

"Not so much; a few details. She asked for the house to be sold and the money to be donated to an orphanage in Bagheria. Everything else she handed to Marcello Maggiore. The gossip in the *città bassa* is that they were related in some way." Talaia smirks; a patronising expression that suggests he finds the islanders a touch parochial for his taste. "Of course, only you would know the truth in this story." He shifts in his seat. "But, I have always thought it is better for people to have something to talk about."

"Better than what?" Ric asks.

"Oh," he shrugs, "nothing or perhaps something less attractive. In Sicily we say *Cu è surdu, orbu e taci, campa cent'anni 'mpaci*: he who is deaf, blind and silent will live a hundred years in peace. People say this is the vow of Omertà, but I like to believe there are many things the ears are better not to hear."

Ric is faintly amused, "What you're saying Maso is that whatever Valeria wrote in her last letter, you don't intend to share it with me."

He nods, smiling, but reconsiders. "Oh, in her letter, La Signorina Vaccariello asked for forgiveness; but generally, not for any one particular impropriety."

"Not one in particular?"

Talaia chews his lip.

"Take all the time you need, Commissario. I'm sure it hasn't escaped your notice that I now have time to spare. Unless of course you think I should be concerned about the price Candela's men have put on my head?

Ric pauses, but when Talaia doesn't respond, he continues, "When Marcello took me over to Vulcano, he told me that the latest rumour running round the *città bassa* was that Palermo had sent someone to decommission me."

"Oh, you don't want to believe every little piece of gossip, Ric. Who knows how they start or from where they come?"

Ric pauses again, thinking, "Officer Paolo?"

"What about him?"

"Didn't Old Nino say his mother lives over at San Calogero?"

The little Commissario does not look up as he replies, "I believe she does."

Ric shakes his head and chuckles, "Who needs the internet when you've got the bush telegraph?"

Talaia still doesn't look up.

Ric pats the policeman rather affectionately on his shoulder, "Well, Maso, now that Il Velaccino has repaired the Mara and she is back in the water, you don't seem too interested in when or where I go next. By which I take it that you no longer have any interest in who may have shot Girolamo Candela or who murdered Claudio Maggiore, or even how Ciccio Ferro met his end?"

The little Commissario sighs, "Ah, the poor, unfortunate Ferro Francesco. It seems he was asphyxiated by a cloud of sulphur gas. You know there are signs all the way up to the crater of the Fossa di Vulcano warning people not to get too close to the *fumarola*. He was careless. What more needs to be said?

"In the case of Signor Maggiore Claudio, we have no corpse therefore there is no crime to investigate. His disappearance will be a matter of conjecture for many years to come. Perhaps it is better for him to be thought of in this fashion. But with regards to Signor Candela?"

He studies his hat for a moment. "You remember me telling you that our forensic laboratory found a curious, oily substance on the Beretta?"

"I do."

"This substance, they believe, was present on the cloth which the perpetrator used to wipe your gun clean of prints; except of course that whoever wiped it clean was clearly not a professional. We know this because your partial thumbprint was near the muzzle—"

"In your dreams, Maso," Ric groans.

Talaia smiles, but again doesn't lift his gaze from the table, "Mm, perhaps so. But, this substance: our forensic department has now had sufficient time to examine it properly and they have ascertained that it is a form of *crema di mani*: a hand cream. Perhaps more importantly, the type of hand cream a woman would use. To be more exacting, the name of this cream is Ortigia Lime Di Sicilia."

411

The name is familiar to Ric and he recalls his first meeting with Old Nino. Ortigia was Valeria's perfume; it was the scent by which Old Nino recognised her.

"Imagine that," Talaia says, all too aware Ric is hostage to his thoughts. "A perfume from a company founded by a British woman, named after an island near Syracuse and found on a gun used to commit a murder in Lipari."

"Yes," Ric agrees. "Imagine that!"

They sit in silence and observe the townsfolk as they go about their business: Alfredo, in his fish-laden *Ape*, potters down the Corso as Maurizio, with his array of vegetables on his, potters up.

"I have found, Ric," Talaia continues, a vague inevitability creeping into his tone, "that when it is possible to avoid forming judgements, it is better not to. As I was beginning to tell you before La Signorina Vaccariello interrupted us, Giambattista Basile, a courtier and soldier of the eighteenth century, wrote a number of fairy tales. Amongst other important works, he was responsible for the original versions of *Rapunzel* and *Cinderella*. However, in *Il Corvo* – *The Raven* – a story from his collection *The Tale of Tales*, he observed that all human judgement is false and perverse. There is much truth in this simplicity, don't you think?"

Ric is taken with the feeling that the little Commissario is gloating, only a little perhaps, but gloating nevertheless.

"And what of your ancestor?" Talaia asks. "What judgement have you reached regarding Antonio Sciacchitano and his empty grave?"

Ric sighs, "My *uomo integerrimo*? My solid citizen? Well, Maso, I think we'll let that sleeping dog lie. I know most people think there is nothing but silence to be found in a grave, empty or otherwise, but these past few days I've learned they are far from silent. After all, where better to keep secrets than a grave?"

About the Author

Peter Crawley was born in Chiswick in 1956. He was educated at Cranleigh School in England and at the Goethe Institut Freiburg-im-Breisgau in Germany. He spent much of his youth in Germany, Austria, France and Corsica. Upon leaving full-time education, and after a short period with the army in Germany, he worked in Stuttgart, as a translator, and on luxury motor-yachts in and around the Mediterranean and the West Indies. After further travels he started his own business dealing in Mercedes-Benz in London's West End. He has now returned to writing full-time and his first novel, *Mazzeri*, a novel of Corsica, was published by Matador in July 2013. *Boarding House Reach*, his second novel, was published by Matador in June 2014. Peter Crawley is a former transatlantic yachtsman and historic motor racing driver. His interests include his family, his research and writing, and skiing. He lives in Chertsey, Surrey, with his wife, Carol. They have three daughters.